QUEEN
OF THE
DARKS
THINGS

ALSO BY C. ROBERT CARGILL

DREAMS AND SHADOWS

PRAISE FOR C. ROBERT CARGILL

"Powerful . . . Brimming with philosophical conundrums and littered with myth and lore, Cargill's world is abundant in detail and imagery in the service of the story. Not a page is wasted . . . Colby's journey through a world of demons and fears made real will keep readers entranced."
—*Publishers Weekly* on *Queen of the Dark Things*
(starred review)

"Exceptional world building, sure-handed plotting and well-rounded characters (even the nasty ones) abound, and the whole impressive enterprise moves smartly along . . . A mesmerizing and highly original debut."
—*Kirkus Reviews* on *Dreams and Shadows*
(starred review)

"[T]his is a fantasy about mythmaking, learning the uses of power, and living with the consequences of one's behavior. Recommended for readers of Lev Grossman's *Magicians* series and Neil Gaiman's adult contemporary fantasies."
—*Library Journal* on *Queen of the Dark Things*

"Cargill's screenwriting chops bring to life a vivid mix of real and imagined folklore in his fantastical second novel. While the mix of urban fantasy, Guillermo Del Toro–like monsters and academic explanations of this magical world shouldn't work, it absolutely does. . . . [T]he story takes us happily deeper into a completely unique world."
—*RT Book Reviews* on *Queen of the Dark Things*

QUEEN OF THE DARK THINGS

C. ROBERT CARGILL

HARPER **Voyager**

An Imprint of HarperCollins*Publishers*

Harper Voyager and design is a trademark of HCP LLC.

QUEEN OF THE DARK THINGS. Copyright © 2014 by C. Robert Cargill. All rights reserved. Printed in the United States of America. No part of this book may be used or reproduced in any manner whatsoever without written permission except in the case of brief quotations embodied in critical articles and reviews. For information address HarperCollins Publishers, 195 Broadway, New York, NY 10007.

HarperCollins books may be purchased for educational, business, or sales promotional use. For information please e-mail the Special Markets Department at SPsales@harpercollins.com.

A hardcover edition of this book was published in 2014 by Harper Voyager, an imprint of HarperCollins Publishers.

FIRST HARPER VOYAGER PAPERBACK EDITION PUBLISHED 2015.

Designed by Paula Russell Szafranski

Library of Congress Cataloging-in-Publication Data has been applied for.

ISBN 978-0-06-219046-8

15 16 17 18 19 OV/RRD 10 9 8 7 6 5 4 3 2 1

FOR JESSICA,

BUT THEN, THEY'RE ALL FOR JESSICA

ACKNOWLEDGMENTS

My editor, Diana Gill, once told me that the second book is the hardest of them all to write. She wasn't lying. The book you hold in your hands now comes after the longest, hardest literary slog of my life. It isn't the book I set out to write, but it is the book I wanted to write all along. And it couldn't have fought its way to you without the efforts and support of a number of amazing people. Everyone should be so lucky as to be surrounded by the likes of these, each of whom I would like to thank now.

First and foremost, I have to thank Diana, whose near psychic ability to steer me in the right direction without directly telling me where to go continues to mystify me. She is my Mandu. And I never would have found this book without her. She also knows how to find the very best food in the world, regardless of what city she finds herself in. So trust her on that if you ever get the opportunity. And, of course, I have to thank Simon Spanton, my Diana across the pond. His passion for the written word and his faith in me always give me something to aspire to when I find myself on the darkest, toughest nights. I've said that before, but it bears repeating.

Thanks to my tireless publicist, Jessie Edwards, who I learned, only hours before this writing, fought for the chance to work on my books. That requires a level of thanks that I do not yet quite have the words to express. Her patience and devotion to answering e-mails within minutes helped guide this first-time author through the terrifying trial of a first release and book tour. And to the Weirwolf Jon Weir, who did the same for me with gleeful abandon overseas. Thanks to the outstanding team at Voyager: Kelly O'Connor, Shawn Nicholls, Dana Trombley, et al. And with equal measure thanks to the team at Gollancz: Sinem Erkas, Charlie Panayiotou, Jenn McMenemy, and all the rest. All of you folks make this more fun than it has any right to be.

Thanks and much love to my agent, Peter McGuigan, who continues to be a rock star, doing things that you think only half-crazed, angry agents can do, but with swagger and a genuine smile that earns the trust he so richly deserves. He's the real deal. As are Kirsten Neuhaus and the amazing team at Foundry. Thanks to my manager, David McIlvain, whose voice guides me through the hardest decisions, but who always seems to call with good news. He was the first person in my career who believed in me before he really knew me, and I'll never, ever forget that. And, of course, his confidant, Mac Dewey, another early believer.

Thanks to my readers: Jason Murphy, Rod Paddock, Will Goss, Paul Gandersman, Peter S. Hall, Luke Mullen, and Brian Salisbury. The value of your brutal honesty is matched only by the warmth of your friendship. I love you guys. So drinks. Friday. Salisbury and Mullen's house. I'll bring the scotch.

Thanks to Lee Zachariah, my man from Oz, who helped with the lingo and the research on the little bits that were vital to get just right. Thanks to all my friends in the industry, too numerous to name, who have ever sat me down, gifted me with advice, shown me the ropes, and tweeted or talked about my work. You know who you are. Thanks to Tim and Karrie League and the staff of the Alamo Drafthouse who not only supported my book and movie but have also provided the venue for many of the greatest nights of my life. And thanks to my partner in crime, Scott Derrickson. He makes me a better writer every day. The world has yet to see the full extent of his talent. But it will. It will.

Thanks to my wife, my life, my breath—Jessica. She believes even when I no longer have the strength to. Every love story I write is really all about her. And for good reason. She is everything.

Thanks to everyone who came out for my first tour, who bought the book sight unseen, or who followed me from my previous endeavors. Thanks to those amazing people who have approached me at signings with copies of the book they bought after having borrowed it first from a library or on loan from a friend. Thanks to everyone who reviewed, tweeted, or blogged about it, and especially to the booksellers who put it in the hands of their customers with an eager gleam in their eyes. All of you make my heart swell with joy with every kind word you share.

And you. Yes, you. This is a second book. If you're reading this, then odds are good that you read the first one. Taking a chance on a first-time author is a grand thing, particularly to the author. But giving them a second chance is something else altogether. You are the people this book was written for. So thank you. I hope I don't (or didn't) let you down.

And lastly, thanks to Deputy So-and-So of the local police department, whose research made this book possible.

CHAPTER 1

SHADOWS OF THE *BATAVIA*

OCTOBER 2, 1629

Jeronimus Cornelisz didn't believe in the Devil, but the Devil sure as hell believed in him.

How he, an apothecary by trade, found himself working as an undermerchant aboard the *Batavia* in the first place was something he cared not to discuss. It was a tale of woe involving a dead child, bankruptcy, and the jailing of a close confidant whose radical ideas had taken root in a few too many prominent hearts. But Jeronimus did talk. A lot. He was of fair complexion, with dark hair and darker eyes that, coupled with his charisma, made it hard to break loose of his gaze. So when he talked, you listened, whether you cared for what he had to say or not.

"God does not mock us," he said, staring off into the crystal blue sheen of the sea. The sun was high, the sand warm across the top of his feet as he and six of his fellow sailors shuffled across the beach. The seabirds cawed in the air around him, the waves lapping the shore. It was as beautiful a day as ever there was. He nodded, squinting in the sun. "He smiles upon us. Loves us. Wants us to be happy. He demands not servitude, but experience. Gifts us with urges. Rewards us with pleasure. Satisfaction. Wholeness. Why is it that a man feels no ecstasy when he prays? There, on his knees, in congress with his maker, he feels nothing but what he pretends to. But a man on his knees, in congress with a woman, feels more alive than ever. Every inch of his body sizzles with joy, and when he explodes, he becomes one with the whole. In that moment, and only that moment, a man knows absolute peace, free of want, free of fear.

"All the things that bring us ecstasy are banned, held captive by the new Pharisees. They put their pope on a throne of gold and silver and let him rework both history and the word that was passed down to us through their lips. And the lips of those before them. And of those before *them*. And the longer the word of God stays on earth, the longer it is corrupted to justify the illusion. Make no mistake. They hold hostage everything we hold dear to maintain their own control of it. Even the pope has his whores." He turned to look at his burly shipmate, shuffling close behind him in the sand. "Have you ever fucked a whore proper, son?" he asked him.

"What?" asked the man, looking up from the ground.

"A whore, son. A whore. Have you ever dropped a few guilders in the cup of one after dropping a few in her box?"

The man grunted, nodding, as if it was a stupid question. He was a sailor. Of course he'd been with his fair share of whores.

"When she shined your knob, who did it hurt? No one. That's the Lord's work. Pleasure for one, rent and food for another. Why would He condemn us to Hell for that? The Pharisees tell us that a roll with a lady is all it takes to burn forever in a lake of fire. But if the Lord has a plan for us, really has a plan for us all, why would He plan for us to go to Hell? To burn. To suffer. What God would do that? Not one who loves us. One who loves us has created an afterlife, a place where we are free from pain, free from suffering, and only know the orgiastic joy of blissful wholeness."

"So you're saying there ain't no Hell?" asked another sailor, following a little farther back.

"I'm saying that not only is there no Hell, but no Devil. He's a ghost story meant to keep the finer things in life under lock and key in our captain's, our captor's, bedchamber. God wants only for us to do what makes us happy. He sorts out the rest."

The second sailor spoke up again, this time leaning closer. "You're saying it's okay to kill?"

"Why wouldn't it be? Killing someone only sends them to the great reward, right? And taking from someone only encourages them to take for themselves. Have you ever looked closely at the Ten Commandments?"

A third sailor spoke up. "There are no Ten Commandments south of the equator. Every sailor knows that." He laughed, though no one laughed with him.

"But do you *know* them?" asked Jeronimus of the third sailor, unfazed.

"I know them," said the sailor, soberly. "By heart."

"We all do. But have you ever thought about them? The man in charge goes up a mountain and comes back down with ten rules that keep him and his rich friends rich and in charge. Do not steal, do not murder, obey your elders, do not covet their wives—of which they had many—do not speak ill of the Lord who passed down these laws nor dare to question or speak for

Him, worship no other god who might make other laws. These aren't rules to keep us free, they are rules telling you to know your place and take only what the rich deign to give to you. These are not the laws of God, they are the laws of man designed only to rule over other men. God wants us to be happy. God wants us to take what we want. God wants us to rule for ourselves. The only way to truly be free is to free yourself of your own conscience."

"That's easy to say now," said the soldier farthest in back. "But let's see what you say in a few moments' time."

Jeronimus smiled wide, his teeth speckled with bird guts, several chipped or missing from a few too many beatings. "Aye," he said. "More to the point, in a few moments' time, we'll see just how right I am after all."

The seven looked out together over the island—a flat, mile-wide coral sand wasteland, no more than three feet above sea level, devoid of bush or tree, surrounded by the Indian Ocean, its only markers three shoddy wooden gallows, constructed from the skeleton of the *Batavia*, which itself was wrecked and battered to pieces by the tide a scant half mile away. Beside the closest gallows was a barrel, and beside that a box on which sat Wiebbe Hayes, captain of the guard, his chin held high, a sly, proud smile on his lips, hammer and chisel in his hands. Behind him stood Fleet Commander Francisco Palsaert—a boorish, sweaty gnome of a Dutch East India Trading Company man who rubbed his fat little fingers together, grinning like a child molester.

"Cornelisz," he said. "You're up."

Jeronimus knelt before the barrel, placing his left hand atop it, eyes cold and expressionless. "I'll be back for these later," he said to Hayes.

Hayes nodded, placing the chisel squarely on Jeronimus's wrist. "Jeronimus Cornelisz, you have been tried and convicted of mutiny, complicit in the deaths of one hundred and twenty souls. Your guilt is not in doubt. Have you anything to say before your sentence is carried out?"

"Yes. Had fortune favored me just a little more, it would be your hand up on this barrel, Hayes. Not mine."

Hayes nodded knowingly. "Though I doubt you would have granted me the courtesy of the barrel."

Jeronimus flashed the hint of a smile, concealing it as quickly as it came. "You're probably right."

Hayes brought the hammer down.

Jeronimus neither winced nor cried out as the chisel severed his hand from his arm; he didn't even blink. He simply stared into the soldier's eyes as he removed his gushing stump from the barrel, placing his right hand directly atop the dismembered left.

"Remove the hand," ordered Palsaert.

"No," said Jeronimus flatly. "They're a set. They stay together."

The hammer came down again, separating the second hand, Jeronimus once again making nary a sound.

A soldier grabbed him by his armpits, hoisting him back to his feet, and then led him to the gallows where a crudely assembled ladder awaited him. Jeronimus climbed up, step by step, the ladder creaking beneath him, bowing his head for the executioner to slip the noose around his neck. Palsaert stepped forward, boisterously offering a morsel of civility. "May God have mercy on your soul."

Jeronimus looked up, smiling, blood spurting from two dismembered stumps. "He already has."

The executioner kicked the ladder out from under him. The mutineer dropped less than a yard; not quite far enough to kill him, just far enough to tighten the rope. There he spun, slowly choking, head swelling up like a cherry tomato, his toes stretching, scraping barely, cruelly, at the sand inches beneath his heel.

Then, one by one, Hayes took the right hand of each of the remaining sailors before he was led to his own noose, to spin and choke slowly in the sun. Each spat a curse at Jeronimus before his own ladder was kicked out from under him, and while no one would ever speak or write of it in their accounts, many thought to themselves that day that they saw Jeronimus smile each time they did, even as the life was slowly choking out of him.

And once the last man had been hung and the life finally drained from his body, Palsaert, Hayes, and the remaining soldiers each made their way to the boats one by one, leaving the conspirators behind to rot where they died.

On the shore, sitting in a boat of their own, Wouter Looes and Jan Pelgrom de Bye waited in chains, their hands cuffed to their feet. Looes was a grizzled sea dog covered in scars, a willing mutineer and right-hand man to Jeronimus; Pelgrom was a thin, blond, eighteen-year-old cabin boy who had only committed one murder—and that under duress. While each of the other mutineers had lied about their involvement or intent in the mutiny, these two fell upon their knees before the seaside court and begged its mercy. Palsaert granted it, though the extent of his mercy was questionable.

"You see the fate you escaped?" asked Palsaert of his captives.

Both men nodded silently.

"Let those images fester, gentlemen. For while your fate is in your hands, know that no manner of death could be as awful as that." He turned to Hayes. "Unshackle them." As Hayes did, Palsaert raised a stiff arm to the horizon and continued to speak. "Eighty-odd kilometers from here is a land filled with monsters and savages. No civilized man has settled it. Maybe you'll make it; maybe you won't. Your lives are your own now. The only thing I promise you is that if I ever see your faces again, I will have you hanged before the sun sets on that day. Good-bye, gentlemen. May God have mercy on your souls."

He motioned to Hayes who gave the boat a good, swift kick into the water. Looes and Pelgrom immediately set to rowing, knowing that what little food and water Palsaert's meager mercy had granted them would be gone before they saw anything resembling land. It would take only minutes for their small craft to vanish into the horizon and their names into legend.

And once they were gone, Palsaert gave the order and the last remnants of the crew of the *Batavia* set back out for Java, never to set eyes on these islands again.

THE HANDLESS SHADOWS hung long in the noonday sun, lifeless as their bodies, slightly twitching, swaying in the breeze. Slowly, as the boats sailed away, the shadows' twitches became more pronounced. And then they became movements. And the movements became dancing. And finally the shadows wrestled away from their bodies, loosed from the moorings of their mortal shells, free to roam and stand up on their own, no longer bound to the flat of the ground. They stood up, square faced, boxy, and malformed, racing for the nearest pools of shadow before the sun could strike them down.

They hid in the dark of the barrel and of the rocks and of the shadows of the posts that held up the gallows. There they waited, watching as their old bodies swayed, shadowless, birds swarming to pick them apart, tearing out their innards, pecking out their eyes. And once the day had run its course and the sun had sunk slowly behind the sea, and the boats had all sailed far, far away, the shadows crept out into the night looking for their hands. But they were nowhere to be found, having been carried off hours before by the birds.

Disappointed, with the moon rising on the water, the shadows turned into crows—their feathers formed from darkness, their eyes a shiny black—flapping off beneath the stars toward an island thousands of miles away. Java.

Ariaen Jacobsz was strong. He'd endured torture, threats, and all manner of inquiry. And as a captain and skipper of the *Batavia,* it would take more than the accusations of known mutineers, murderers, and thieves to have him executed. The company needed him to confess. It was the last privilege his station would afford him. Jacobsz would never give them the satisfaction. No matter how guilty he truly was.

His cell was small and windowless, stuffy with the sweat of tropical air and body odor. No torches were lit this low beneath the castle, the dungeon always as black as night could get, even when the sun was highest in the sky. It was a miserable hole deep in the earth, but it was a damn sight better than hanging handless in the sands of an island with no name.

"Jaaaaacobszzzz," said a whisper outside his cell, waking him from a shallow sleep.

"Keep it quiet out there," he called out to his fellow cell mates farther down the hall. "I'm trying to sleep."

"Jaaaaacobszzzz."

"What is it?"

"We had a deal," said a voice from behind him.

Jacobsz turned around, looking for its source. "What?" Then he heard shuffling from all sides. He wasn't alone, but as dark as it was, he couldn't make out anyone, or anything. "Who is it?"

"Yourrrrrrr crewwwwwwww."

Hands grabbed him from the darkness, clawing his flesh, dragging him backward, choking him. Then, in unison, they heaved him, and he felt the dry, chafing burn of a rope coiling tightly around his neck.

"No! Not like this!" he cried. "Not like this!"

"Exactly like this," said Jeronimus, now a misshapen shadow of what he was. "Take his hand, boys! And spare him the courtesy of a barrel."

The next morning his jailers would find him hanged from the ceiling, his right hand severed and missing. The cell was locked when they found it, and the guards swore that no one came or left in the night. No report was made and, since Jacobsz had no kin anyway, no one was ever notified about the mysterious death. And with so many of the conspirators spread out, already serving on new ships or condemned to different prisons in the region, no one took notice of just how many times this manner of death would repeat itself for an untold number of the mutineers of the *Batavia*.

CHAPTER 2

THE MISSING MAN MARCH

AN EXCERPT FROM THE *AUSTIN CHRONICLE*
BY MARTIN MACK

The air was thick, muggy, and dank with downtown sweat. If you were paying attention, you could feel something in the air. But like a sudden summer storm, few saw it coming until it was pouring down around them. That night, in a cramped, seedy little bar on Sixth Street, a rock god came out and greeted the audience with the deafening strum of his guitar. And now, six months later, a hundred thousand hipsters all claim to have stood among a couple of hundred.

It was an odd crowd, a smorgasbord of the Austin music

and critical elite mingling among friends, family, and fans of the other bands. Scenesters and tastemakers tripped over one another at the bar. I even saw Cassidy Crane nodding along in back.

I'll admit, I wasn't expecting much. I'd seen Limestone Kingdom several times before and they were terrible. Thoroughly mediocre twaddle starving on the outskirts of a rock apocalypse. But they had an in with the manager, opening often for far better bands. So when Ewan Bradford stepped out onstage, I rolled my eyes and ordered another beer. It was going to be a long night.

Or so I thought.

That first chord rattled my bones, resonating in my gut. And then Limestone Kingdom exploded, playing what would become the anthem for an entire city.

You've seen the videos online. You've listened to the hastily recorded tracks. You know what I'm talking about. Sort of. You know how good the music is, but even words fail to capture just how captivating Bradford was. You couldn't take your eyes off him. I must have seen that guy sling ice as a barback dozens of times, but that night was the first time I really saw him for what he was.

A rock god.

But that was it, the last we'd ever hear from him.

There would be rumors of a fight. Blood on a brick wall that police found to be "inconclusive." Talk of a girl—whom no two people could even agree as to what she looked like—walking him out of the club. But no clues. No real leads. Ewan Bradford walked off that stage never to be seen again. His band members haven't heard from him, and the label that later signed them (with Bradford in absentia) has a standing reward for information leading to his whereabouts. But at the end of the day, all we have are sightings of guys who look like Bradford, or sound like Bradford, but none of whom can actually sing like Bradford.

He's out there somewhere. And I think he's alive. I think this is the biggest viral campaign in the history of rock music, playing out in blogs and alt weeklies the world over. Ewan Bradford is out there, smiling, laughing, checking as the hit counts climb on every video his fans post.

The real question is: will he ever show his face again?

Chapter 3

The Stacks

Martin Mack was the consummate rock writer. Though small in stature, he carried himself as if he were the tallest person in the room. He wore leather jackets over black, faded rock tour T-shirts from bands few had heard of, above jeans that were always five minutes ahead of the latest style. His head was shaved close and had been for as long as anyone could remember. No one knew exactly how old he was, but he was old enough to have been around and young enough that he still was. He knew all of the underground, backroom secret spots there were in Austin, which meant he also knew how to find Puckett's Stacks, which is exactly where he found Colby Stevens.

Colby looked up as he entered, at first unaware of who he was. "Can I help you?" he asked. Colby looked grizzled, tired, a world-weary twenty-two going on forty-five. His red hair grew out in long shaggy tufts, longer than he liked it, but not long enough to remind him to bother getting it cut. His gaunt face and sunken eyes oversaw a field of red-brown stubble, almost thick enough to distract from his pointy chin. But it was his expression that was the most damning thing about him. Sullen, beaten, like a tool worn all the way down. He had the look of a man who just didn't give a shit anymore.

Fortunately for him, most people took that as a sign that he'd simply worked in retail a little too long.

Martin smiled, speaking with a soft, friendly tone. "Yes, yes you can. I'm looking for someone. Colby Stevens."

Colby froze for a second. *People* didn't come looking for him. Things, yes; people, never. "I'm Colby," he said, cautiously.

"Of course you are. I'm with the *Austin Chronicle*."

Colby nodded, now recognizing him. "You're Martin Mack."

"You know my stuff."

"Only your recent work."

"Then you know why I'm here."

"I have an idea. I know what you're writing about, but not why you would want to talk to me."

"You were one of Ewan's friends."

Colby nodded. "Yeah, so you'll understand if I'd rather not talk about him."

"People want to read about him."

"No. People want to listen to his music. The only reason they keep reading about him is because you've convinced them he's faked his own death."

"You don't think he did?"

"Man, how would I know?"

"Because," said Martin, "you were the only person outside the band who appears to have spent any time with him."

"Aside from his girlfriend, you mean."

"Nora."

"That's the one."

"Did you know her?"

"No. She was a well-kept secret." Colby slipped a book off the shelf, a tattered, dog-eared copy of Hunter S. Thompson's *Hell's Angels* with a crippled spine and no dustcover. He held it up as if it were what Mack had come looking for.

Mack grimaced. "I've already got a copy of that," he said.

Colby's expression didn't change. He merely opened it to the title page without looking, turning it toward Mack as he did. Martin Mack's eyes grew wide, his jaw slowly going limp, his teeth almost whistling as the air rushed in past them. "Is that a . . . signed Thompson?"

"A signed first edition."

"How did you know?"

"What? That the rock writer at the local alt weekly has a thing for Hunter S. Thompson? Call it a hunch."

"It's a bit beat up and a little the worse for wear, don't you think?"

"You mean like Thompson himself? Yeah. It's kind of perfect, isn't it?"

Martin Mack grinned like an eight-year-old seeing boobs for the first time. "Okay, how much?"

"It's on the house."

"Bullshit."

"I'm paying for it. If, and only if, this is the last time we see each other."

"That's not cool."

"What's not cool is you coming in here and asking me questions about a friend I haven't seen in a long time. Someone I miss. Someone I'm afraid I'll never see again. And while I appreciate what you're doing—for his music—I gotta tell ya, it hurts like a son of a bitch to even think about. So please, for the love of God, cut me a little slack and leave me alone."

"You think he's dead, don't you?"

Colby glared at Martin Mack, thinking long and hard about his choice of words. "I think that with all the attention he's gotten, with all the stories you've written about him, with all the people clamoring to see him live, there isn't anything else in the universe that could keep him off a stage."

"Can I quote you on that?"

"Only if you don't use my name."

"Why not?"

"Some of us, and I'm just speaking for myself here, don't want to get famous off the dead."

Martin grimaced. "I think he's still around. He's just in hiding, waiting for the right moment to come back."

"Maybe you're right. But if he does, he better not show up here."

"You don't want to see your friend again?"

"Of course I do. But I've shed a lot of tears over that man. And anyone who would do that to a friend isn't really very much of a friend at all."

Martin nodded solemnly; it was a fair point. "I'm sorry to have bothered you." He turned to leave.

"Wait."

Martin perked up, imagining for a second that Colby had changed his mind, and turned back around. "Yeah?"

"You forgot your book."

"Oh. Yeah. Thank you."

Colby handed him the book and Martin slowly made his way out of the store.

The bell on the door tinkled, and the store fell silent once more. Colby slumped onto the ground in a heap, weeping. Tears erupted, warm and glistening, down his cheeks. He sobbed openly, sure that he was alone. It was the first time in months that he had cried, and it was only then that he realized just how much he had let the emotions build up.

He sat on the ground, his back to a bookshelf, rocking back and forth, running his hands through tufts of red hair, for a moment completely unguarded. Then the door tinkled again. Colby swallowed hard, quickly wiping his cheeks with his sleeve. "I'll be right with you," he said, spitting out a mouthful of swears beneath his breath.

He stood up, haphazardly collecting himself, took a deep breath, and walked around a bookshelf to the front of the store.

There stood a woman in her early to midthirties, very beautiful, clearly someone who had once been unbearably gorgeous, but was concealing the ravages of fatigue and sleepless nights with an oversize pair of sunglasses and a little too much makeup. She was frayed around the edges, nervous even to be there. Her clothing was expensive, her purse even more so. Everything about her shouted *trophy wife* at the top of its lungs. She looked over at Colby, slipping her sunglasses off to better see in the basement bookshop, immediately noticing his swollen eyes and tear-stained cheeks.

"I'm sorry," she said, fumbling to return her sunglasses to her eyes. "I can come back."

"No, no, no," he said, pointing to his eyes. "Allergies. The molds are killing me this year. How can I help you?"

She looked around to see if anyone else was in the shop, certain that this young man was not who she was looking for. "I'm looking for someone named Colby . . ."

Colby's gaze fell to the floor. *Crap.*

CHAPTER 4

THE BILLBOARD PSYCHIC

The billboard was large, colorful, and could be read clearly from the highway. PSYCHIC READINGS AND SPIRITUAL GUIDANCE. WALK-INS WELCOME. In the window hung a neon OPEN sign, lit and buzzing. It was a quaint little house, a faded blue box with a porch much fancier than its plain design seemed to deserve—large white columns reaching up to support an unimpressive overhang. There was something about it that felt like it belonged on the outskirts of a plywood-and-plank Wild West movie set instead of along a side street overlooking an interstate. But there it was. Cheap. Tawdry. Looming like a ten-dollar whore beckoning the curious to take a chance and see if it was worth the money after all.

It reeked of sadness and disappointment.

But Carol Voss was desperate. Her hands trembled as she pulled the keys from the ignition and fumbled them into her purse. This wasn't the sort of place she expected to find herself. It was the last place in the world she wanted to try. It was also the last place she had left to turn to.

As she stepped out of the car, she gave one last thought to turning back. Then she heard the wail again in the back of her mind, a chill running up her spine, shivering, gooseflesh prickling across her skin. There was no turning back now. What was waiting for her back home was far worse than any humiliation she might face inside. Here was only the chance to waste her money, which she had plenty of. She might as well give it a shot.

The inside of the house was a cramped cluster of beads and fabric, the air thick with incense, almost every square inch of real estate covered in iconography. It smelled of smoke and mirrors and cheap theatrics. Just beyond the door, just as you entered, stood a lit glass case stocked with candles, crosses, crystals, and stones, a cash register sitting on top with a credit card machine plugged into the side. *This wasn't the home of a psychic,* Carol thought. *This was a gift shop for the gullible.* She clenched her fist nervously, and was turning to leave, when a woman's voice called from behind a curtain.

"Be right with you," she said.

Carol stopped. She'd come this far. So she waited a moment longer.

"How can we help you?" asked a young woman before she'd even finished rounding the crushed red velvet curtain. She was pretty, and her dark, thick hair draped over the olive skin of her bare shoulder.

"I'm here to speak to . . ." Carol trailed off, searching for the words. "The psychic."

"Mother Ojeda. My grandmother," the girl said, nodding. "About your future?"

Carol shook her head gravely. "No. About a problem I'm having now."

The girl nodded, understanding. "Of a worldly nature or . . . a spiritual one?"

"The . . . the second."

The girl's eyes squinted a bit. "One moment, please." She turned around, vanishing again into the back of the house.

Carol waited, her hands tucked together in front of her, fidgeting nervously with the buckle of her belt. She tapped her foot and chewed the inside of her lip. For a moment she thought about slipping out the door as quietly as possible. Then the girl reappeared.

"Right this way, Mrs. . . ."

"Voss. Mrs. Voss."

The girl walked back behind the curtain, this time towing Carol behind her. The back of the house was a little less cramped, a dining room converted into a gaudy séance chamber. There was a large oak table covered in heavy cloth topped with a much thinner silk overlay. Atop it were a number of candles, all burning. Several carefully placed spotlights cast grim shadows on the walls, highlighting an empty chair next to the room's entrance, a spot on the table where a tarot deck rested, and a chair immediately opposite the first. Sitting in that chair directly across the table was Mother Ojeda, an old Hispanic woman, her thick black hair braided, disappearing behind her into a woven shawl that rested on her shoulders.

She stared at the table, not looking up as Carol entered.

"Grandmother, this is Mrs. Voss," the young girl announced.

Mother Ojeda nodded with a smile. "Thank you, Celesta," she said, her accent thick, dripping with old Mexico. "Have a seat, Mrs. Voss."

Carol sat down in the empty chair.

"My granddaughter tells me you have a problem."

"Yes. I do."

Mother Ojeda picked up the tarot deck, shuffling it in clumps. "What kind of problem do you have?" She laid down a card, shaking her head. "Hmmm."

"Something is . . . haunting my . . . my home."

"A spirit? Hmmm . . ." She laid down another card, then frowned, looking up strangely at Carol. "Have you seen this spirit, or merely felt it?"

Carol hesitated, her eyes darting around nervously, her hands sweating. "I've seen her," she said. "And heard her."

"Heard her? Moving things you mean?"

"No. Screaming. Wailing. Crying." She paused. "Speaking."

Mother Ojeda laid down another card, looking mildly confused about the card facing up at her. "What did she say?"

"Nothing in English. I couldn't understand it."

Mother Ojeda was quite serious now. All of her theatricality and pretense had vanished, her accent fading with it. "What does this woman look like?"

"She's tall, very thin. Skeletal. Her arms look longer than they should be. Bony, with elongated fingers." She shivered a bit, the words getting harder to free, mired in the pits of terrifying memories. "She has long black hair and her eyes, they're gouged out. Holes with something glowing behind them. Like coals."

Mother Ojeda clasped her hands together, wringing them tightly. "The words she spoke. Can you remember them?" She placed a final card, her eyes wide and unbelieving.

"I miss hee ohs."

"¿Ay, mis hijos?"

"Yes! She just kept screaming it. Over and over. What are the cards telling you?"

Mother Ojeda looked solemnly upon her. "That you're not lying."

"Why would I be lying?"

"Mrs. Voss, do you have children?"

"Yes."

"Two boys?"

" . . . Yes."

"Both still young enough that they need a sitter?"

Carol nodded.

"And you have a home by the water, don't you?"

Carol eyed her suspiciously. "Now wait a second, how did you know that?"

"By the river?"

"The lake."

Mother Ojeda shook her head. "The lake is just a river dammed up. You have found yourself at the mercy of a terrible spirit. La Llorona."

"Is it dangerous?"

Mother Ojeda nodded. "Once there was a beautiful young woman, every bit as stunning and radiant as yourself. But she was unmarried, widowed, her husband having died in a terrible accident, leaving her to take care of their two children—both young boys—on her own. She was in love with a wealthy merchant who, while having feelings for her, did not want to marry her. Instead he told her that he did not want children and thus *couldn't* marry her. This broke her heart and, desperately lonely, she went home, took both of her boys out of their beds, walked them down to the river, and drowned them both right then and there.

"She went back to the merchant, overjoyed at her new freedom, and told him that they could finally be together. Horrified by what she'd done, he immediately rejected her, saying that he never wanted to see her again. This destroyed her. She begged and pleaded for him to reconsider, but he wouldn't have it. He refused even to see her. Now even more heartbroken than before, she hanged herself.

"When her spirit arrived in Heaven, God met her at the gates and asked her where her children were. She shook her head. 'I have no idea,' she said. 'I thought they were with you.' God said, 'No, I haven't seen your children. Go back to earth and find them. You cannot come into Heaven without them.'

"The woman was distraught, confused. She had no idea where her children were. So she came back to earth and began scouring the river. But they were nowhere to be found. Eventually she realized the current was too strong and she would never find them, so she hatched a plot. She needed two boys who looked like hers that she could pretend were her own. She would take them, walk them down to the river, drown them like she had her own children, then march them up to Heaven to prove to God that she knew where her children were.

"That woman is La Llorona. She wanders the world still, up and down the length of the Colorado, looking for her little boys—or ones who remind her of them that she can claim as her own—crying out, '¡Ay! ¡Mis hijos! Oh! My children!'—so she might finally get into Heaven. And now she has her eyes on your little boys."

Carol stared at her incredulously, both horrified by the story and unsure of what was coming next. For a moment her brain spun dry, unable to process what was happening. Then reason began to take hold. She narrowed her eyes. "How much is this going to cost me?" she asked.

Mother Ojeda shook her head. "Nothing."

"What do you mean nothing?"

"Nothing," she said again, waving her hand as if refusing money. "I can do nothing at all for you."

"Wait. What do you mean you can't do anything?"

"This is beyond my gifts."

"Then what do I do?"

"Go home. Keep your children away from the water. Don't let

them anywhere near it. Keep the doors and windows locked at night. If there is a knock at the door after sunset, don't answer it. Do you smoke?"

"No. Of course not. I have children."

"Then consider starting. A lit cigarette in the hollows of her eye sockets will chase her away."

Carol leaned back in her chair. "This is ridiculous. You're pulling my leg."

Mother Ojeda shook her head, eyes cold and narrow, pointing sternly at her. "Have you really seen her?"

"Yes," she said, swallowing hard.

"And have you really heard her?"

Carol nodded. "Yes. I have."

"And as I sit here and say that I believe you, you don't believe me?"

"Isn't there something you can do? Don't you speak to spirits? I read that you speak to spirits."

"I do speak to spirits. But I will *not* speak to her. There is too much evil there. Too much danger in even looking her in the eyes."

"What *can* you do?"

Mother Ojeda took a deep breath, considering her next words very carefully. Then she reached behind her to a nearby end table and pulled from it a pen and a scrap of paper. She began writing. "The spirits, they speak of a boy. One said to be able to wipe a spirit clean off the earth for well and for good. One who scares them so much they won't speak his name loudly out of fear he might notice them. His name is Colby. He works in a bookshop. Here is where you'll find it."

Carol took the slip of paper, tears forming in her eyes. "I don't . . . I don't know how to thank you."

"Go home, kiss your boys. Love them and raise them to be good men. And whatever you do, do not let them anywhere near the water."

"HER NAME IS Beatriz," said Colby. "She's been walking up and down the shores of the Colorado since the fifties."

"So the story? It's true?" asked Carol.

"Parts of it. There are a lot of stories, few of them entirely true. But that's the point of stories, I guess. The part about her drowning her sons is true. That and the part about her walking the earth looking for children who remind her of her boys. But the part about God is superstitious bullshit. God doesn't make creatures of the night. We do. Beatriz made herself out of her own madness and guilt. That's all that's left of her now. She's a shadow of everything that was wrong with her, walking, feeding, wailing."

"So you know her?"

"Yes."

"And you'll stop her?"

"Well . . ."

"Well, what? I can pay. My husband does very well—"

"It's not about money."

"You work in a bookshop. And it's always about money."

"Ma'am, I'm going to stop you right there."

"No. No," she said, waving an authoritative finger. "I am not taking no for an answer. These are my boys we're talking about. They are the point of my whole life. They are everything. I will give you whatever you want—anything—if you protect them for me. So quit negotiating and name a price."

"Look, ma'am—"

"Carol," she said, bringing herself half a step closer, her eyes softening.

"Carol. I'm not an exterminator and this isn't a raccoon in your gutter. La Llorona are exceptionally dangerous creatures. They don't just go away when asked. I don't know what you think an exorcism is, but it's not about shouting loudly and sprinkling holy water. It's about doing battle with something made of hate, anger, and fear. You're asking me to risk my life."

She took another half step closer, putting a gentle hand on his upper arm, sliding it up into the short sleeve of his shirt. "I'm asking you to save my sons."

Colby gulped. Women didn't get this close to him; women didn't touch him on his upper arm. "Ma'am."

"*Carol*."

"Keep your sons away from the water. Buy some dried tobacco leaves and keep them burning outside your door after sunset. That's the best I can do."

Carol's eyes hardened again, just for a moment, as she reached into her purse for a scrap of paper and a pen. "Here's my number. You call me when you figure out what it will take to get you to do better than that." Then she turned quickly, making her way out of the shop before she found herself hiding her own tears.

Colby crumpled the scrap of paper in a tight fist, slid it into his pocket, cursing once more beneath his breath. He shook his head. Those boys had a week, at best, before they turned up in the river. But that wasn't his business. Not anymore.

CHAPTER 5

KEEPSAKES AND MEMORIES

Ewan Bradford, once Ewan Thatcher, had been dead six months now—the pike that killed him resting on two pegs drilled into an otherwise empty wall. The blade was clean, polished, not a hint of the blood it spilled still anywhere on its haft. This was the pike that took the hand from a changeling, slew that changeling's mother in a lake, pierced the heart of a Leanan Sidhe, and, most important, robbed Colby Stevens of his longest, and best, friend. It pulsed with that power, having grown stronger with each strike, the legend surrounding its deeds still nowhere near doing justice to its potential.

And Colby Stevens hated it. He sat across from it on his couch, staring, remembering the feel of it in his hands, its heft, the way it swung. He'd made it. Though he hadn't forged it himself, it only existed because of him. And now it stood monument to the worst night of his life. Colby rubbed his chin, thick, abrasive stubble like sandpaper in his hands, and he thought of his friend.

"Are you going to stare at that thing all night, boss, or are we going to go for a walk?" asked Gossamer, the golden retriever resting his head on his front legs in front of the couch. The dog's thick, red coat was well groomed, his face developing only the hints of a white mask in the fur around his muzzle and brow. Colby looked down at him, roused at once from his daydream.

"What?" he asked.

The dog spoke again. "I said, 'Are you going to stare at that thing all night, boss, or are we going to go for a walk?'"

"Oh. I don't feel like going out tonight."

Gossamer flipped his tail a bit, thumping it on the floor impatiently. "I want a beer."

"We have beer here."

"I want a sausage."

"We don't have sausage."

"I guess that means we have to go for a walk then."

"Gossamer, we're not going for a walk."

"What? Are we going to sit here all night, staring at a thing on a wall?"

"You used to do that all the time."

"I only stared at things that moved."

"I'm sure it makes all the difference."

Gossamer grimaced. "Have you ever watched a possum shimmy along a telephone wire? Knowing that at any moment it could drop into your yard for you to play with?"

"No."

"No, you haven't. You don't know. Don't judge. I want to go for a walk."

"And I want to stay here. And stare at a thing on the wall. It's why people buy houses. So they can sit in them. With their things. And stare at them."

"I want a beer. And a sausage."

"I never should have helped awaken you."

"You didn't have a choice. I was waking up without you."

"I should have let you become a Black Dog."

"That's racist."

"That joke is still not funny."

"It is to dogs."

"WHY ARE YOU BEING SO ANNOYING TONIGHT?"

"Because. I want you to stop thinking about him."

Colby looked sadly down on Gossamer, his gaze softening. "Oh."

"Yeah. Oh. We've got to get out of this house."

"He was in the paper again."

"I know."

"And how would you know that?"

"Because this is what you always do when he's in the paper. Or on TV. Or the radio. You mope, you pout, and you stare at the wall. Why don't you get rid of that thing?"

Colby shook his head. "It's too powerful. In the wrong hands it can kill even the longest-lived of creatures."

"But it's safe here?"

"Of course it is. It's got you to protect it, doesn't it?"

"That doesn't exactly instill confidence in me, you know."

"I know. But what do you want me to say? That I'm the great Colby Stevens? That I can evaporate a soul with a dirty look and no one in this town wants to fuck with me?"

"I'd rather you not. That conversation usually ends in an entirely different style of self-loathing."

"You really are being a pain in the ass today."

Gossamer nodded, nuzzling against Colby's leg. "I know."

"A walk?"

"Yes, please."

"I'll get the leash."

"That's not funny."

"It is to people."

COLBY AND GOSSAMER sat on the edge of the building's roof—one of the tallest in the city—looking out over the slowly drifting lights of distant traffic on the highway. There were no angels out tonight, not on the rooftops. They kept their distance now, their eyes narrow and trained, watching from blocks away before slinking off to conspire about how best to take back their rooftops. Below, the city slowly swelled with the overeager sober of the early night. It would be hours before it vomited them back out in a stumbling stream of swerving, giggling mess.

This place was familiar, sacred. It held wisdom that Colby tried in vain to tap into, with answers, it seemed, that could only be loosened by the tongues of angels.

"I hate it up here," said Gossamer, warily peering over the edge.

"You don't hate it. Stop being dramatic."

"I don't like it."

"You're the one who wanted a walk."

"Walk. Not a climb."

"We took stairs."

"You *climb* stairs. I don't like stairs. Medieval contraptions built for things with far longer legs. Maybe if there were an elevator—and a railing—I might like it up here. But there isn't and I don't."

"Well, I like it. I had a really good talk up here once."

"The one with the drunk?"

"The angel. Yeah."

Gossamer growled a little. "That guy's a dick."

"He's not a dick. We just don't see eye to eye anymore."

"He's a dick. I don't like the way he and his friends treat you."

"Maybe they have good reason. You don't remember that night," said Colby.

"Don't be that guy. Not tonight, boss. I remember it well enough. You did what you did, what you had to do. We have to move on."

"I'm trying. But everyone else wants to remind me."

"Nobody makes you read the paper."

"I should be able to read whatever paper I want."

"Boss."

"He was on the cover. They're all over town. What was I supposed to do?"

"Boss."

"Shut up, Gossamer. You haven't soaked up enough dreamstuff to be smarter than me yet."

"You don't have to be smart to know better than to read stuff that you know will piss you off."

"Lots of people do it. Every day."

"They're not smart either."

"Maybe they want to be mad. Maybe they want to read the events of the day and feel somehow involved with them. Maybe they think being mad keeps them involved."

"You think?"

Colby looked over at Gossamer, the dog's eyes big and brown, peering back at him with a mix of love and pity. "Shut up, dog."

"Don't *dog* me. It's patronizing."

"That's why I do it."

"That's not what a good friend does."

Colby grimaced, insulted. "What would you know about being a good friend?"

Gossamer straightened up proudly, showing off, his head

high, his gaze regal, reddish fur blowing in the light breeze. "Man's best friend."

"That joke is still not funny."

"It is to dogs."

"Sometimes I think you just say that. I don't think dogs tell jokes."

"Are you kidding? Dogs love jokes. We're just not very funny."

"That I believe."

Then, at once, the rooftop darkened, dimming like someone had snuffed out a dozen candles. Colby sniffed the air. Something familiar. A hint of musk and despair drifting in.

"Bill?" he asked.

Bill the Shadow—his coat long and dark, his shadowy face hidden beneath the gloom of his wide-brimmed hat—slunk in from out of the night. The rooftop darkened further still, the ever-present cold murk that followed him settling in, filling the nooks and crannies with puddles of night. "Yup."

Colby didn't turn around. "What are you doing up here?"

Bill sat down next to Colby, dangling his misty, insubstantial legs over the side of the building. "Not your rooftop," he said, striking a match, lighting a cigarette. He cast the charred remains of the match away with a flick of the wrist, watched as it sailed down out of sight.

"I never said it was. I just thought . . ."

"What? That I hated you like everybody else?"

"Well, yeah."

"Nah. Just wanted to give you your space. A night like that, well, it sticks with you. Wanted to make sure you had time to get your shit together." He paused, staring out into the city. "Did you get your shit together?"

"No," said Gossamer.

"My shit is together," said Colby.

Bill nodded, peering at Colby from behind his cigarette. "I

know you've got to have some hooch on you," he said. "You always have good hooch on you."

"Do I look like a liquor cabinet to you?"

"No. You look like a man who could use a drink with friends."

Colby reached behind him into his backpack and, without looking, fished out a bottle of bourbon. He unscrewed the cap, taking a pull off the bottle. "Give me one of those smokes."

"Deal." Bill produced a cigarette from the back of his trench coat, swapping it for the bottle. He quickly looked it over, eyeing the label. "Aw, hell. This ain't bad, but it ain't the *good stuff.*"

Colby snapped his fingers, lighting a flame at the end of his thumb. He lit the cigarette then shook out the fire. "The good stuff always came from Old Scraps."

Bill closed his eyes, nodding sadly, raising the bottle into the air. "To Scraps." He took a drink and handed the bottle back to Colby.

Colby took another swig. "He was a hell of a bartender."

"*Hell* of a bartender."

Gossamer looked longingly up at Colby, whimpering a little.

"What?" asked Colby. "You hate bourbon."

"I was promised beer."

Colby rolled his eyes, passing the bottle back to Bill. He reached behind himself again, this time fishing out a cold bottle of beer and a dog bowl from the pack. With a quick twist he popped the bottle cap off, sloppily filling the bowl.

"Careful," said Gossamer. "Pour it along the sides."

"Maybe you should pour it," said Colby.

"I don't like it foamy."

Bill took another drink. "I see you two have become close. Is he your familiar now?"

Colby nodded. "Yeah, kind of."

"Wait, you mean there's a name for this?" asked Gossamer.

"Yeah," said Bill. "There is. Colby, you didn't explain any of this?"

Colby put the dog bowl in front of Gossamer, who immediately began lapping up the beer. "Some of it," he said. "But he's still learning. I didn't want him to get the wrong idea about our relationship."

Gossamer looked up from the bowl. "What's not to understand? We're best friends."

"Exactly," said Colby. "And that's how it's going to stay."

Bill took a drag off his cigarette, exhaled, took another drink. "Okay."

Colby looked over at Bill and shook his head silently. Bill took the hint.

The three sat quietly for a moment, Colby and Bill smoking, passing the bottle back and forth, watching the lights on the highway, Gossamer's incessant lapping the only sound. The night was humid, but cool, a breeze floating in off the lake. The stars were out, the moon's thin crescent waning, absent a cloud in the sky. It was beautiful.

"So why don't you hate me like everyone else?" asked Colby.

"I can't think of a good enough reason, I guess," said Bill. "I mean, it's not like I think you're going to nuke me for hanging around like everyone else does. And, well, we've got a lot in common."

"What do we have in common?"

Bill's gaze lingered for a second. "We're both monsters." He took a long, deep drag off his cigarette, leaned his head back, and exhaled a slow, steady stream of smoke. "You see," he said, still staring up at the stars, "I don't scare little kids. I don't murder chaste virgins caught out alone at night. I just feed on monsters. The soiled. The unclean. The deeper and darker the hate or fear or self-loathing there is, the more delicious the meal. Now you might look at some of the people I feed on and say that they didn't have coming what I did to them, but you couldn't for a moment argue that they were without sin, without fault. That the world ain't just a tiny bit better without them."

"Yeah? And?"

"And your friend over there didn't just awaken on his own. This city doesn't have enough dreamstuff for that. Not anymore. You used the energy of a redcap."

"You're gonna hold me to the death of a redcap?"

"I might," said Bill.

"He crossed over the city limits. He knew the rules."

"The rules you laid down. You murdered that redcap and you used the energy for your own ends."

"I'm not a monster."

"Monsters with purpose. That's what you told Yashar. Monsters with purpose."

Colby took another drink. "Shit. I said that, didn't I?"

"You did. We're monsters, Colby. But you're one of the good ones. You mean well. You want to protect the innocent by devouring the unjust. You take that darkness on to yourself and you carry it with you day in and day out. I've been around a long time. I've seen my fair share of darkness. I've taken a lot of it on to myself." He paused, lost in thought for a moment. "There's a reason you've never seen my face."

Colby nodded, stabbing out his cigarette beside him on the ledge. "Well, if I'm gonna be a monster, I might as well surround myself with the best sort of them."

Bill nodded. "You're goddamned right about that. Thanks to you, that's just about all that's left in this city."

"I try."

"It won't last. It never does."

"As long as I'm here, it will."

"No one lights a candle in the daytime, Colby. Men dream up their monsters for a reason."

"So they can have windmills they feel good about tilting at?"

"Something like that," said Bill, lighting up another cigarette with the end of the old one. "Why are you up here?"

Gossamer stopped lapping at the beer. "He was in the paper again."

"Ewan?"

"Yeah," said Colby.

"He's gone. No coming back from that."

"You think I don't know that?"

"No, I think you believe that if you keep him in your heart, some piece of him will still live on."

"Yeah. Maybe. What's wrong with that?"

"It's horseshit. The only thing that lives on is the part that makes everyone they left behind who they are. And right now all that's making you is miserable. The kid got a whole lot more life than he was destined to. Touched a lot more people than he ever would have. All that was you, not him. All that's left of him is a lead weight dragging you down."

"I didn't come here for a lecture."

"Yeah you did. You were just hoping it'd be from him and not me." Bill pointed off into the night then formed a shadow puppet of a bird, flapping off, his hands actually vanishing into the dark as he did. "If that fucking angel had any real answers, he wouldn't have fallen and he wouldn't be drinking himself into a stupor. He's not going to forgive you, Colby. No one will. You shouldn't expect them to. You shouldn't want them to. And you don't need them to."

Colby nodded, swallowing. "It's just that—"

"It's just what?"

"He's the closest I've ever come to talking to . . ."

"Talking to . . . ?"

"Talking to God."

Bill shook his head, the light ever shying away from the features of his face, no matter the angle. "Shit. He's never talked to God. God doesn't talk to angels. Not for a long time. Why do you think so many of them jump?"

"I thought there would be answers, you know? When I was a kid."

"There are answers. You just don't like them."

"But there are always more questions."

"Yeah. If there weren't, what the hell would be the point? You don't need more answers, Colby. You don't need approval. The only thing you need . . ." He trailed off, taking another pull from the bottle. " . . . is to figure out where the hell Scraps was getting the good stuff. Because, seriously, this ain't cutting it."

Colby reached into his pocket and pulled out the small, crumpled scrap of paper he'd been given by Carol Voss. Then he slowly unwound it, straightening the creases, staring at the number, letting his eyes glaze over as he drifted off in thought. "No. No, it's really not."

CHAPTER 6

ON DISBELIEF

AN EXCERPT BY DR. THADDEUS RAY, PH.D., FROM
HIS BOOK *THE EVERYTHING YOU CANNOT SEE*

Disbelief is perhaps the single greatest weapon in the arsenal of anyone trafficking in the arcane. Versatile, powerful, and, most important, final, it is a last resort meant only for when there is no other recourse but the permanent destruction of a thing. Against truly frightening, nigh immortal creatures, sometimes it is the only option. But it is neither clean, nor easy, nor sometimes even possible against certain beings. And it certainly isn't recommended except under the strictest and direst of circumstances.

Disbelief is, simply put, the art of reweaving the dream-stuff comprising one being into that of another, more harmless form—literally believing it to be something else. You can, with the right focus and understanding, convert a redcap into sunlight or an angel into a breeze. At advanced levels of understanding, one can even convert that dreamstuff into more useful constructs, fueling spells or creating new life. As most beings that can achieve some semblance of physicality actually contain elements and particles other than dreamstuff, there are often physical components left behind—manifesting as smells, feathers, or flower petals—often drawn together as side effects of the disbeliever's own imagination.

The concepts behind disbelief are simple and build upon the nature of dreamstuff as has already been discussed. Dreamstuff collects together, forming the will or consciousness of a being that can then exert its own will upon other nearby dreamstuff, altering it into a form that it wishes or believes to exist. The stronger the will, the greater its exertion on nearby dreamstuff. Thus, the struggle in disbelief can quite literally be described as a battle of wills. The disbeliever is restructuring a being's essence while that being is trying to maintain its own form through its belief in its own existence.

The danger of disbelief—besides the fact that you are disintegrating a living, conscious thing—is that some beings are very good at resisting such attempts. Strangely enough, the beings best adapted to resist disbelief, almost counterintuitively, are the lesser forms. Disbelieving complex forms like fairies, genius loci, angels, or djinn is fairly simple unless they are adept in defending themselves from such attacks and are given ample time to prepare themselves in the moments before. They are, after all, beings of complex emotion and, though nearly, if not completely, immaterial, they are made up of as many working, moving parts as we are—even if those parts are entirely made up of energy.

No, the hardest beings to disbelieve are those made up almost entirely of a single emotion. Hate, anger, love, sorrow—these are not the kinds of emotions easily diminished by reason. They are stronger than disbelief. Your urge to disbelieve them must be significantly more powerful than their belief in their own existence for it to work.

Beings of hate, beings of love, beings of sorrow and loss; these are creatures that exist only to fuel and feed their emotions. They exist as a means to an end. And those creatures resist with a willpower that few can override. It is why most religions teach their holy men to exorcise rather than to destroy; the beings they are sent up against are creatures of such powerful emotions that they can only be sent away. This is not to say that they cannot be disbelieved, but simply that they cannot be disbelieved by you.

CHAPTER 7

BEATRIZ

You're going to what?" asked Gossamer. "No way. Not without me."

Colby shook his head as he grabbed small tokens and materials from around the house, stuffing them into his backpack. "I can't take you. Not this time. It's too dangerous."

"If it's too dangerous for me then it is definitely too dangerous for you."

"I promised I'd help. Besides, Beatriz knows the rules. She shouldn't be here. Not in Austin. This is my city and no one takes children in my city."

"Are you at least taking Yashar with you?"

"No."

"Bill?"

"Definitely not. There's no telling what he would do."

"At least take the pike."

Both looked over at the wall, the pike still resting on its pegs. "No. No freakin' way. That thing stays here."

"You might need it."

"I don't need something that dangerous."

"What if you can't just disbelieve her? She's old. She's powerful. If she is more emotion than reason—like *he was*—you might not be able to just make her go *poof*!"

"I can handle her."

"By talking to her?"

"There are ways to handle spirits other than just disbelieving them. She has her weaknesses, her own fears. If she doesn't listen to reason, I'll find a way to get her gone. I've destroyed far more powerful spirits than her before."

"That's the kind of cockiness that gets people killed."

"Goddamnit, Gossamer! She didn't listen. I told them! I fucking told them! Stay. Out. Of Austin. She was there, Goss. She was there the night they tried to sacrifice him. She was there the night they killed him. That she still walks the earth is only because I didn't destroy her when I had the chance, and this is how she repays my kindness? By trying to drown children in my fucking town?"

Gossamer cowered, his tail creeping in between his legs. "Your . . . kindness? Are you serious?" He shook his head. "Are you listening to yourself?"

"Are you fucking with me?"

"No. Not even a little bit. I get where you're coming from and I know how angry you must be, but do you really think that sparing her life from your own rage means she owes you anything?"

"Shut the fuck up. I didn't ask you."

"I don't know . . . I don't know what to say. Maybe you need this. Maybe you need to go out and kill something. It's been too long. Maybe Bill was right."

"About what?" Colby stared at him, thinking back. "That I'm a monster?"

Gossamer shrugged, his fur bristling.

Colby glared for a moment, seething. Then he took a deep breath. And another. And another. Rage seeping away. "No. You're right. I'm going about this all wrong. I'm not out to kill Beatriz, I'm out to ship her off, send her back up the river away from those little boys. I can't forget that."

"Take someone with you. Please."

"Not this time. This I have to do alone."

CAROL VOSS'S HOUSE was much larger than Colby had expected. When she'd said money wasn't an issue, he assumed she was exaggerating. While he had spent time around all manner and sort of supernatural creature in his life, he'd spent very little time around the wealthy except when picking through estate sales—and those were almost entirely run by separate brokers. She seemed normal, just an average everyday mom worried about her kids. As it turned out, Mr. Voss did in fact do *very* well for himself. Their house was on the expensive side of the river with a Brazilian hardwood boat dock and a view of Mount Bonnell that only a privileged few could afford.

The lawn stretched out long and wide from the back of the house, thick, lush, a shade of green brighter than most of the other lawns this time of year. The grass was firm, uniformly cut, springing back into place with each step, carefully manicured trees growing at perfectly measured intervals. The lawn looked less like someone's backyard and more like the set of a catalog photo shoot.

Colby stood in the expansive backyard, looking out over the river, the sun setting behind him, waiting for twilight. Shadows crept closer and closer to the water, the sky exploding in pinks and purples. From where he stood, Colby could see the crowds atop Mount Bonnell, watching the sky, waiting for the sun to wink out behind the hills.

And as the hills swallowed up the sun, and the tourists returned to their cars, and the night began to set in over the river, darkness swelled beneath the waves. Colby sat pensively in the grass, waiting for the moment when twilight shifted to dusk. That was the moment that shadows came out, when Beatriz the La Llorona would show herself.

And there she was. Standing, dripping, hollow eyes burning, knee-deep in the shallows of the river. She stared out, her mouth dangling in some silent howl that had yet to catch up with her, her gauzy linen dress soaked through, clinging to her every curve. Her body was still a sultry twenty-four, lusty, hippy, dangerously seductive. But her face was ghoulish, a wrinkled prune wrapped around yellowed, mossy teeth and embers peering through clawed-out sockets.

She took one sloshing step forward, cocking her head to the side at Colby, her howl finally catching up to her, a shrill, angry cry like bitter wind scraping through dead trees. Then she moved again, and again, her entire body lurching forward with each awkward, splashing step, her feet digging in and out of the river mud beneath. Her hands, soaked, freezing, and pale, were unmoving, clutched in a clawlike rigor, dead nubs at the end of stiff arms. Beatriz moved like the dead should move.

She tried to step around Colby, pretending he wasn't there. Colby carefully sidestepped. Beatriz grimaced angrily, surprisingly able to become uglier and more horrifying than before.

"*¡Ay! Mis hijos!*" she wailed.

"No, *ellos no son tus hijos,*" he replied in slightly accented Spanish. *No, they are not your children.*

"*They are my children, and I need them!*"

"*No. You need to leave, to return to the water. You know my rules. I'm asking nicely. Please leave this family be.*"

"*No! I will not leave without my children! I need them. I am so alone.*"

Colby stood at the edge of the water, the night getting darker around him. He reached into his pocket, pulling out a pack of cigarettes and a finely etched silver Zippo covered top to bottom with arcane symbols. "*I'm going to ask nicely one last time,*" he said.

"*Colby, I need my children.*"

Colby flipped a cigarette into his mouth, flicking the lighter, and lighting his smoke in one fluid motion. "*Those aren't your kids, and you know it, witch.*"

Beatriz tightened, her arms drawing close, her fingers becoming long and sharp. She hissed and the air around her chilled, frosting the water on her skin. Then she took another sloshing step forward. Colby took a long, slow drag on his cigarette, blowing the smoke in her face.

She recoiled, covering her eyes with the inside of her elbow.

"*I have two rules, Beatriz. And you know them. One: Austin is off-limits. Two: you come for the children, I come for you.*"

Beatriz lunged at Colby, hissing, slashing at his face. Colby fell backward to the ground, landing hard on his ass.

She clawed at him and he jabbed his cigarette at her eye sockets.

Beatriz jumped back, again covering her face.

Colby focused upon her, trying to break her dreamstuff apart. He felt cold, lonely hate. Misery. Anger. "Shit."

"*I'm so hungry, Colby. It consumes me.*"

"*I know.*"

"*I need them. I need them.*"

"*I know,*" he said again.

"*Let me have them and I will leave. I promise.*"

"*I can't do that. I can't let you drown those little boys.*"

"*I won't, I promise. But I need them.*"

"*You're not taking those boys.*"

Beatriz cast her arms back and leaned in with a wild, uncontrolled hiss.

Colby stabbed at her with the lit end of his cigarette, causing her to recoil once more.

"*That cigarette won't stay lit forever.*"

It wouldn't. He had to think quickly. "*You can't have those boys, Beatriz . . . because you have two of your own. Where are they?*"

She shook her head. "*I don't know.*"

"*You do. You know where they are, Beatriz.*"

"*No. I don't.*"

"*You do. Think back. Think hard. Where are they?*"

"*I don't know!*"

"*You know where they are, Beatriz, because you drowned them. You drowned your little boys!*"

"*I didn't! No! I don't know where they are!*"

"*Think. Think. Think back as hard as you can. Where? Are? Your boys?*"

Beatriz stopped her clawing and flailing for a moment, tilting her head, lost in thought. Colby could feel the confusion, the lack of conviction and certainty. Beatriz was bubbling to the surface of all that hate. She was beginning to reason, beginning to think back through frozen memories decades old and drowning.

Colby focused once more and the embers in Beatriz's eyes became flames. "*Noooo!*" she screamed, flaring up, a green flame swallowing her whole, boiling away her flesh.

Beatriz vanished with a slight sizzle, the smell of cheap perfume and rotting fish the only lingering reminder that she'd ever been there.

Colby rose to his feet, dusting himself off, and flung the lit cigarette out into the water. It was done. He took a deep breath and staggered slowly toward the house.

He knocked on the back door and Carol answered almost instantly. Colby's eyes were cold, disappointed.

"You were watching?" he asked.

Carol bit her lip, playing coy.

"I told you not to watch."

"I know, but . . . I was worried." She paused for a second, then asked, "Is it done? Is she—"

"Gone? For good. She won't be back."

"Oh my God, thank you!" She burst into tears, throwing her arms around him. "You saved my babies!"

"You're welcome. Now for your end of the bargain."

Carol pulled away and nodded, wiping tears away from her eyes. "Are you sure I can't pay you?"

"There's no comfort in the world I need that money can grant me for very long. Besides, like I said, I do all right. This is the one thing I can't really get. On my own. You know?"

"It just seems so—"

"Yeah. But a deal is a deal."

"Come on in," she said, stepping back, welcoming him inside. "My husband is with the boys upstairs. We won't be bothered."

The back door led immediately into the kitchen. Colby walked in and breathed deeply. He pointed at the simple wooden kitchen table. "Right here?"

"Is that okay?"

He nodded. "It is."

"Can I get you something to drink?"

"Coffee would be great. Black."

"Is French press okay?"

"Perfect."

Carol began nervously making a cup of coffee. She turned around. "This seems, I don't know . . ."

Colby smiled awkwardly, nodding. "Look, I don't meet a lot of *people* doing what I do. And I certainly can't talk to them without feeling like I have to hide who I really am. Words can't explain the loneliness I feel on any given day." He stabbed a single finger in the air. "There's one thing, and only one thing, you can do for me that makes what I just did out there worthwhile. I want to sit down at that table, have a nice cup of coffee, and eat dinner with a very nice woman whom I don't have to pretend around. I don't get a lot of home-cooked meals and whatever that is, it smells delicious."

"It's lasagna."

"Perfect."

Carol smiled. "Black, you said? The coffee?"

"Yes, black. Thank you."

She handed him a mug of dark, steaming coffee that read #1 MOM on the side. Colby looked at it, gripping the handle a little tighter as he read, then took a sip. He could never tell the difference between expensive coffee or the cheap stuff, but this was delicious. It was probably expensive.

"How big a slice do you want?" she asked. "The lasagna, I mean."

"As big as the plate." Colby sat down at the table with his coffee and took a deep breath, relaxing. "So. Carol," he said, as chipper as he could muster. "Tell me about your day."

CHAPTER 8

THE PRETTY LITTLE GIRL IN THE PURPLE PAJAMAS

Once upon a time there was a pretty little girl in purple pajamas, all of eleven years old, who appeared not as she saw herself, but rather as she wished she could be. Her dark hair shone in the starlight, her smile shone in the moon. She had left her body at home once again, a silvery wisp trailing behind her as she moved, the thread connected at the base of the back of her skull, winding all the way back through the barren wilderness to her bed, hundreds of miles away.

She was faster without her body. Taller. Of slighter build.

There were no imperfections, no unsightly scars, nothing at all to distinguish her from any other girl in the world. The pretty little girl in the purple pajamas was normal. Unburdened. Happy.

And it was a beautiful night.

She was deep in the outback again, well past the black stump, hunting bunyip barefoot over sandblasted red stone fields. While the pretty little girl in the purple pajamas had seen a lot of strange things out here at night, she had never seen a bunyip. And that was something she was very much hoping to change. The stories said they were big, scary, hairy, and mean, able to drown a man by raising the lake water while he slept if he dared to camp too close. But she was clever. And she was fast. And there wasn't a spirit yet that dared try to catch her that had been able to.

Stars burned brightly in the black sky, splayed out from end to end unblemished by clouds or lights. Below, only campfires pockmarked the desert before her. She raced from water hole to water hole—each sometimes dozens of miles apart—looking for a bunyip lurking within its depths. But she found nothing but a glassy reflection of the sky staring back at itself. And as the night approached its darkest point, she knew it was time to give up the hunt and visit the one friend she'd made this far out in the desert.

The Clever Man.

She looked out over the vast, black expanse, glancing at each fire in the distance until she found one that felt familiar. Then she raced across the dark, her feet barely touching the ground. Rocks. Shrubs. Lone trees. All blurring together. Then fire, the one she was looking for.

The Clever Man sat before it, alone, smiling brightly, his eyes flickering with firelight. His hair was thick, curly, black—the ends dusted with a light gray, his temples a silvery white—his skin a rich, sunbaked brown, only a small, tanned cloth providing any modesty. He did not look up, and instead tended the fire with a small stick, speaking only to the night.

"Have you seen it yet?" he asked.

The girl in the purple pajamas slumped down on the ground beside him, frustrated. "Nooooooooo. Not yet."

"He is wily. Wilier even than you. You will have to be very patient; he will not so easily show himself. Just wait. The first time you see one, nothing will ever be the same."

"Okay," she sighed. Then she perked up. "So, is he here yet?"

"Is who here yet?" asked the Clever Man.

"The Dream-hero. You said he was coming."

"He's coming. But he's not here yet."

"Why not? What's taking him so long?"

"It's not his time."

"But it will be? Soon?"

"Very soon."

"I can't wait."

"You can wait."

"You said it was my destiny. I can't wait for my destiny."

"He is not your destiny."

"But you said he was!"

The Clever Man shook his head. "No. I said he was destined to arrive and you were destined to meet him. What he brings with him is a choice. What happens to you will not be *his* doing, but *yours*."

"But he *is* coming?"

"Yes."

"Soon?"

"Very soon."

"I can't wait."

The Clever Man laughed. "You two are very much alike. In so many ways. So many small details about you indistinguishable from the other. So many children in this world so eager to end their childhood. So ready for the future. Never ready for the now."

"I'm ready for the now."

"You hate the now. You spent the whole night looking for the bunyip, didn't you?"

"Yeeeeeesssss. But you told me to."

"Never. Never did."

"Yes, you did."

"I said once you see the bunyip . . ."

"Nothing will ever be the same."

"So why hurry?"

The pretty little girl in the purple pajamas pouted. She knew the answer. The Clever Man was right. He was always right. "I like the now. I just like the now out here better. I wish I could stay out here."

"Wishes are dangerous. Especially for a spirit as powerful as you. You are exactly where you need to be to become exactly who you are supposed to become. Too many people be saying *I wish I was this* or *I wish I was there* and not enough people saying *I will be this here and make this place better*. If you want to like better the now, you should think more like that. You are too beautiful a spirit to wish you were prettier, too powerful a spirit to wish you were stronger, too quick a spirit to wish you were faster."

"You don't know I'm pretty."

"You are very pretty," said the Clever Man.

"You've never even see me, not really."

It was true. He hadn't. He'd only seen her spirit. "I am a Clever Man," he said. "I do not need to look at you to see you."

"You don't, do you?"

The Clever Man smiled wide, shaking his head. He took a deep breath, the kind he took only before launching into one of his stories, and then, with a stiff finger pointing into the night like an exclamation point, he began one. "Long ago, when the earth was still being dreamed, only seven women possessed the secret of fire. They carried it with them at all times, burning at the top ends of their digging sticks. All the fellas were very jealous of their secret and wanted it for themselves. And no fella wanted it more than Crow.

"Crow was a clever trickster. He knew that the women loved to eat termites right out of the mound, but that they feared snakes more than anything else. So Crow flew all over creation and picked up every snake he could find. Red ones, black ones, yellow ones! Red, black, and yellow ones! Then he tied them all into a knot, burying them deep within a termite mound. They wriggled and wiggled and tried very hard to untangle themselves, but even those that managed to break free could not go far underground.

"Then Crow flew to the women, telling them of the large, virgin mound he'd found out in the desert. The hungry women rushed to the mound, but as they dug into it with their sticks, it erupted with snakes. The mass wriggled apart all at once and there were so many snakes that the ground itself seemed to move and wave like the sea. The women were so scared they dropped fire from the ends of their sticks and Crow, waiting for this, collected every single bit of it. He laughed as he flew away with all their fire.

"Crow spent a lot of time after that tending the coals he kept his fire alive in. Soon it became all he would do. All men of the earth wanted his fire, but he would not share it, for without it he would no longer be special. Then one day a Clever Man came to take his fire, calling Crow names, making fun of him. Crow became enraged and angrily hurled a coal at the man. But Crow did not notice that the man was standing on a patch of dry grass upon which Crow himself also stood. The Clever Man moved and the coal missed him, setting the grass on fire.

"Crow, afraid he would lose his fire to the man, stayed instead to protect it, but was burned up, consumed by the grass fire surrounding him. Everyone thought he was dead, but Crow could not be killed so easily. From the flames he emerged, smoky, singed and black with soot. He laughed, carrying with him a single flaming stick. He had protected his fire. But to this day, Crow remains black, everyone seeing him not as he was, but for what he had done.

"You are a very powerful and clever spirit. I do not see you as you are; I see you only for what you have chosen to do. And you have chosen to be very beautiful. Your spirit is a good one. A well-intentioned one. It will be tested. But when the tests are done, I think you might be more beautiful than ever."

"Is the bunyip the test?" asked the girl.

"The bunyip? He is only the first of many." The Clever Man looked up, his smile fading, staring sadly off into the distance. "Oh," he said. "It looks like our time together is over."

The pretty little girl in the purple pajamas reeled back in horror, eyes wide, the silver cord connected behind her to the base of her skull pulling suddenly taut, flinging her backward into darkness. The night shot past, stars streaking, the fire a pinprick swiftly winking out. She screamed and the night disappeared.

For a second there was only black.

HER ALARM CLOCK roared, its dingy yellowing plastic rattling, ancient gears grinding as the tinkle of it slowly wound down. Kaycee blearily rubbed her eyes, the glare of the campfire still etched in them. The gentle rays of a very early dawn peered, grayish blue, through rusting, bent blinds tangled in knotted cords. It was morning again and her walk was over. She hammered a balled-up fist down on top of the clock, sneering, just a little, her cleft palate splitting enough of her upper lip to show nothing but gum and teeth all the way up to her nose.

Her eyes adjusted, the dull, pale hues of the physical world growing crisp and sharp, like a TV antenna being twiddled into place. Nothing twinkled or glowed or scintillated, rippling with unearthly colors. It was static, cold, dirty, and old. The waking world was just about the most awful thing Kaycee could imagine. In the dream she could be whatever she wanted; here she was what everyone else thought she was.

Swinging her legs out from under the covers, she put her right foot down on the floor. Her gnarled club of a left foot followed soon after—swollen, twisted, with tiny malformed nubs protruding like warts where her toes should be. She still wore her purple pajamas, though they were ratty, tired, frayed around the cuffs, two or three sizes smaller than they should be, meant for a girl far younger. The buttons clung on for dear life and the shoulder rode a bit higher up the arm than it should, but they held, their yellow stars now brown with stains and infrequent washing.

Leaning onto her good foot, she pushed herself upright, lurching forward in a drowsy zombie shuffle out into the hallway. Kaycee ran her hands through her curly, matted black hair, tugging hard, trying further to shake the dream.

Across the house, the television rattled on about an accident—a twelve-car pileup—sunny voices struggling to sound strained. The words ran together through the thin, water-stained walls, Kaycee not caring enough yet about the day to bother trying to parse them out. She walked down the stairs, into the living room, past the television, straight on through the wall of stink where lingering stale smoke mingled with rum and a night's worth of sweat. There, in his battered, threadbare easy chair, snored her father, an open bottle and half-full glass on the end table next to him, a twitch and a half away from being knocked over.

Wade Looes looked like a washed-up boxer, a mountain of

muscles sculpted from tossing boxes, hands calloused, chewed raw from years of canning fish. His face was chipped with scars, his brow thick, his jaw thicker, his skin a creamy coffee brown. At rest, he looked angry; when angry, he looked monstrous. He snored away in the chair, snorting occasionally like the sound of a bad transmission slipping gears.

Kaycee reached behind the lamp, pulling out the funnel she kept there, and slotted it into the bottle of rum, dumping what was left in the glass back into the bottle. They weren't rich enough to throw out good rum like that. She wished she could dump the whole bottle out, pour it down the sink and be done with it. She'd done that before. He was always so drunk when he fell asleep that he simply thought he'd polished off the whole bottle himself. Do this enough, she thought, and he'd stop drinking for sure. But Wade always went right back out, with whatever money he could scrape together, and bought more.

So she stoppered the bottle back up, slipping it between the end table and the chair, praying silently that this would be the last time she had to.

"Dad," she said, gently tugging at the sleeve of yesterday's work shirt. "Dad. Wake up. Sun's comin' up." Her father shifted in his chair, groaning against the morning. "Dad, come on. I gotta get to school. You gotta shower still. Sun's comin'."

His eyes shot open, confused, a smile creeping slowly across his lips as his daughter came into focus. "Morning, darlin'," he said, reaching up to stroke the deep brown of her face. "You have good dreams again?"

She nodded. "Yes, sir."

"Good. I reckon you deserved 'em?"

"Yes, sir."

"All right," he said, settling back into the chair. "Well, Dad needs a few more minutes' sleep. So why don't you—"

"Nuh-uh. You gotta get ready for work. Go take a shower. I'll make breakfast."

Her father smiled, face buried in the chair cushion, peering up at her with a single, squinting eye. "You know Dad's still a little drunk, don't you?"

She nodded sadly. "The shower and coffee will help."

"Okay," he said, grunting as he stood to his feet, leaving behind a cushion soaked with rancid drunk sweat, its stink wafting up after him, chasing him down the hall. "But only if you fry the eggs. Will you fry the eggs?"

"I'll fry the eggs."

"Over easy?"

"Over easy."

He staggered slowly into the bathroom, calling back over his shoulder. "Kaycee Looes, you're the best thing to ever happen to me."

Kaycee smiled a little, wishing that were true and not just the rum talking. But she knew better.

Then she limped into the kitchen to make breakfast, mindful they were still days away from the next paycheck, knowing that she should probably scramble the eggs instead of frying them, watering them down with a little more milk than she'd like. Fortunately for her, the bread was about to turn, so she had no choice but to make extra toast, plumping out breakfast enough to keep them both full until lunch.

Her father slipped in, skin still steaming from the hot shower, curly black hair tousled and slick, eyes twinkling at the thought of sizzling eggs. "What's with all the toast?"

"About to go stale."

"Good. I like toast."

"You better. It's that and the eggs until lunch. Drink your coffee."

He sipped at the mug, face souring a little. It wasn't good.

But that was hardly Kaycee's fault. So he hid his displeasure, muscling down as much as he could stand without burning himself. Kaycee held the scalding-hot skillet above his plate, oil popping, thick egg white bubbling up, sliding two eggs off with a warped old spatula. Her father looked up, eyes pleading. "One more?" he asked.

"You want eggs tomorrow?"

He nodded.

"Then you only get two today."

"Okay," he said, looking down sadly.

"Eat 'em slow."

Wade took a small bite of dry toast, smiling, twitching an eyebrow playfully at his daughter. She smiled back, slid a single egg onto her own plate, and put the skillet back on the stove.

The two ate together in silence, Wade trying to sober up, wishing he didn't have to, Kaycee trying not to think about the fact that this was going to be the very best part of her day. They powered through the dry toast and the bad coffee, but the eggs were perfect. Piping hot, lightly salted, a dash of pepper. They slid warm and greasy into the belly, at once sobering Wade up.

It was morning again, and he was ready to go back to it. He kissed his daughter on the cheek, wrapping his massive arms around her, then headed out to catch his ride back into town.

Kaycee quickly cleaned the kitchen then readied herself for school—a quick shower and a few strokes of a brush through her hair before tossing on a clean shirt and a pair of shorts. Then she slipped a sandal onto her one good foot, turned off the television, locked the front door, and walked out to the curb to wait for the van to school.

She stood there, staring at her shadow on the ground, the bland, dingy colors of the dry earth stinging in the harsh Australian morning sun. The van always picked her up last, already overflowing with kids. Kaycee dreaded seeing them, hated the moment when the van pulled up and the doors opened and not one of them looked out the window or up at her as she passed them. They weren't cruel. No one would utter a word about her foot or the split in her lip. There would be no name calling, no harassment. Instead it was as if she wasn't even there. The invisible kid meant for the seat no one else dared sit in lest they be forced into eye contact or to exchange a few uncomfortable words.

Sometimes she wished people would say something, make fun of her in some shape or form, if only so she could put them in their place; if only so she could feel like they saw her. She hated being awake. She hated the world outside sleep. In the dream, she could be whatever she wanted; here, she was what everyone thought she was.

And that was nothing. Nothing at all.

CHAPTER 9

ON KUTJI

An excerpt by Dr. Thaddeus Ray, Ph.D., from his book *Dreamspeaking, Dreamwalking, and Dreamtime: The World on the Other Side of Down Under*

Shadows are not necessarily spirits of the dead, though they are formed by the painful, agonizing, or tortured death of a human being. But these are not the persons themselves, merely reflections of the very worst or most powerful parts of them. While it is true that they are comprised of dreamstuff squeezed from a deceased soul, they are not beings of memory, intellect, or experience. They are beings of deep emotion and fear. They are monsters born of lingering hate, pain, or agony.

Shadows do not exist to achieve goals fostered in life—at least not in the way they were initially intended—but rather to carry out some new mission to assuage the painful scars that forged them. These are scars that never heal, wounds that never close. Shadows press on like Sisyphus, forever clawing at the night, continuing to do the same terrible things over and over again until they have no dreamstuff left to press on any farther.

Some shadows, like boggarts, become mostly sentient. Most of the time they behave as they did in life, albeit with much more pronounced traits or quirks. The only point at which their shadowy nature becomes a hindrance on their personality is when they feed or fight. It is in those moments that their lack of humanity shows through and their truly terrible natures bubble to the surface. One can live in close proximity to a boggart for quite some time without ever feeling in danger or actually being in danger for that matter. But shadows are comprised of darkness, and eventually they must succumb to that.

Other shadows, like La Llorona, are much more feral than their more humanlike cousins. These creatures are formed from women destroyed by their own grief and madness, and thus that is all that remains of them. They wander the earth, reliving their final moments, trying desperately to get it right this time around. Their memories are short, their personalities only approximations of humanity, their attempts to imitate behavior existing only as a self-defense mechanism. They seduce men to keep them from becoming a threat and they use whatever guile they can to gain access to children they can drag into the water.

Kutji, on the other hand, are somewhere between these two extremes.

A kutji is a shadow native to the deserts of the outback. Often appearing warped and distorted, they are shaped as their shadow hung at the moment their body passed. This leaves them ranging in appearance from short, squat, and square to tall, lithe, and gangly, possessed of limbs the length of a grown man. Their bodies are made entirely of darkness and thus they are terrified of the sun, living in holes, cracks, or under rocks and abandoned vehicles. If caught away from their haunts near dawn, they will take shelter anywhere dark and hide until the sun sets once more. Exposure to sunlight boils them away almost immediately and, once destroyed, they will never return. While artificial light is painful to them, it poses no real threat and they will endure it if the reason is good enough.

Kutji are usually formed as the result of violent, unjust, or unwelcome death. It is very rare for a peaceful or accidental death to result in forming one. Most often they are formed by the fear and anger building up over a short period of time between learning of their death and experiencing it. In that moment, the dying think of all the things they left unfinished, all of the anger they have for the person killing them, and they cling to that rather than finding release. The moment their soulstuff is released, if an area is as particularly rich in dreamstuff as the outback is, a kutji can be formed.

They do not exist as they did in life. Their wit, their passionate desires, and their quirks remain, but their humanity is stripped from them, so much so that they don't even bother to imitate it. They are in thrall to their desires, trying again and again to achieve the unattainable satisfaction of completing whatever task eluded them in life. Oftentimes this can be the accumulation of wealth, satiating sadistic urges, or getting revenge for some slight done to them. On rare occasions the task can be specific, like getting hold of a certain item or killing an individual. But like many spirits, the kutji lose their way over time and those desires become blurred, muddled, sometimes confusing one object with another.

The kutji cannot be satisfied. It is their curse. They walk the earth, fearing the light, convinced that completing their task offers some great reward. Whether it be death, a respite, or a return to the land of the living, they each pine for something and think achieving it will grant it to them. But it never does.

However short of memory they might be about their reason for being, they are both long of memory and extraordinarily patient. A kutji will work for years, even decades, on a single task. But unable to affect many things in the mortal world, they often must turn to dreamspeakers or anyone else able to peer past the veil. With these people, the kutji often strike bargains, offering to do dark deeds or help gather the dreamstuff to perform magic. Dreamspeakers, better known as Clever Men or shamans, have learned over time to cultivate relationships with local kutji and call upon them to do whatever they need done, often unaware of the kutji's true motivations. In truth, these motivations rarely affect the dreamspeaker, as it is customary for the first deal struck to be one of nonaggression.

Kutji, like many spirits, are bound to their own word. As certain memories fade, so too do the details surrounding such an agreement, leaving behind only the prohibition or promise and an understanding that this prohibition or promise is sacred law. Breaking such an oath is like deciding to put your hand into a fire, or to jump from a cliff, or to cut off your own foot. They believe doing so is the key to their undoing, no matter how small or insignificant the agreement might be.

Unlike more terrifying menaces, kutji aren't particularly violent or directly malicious. More often than not, a kutji's requests will seem ridiculously simple, almost mundane. Sometimes they serve no other purpose than to fulfill a desire or habit they performed in life, like drinking or smoking. But it is wise not to take all of their requests lightly, for they are playing a long game. It is possible the small task you perform for them in the physical world is the puzzle piece they need to do something terrible far down the road or is meant to bring some harm to the person performing it. In fact, you can almost always be assured that it is. One should never agree to a kutji's terms before thinking through what they are asking for.

While kutji often appear as spirits, they can show themselves in a number of different forms, ranging from animals like kangaroos, crows, owls, eagles, bandicoots, emus, and snakes; they can also manifest as dust storms, rain clouds, or even thunder. They can also possess these creatures in order to travel over great distances or appear to those who cannot perceive their spirit forms easily. Their powers over the souls of others allow them to possess human beings, at a great cost to their own energy, infect others with disease, or even cause death.

But kutji rarely bother those who cannot see or hear them, for they find them to be of little use. The only time one can expect to be bothered by one is if you somehow play into achieving their goals. As long lived as kutji are, these are not goals it is easy to simply blunder into. On the rare occasion that you find yourself the target of a kutji's intentions, all bets are off. It is cases like these when any reports of aggression or deliberate malfeasance arise. They are beings with hazy memories, and without remorse; expect little quarter.

CHAPTER 10

AUSTIN

Colby meandered into the bar with a belly full of lasagna and an ass still sore from his awkward, painful landing in the grass behind Carol Voss's house. He didn't want to go home yet, but he didn't want to be around the denizens of the Cursed and the Damned either. So he quietly slid into a small bar, hoping to blend in with the flimsy plywood and ironic neon.

He ordered a cheap Mexican import served with a lime in the neck of the bottle and made his way out through a metal door to the back patio. Limestone walls ranging from knee high to almost ten feet tall surrounded a courtyard littered with cheap metal tables, a chain-link fence boxing in the rest. It was a nice, quiet place to have a beer and ignore the rest of the world. There were no demons, no angels, no djinns.

Just a blonde. A beautiful, heartbreaking blonde.

And she was sitting alone.

She was slender, tan, freckled, blond hair spilling out from under a braided-cord straw cowboy hat, wearing a black T-shirt with the sleeves ripped off, faded blue jeans, and hand-painted sneakers. One arm was smooth and bare while the other was a complete sleeve of brightly colored tattoos. The corners of her mouth twitched into a slight smile when she saw Colby and it felt as if the whole patio had brightened at once. Her delicate fingers fondled a local craft brew and she bit her lip slightly.

It was a slow night and they were otherwise alone.

The blonde traced the rim of her bottle with a single finger and watched as Colby took a seat a few tables away. He tried not to look at her, clumsily trying to show that he wasn't creeping up on her.

"That's not really a Mexican beer, you know," she said.

Colby looked up, a little confused. He'd been thinking of a dozen different ways she might shoot him down and had no idea how to react to her speaking directly to him. He swallowed hard. "Um, huh?"

"The beer. It's not Mexican."

Colby looked down at the beer in his hand. "Oh. I didn't know that."

"Yeah, they make them in San Antonio from a Mexican recipe and just put imported on the bottle. It's the same guys who make all the cheap stuff."

"What's that?" he asked, pointing at her own beer.

"Local."

"You like it?"

"It's pretty much the same shit you're drinking, only more

expensive." She stood up and took a few graceful steps over to his table and pointed at the empty chair beside him. Not across. Beside. "May I?"

"Uh, yeah! Yeah!"

She plopped down in the chair far less gracefully than she'd walked and took a swig of beer. "It costs more, but the money stays here in town, puts guys I know to work, so it's worth it."

"Oh, local economy and all that."

"I'm Austin," she said, raising her beer.

"Colby," he said, raising his.

"You know, I gotta say, I imagined you much more well spoken than this."

"I'm . . . I'm sorry."

"It's okay. Do I have you flustered or are you just normally like this around people?"

"I . . . well . . . yeah. It's you."

She smiled, reaching into the hip pocket of her jeans. "I can dig that. Just as long as the conversation gets better as the night goes on." Austin pulled out a small bag of weed and a pack of papers and, without a thought, began rolling a joint.

"What are you doing?"

With a quick lick and a twist of her wrists, she wrapped the paper up tight into a perfectly formed spliff. "Rolling one up. You wanna share or would you like your own?"

"Uh, no. Um, thanks though."

Austin laughed. "I never pegged you for a prude." She lit the joint and took a quick puff.

"I'm not a prude. It's just, we're out in public."

She held her breath for a second, then exhaled loudly. "There's not a cop within three blocks of this place and not one who will walk by for another . . . fifty minutes, give or take."

"That's a little specific."

"They have schedules. Routines. Habits. Lots of things that

keep them in other places and then bring them here. But nothing that will bring anyone here anytime soon."

"Well, what about the bartenders?"

"The *bartenders*?" she asked. "Have you ever known any bartenders? Our biggest concern then is bogarting this. You worry too much."

"And you seem pretty relaxed."

"Trust me. It's still, like, forty-nine and a half minutes before anyone comes by. Maybe forty-nine even."

Colby pursed his lips. "Who are you?"

"You still don't recognize me, do you?"

"Not even a little. Do we know each other?"

She shook her head. "No. We know *of* each other. I've read your books. I've seen you around. But *know* . . . ?"

Colby's jaw dropped open. "Wait, you're—"

"Austin."

"*The* Austin."

She smiled. "No. Just Austin. There's no *the*."

Colby gawked at her for a moment, stunned speechless.

She took another drag off the joint, held her breath deeply for a moment, letting Colby wrap his head around what was going on, then exhaled. "You sure you don't want a hit of this? It's amazing stuff."

"No, really."

"Aw, Colby. I thought you were cool."

"No you didn't. No one thinks I'm cool."

"Okay. I didn't. But I did hope you would get cool-*er*."

Colby sipped his beer, the wheels turning in his head. "Wait a second. Why haven't we met until just now?"

"Because we never had to before today." Her eyes turned cold and serious. She wasn't playing around anymore. "You crossed the line tonight, Colby. It wasn't your place to do what you did."

"Is this about . . . is this about Beatriz?"

"Of course it's about Beatriz. What else have you been up to tonight?"

"That's between her and me."

Austin shook her head. "There isn't a *her* anymore. Now it's just you and me. You may want to be the sheriff of this town, but you ain't the sheriff of this town. There's only one sheriff. And she might have to ask you to leave if you can't get your shit together."

"I can't believe what I'm hearing. You knew about her?"

"Yeah."

"What she was up to?"

Austin nodded, the joint six inches from her face. "Yeah."

"And you were just going to let those kids die? You would have let that thing drown them?"

"Of course not," she said, slightly offended. "Vincent and Taylor are wonderful boys, both with bright futures. More important, their mother is a sweet, wonderful woman who would do anything for them. I wasn't going to let Beatriz harm a hair on their heads. I couldn't do that to Carol."

Colby took a sip of his beer and glared at Austin. "And just how did you plan on stopping her?"

"They're still here, aren't they?"

"Yeah, but not because of you."

Austin grinned. "Really? How did Carol find you again?"

Colby leaned forward pensively, his eyes narrowed. "She said a psychic told her, but wouldn't say who."

"Mother Ojeda. Nice woman. Has the gift. But not quite like you. She hears things sometimes. Sometimes it's mild schizophrenia mutating shit she heard on TV. Sometimes it's me, telling people what they need to hear."

"So what you're saying is that you brought Carol to a psychic and the psychic told her where to find me because you knew I would show up and kill Beatriz."

Austin did the mental arithmetic, tracing her work on the air with a single outstretched finger. Then she nodded. "Yes. That's exactly how it happened."

"And you're pissed at *me*?"

"I know it doesn't make sense, Colby. But I don't have to make sense."

"Why? Because you're a woman or something?"

"No, idiot," she said. "Because I'm a god." She paused for a moment, eyeing him up and down. "Or what *you call* genius loci." Then she smiled. "Like I said, I've read your books."

"But why did you just chew me out for stopping her after you set it up so I would?"

"Because we needed to meet. We needed to have this conversation."

"I can't believe this shit."

Austin killed the last few swigs of her beer and slammed it down on the table. Then she took another toke of her dwindling joint. A waiter appeared with a beer for both of them, setting them down on the table.

"Hey," he said to Austin. "You mind if I hit that?"

"Be my guest," she said. "Don't bring none unless you want to share."

"My kind of lady." The waiter took a few quick tokes, holding them in, then gave a wave on his way back to the bar, exhaling just before walking inside.

She smiled. "That's Brad. He was having a rough night earlier. Nice guy. There's a girl a few streets over named Felicia. Her ex called her fat in the middle of their breakup. She's not taking it well. I'm going to let her stagger over this way and she and Brad are going to have a very nice few hours together."

"A drunk hookup?"

"He's gonna consider the night a good one, she'll wake up remembering some cute bartender couldn't keep his hands off her, and even though they'll most likely never see each other again, it will put them on the path they need to be on. But you wanna know the kicker, Colby?"

"What?"

"I'm not making either of them do anything. I just know them. Intimately. I know the mistakes they'll make when they're presented with the options. And by manipulating a few traffic lights, breaking a high-heeled shoe or two, and distracting someone long enough to run a stop sign, I can put two people in each other's arms in order to change their lives for the better. But it's not always about hookups or good times. Sometimes it's about murderous spirits. Sometimes it's about wizards who think it's their job to patrol the streets to keep the night safe for children.

"What you did the night the fairies came for Ewan was your business. They made their bed. You did what was just and right for you to do in that situation. I've got no beef with that. And until now you've been all talk. I've certainly got no beef with *that*. But tonight you crossed the line from tough talking to instigating. I played my part, which is why we're talking over beers and a joint—and really, you should try this, it's really good shit—instead of having it out in the mud behind Carol's house."

Colby finished his beer and then grabbed the other. "So why exactly did we need to talk?"

"So I could tell you never to do that again. I don't care how you go about defending yourself. But the vigilante act ends tonight."

"I'm sure you're telling everyone that Austin is back on the market and the buffet is open, then?"

"Are you kidding me? I'm not saying shit. I love that those prissy Limestone Kingdom pricks are staying where they belong out in the woods. I just can't have you gunning them down in the streets if and when they do come to town." Austin took one last hit from the roach, finally cashing in her joint. Then she looked at Colby with soft, gentle eyes. "Like I said. I don't have to make sense."

Colby shook his head, a hand to his temple.

Austin stood up and slammed down the remainder of her beer. "Besides, it's rare that I get to share a beer with a man I don't have to pretend around. Know what I mean?" She winked, then shook her head. *"Because I'm a woman?* Jesus, dude. You are not single by accident, that's for damn sure." Then she vanished from where she stood, leaving Colby confused and alone on the patio, fumbling for the words to apologize.

"Damnit," he muttered, thinking about how hard his heart was pounding. "That's inconvenient."

CHAPTER 11

ON GENIUS LOCI

AN EXCERPT BY DR. THADDEUS RAY, PH.D.,
FROM HIS BOOK *THE EVERYTHING YOU
CANNOT SEE*

As discussed earlier, dreamstuff accumulates, giving birth to creatures born of whim or, in extreme cases, transmuting a creature's dreamstuff from one form into another, as in the case of a dying human turning into a spirit, a shadow, or a fairy. But not all things created as such are conjured directly out of the imagination of those nearby. In many cases, as with the genius loci, dreamstuff coalesces into a form representative of the area around it. These creatures become arbiters or wardens of the area they inhabit, embodying the very essence of the land itself and the people who live upon it.

The name genius loci comes from the Latin, which originally described local gods, specifically household gods, or those that governed over small towns or islands. Greeks and Romans often recognized these genii as godlike beings, telling and retelling the stories of their governance or misadventure as part of their oral history. As was the case with many cultures of the day, the stories would be absorbed into other communities and ascribed to their own genii. Thus rose the tales of the Greek and Roman pantheons, which in all likelihood were based on the accumulated tales of hundreds of different beings and creatures.

A genius loci can take many forms, from the green men or living trees of the forests, to leviathans of the sea, to dust devils of the desert, to creatures that look and act every bit like the human beings they represent and protect. Each locale creates the protector it wants or needs, whether or not they know what they're asking for. But once born of dreamstuff, the genius loci possesses a mind and will of its own and thus can affect its surroundings just as much as its surroundings affect it.

Often, as is the case with fairy communities, the genius loci will interfere directly with the events transpiring around it. This can involve acting in the place of a king or governor, as a knight or protector, or in some cases, simply overseeing a council of the beings it represents. Other genius loci, like those representing large cities or particularly powerful locations—like castles or islands—tend to act indirectly, skulking in shadows or amongst the populace, gently manipulating the area around it with small, imperceivable changes. This can be as subtle as gifting a person with sudden inspiration or causing a car to stall, delaying them or forcing them into an unplanned encounter, or as obvious as an earthquake or large-scale riot.

Most large-scale cities tend to create people, albeit people with an extraordinary amount of control over their surroundings. The personality of this being tends to be entirely representative of the culture around it, looking, sounding, and acting in the purest, most common, easily recognizable fashion. The genius loci of Manhattan, for example, embodies the essence of the true New Yorker, while that of Seattle is much more subdued.

Unlike most beings of dreamstuff, however, genius loci have incredibly short life spans, some living as long as a few decades while others live only a few short years. As the culture around it changes, the genius loci too begins to change, and as it shifts from one era to the next, it must re-create itself, becoming something entirely different from what it was before—something more representative of the new era. For example, the genius loci that oversaw Manhattan was very different in the sleazy Times Square era of the late sixties and seventies from what it is in the family friendly, commerce-minded era of the time of this writing. While a genius loci might keep many of the same traits, enough of it changes through each incarnation that it re-forms as a different being. Look, style, demeanor, and even gender might change as a result of its ever evolving surroundings.

Genii should always be treated with the utmost respect, as they are creatures to be feared. When encountering one you must always remember that you are on their turf, playing by their rules. When destroyed they will re-form, and when they do, they will remember exactly who wronged them.

CHAPTER 12

BACK TO THE CURSED
AND THE DAMNED

The Cursed and the Damned was as lonely a place as there was at this time of night. For all its business, it might as well be out in the mists of the moors or well off the highway in the barren Arizona desert. It was in the dead center of downtown, in the middle of everything, but there were few beings inside Austin left across the veil to enjoy it.

The only reason Yashar even kept it running at all was as a silent eulogy to Old Scraps. He stood there all day, most days, staring over the cheap, depressing innards of the place—its bulbs dangling uncovered on long cords from the ceiling, its gray concrete walls, mismatched tables, boxes and barrels in place of most chairs—occasionally wiping the counter out of habit, thinking about what this place *used to be*. Every once in a while he'd be reminded that some things just needed to be put down or left alone long enough to die. And every time that thought crept in, he thought about the times he and Colby spent drinking themselves into a stupor, the smell of Bill's smoke from the back corner, the sound of drunken angels laughing and falling out of their chairs, having to be hoisted back upright before ordering another round.

And in that moment he remembered why he was serving as life support for an ailing friend, keeping it alive long enough to see the last few good days it had left. This would prove to be just such a day.

Colby threw back the whiskey as if he was putting out a fire. In a sense, he was. He was still shaken, rattled, his heart pounding, gut lurching, fists clenched tight. All the color had drained from his face and he trembled—just a little—reeling from his encounter with Austin.

Yashar leaned over the bar from the other side, bottle at the ready, leather jacket and dangling baubles clanging on the countertop, eagerly hanging on Colby's next words. "Well," he said, as Colby lowered his glass. "What's got you so spooked?" he asked, pouring Colby another few fingers of whiskey as he did.

"I met her," said Colby.

"Who?" asked Bill the Shadow, looming darkly in the corner of the bar.

"The girl of your dreams?" asked Yashar with an interested smile.

"Worse," said Colby. "Austin."

Yashar leaned in a little closer. "Austin who?"

"*Austin.*"

Yashar sighed, deflating. "Oooooh. It's about time you met her."

"Yeah, Colby," said Bill. "How the hell have you gone this long without running into her?"

"She's cute—," said Yashar.

Bill nodded, interrupting. "Yeah, she is."

"But she's nothing to get in a twist over." Yashar recorked the whiskey. This wasn't a story warranting the good stuff.

Colby slammed back the whiskey once more, shook his head. "She's pissed at me."

Yashar eyed him suspiciously. "And how did you manage that?"

"I killed Beatriz."

Yashar and Bill traded troubled, disbelieving glances. Then Yashar slowly uncorked the bottle and walked back over to Colby. "Say that again?"

"I killed Beatriz La Llorona. And Austin wasn't too happy about that."

Yashar poured Colby another glass of whiskey, filling it almost to the top, then looked at him darkly. "Did she have it coming?"

Colby nodded. "Yeah. She had it coming."

Yashar nodded in return. "Bill? You knew her, right?"

Bill nursed a beer, nodding. "Yeah, I knew her."

"And?"

"And the kid's right. She had it coming. Crazy. Half starved. Damaged from the moment she showed up. She never gave the world a damn thing except drowned kids. The river is better without her."

Yashar shook his head. "Then why the hell would Austin be pissed at you?"

"Because I'm not the sheriff of this town," said Colby. "She is."

"And she asked you to leave town?"

"Nope."

"Then what's the problem?"

Colby took a deep breath. "Like you said. She's cute."

"Aw, hell." Bill groaned.

"Damnit, Colby," said Yashar.

"What?"

Yashar put the cork back in the whiskey. "I thought this was serious."

"This is serious. You've been telling me for years that I should find a girl. I finally find one and not only does she threaten to kick my ass out of town, but she's also powerful enough to do it. To make matters worse, she's the reason I ended up killing Beatriz to begin with."

"Wait. You're going to have to explain the last part," said Yashar.

"Yeah," said Bill. "I'm a little lost as well."

Colby sipped from his glass. "A woman came to me for help. Said she was being plagued by La Llorona. She got my name from a psychic."

"Mother Ojeda?" asked Bill.

"Yeah," said Colby. "How'd you know that?"

"The billboard psychic. One of the only legit working spiritu-alists in town. She's exactly who Austin would use."

Yashar's eyes grew wide. "Shit, Colby. You got played."

"Yeah, I did."

"And that . . ."

Colby shot a longing glance across the bar. "Intrigues the hell out of me. Never met anyone before who could play me, put me in my place, and make me feel like I deserved it."

Bill laughed and sipped his beer. "Kid's in trouble all right, Yash. Let the whiskey flow."

"Colby," said Yashar. "Did she threaten you?"

"Directly?"

"Yeah."

"No. It was more of a warning against future endeavors."

Yashar nodded. "So she got what she needed out of you and that was that, right?"

"Exactly."

"Then you're in good shape. Austin is good people. That's her thing."

"Her thing?"

"Yeah. Every loci I've ever met has had a *thing*. An ethos. A sense of purpose driven in one direction or another. It's what they impart to their people. For some it's progress. For others it's war. Some want isolation, others celebration. For years Austin was a bit of a party girl. She likes her beer and she throws amazing parties. But she's mellowed. Her thing has become less about the fireworks and more about the company, if you know what I mean. She wants her legacy to be a town where everyone feels welcome and nobody messes much with anybody else."

Bill lit a cigarette. "Yep. She once told me that she wanted this city to feel like the buzz before the drunk. Laid back and worry free."

Colby grimaced. "That doesn't sound like the girl I met at all."

"Really?" asked Yashar. "And where did you meet your dream girl?"

Colby hesistated a moment. "At a bar."

"Was she pissed?"

"No. She . . . she was actually kind of flirty."

"Uh-huh. Was this the easiest piece of ass chewing anyone's ever given you?"

Colby stared down at the bartop, nodding.

"Then it sounds exactly like Austin."

"S-so, then . . . ," Colby stammered a little, swallowing hard. "H-h-h-how do, how do I . . . how do I tell her . . . ?"

"Oh, sweet merciful Christ," said Bill. "This is happening."

Yashar pointed a stiff finger at Bill. "Cut him some slack."

"Nope. Not this time." Bill took a drag off his cigarette then drenched it in the backwash at the bottom of his beer. He stood up and put a firm hand on Colby's shoulder. "She's loci. She knows. Don't be such a bitch about it." Then Bill faded into the shadows, vanishing from the bar.

Colby and Yashar sat in silence for a moment, each taking turns sipping their whiskey.

"He's right, you know," said Yashar. "She knows."

"Well, then, what the hell am I supposed to do about it?"

"Nothing. You don't do anything. You've dealt with loci before."

"Yeah. I've fought with them. Argued. Made peace. Avoided them when I've had to." He paused, cocking an eyebrow. "Blew one to pieces. But I've never asked one out on a date."

"It's kind of the same thing, actually."

"I'm being serious."

Yashar nodded apologetically, pouring more whiskey into Colby's glass. "I know you are. And I'm trying, really. But, well, I've known you since you were eight."

"And?"

"And in all that time, you still don't understand women any better than you did then."

"The hell I don't. I . . . get . . . women."

Yashar took a sip of whiskey, never breaking his stare, not once so much as blinking.

"I . . ."

Yashar took another sip.

"Tell me everything you know."

"Are we really going to have the talk . . . ?"

"Don't make this harder than it already is."

" . . . because this could take a while."

"Tell me. Everything."

Yashar pulled two ice-cold beers from under the bar, effortlessly popping off the bottle caps. "In that case, we'd better slow down on the hard stuff."

CHAPTER 13

BUSINESS

Swallowed whole and deep by night, the Clever Man stalked quietly through the bush, listening rather than looking. He knew the land, every nook, every cranny, every rock, every shrub. The stars were out, bright beacons guiding him along the songline. The only thing that could surprise him here would be on the move. So, sound; he listened for sound.

He heard them at a distance—a mob of chittering spirits, rolling across the land like a storm, their scuttling bodies tearing through the night with purpose. High-pitched hoots, catcalls, guttural mumbling in incomprehensible languages, moans about half-forgotten agonies. They were headed right for him. He took a deep breath, bracing himself, closing his eyes.

Slowly he drew the bullroarer from his pouch—a carefully carved and painted piece of wood at the end of a frayed, time-worn cord. Then he whipped it around, one end of the cord wrapped tightly around his hand, slinging it through the air like a propeller. At first it hummed, then it sang, finally it screeched such terrible sounds, like a thousand souls loosed from their bodies all at once.

The mass of creatures swarmed in the blackness, surrounding the Clever Man on all sides, unseen, moving around him like a swirling school of fish, roiling just out of sight. A single shadow emerged, its thin, wispy arms nothing but nubs without hands, struggling to approach through the mind-shattering cacophony.

At first he could not see them, but they struggled against the dream, aching to speak. The shadow slunk into the starlight, creeping warily in case the Clever Man lashed out with a bit of unexpected magick. It was as if he was finally able to focus upon the things one sees out of the corner of one's eye only to realize that it still didn't look like anything at all.

"This soul is not for you, spirits," said the Clever Man over the howl of his bullroarer.

"We don't want your paltry soul," said the handless shadow, his mind reeling, manner unsteady, voice like air leaking out from a pinched balloon. "We come for larger prizes. We come with business."

"You have nothing I want."

"Oh, but we do," it hissed. "We doooooooooo. We can offer you a great many things. Riches. Power."

The Clever Man's expression remained blank, entirely loosed of emotion, as if he had no interest in anything at all. "These things do not interest me. Who are you, kutji? Who are you really?"

"No one. Just shadows."

"Your name, kutji. What were you called in life? Tell me or this conversation is over."

Mulling it over for a moment, its mind befuddled by the bull-roarer, it said, "Jeronimus. My name was Jeronimus. And these were my crew." The handless shadow waved his stump, presenting his drifting legion as they slowly melted in from out of the night, nearly formless, like nightmares crafted into dolls and blown awake by the last breath of dying gods, each half a dream of what they might have been.

"And who is your master?"

"We have no master."

"Who created you?"

"A spirit of great power."

"And who is this spirit?"

"A spirit of great power."

"You said that."

"A spirit of such great power that we dare not speak its name."

"Now that," said the Clever Man, "interests me." He sat down, cross-legged, a wry smile on his face, his arm still whirling the bullroarer. With its name he had power over the spirit now; it could not hurt him. For a time. He swatted at the air, commanding the spirit to sit. "And what business could be important enough to involve me?"

Jeronimus smiled, his black shadow grin carving deep cuts in the angular box of his face. "There is a dreamwalker that visits you. We want her."

Shaking his head, the Clever Man waved the spirit off. "Catching dreamwalkers. Tricky business."

"We don't need you to catch her. We have plans for the catching. We need you to keep her in the dream, keep her from running off to wake up."

"Oh," said the Clever Man, making scissors with his fingers, cutting invisible string. "I know exactly what you mean. This can be done. But still, very dangerous. She's a powerful spirit. Very strong. Very clever. Why do you need her?"

"Because she is ours."

"If she were yours, you wouldn't need my help."

"She belongs to us. She is the last of the blood promised us."

"And when you have this blood?"

"We will be free."

"Why don't you just kill her and take the blood you're owed?"

Jeronimus raised both his shadowy stumps. "Because we haven't all our hands to kill with. She will help us find them. Then, when her body fails, she will join us."

"And you will be free."

"Yes."

"This is dangerous. My price is steep."

"Name it," said Jeronimus.

"Yes, name it," hissed the crowd of shadows.

"From this day on, you may never harm anyone of my dreaming."

"Done. Agreed!" Jeronimus's smile broadened. This was an easy bargain.

The Clever Man shook his head, holding up his free hand. "I'm not finished." He spun the bullroarer faster.

The shadows writhed impatiently. "What else?" asked Jeronimus, his enthusiasm fading. "Name your full price."

"You may never again enter Arnhem Land. It is forbidden to you. If you step one foot on it, you forfeit your spirit to me."

"Yes, yessss. Agreed."

"Agreed!" promised the crowd.

"And," said the Clever Man, looking very sternly at Jeronimus. "I demand the sacrifice of one of your own."

"What?"

"One of your shadows." He pointed at one standing toward the front of the throng. "That one. Bring him to me and we have business."

The nominated shadow shrieked. "What? No!"

Jeronimus turned to look at the shadow of his crewmate then looked back at the Clever Man. He nodded coldly. "We have business."

The pack of kutji descended upon their brother, each grasping him with their one good hand.

"No! Not me!" shrieked the spirit. "I've been faithful."

"Your sacrifice will not be forgotten," said Jeronimus.

The kutji dragged the shadow to the Clever Man who at once flicked his wrist, whipping the bullroarer to a full stop in his hand. He lowered his arm, pointing the tip of it at the shadow. He began to sing, the words deep, abrasive, cutting into the night with the howl of rising winds and the rippling of the dream around them.

The sacrifice screamed, its voice breaking, distorting, its essence siphoned directly into the Clever Man's artifact. The shadows scurried backward over the broken, rocky ground, terrified at the sight of their brother's demise.

And then all went silent, the night returning to a soft and gentle peace. The shadows did not speak nor chitter nor sigh in any way. They were too frightened by what they had seen.

The Clever Man nodded respectfully. "I agree to cut the cord of the dreamwalker and deliver her to you. Are we agreed?"

"We are agreed," said Jeronimus.

"We are agreed," said the rest of his crew.

"Good," said the Clever Man. "Do you know what she looks for at night when she walks?"

"No," said Jeronimus.

"She seeks a bunyip. Find the one that wallows nearby and show it to her. I will do the rest."

CHAPTER 14

OROBAS AND AMY

Goddamnit, Ewan," Colby muttered into the night, his words slurred into an unintelligible blur. He was mumbling incoherently, his head dizzy; his face fuzzy, numb; his lips slapping against each other just to see if they were still there. He was drunk. Completely trashed. Somewhere between beers with Austin, half a bottle of whiskey with Yashar, and a few more slow beers for good measure, Colby was lucky to be upright. Though upright was being a bit optimistic.

He was stumbling, stammering, cursing randomly. And somehow he'd found himself alone, out in a field, in the middle of the Limestone Kingdom.

There, off in the distance, Colby could make out his friend, smiling, waving, beckoning him to come back. But he couldn't go back. There was no going back.

"Fuck you, Ewan, you fucking fuck." He stumbled to his knees, his palms slapping the ground in time to prevent him from going face-first into the cold, dewy grass. "I trusted you. You were *pissed at me*? Pissed at *me*? Because I didn't tell you shit? Well, you kept her from me, buddy. Your little girlfriend got us all in the shit, didn't she? That's what they do. It's how they get us."

Colby lowered himself to the ground, then rolled over on his back, staring at the stars, still yelling out to the spirit in the field.

"How fucked up is it that of all the monsters we dream up, the ones that are the most dangerous, the ones that we fall most easily for, are the women? The ones that want us to dance or to fuck or to kiss or to, or to, or to whatever, you know. You know what I'm talking about. Those. They're fucking dangerous. I told you. I mean. Not directly. But I told you. But you didn't listen. And here we are. You with your girlfriend and me all alone. Again."

Colby sat up and spun himself around on his ass to be able to see Ewan. But the spirit was gone.

"Where the fuck did you go? I know you're out there. There's more to you, isn't there? More than just what's playing on a loop like a broken fucking record replaying the best part. There's got to be more. You're not that. You're not that happy little boy. You were only that happy little boy for like five fucking seconds, but that's how you're going to spend the rest of my life? Waving like a fucking moron?"

He stopped, burping slightly, his insides roiling, stomach muttering as loud as he. "Hold on," he said, his throat tight, stifling his speech. Then he vomited, puking up a mess of booze and cheese. "Oh. Lasagna was a mistake." The world began spinning more violently than before. "Hold on, Ewan. I need to find more grass. Better grass."

Colby crawled on his hands and knees through his own mess, finally collapsing a few feet away. He stared at the tilt-a-whirl sky, calling out into the night again.

"That's the worst part, you know," he said, screaming at the stars. "I know so many people who used to be dead, I mean, dead who used to be, well. You know what I'm saying. Spirits of people who are dead now. Some things can become other things. But not you. You're just an echo. A memory. You only say things that made sense a lifetime ago. And that's all you're ever going to say. You'll never make me laugh again. I can't even tell you about Austin. I mean, I can. But you aren't listening. You aren't there. You might as well be ashes in a jar."

His eyes glazed over with tears, his garbled rambling punctuated with weak sobs, occasional hiccups serving as misplaced commas.

"You just had to fall in love with that girl. A smile and a pair of tits dreamed up to wring the life out of you. Well, fuck you! Fuck you for being there for her and not me. She tried to kill you with the rest of them and you chose her. I was your friend. I was the one you were supposed to be there for. But you chose her. You. Chose. Her."

The night, already quiet, got quieter still. The buzzing insects dropped their songs and crawled deep into the earth. The wind stilled, the leaves holding tight, trying their best not to rustle. The air grew thick, heavy, damp, an unnatural chill setting in with it. Something was very, very wrong.

"Ewan?" asked Colby, tilting his head up toward the forest.

"No," oozed a voice so deep and menacing that it sounded almost as if it came from everywhere at once. Then the whole world screamed—damned voices begging for mercy, moaning, bellowing, crying out—a tinny, AM radio broadcast from the bowels of Hell, wails like static, distorted, breaking up, shivering the land itself. Trees stiffened like hairs on the back of the neck. Everything alive quivered like it had something to fear.

The universe tore open and Hell spilled out, for a brief moment becoming one with the field.

Colby tried five times to sit up, aggressively rocking himself upright, before managing with the sixth to prop himself on wobbly arms. The night around him flickered as if by campfire, trees blinking on and off, a dancing murk writhing behind them. It took Colby the better part of a few beats to even take it all in.

Then all, once more, went silent.

Before him, across the field, stood a man burning from head to toe, fire licking the ground around him, air bending, melting in the heat, a long blazing ribbon rippling off the back of his head like hair fluttering in the breeze, embers like dandruff spiraling away. His flesh was charred and smoking, the deep blue of well-fed flame, bits dripping to the ground in waxy globs before boiling away on the earth. He was like a candle melting in a house fire, its wick burning futilely above.

Beside him stood a horse whose hair was the black of the deep, dark nothing, as if it were a shape torn out of space with all the stars plucked out, only seen because of the light reflecting off everything else around it. It whinnied and stamped, the void of its mane caught in the same strange wind guiding the embers.

Colby knew at once who and what these things were. "No! Nononono. I didn't summon you. I want no part of you. Get out. Get away!"

"Colby," said the Horse, its voice carved out from the sounds of a stampede. "Do you know who I am?"

"I don't know you. I don't want to know you. Leave me be." Colby tried to push himself to his feet, only to end up on all fours, his ass the high point of a failed arch.

"But you do know us," said the man on fire, his voice hissing, sizzling, popping. "You know us well."

Colby crab-walked forward to a tree, climbing himself upright along the trunk. "I've never met you," he said, his fingers still gripping handfuls of bark.

"But you know our stories. Our names."

"No! You are Mr. Johnson," he said of the blaze. "And you are Mr. Miller," he said to the Horse. "And I did not summon you. There are rules. Rules to all of this. And I didn't call for you."

"You didn't call for us," said the Horse. "We're calling for you."

Colby turned his head, averting his eyes, squinting them shut. "I'm asking you to leave me. Leave me be. I'm way too drunk for this."

"That's why we're here," said the man on fire. "You wouldn't speak to us sober."

"I won't speak to you now."

"We're here to ask of you a favor."

Colby looked back, but not directly. "I grant you no favors. You will not be in my debt nor will I ever be in yours. *Go. Away.*"

"You can help us willingly, or not so willingly. We can make things very hard on you."

The Horse held his hand up to his companion, trying to wave off the threat, then took a few steps forward.

"That's far enough, Mr. Miller."

"My name is not Mr. Miller, it is—"

"Don't say your name."

"Don't you want to know for sure?"

"The best that could happen is that you're not really who you appear to be. There's no need to confirm it. Hopefully I'll forget all this by morning."

"There's very little chance of that," said the man on fire. "What we're about to tell you will be hard to forget."

"Impossible to forget," said the Horse.

"Yes, quite impossible."

Colby pushed himself to his feet, eyes still averted, turning his back on the interlopers. "I don't want to hear this. This has nothing to do with me."

"This has everything to do with you. Now, do you know why they sent *me*?" asked the Horse.

Colby walked away, speaking only over his shoulder, his feet unsure. "Because you can't lie."

"I cannot."

"Then go back and tell the other seventy the truth. I won't talk to you."

"We are sixty-seven now. Five of us are missing."

"I don't see how that's my problem."

"The one who took them is someone you killed a long time ago."

"You're mistaken. The things I kill, they don't come back."

"Some deaths are slower than others," said the Horse.

Colby continued his stagger, the world spinning so hard and so fast now that it took everything he had to not fall over face-first. "You're only supposed to speak the truth, Mr. Miller, not in riddles."

The man on fire spoke up. "The five we're looking for were in Australia when they disappeared."

Colby stopped, but the world kept spinning. His stomach lurched forward as if it were still moving, and he threw up again before doubling over and, finally, passing out in the grass.

CHAPTER 15

THE SEVENTY-TWO

AN EXCERPT BY DR. THADDEUS RAY, PH.D.,
FROM HIS BOOK *THE EVERYTHING YOU
CANNOT SEE*

If one wishes to live a long, prosperous life, then one should never dabble in the darker arts. In this book I have warned many times against treading into the unfamiliar waters of the arcane or the occult. No doubt few who read this will heed such warnings. But even if you do not, even if you see this as nothing but a road map to the unseen things you wish to experience firsthand, heed this: do not, under any circumstances whatsoever, attempt contact with the Seventy-two.

I won't name them by name, nor will you find them cataloged as you do in the apocryphal texts, *The Lesser Key of Solomon,* or throughout Crowley's flawed manuscripts. Even their names have power. Just speaking them too loudly can damn you. They are a motley lot, demons and their unholy spawn, djinn and fallen angel alike. Nine kings of Hell, six princes, nearly two dozen dukes; the rest an assortment of counts, marquis, presidents, and knights. And while not all of them are evil, not one of them can be trusted. They were cast together for far too long and have gone to immeasurable lengths to keep their truths hidden. They do not want you to know the truth about them and they see to it that anyone who learns too much comes to a terrible and untimely end. What I share with you now, while true, is what you could simply have culled from millennia-old documents, the Koran, the Bible, the Torah, and myths and stories all surrounding the greatest king of the old world. Solomon.

Thirty centuries ago, long before the veil dropped and all things supernatural still walked in the sight of man, Solomon was named king at the death of his father, David. Undisputed is the fact that Solomon became quite the trafficker with demons. He could summon them, bind them, and force them to do his bidding. The oldest of the stories about him tells of the thirty-six demons he bound into service to build his great temple, using them to cut stone and assemble unearthly masonry, sentencing the most foul and disgusting of them to fetching water or digging ditches.

While the specifics of what drove Solomon to gather together the Seventy-two differ from story to story, the result is always the same. Solomon used his powers to summon and command seventy-two different creatures—not, curiously, all of the same creatures he had previously bound into service—and sealed them in a large brass container, which he then had sunk into the deepest part of the sea. The container was marked from top to bottom with Solomon's own seal, a mark said to keep anything supernatural from opening or even finding it. There it rested at the bottom of the sea for hundreds of years, the Seventy-two creatures within bickering, fighting, and ultimately making peace with one another, promising that if they ever were released, they would ensure that such a thing could never happen again. It would not be until hundreds of years later, when the Babylonians would discover the location of the vessel and break it open, thinking it to contain a portion of Solomon's riches, that these creatures would find freedom. In a few short years, these starving beasts would set into motion the collapse of an entire empire, each honoring his pact to protect his fellows while they corrupted and fed on Babylonian souls.

While contained, peace reigned for forty long years in Solomon's kingdom, no otherworldly creature daring to so much as raise a stern voice against Solomon and his rule. Upon his death, however, all bets were off. Several djinn snuck into his palace during the royal funeral and forged a number of dark works, each penned and signed with Solomon's name. Theory has long held that they did this to discredit him, to make a mockery of his rule and have him branded a sorcerer who had turned his eyes from God. These works would be stolen, copied, and disseminated by sorcerers for the next three thousand years, their wealth of information not only keeping the existence of these foul creatures known to mortals—thus strengthening them—but written in such a manner as to misrepresent the details of their weaknesses and the various ways in which they could be bound or pressed into service.

The truth is, there are few ways to truly bind them, all of them dangerous. The rituals contained in the many occult texts chronicling them teach the reader not how to summon them, but instead only how to get their attention. A member of the Seventy-two doesn't always come when he's called. Instead, he only chooses to visit those he feels he can use or corrupt, those who would pose no real threat to their existence. Aleister Crowley's great many deeds and accomplishments in his field come not from his own power or knowledge, but rather from his ignorance that his visitors found him to be an interesting tool through which they harvested the souls of thousands of knowledge-seeking neophytes.

These demons, and their spawn, feed directly on the misery of others. The mistake most often made about them is that they gain their power from sin. Sin is relative. It exists only in the mind of the sinner. In times past, consuming shellfish or tattooing your body was sinful; in others, uttering certain words or lighting fires on the wrong day. Demons don't measure a person by their sin. They measure them by their guilt. Thus demons rarely have any interest in the truly wicked. Instead they level their gaze at those who might later regret their actions, or whose stomachs turn at witnessing the results of their choices. That feeling you get after cheating on a spouse or stealing from a good friend—that's what they feed on.

Remorseless sorcerers are rarely afforded the courtesy of a visitation. The noble, or the good, or the well intentioned? Those are whom the Seventy-two seek to feed upon. Those are the ones whose calls they will answer. And they will not hesitate to pretend that they might actually in some way be bound or rendered harmless.

Do not talk to them. Do not speak or write their names. Draw no attention to yourself and never ever be so arrogant as to think you can get the better of them in a deal. You will not. These deals are their profession and they have been making them since before the rise of the pyramids. Traffic with them only if you desire a swift death preceded by intense suffering, or a long-drawn-out existence pained by regret.

CHAPTER 16

A FIELD OF BAD CHOICES

Colby's eyes opened wide, the light of the sun already strong on his face, a chirping cacophony of birds bursting into his ears like a TV blaring suddenly in the middle of the night. He shot up straight, sitting at a perfect ninety-degree angle, feet straight out in front of him, completely unaware of where the hell he was. His head thundered; his throat dry, cracking; his eyes stinging.

His thoughts were muddled; he couldn't process what he was seeing very well at all. Trees. Trees everywhere. Grass. A limestone outcropping. The field.

Holy shit. The field. He knew where he was.

"Morning," soothed a voice from behind him.

Colby whipped his head around quickly, immediately regretting his decision. He squinted, pain stabbing him between the eyes, headache murdering his thoughts. "Fuck!" A silhouette stood between him and the sun. Rigid, honed muscles. Copper skin. Deerskin tunic. Broad, friendly smile.

"Someone lost a battle with a bottle last night."

At once Colby recognized him. "Oh shit. No. No, no, no, no, no, no."

Coyote waved his hands. "Relax. Truce. I'm here with good intentions."

"You don't have good intentions."

"I have the best of intentions. You just won't ever live long enough to see them realized."

"What do you want, Coyote?"

"To wake you up, pat you on the ass, and send you on your way before things get ugly around here."

"Excuse me?"

"Half the kingdom heard that little show you put on for us all last night. And there were a number of folks who thought taking advantage of your being passed out might be the best solution to their problems."

Colby snapped his head back and forth, glancing wildly around, once again regretting doing so. "Ahhhhh!" He cradled his head in his hands, the hangover pulping his brains with each pound inside his skull. "Why didn't they?" he moaned into his hands.

"They realized that you might wake up. And I reminded them that the only thing more dangerous than an angry Texan was a drunk one. They thought better of it."

"You think?"

Coyote crossed his arms, his tone slightly more serious. "They are exactly where they are supposed to be. You're the bear spoiling the picnic."

Colby squinted, slightly embarrassed. "I am, aren't I?"

"Yes. You are."

Colby swallowed, his throat prickly and dry. "Is there water?"

"This way." Coyote reached down, and taking Colby by the hand, helped him to his feet. He motioned, and Colby followed, walking casually through the sagebrush, past live oaks, toward a nearby stream that babbled louder the closer they got. "Look, Colby," Coyote continued, "I feel that I owe you. And while I've never lied to you—well, never lied to you about you—"

"Have you lied to me about you?"

"I lie to everyone about me."

"But wouldn't that have to be a lie?"

Coyote smiled wider, squinting coyly, shaking his head. "No. Because I don't always lie. I only lie enough to make sure no one knows the truth. The rest of the time I'm on the level." Then he cocked his head to the side, qualifying. "Mostly."

"And what horseshit do you have for me to shovel today?"

"Horseshit?"

"You're not here as a friend. You want something."

"Of course I want something. This time around though, I want what you want."

"And what's that?"

Coyote stopped smiling, the effect of which seemed to dim the harsh bright light of morning. Colby had never seen him not smile, never so much as heard of him not smiling. The old man brooded for a moment, his eyes growing deathly serious, his copper skin creasing unpleasantly. "I want you to survive this."

Colby panicked, his chest tightening, his heart pounding suddenly. Every muscle in his body tensed up. "Survive what?" He looked around for an ambush, something waiting behind the trees. But there was nothing. Only himself and Coyote. He stopped, but Coyote kept walking, waving for Colby to follow.

"Last night. Your visitors. The demons."

Colby searched his memories, unsure for a second what he meant. And then it all came flooding back. He rushed to catch back up to Coyote. "What do you know of it? You saw them?"

"Of course I saw them," said Coyote. "We all saw them. And we felt them before that. Their very presence warps the space around them, changes the rules. Hard to miss. It was the only interesting thing to happen out here for weeks. It was practically theater." He paused for a beat. "They need you for something."

"That much I remember."

"What a demon cannot do for itself, but wants done, most often shouldn't be done at all."

Colby cradled his head in his right hand, trying to discern how much of what he couldn't understand was being muddled by the hangover and how much of it was just Coyote fucking with him. "I don't understand," he said at last, resigned.

"No. You don't. And you won't. Not for a while yet. But when you do, you're going to realize just how deep in this you are. Here we are."

The stream was narrow, hidden past a steep, rocking incline, cutting through the land like it had been dug out by hand. Colby fell to his knees and began cupping water into his mouth. It was spring fed. Pure. The only thing ruining it was the taste of the night before.

"When do I get to understand?" asked Colby.

"That's up to you."

"So you're not going to tell me." Colby stood up, his belly sloshing with fresh water. "All due respect to the great and powerful manitou, but I can't take this shit this morning. I'm not going to remember half the stuff I actually even understand coming out of your mouth. If you want to mess with my head, you're going to have to speak slower and be more specific."

Coyote nodded, intrigued. "I'll tell you this much: they mean to use you. If you do everything exactly as they ask, you'll live through it, but you won't be happy about it."

"And if I refuse?"

"It'll be worse. Either way, something terrible is coming for you."

"Something terrible?"

"The past."

"If you know something, just tell me. They said Australia. This is about her, isn't it? This is about what I did there."

Coyote nodded. "And a lot more. This goes back a long time. There are games within games going on, bargains within bargains that have yet to see their end. These things, they have intentions so vast and alien that you'll never be able to wrap your mind all the way around them, but even those get trumped by the bargain they made with themselves. Several of them are in trouble, which means they are all in trouble. And they will do whatever it takes to get themselves out. Right now that means using you."

Colby balled up his fists, knuckles white, jaw tight, teeth grinding together. "Why can't anyone ever be straightforward with me? Why do you all have to use me?"

"Because you try so hard to be good."

"Because I'm good?"

"No. Because you try to be. The good just are. The ones who try are much more easily manipulated. It's a special kind of self-ishness. You always know what someone who tries to be good will do when given a choice. It makes it very easy to set up a field of bad choices. If you can make one of the bad choices look like the *good* thing to do, you know that the man trying to do good will do it. Entire nations have been led to genocide and butchery that way."

"And I slew a number of fairies that way."

Coyote beamed with pride. "Yes. And you destroyed La

Llorona that way. And you saved a child from the knife that way. And you've done countless other things in the name of goodness that other creatures wanted you to do for them."

"And now the demons want their turn."

"Another field of bad choices, none of them good."

"So what do you want out of all this?"

"For you to make it through to the other side."

"Because I have some kind of *destiny*?"

"Destiny is a crock, Colby. It's the fairy tale the successful tell themselves to make it seem like they have God or the universe or whatever on their side. Nothing is predetermined. And no one can see the future. Not really. Some of us are gifted enough to see past the lives and the fictions and just see the machine. We can tell you what the machine does, what happens when you turn it on. One gear turning another that turns another. That's the machine. But it doesn't mean we can see the future, can tell when one of those gears will give out and the whole thing will break down. But we can see the long game, one stretching out for decades, centuries, sometimes millennia. Some of us serve ourselves. Some of us serve a higher ideal. But some of us just serve the machine. We keep it running, doing what it is supposed to do, doing what we're supposed to do, because it's our job to keep it running, to make sure those gears fall into place, to replace them when they're about to fall apart."

"And I'm one of those gears."

"One of the most important gears. Or you will be. You can be. If you don't fall off the machine first."

"So you can't see the future?"

"I can see *futures*. I can see the maybe that exists if everything stays the same. But there is no future. Not yet. The future is just a now waiting to happen that may or may not ever arrive."

"Why does this all sound so familiar?"

"Because you've heard it all before. You just weren't listening the first time around because you didn't like the answer."

"You're the second person to say that to me."

"Oh? Then maybe there's something to it."

"So you're going to tell me what you want me to do? Or am I supposed to guess?"

Coyote shook his head, chuckling. "Colby, if I told you what you would become one day, you would do all the wrong things just to spite me, no matter how important a role you play. You believe too much in freedom. In choice. What you don't realize is that you've already made your choices. Now you just have to live through them."

"You mean *with them*."

"No. No I don't. Your wishes are your wishes, whether you make peace with them or not is entirely your business. Whether you live to see them out is what concerns me."

Colby sighed long and deep. "So what am I supposed to do?"

"If I tell you, then it's not really a choice. And if it's not a choice, it means nothing."

"Fuck you and your riddles and this headache. I can't take your shit when I'm not hungover; I sure can't handle you right now. Please. Just leave."

Coyote smiled wide, his teeth glistening in the morning light. "You know what's really going to piss you off, Colby Stevens?"

"What?"

"When the headache is gone and your mouth doesn't taste like that and you can finally think straight for the first time all day, you're going to think back on this conversation and you're going to wonder. You're going to wonder hard. And you're not going to know whether I've been messing with your head this whole time."

"Oh, I hate you."

"And if that weren't bad enough, when you remember that I didn't tell you to do anything at all, you won't have any idea what to do."

Colby buried his head in his hands and swore a string of unintelligible curses so long and unappealing that even Coyote blushed.

"Don't trust anyone to be who they appear to be, Colby. Not even me. I'm not your friend." He patted Colby on the back, squeezing his shoulder warmly. "I got you a half hour to leave the border of the Limestone Kingdom. That was ten minutes ago. I suggest you start walking now. I'd use the trees." Coyote turned, walking away.

"Hey, Coyote."

"Yeah?" asked Coyote over his shoulder.

"Thanks."

Coyote smiled one last time, then nodded so sadly that even the smile was unable to hide it. And with that, he was gone.

Colby looked around, expecting for a moment to catch the hint of a pointed ear or the flash of a red cap behind a bush or in the trees. He didn't trust the things of the Limestone Kingdom and he supposed he never would. If they'd promised him twenty more minutes of peace, they'd be waiting to kill him in fifteen. There wasn't much time, so he took a shallow breath, reaching out with his thoughts, wading deep through the moist earth, looking for the oldest, gnarliest roots he could find. Then he turned and walked full speed into a fat, ancient oak, disappearing into its trunk, vanishing completely.

CHAPTER 17

CITY OF THE DAMNED

The most foolish mistake man often makes is believing that evil lurks only in the darkness. There is no safety in the sun. Only shadows fear the sun. And shadows are just the dark reflections of daylight. True evil is as at home in the bright light as it is in the darkness. And it has no qualms about snatching you right out in the open.

Colby's headache hadn't subsided. Though it hadn't gotten worse, it sure felt as if it had. His head continued on like an out-of-sync kettledrum, his mouth like he'd been eating a litter box. But it wasn't the worst hangover he'd ever had. Thus far, on the walk home, he'd only sworn off drinking four times. Some days he'd already managed that before breakfast.

He wandered in through the west side of town, up through the forests, past the suburban sprawl, and on into the oldest parts of the city. The trees were ancient here in comparison to outlying Austin; they were older than many of the buildings sprouting up as the city yawned and stretched its arms. The buildings were clustered together, tightly packed along the streets. It was greener here, homier here. And yet he was mere blocks from the newest buildings, towering slabs of condos swallowing up whole city blocks.

This was a place where he was used to seeing old spirits. Most of them were echoes, remnants of people long gone. Sometimes they were angels, demons, nightmarish things of all kind and sort, perched on ledges, stalking prey, sitting along the lake. For the most part, he'd stopped paying attention to them. They were like the faces of people on the bus. You see them, but you don't really *see* them. They're just background, so much static to be filtered out. But sometimes, just sometimes, he saw things that were just downright out of place.

And that's what he saw as he closed in on downtown.

An old man, untamed beard yellowed with age, clothes ragged and worn, riding a crocodile.

Now, this being Austin, Colby's first thought was how had someone managed to get a license for a crocodile? *That had to be illegal.* Then, as the haze of his pounding head cleared a bit, and his memory kicked into gear, it dawned on him that this was no man at all. And he realized just who, and more important, what this man was.

He was Agares, another of the Seventy-two, ruler of the eastern portion of Hell. Or so the story went.

He was decrepit, hair having fallen out in patches, drowning in wrinkles, hands speckled with liver spots, jowls drooping below his chin, beard holding on for dear life. His expression was cruel, hateful, like he was pissed at just being alive. And the crocodile beneath him seemed every bit as old, scales thick, scarred; teeth ocher with plaque, chipped, a number of them missing—no doubt left long ago in prey. When Agares laid eyes on Colby, his scowl became harder, sinister, as if he was ready to charge and kill Colby for no other reason than he didn't like the look of him.

Then the demon raised its hand, giving a slight little wave, and sat still, watching Colby walk past.

Colby's heart raced. He didn't know what to do. This was uncharted territory for him. Before last night he'd never seen a single one of the Seventy-two. Now one was strolling through Austin as if he was going to the corner store, and waving to Colby. A duke of Hell was a powerful thing; there was no fighting it were it to come to that. So Colby continued walking, trying to pretend he didn't see it.

Agares never took his eyes off Colby, not for a second, not until Colby had walked out of sight around a building.

Colby felt relieved, terror subsiding. He didn't know why the demon just let him pass, or why he was even here at all. Frankly, he didn't care to know; he just kept walking, pretending it hadn't happened.

Until it happened again, a few blocks deeper into the city.

This one Colby could not mistake for anything other than what it was. A large, strong, black wolf, its muscles bulging, fur sleek and full, bearing a rider, an angel, sprawling feathery white wings, china white skin, and the large, bulbous, brown feathered head of an owl. Andras, great marquis of Hell, sower of discord and confusion. In its hand it wielded a massive sword that gleamed in the shadows; with its other hand it pointed at Colby, a single, extended finger tracking him as he walked in its direction.

The owl-headed beast stared at Colby with its beady black eyes, its beak unmoving, its feathers ruffling as if it was ready to pounce. But he didn't move. He just stood there, staring, his wolf growling softly, just loud enough for Colby to hear.

And Colby kept walking, eyes down, the icy-cold glares of demons piercing any semblance of bravery. His insides quivered, turning to jelly, knees weak, breath short, chest caving in. If they wanted to kill him, they could and they would. But they didn't. And that's what scared him most. Whatever this was, whatever they had in mind, they wanted him to know that he was in their grasp whenever they wanted.

Pressing forward, deeper into the city, his pace quickened, trying to shorten the time between himself and the Cursed and the Damned. He thought about slipping into a tree, but there were too many people watching. That was the kind of attention he didn't need. So he hoofed it, uneasy with the knowledge that an owl-headed wolf-riding demon might be right behind him, steps away from cleaving him in two and dragging his soul straight down to Hell.

Eyes down, stride long, steps furious.

He stopped at a crosswalk, waiting for the light, looking around nervously.

The light changed and he sped across the street as fast as he could without running. Then, as his foot touched the curb, a voice called out, grating and malicious, its bass and tenor reverberating through his bones as if they'd been struck by a tuning fork. "Colllllllllbyyyyy."

He turned and saw the king of terrors, Asmodeus, a three-headed titan of a man, one head like a bull's, another like a ram's, the centermost that of a man, hideous, distorted. All six of its eyes cut bitterly into Colby from across the street. In front of Asmodeus stood an ordinary man, dressed for work, waiting, having just missed the light. Asmodeus approached from behind, walked right into him, melding until they were one, the demon no longer visible.

The man convulsed, shaking from a seizure, limbs twisting in odd directions, head nearly snapping atop his neck. Then the shakes calmed and he settled, the demon inside shifting uncomfortably as if trying to get a new suit to fall right. He put a single foot forward and stepped into traffic.

The light changed, a speeding truck slamming into him. The man was thrown like a rag doll, his bones powdered all at once, but the demon still stood in the place he had stepped out of. The truck screeched to a cockeyed stop, never having had the chance to brake before hitting the man, driving right through Asmodeus, all three of the demon's heads smiling. He stood there as the chaos of the accident unfolded around him—people screaming, the driver rushing out yelling obscenities, traffic coming to a standstill before the body even stopped rolling—but Asmodeus never took his eyes off Colby. He just wrung his hands, cracking his knuckles, savoring the look of horror on Colby's face.

Colby ran. He didn't have time to play it cool anymore, didn't have an ounce of bravado left. Though his head still pounded and his throat was still raw and his stomach toppled like a carnival ride, he didn't notice, not a bit. All he knew was fear. Hell was coming for him, they were sending him a message, and it was reading loud and clear.

They were not going to let him go; they were not going to let him say no. He was theirs, and if they didn't want him to get out of this alive, he wouldn't.

He rounded a corner to the final stretch to the bar—a straight shot of only a couple of blocks—legs pumping like a track star.

And then he slowed, his muscles pulling him to a painful, sudden stop. He stood there on the sidewalk, eyes agape, mind reeling, entirely unsure how even to process what he was seeing.

Madness. He saw pure madness.

The buildings, the streets, this whole section of sun-drenched city, was lined from top to bottom with dozens of the Seventy-two. Demons and angels with forms as mind bending as any you could imagine. Angels with animal heads, dragons, serpents, jungle cats with wings and serpent tails, three-headed dogs, hounds with the faces of men, men with the faces of hounds. And everything in between. They stood along the sidewalks, on the ledges of buildings, lined the rooftops above him. Dozens, perhaps all. Colby couldn't tell. All he knew was that he recognized them, each and every dangerous one. He knew their names; he knew their deeds; he knew that every last one of them was staring right at him, never for a moment taking their eyes off him.

Not a one said a word. They stood silent, vigilant, faces cruel and emotionless, watching, waiting to see what he would do.

Whatever this was, whatever they wanted him to do, it was big.

He knew it was important when they sent two greater demons. Now he was staring down what might be all of them.

There was no talking his way out of this now.

He took a deep breath, steadied himself, and started walking. *Just a few more blocks*, he thought. *Just a few more blocks.*

The demons, silent and unmoving, just watched.

CHAPTER 18

HAIR OF THE DOG

One of the only things more depressing than the current state of the Cursed and the Damned was seeing it cower in the alley from daylight. Though it had no windows, there was something about the harsh, stinging light of midday waiting just outside the door that made it all the more sad. Bars were places meant to be refuges from the dark, not suppliers of it. While it was easy to forget the time of day, and buy into the shadows of the piss-poor lighting and dim booths, all that goodwill went away the moment you stepped into the bustling afternoon of downtown.

It was enough to kill a buzz if you did it wrong.

And the only thing worse than all this was seeing that bar, in daylight, through the angry throbbing buzz of a hangover, knowing what hell waited on the streets and rooftops outside.

Colby nursed his headache with a shot of whiskey and a tall sweating glass of ice water, his fingers trembling, struggling to find the words. Few things ever shook him up. He'd just met, for the first time, most of them.

The bar was empty, morbidly silent. Gossamer was curled up in the corner behind the bar, lying atop a rubber floor mat ringed with holes, keeping quiet, trying to keep up.

Yashar leaned forward on the counter, peering across the bar, eyes narrow, concerned. "Which two actually spoke with you?" he asked, his tone as nervous as it was curious.

Colby sipped his whiskey, staring dead-eyed back over the bar, his red hair still slicked to the side of his face with last night's sweat. "The Holocaust Man and the Horse."

"Holy . . ." Yashar picked up a glass and began to clean it with a fresh rag. He needed something to do with his hands. It made no difference that the glasses were already clean.

"Yeah."

"Tell me the Horse did all the talking."

"Some of it."

"Because you know he can't lie."

"I know."

"What did they say?"

Colby took another sip, steadying himself. "Something's happened to five of the Seventy-two."

"Happened?"

"They've gone missing."

"And they've mistaken you for a private detective? What's that even mean?"

"I guess they imagine I'm somehow involved."

Yashar shook his head. "Bullshit. You're either involved or you aren't. These aren't the kind of folks who get that sort of thing wrong. So which is it?"

"Which is what?"

"Are you involved or are they trying to involve you?"

"A little bit of both I suppose."

"Colby, what aren't you telling me?"

"Australia. They said it had something to do with Australia."

Yashar backed away from the bar, dispirited, beginning to understand. "That's not good. That means—"

"That could mean a lot of things."

"No. That can mean only one thing."

"I'm not going back to Australia," said Colby.

"Of course you're not going to Australia. No one goes to Australia."

"Now what is *that* even supposed to mean?"

"It means no one goes to Australia anymore. The whole continent's gone dark."

"Gone dark? That's not possible. How does that even happen?"

Yashar hesitated, pursing his lips. Colby's chilly glare wore him down without much effort. "Anyone magical who goes in doesn't come back out. No one's heard anything for months."

"Why is this the first I'm hearing of it?"

"Because no one wanted to tell you. I certainly didn't."

"And I didn't know," said Gossamer, peering up from behind the bar.

Colby snapped his fingers. "Is that what happened to the five? Were they . . . ?"

Yashar shook his head. "I don't know. No one said anything about the Seventy-two. But then, no one ever says anything about the Seventy-two unless they have to. If Orobas and Amy came to visit you—"

"Don't say their fucking names!"

"I know them, Colby. I've known them for a thousand years. I can call them by their names. You've got their attention. No use hiding from them now."

"That's not how it's supposed to work. I didn't—"

"You didn't what?" asked Yashar. "Summon them?"

"Yeah."

"No. You just brought the Wild Hunt across and offered it souls."

"That . . . that's not . . ."

"That's not *how it's supposed to work*? Colby, that's exactly how it works. That's how it's always worked. Damnation is a hook with bait. It looks like a meal, but there are no free lunches. Not in Hell."

"The Wild Hunt came to me. Threatened me. Demanded a favor of me."

"And now you're going to be pissed at the demon for knocking on the door so you don't have to deal with the fact that you're the one who let him in?"

"Look outside. They're knocking again."

"You can't help them. And you can't look into this. You have to let them clean up their own little mess. Let them stand outside all day and night if they have to."

"That's the plan. But then—"

"Then what?"

"There's something Coyote said."

Yashar's face went cold. He reached under the bar for a tall glass, unstoppered the best bottle of whiskey within reach, and filled it to the top. "Coyote? You didn't mention Coyote."

"He was waiting for me when I woke up."

Yashar took a big swig. "What did he say?"

"You're not really going to guzzle the good stuff like that, are you?"

"Colby—"

"Because that's really good stuff, and if you're just going to drink it like soda—"

"Colby—"

"You might as well be drinking the cheap stuff—"

"Damnit, Colby! Forget about the goddamned whiskey. What did he say?"

Colby paused for a moment, sipping his own whiskey. "He talked in riddles, mostly. Said he was looking out for me. Not to trust anyone. Then, by the end he told me that he hadn't really told me anything at all, and saying that would fuck with me later."

"That's fucking with you now, isn't it?"

"It really is."

"Because whatever Coyote tells you to do—"

"You should do the opposite. Unless he knows you know that. Then you can't so much as get out of bed without doing what he wants."

Yashar finished the rest of his glass and began to pour another. "What the hell are we going to do?"

Colby looked up at Yashar, a hair confused. "We?"

Yashar nodded. "This is no small affair, Colby. This is the Seventy-two. But what scares me most isn't their involvement."

"It isn't?"

"No. What scares me is that this isn't a problem they can deal with themselves. Something like this should be self-correcting."

"Self-correcting?"

"It means . . . take you, for example."

"ME?"

"Yeah, you. Limestone Kingdom. You did a pretty good job of peeing in their Wheaties. Really shook things up out there. Those guys totally hate you."

"Thanks for the refresher course."

"What do they do now that they want you gone?"

Colby shrugged, unsure where this was all going. "Get together, maybe. Come for me in the middle of the night."

"Too risky. Good way to lose a lot of friends. No, someone like you, you just wait it out. One of three things is going to happen. One, maybe you get too big for your britches and run afoul of something you can't handle. Splat. Two, you mellow out, grow up a little, and work things out with the initially wronged parties. Peace reigns throughout the land. Or three, since the problem is mortal in nature—"

"They'll just wait for me to die," said Colby.

"They'll just wait for you to die," said Yashar, nodding. "So riddle me this: what could possibly be so powerful that the scariest hombres in all the land want no part of it, have no hope for peace with it, and don't think they can outlive it?"

"They said it was something that I killed. That some deaths take longer than others."

Yashar nodded again. "You know who and what they're talking about, don't you?"

"I think so."

"So who said what?"

"What do you mean?"

"You said the Horse didn't do all the talking. Which one of them said what?"

Colby hesitated, the fog of the last night's drinking rolling in over the memories, enveloping them, the crisp horror of etched-in shock becoming blurry shadows in a drifting haze. He remembered a man on fire, the way the flames flickered and shifted in the night. The way the embers fluttered on the breeze, delightful dancing little fragments of the damned. And he remembered a horse so black that it stood apart from the darkness. But the words, the words eluded him. "I don't . . . I can't quite remember. I remember the gist of what they said, but not who said it."

"These two didn't happen upon you by accident. They were chosen to speak to you. They no doubt discussed exactly what to say before they ever showed up. These aren't just schemers, Colby. They are the greatest schemers. Seventy-two of the most cunning, underhanded backstabbers the world has ever known. They'd already thought well past this conversation and on to tomorrow before they ever stepped foot in that field. Of the sixty-seven they had, they chose Orobas and Amy. Why?"

"The Horse and the Holocaust Man. Please."

"Fine. The Horse and the Holocaust Man. One can't lie. The other is still bitter he was tricked into thinking he might one day return to Heaven. Why these two? Why send them to do the talking? There are more powerful spirits. More persuasive spirits."

"Because these are the two I might trust."

Yashar nodded. "Which means?"

"I can't trust them at all."

"Exactly."

Colby finished his whiskey, but it did nothing to soothe the knot in his stomach. He held his glass to the light, rolling it around in his fingers, watching as the glare warped and twisted as it moved. "They're not going to let me out of this, are they? I'm already in it."

Yashar's expression held hopeful aspirations of confidence, only to fall short, the confidence draining with the hope. "I suppose you are."

"This time I've really done it. I've damned myself."

Yashar shook his head. "Don't kid yourself, Colby. You damned yourself a long time ago."

"Yashar, what the hell has she become that it's come to this?"

The two exchanged pained looks, the silence between them pregnant and brooding.

"Guys?" asked Gossamer. "What the hell happened in Australia?"

CHAPTER 19

DREAMTIME AND
THE LAND OF DREAMS

AN EXCERPT BY DR. THADDEUS RAY, PH.D.,
FROM HIS BOOK *DREAMSPEAKING, DREAM-
WALKING, AND DREAMTIME: THE WORLD ON
THE OTHER SIDE OF DOWN UNDER*

Western arrogance puts the cradle of civilization squarely in Mesopotamia, the root of our writing, storytelling, and technological achievements stemming from thousands of years of culture emerging from that region. And yet while our core beliefs stem from the original tales passed down around the campfires of that region, our history covers only a surprisingly short amount of time.

The Aboriginal tribes of Australia, on the other hand, constructed no great monuments, contributed no technological achievements, and offered no contribution to our emergence into history. Instead, in place of that, they possess an oral tradition stretching back tens of thousands of years. While thousands of years of man rose and fell before telling their story in clay, the Aborigines share tales of 25,000-year-old volcanic eruptions and the flooding that took place after the melting of the Ice Age. In fact, they share entire tales that take place on land that now rests at the bottom of the sea.

This is a culture that did not push forward on the cutting edge of technology because it focused instead upon mastering the power of creation. No other culture in the history of man has so understood the nature of its own surroundings, a fact mostly due to their entire culture evolving around respecting, protecting, and mastering what they live upon.

To listen to the tales of the Aborigines is to hear histories older than any text, to hear of heroes who walked the earth before it last froze over. And their tales of creation seem closer to the truth that remains today than any other I've found. To the Aborigines, the world was not simply created, it was dreamed into being. Things became conscious and then consciously began altering their surroundings.

They call it Dreamtime.

Dreamtime is the idea that in the beginning there was a substance of raw creation that beings, or consciousness, evolved from. Every tribe tells a different tale of the creatures that emerged, but the mechanism that follows is always the same. Those beings then walked the earth, imagining, or in some cases singing, things into being. Plants, animals, monsters, places, rivers, people. All came from the Dreamtime. Then, after most of the raw creation was spent forging the world, the beings that made it passed on and left behind a world full of wonder. Thus ended Dreamtime.

To the Aborigines, all land is sacred, for it is a place not only dreamed into being by the ancients, but it is also where the heroes of old walked. They do not merely revere their heroes, they revere the places where those heroes performed their greatest deeds. They revere the places where those heroes were born. They believe the land itself is the most important part of creation, because the land is, itself, the record of all stories.

There are three principal ideas one must grasp in order to understand the basic tenets of Aboriginal mythology: their relationship with the land, their relationship with time, and their relationship with death. Once you have those down, the rest you can pick up fairly easily.

The land. Many Aboriginal men are given custody of a parcel of land, much in the same way boys in regions of Thailand are given baby elephants. They have one job: to watch over it. Now, these men do not own the land, as they believe no one can truly own land. They merely protect it. They memorize every contour, learn the location of every rock and tree. They know which trees and bushes bear fruit and which bear poison. They learn the way the rain falls, where the water collects, and what animals come to drink. They learn the holes where all the snakes live, the caves where animals take shelter. More important, they learn, in song, the history of every important thing to ever happen on that spot of land. These men learn which hero defeated which animal with what weapon on which spot. They learn where villages rose and fell. They learn where people fell in love. They learn all of this and they protect it because it will one day be their job to pass that knowledge on to someone else.

During their time as custodian, these men will be asked to teach the songs of their land to others passing through. They lend them to others, and they borrow others' songs when traveling. But just as no one truly owns the land, no one truly owns the songs either. We do not live long enough to own anything. We merely borrow it.

Time. There was once a psychological study that looked into the way people process information chronologically. Each was given a series of photographs of a person, ranging from their birth to their death, and asked to put them in order. Westerners from countries that read from left to right placed the photos in that order. Middle Easterners from countries reading right to left also ordered the pictures as such. Those from Asian countries reading from top to bottom placed their photos in order from top to bottom. But Aborigines all put theirs differently. Some were right to left, some left to right, top to bottom, bottom to top, diagonally. The researchers were baffled. So they began to ask the participants why they ordered their pictures the way they did.

The answer? The Aborigines were placing the photos east to west. To them, lives are lived with the rising and the setting of the sun. Their story is ordered by the land's relation to the sun and that is how all time is measured.

Death. Aborigines do not, as a culture, fear death. While every tribe tells different stories of what becomes of you after death, each one believes the same basic notion. We are gifted with this life and this body, we borrow our time and sustenance from the land itself, and then, when the time comes, we go back to it. The concepts are similar to those of Native American tribes but with a much more pronounced belief in the story and history of what that life borrowed and gave back to the land.

In short, to them, all life is land, and all land is life. Their duty is to carry the burden of that land's story and gift it to the next generation. In that way the story continues. And as quaint or cute as your Western mind may imagine that is, they have successfully carried stories that predate anything resembling the first Western civilizations. What we know of our history, we learn from archaeologists making educated guesses. What they know of theirs they learn from their fathers, with a trail that leads all the way back to the people who were there.

And knowing what we do of dreamstuff, it is very hard to write off the more creative bits as being mere mythology. On the contrary, their tales of giant rainbow-colored dragons dreaming the world into being might be the closest approximation to the true dawn of man we have on record. The question is, did man evolve and dream those creatures into being, or did they dream us awake?

CHAPTER 20

THE CLEVEREST MAN
IN ARNHEM LAND

ELEVEN YEARS AND NINE THOUSAND MILES AWAY

Colby was all of eleven years old and the Australian sun beat squarely down upon him in a way that would sap dry and kill most children his age. But not Colby. Not only had this little boy weathered the blistering drought of central Texas summers most of his life, but he had also spent the last three years of it walking the earth with Yashar through all manner of extremes. After the first year he'd stopped bothering to complain; by the end of the second he learned to enjoy the variety.

He'd been through blizzards in the Alps, monsoons in southern Asia, the skin-peeling sandstorms of scorching Persian deserts. This was just a little sun. He wore a wispy linen head wrap, sunscreen on his face, and a light robe to keep the sweat from pooling. He'd be fine.

Yashar, on the other hand, didn't fare so well, shuffling more than he walked, his eyelids heavy, his expression one of fevered exhaustion. It looked as if he could pass out on his feet at any moment. But it wasn't the heat weighing him down.

"Come on, Yashar. Pick up the pace," said Colby.

Yashar bristled, his young companion dancing obnoxiously on his last, frayed nerve. "It's not too late to sell you into white slavery. You've still got a few good years left in you."

Colby laughed, knowing enough to understand Yashar was joking, but not quite enough to know what exactly he meant. "Are we almost there?"

"We're almost there."

"We should have hired a car."

"Rented. You're not British."

"Australia. We're in Australia. They say hired here. Hired sounds cooler. Rented means borrowed. Hired means employed."

Yashar grumbled, his voice gravelly and dripping with irritation. "I know what they mean, Colby. I'm not an idiot."

Colby looked up at Yashar, worried. "Yashar, what's wrong?"

"Nothing is wrong."

"You look tired. We should stop for a while and let you get some rest."

"If I stop I'm going to fall asleep. I can't fall asleep."

"Why not? You never sleep anyway. You could use some."

Yashar stopped, gritted his teeth, and took a deep breath. Then he looked down at Colby, swallowing his welling anger, letting it simmer in his gut rather than erupt. "Colby, djinn need to sleep. We don't do it often, only every few years, but when we do, we sleep for ages. Weeks, months, sometimes years. The next time I close my eyes, I will fall deep asleep and I have no idea how long it will be before I wake back up. I need to make sure someone will take care of you before that happens."

"And djinn are cranky when they're sleepy?"

"Yes. Yes we are."

"Wait, are you leaving me?"

Yashar nodded. "Yes, I am. But in good hands, I promise."

"Where are you leaving me?"

"With a friend. Someone who has a lot to teach you. He's the cleverest man in Arnhem Land. And he is walking just a few miles ahead of us."

"How long will I have to stay with him?"

Shaking his head, Yashar's expression fell from one of exhaustion to one of complete uncertainty. "I have no idea. That all depends on what the sleep demands of me."

"Oh," said Colby, not entirely sure what Yashar meant. "Will you dream? When you're asleep, I mean."

Yashar smiled big and broad, his eyes brightening for the first time in days. "Oh yes. We djinn have the most vivid, wonderful dreams. Beautiful women and magical lands, a mixture of all the things we've ever experienced combined with all the things we've ever hoped for. Some think it's where we get our power; others say it is where we go to find ourselves after serving so long the dreams of our masters. All I know is that it feels so real that you are afraid to pull away, afraid to wake up, because you don't really believe you're dreaming. You think it's real, and you're afraid waking up means dying. That's why I think we sleep so long."

"So you'll forget I'm out here waiting for you?"

"I might."

"But you'll come back, right?"

"Of course. I can't sleep forever."

Colby nodded, his smile weak and unconvincing. He was afraid, but trying to be strong for his friend. "Okay. I believe you."

Yashar laughed. "Good thing too."

The two continued walking, the heat getting worse as the sun rose higher. "Are you going to be able to make it much farther?"

"I think so. I have to."

"We should have hired a car," said Colby.

Yashar nodded. "We should have hired a car."

MANDU MERIJEDI BASKED cross-legged in the sun atop an oblong seven-foot-high, red granite boulder, his eyes closed, hands extended palms up, elbows resting on his knees. The sun sat in the sky both perfectly above and behind him, as if placed there deliberately. This was not only Colby's first impression of the man, but also how he would remember Mandu forever. There was something infinitely wise about him waiting there silently for his destiny. So calm. So peaceful. Mandu waited, knowing full well that his life, at any moment, was about to change. And the fact that this did not scare him made quite an impression.

Yashar looked down at Colby, his eyes weary and bloodshot. "Wait here," he said. "No matter what happens, don't leave this spot."

Colby swallowed hard. He didn't like it when Yashar said that.

Yashar stepped forward, took a deep breath, and exploded.

His flesh burned yellow, then gold. He swelled in size and smoked. His head went bald, his muscles rippling, eyes glowing a hellish red. Then his voice boomed like a vocal earthquake, rumbling like thunder, drifting into the desert, scaring bandicoots into their holes.

"MANDU MERIJEDI!" he shouted, the rock beneath Mandu shaking with the sound. "I DEMAND AN AUDIENCE!"

But while the earth trembled, Mandu did not. "You have found him, spirit," said Mandu, quietly. "I am he." He did not open his eyes; he merely breathed calmly, not moving a muscle.

"I HAVE A TASK FOR YOU!"

"What spirit calls me?" he asked as if he did not know.

"YASHAR, THE CURSED ONE, SPIRIT OF THE . . ."

"So much smoke and noise for such a simple spirit. I know who you are. This"—he said, waving his hand around at Yashar as if he could see him—"is not who you are."

Yashar swore beneath his breath. "I HAVE A—"

Mandu opened a single eye, peering mischievously, patting the spot on the boulder beside him. "Yashar, come sit. Come sit."

Yashar sighed, his powerful form deflating. His muscles withered, the glint of his skin fading back into a dark olive, smoke dissipating weakly into a mist before vaporizing into nothing at all. He was once again Yashar the man. Slowly he crawled up the boulder and took a seat next to Mandu. "That . . . that actually is my natural form," he said softly.

Mandu closed his eye, shaking his head, and continued to seemingly meditate. "But that is not who *you* are. You prefer this form. You prefer this voice. The rest of that was all for show."

"It was."

"I don't need a show. I respect your power, spirit."

"I need a favor."

Mandu smiled. "Of course you do. You wouldn't be here otherwise. What brings you so far from home?"

"I bring you a young dreamwalker who needs to learn the old ways."

Mandu opened his eyes, eyeing Colby up and down. Colby's clothes were ratty, beaten and torn by the Australian bush, his face dirty, freckled, and tanned, his red hair wrapped in linen. "But he's a white fella," said Mandu. "And he's not dreaming. He's awake."

"I know," said Yashar.

"You can't teach the white fellas the old ways. They don't understand them."

"This one can."

"No, it can't be done."

"Mandu, I'm tired. I need to sleep. Colby here is in my charge. I need him looked after and I need him to learn the old ways."

"Why the old ways? Why not his own ways?"

"It was his wish."

Mandu looked at Yashar, his eyes confused, incredulous. "What's this?"

"He wants to learn the old ways. He's a good pupil. Fascinated by it all. His wish was to learn about . . . the way things really are. This is where it all began. Wouldn't you agree?"

Mandu nodded slowly, now more curious than indifferent. "What are you offering?"

"Mandu—"

"You know the rules. I do the spirit a favor and the spirit does a favor for me."

"What you ask is dangerous, my wishes, they—"

"I know your curse, so my demand is this: you must never, ever, no matter how long from now it is, grant the wish of a single fella of Arnhem Land. It will stay free of your curse and none shall know the sorrow of your broken gifts."

"And for that you will train the boy? Look after him until I get back?"

"Yes."

"Then I promise," said Yashar.

"Say the words."

Yashar fought through his weariness, clearing his throat, adding a bit of proper, rehearsed seriousness to his tone. "I promise never to grant the wish of a single person of Arnhem

Land, no matter what the circumstances, in exchange for your tutelage of, and promise to care for, the boy Colby Stevens."

"Okay. I agree." Mandu popped to his feet and hopped off the rock, sliding down the side as if he'd done it a thousand times. "'Ey, little fella. Get over here."

Colby rushed over, his eyes wide with excitement. "Yes, sir."

"I'm Mandu."

"I'm Colby."

"So I hear." He motioned back to Yashar, who carefully made his way down from the top of the rock. "It looks like you'll be spending some time here with us. Is that right?"

Colby nodded.

"Okay. Well, we have a long walk ahead of us. Can you handle that?"

"Yes, sir!"

"Yashar, you can rest now."

Yashar sighed deeply, sat down on the ground, his back against the boulder, slowly, but surely, turning invisible.

"Wait!" said Colby, running to his side. "You can't go to sleep yet. I don't know anybody else." He took Yashar's massive hand in his own, gripping a finger with each hand.

"You will," said Yashar, smiling weakly. He peeled Colby's linen head wrap back from his head, ruffling his thick red hair playfully. "You will."

"I'll miss you."

"I would miss you too, but I'll no doubt dream of our adventures." Yashar's eyes fluttered, exhaustion getting the better of him.

"Good night, Yashar."

"Good night, Colby," he rasped before winking out of sight. "Be good for Mandu."

And then he was gone.

"Come on," said Mandu. "Let's walk."

CHAPTER 21

THE CLEVER MEN

An excerpt by Dr. Thaddeus Ray, Ph.D., from his book *Dreamspeaking, Dreamwalking, and Dreamtime: The World on the Other Side of Down Under*

The true power of the songlines is a closely guarded secret, but far from the only one the medicine men of the Aborigine tribes keep from the outside world. These medicine men, known as Clever Men or Men of High Degree, spend a vast majority of their life training in the many secrets of their ancestors. The most important of these secrets is the ability to dreamspeak.

Dreamspeaking is what many in the West refer to as *the sight*, the ability to peer behind the veil and commune with the spirits who live there. Clever Men accomplish this through meditation and ritual. It is a rare Clever Man who natively possesses the ability to see and hear spirits. Those who have such skills are revered as possible dreamheroes, people who have lives that intertwine with powerful spirits and accomplish some great deed as a result. Those with gifts find their way into apprenticeship regardless of birth or tribal standing, whereas most Clever Men are chosen as children for such training as a result of relation to a current or past Clever Man.

A second and much more heavily guarded secret is the capacity to dreamwalk. Dreamwalking is the ability to astrally project, to unmoor yourself from your body, leaving it behind while your spirit traverses beyond the veil. Traveling this way leaves behind a single, thin, often silvery thread that maintains the link between your body and soul. This allows the traveler to freely explore the world in spirit form, perceivable only by other spirits and beings of dreamstuff, unhindered by terrain, distance, or time. If that thread is severed, the spirit may not be able to return to its body and may end up wandering the earth, lost, until its body expires, extinguishing its spirit with it.

Clever Men use the ability to dreamwalk to commune with spirits, with whom they strike bargains or make deals that benefit and protect their tribe. A Clever Man's primary obligation, the whole reason for their being in certain tribes, is to keep the supernatural world at bay and to treat the maladies vexing his people who come into unfortunate contact with creatures beyond the veil.

And this is where the values of the West differ from those of native Australia. A Clever Man's power, his standing as a man of high degree, is reflected not in the power of his spells or in his strength against the supernatural, but rather in his ability to outwit those he comes into contact with. A good Clever Man doesn't have to fight supernatural creatures; he merely needs to convince them to go elsewhere. Thus the very best of the Clever Men prove to be cunning tricksters who employ deceit and guile to turn a spirit's own powers and weaknesses upon itself.

Clever Men are also employed as doctors, but mostly as spiritual healers, exorcising the possessed, cleansing those taken ill by the powers of spirits, or simply granting some sort of spiritual resistance against such incursions. The outback of Australia, which is among the most dreamstuff-rich areas left in the world, provides quite a bit of fuel for aspiring medicine men intent on restructuring the reality around them. However, this is a double-edged sword for a superstitious people. Someone who believes strongly enough that breaking a taboo or invoking the wrath of the land can lead to illness or harm opens himself up to his reality being restructured to just that. These Clever Men are needed to provide healing from the things physical medicine cannot.

This, however, is where the Clever Men of many tribes part ways. For not all Clever Men have the same skills or possess the same talents. Different tribes across the continent ascribe very different powers to their Clever Men, who carefully guard them from others. These gifts range from being able to speak with animals, to manipulating the weather, on to telepathy, cursing others with maladies, or unleashing the fury of spirits upon them.

But none are so powerful or feared as the sorcerers of Arnhem Land, the one territory in all of Australia where sorcery is not only openly practiced but also acknowledged as such. There, in the deepest regions of the Northern Territory, medicine men practice dark arts and outright sorcery to protect their people, collect debts, or avenge vendettas. Theirs are the secrets of soul stealing, an ancient, terrible practice that involves subtle, devious murder by way of capturing and torturing the soul while leaving the still conscious husk of a body behind to slowly die. Here tribes do battle through silent warfare, sneaking into enemy camps at night, stealing the souls of their victims, and leaving them to grow sick and die long after they've returned home. This is when the healer must become the detective and hope to discern such assaults while there is still time to retrieve the soul, if not simply track down the assailant.

Sorcerers of Arnhem Land also possess the ability to step into trees, disappearing as if into mud, and exiting from other trees sometimes miles away. They create illusions that distract or confuse opponents. Some can implant ideas or thoughts as a form of subtle mind control. Others can run at least a meter off the ground, their feet never touching the soil, or summon cords from their own bodies that they can use to climb without the need of a vertical surface.

The most powerful among them even understands the fundamental nature of true sorcery, that being the direct alteration of dreamstuff to be shaped to their will. These men are unbound by convention and lack the restrictions of most Clever Men. Fortunately these men are few and far between and in my travels I have encountered only two men capable of doing such things.

CHAPTER 22

ROCKS AND THROWING STARS

The hot sun blazed down from the heavens, the land seared by its glare. Mandu stood comfortably, naked save for the pouch he carried his valuables in, regaling Colby with half a dozen different tales all tied to the three-foot-high boulder that rested precariously before them. Colby, on the other hand, slouched, his shoulders drooping, interest waning.

"I don't understand, Mandu," he said. "What does this have to do with my walkabout?"

"It's the story of the land. You have to know it to understand the song."

"What do a bunch of old stories about dead people have to do with the song?"

Mandu frowned. "I was told you were curious. That you were clever. That you wanted to learn. But all I see is another silly boy. You want to learn magic but don't want to study it."

"I already know magic," said Colby, his tone pinched and whiny. "It doesn't have anything to do with old stories."

"It has everything to do with old stories."

"No it doesn't."

Mandu smiled, his face vanishing into sunbaked creases and crow's-feet. "Fine then. You know magic so well, perhaps you should teach me. Show me something. Show me some magic."

Colby perked up, the lesson suddenly becoming interesting. "Okay! Watch this!" He reared back, intertwined his fingers, popping his knuckles, concentrating on the air around him. Dreamstuff flowed thick and slow through the land like molasses, unmolested and rich.

Colby focused the energy around him, then let loose.

The air ignited, first fire arcing like lightning, balling up into a small sun five feet in front of him, then darkening, siphoning all the light around it until the tiny sun became a ball of blackness, drinking in the warmth from the earth, no light, nor heat, escaping from its surface. The world began to grow cold around them, dimming the daylight into a twilight-tinged dusk.

Then Colby swayed into a kata, a martial-arts-like dance, with the black sphere swaying before him as if at the end of a string. He clenched his fists and the sphere burst, reshaping into the form of a long, thin, Chinese dragon, blackest of black, seven feet long, soaring across the sand, its tail whipping, drinking the heat from the air.

Finally, it burst one more time, Colby shredding its essence with a gesture, his arms held wide like a gymnast at the end of a routine, small scraps of black evaporating into the returning dry, blistering afternoon swelter.

For a moment he felt overwhelmed, dizzy, his head tingling. He was unaccustomed to weaving dreamstuff this raw, heavy, and abundant. It was as if he'd plugged in a portable radio to the direct current flowing out of an electric plant. Colby had no idea what to do with so much power.

It was all he could do to stem the flow away from what he was reweaving.

Mandu's smile had faded, his eyes wide with shock. As Colby presented himself, sweating, looking as if he was about to pass out, Mandu's eyes swelled with anger. "When the spirit told me of your power, I had no idea you knew so much! And understood so little." Mandu walked toward Colby, putting a fatherly hand on his shoulder, guiding him to sit with his back against the rock.

"Wasn't that cool?"

"No," said Mandu. "You understand the ideas of magic, but have no discipline. You know that lighting oil makes fire, but instead of dipping in a wick for hours of light, you dump the oil out on the ground and light it for a few seconds of fire. That is not how we use the energy around us. It is not how it was meant to be used."

"But that's how you do it. You take it and make something else out of it."

At that moment, Mandu finally understood why Yashar had brought the boy to him. He shook his head, pointing at the boulder against which Colby propped himself up. "Let me tell you about this rock."

"Oh man, the rock again?"

"The rock." Mandu sat across from Colby, his eyes locked with his pupil's, Mandu's demeanor reverent. "Once there was a great but cruel hunter. A man capable of bringing down any beast in the land with a single throw of a rock. He could wing a rock sideways, skipping a stone off the water seven times, and kill a thing across the river.

"One day this man was out chasing some wild thing across the land, all the way to a distant river, and he found himself farther away from his camp than he ever had been. And as he reached into his dilly bag for a stone to kill the thing dead while it drank, he saw the most beautiful woman he had ever seen, bathing in the river. He whooped loud, getting her attention—and also the attention of the beast—then flung his rock, hitting the thing right between the eyes. It dropped dead right there.

"Well, the hunter then slung the kill up over his back, crossed the river, took the girl by the hand, and asked her to lead him to her camp. There he approached the elders—all well past their prime—and asked to wed the girl from the river. Now, this camp had a problem. The past two generations had produced very few boys, and of those boys, few were worthwhile hunters. But here was a man who could kill such large beasts with a single stone. Though he was arrogant and brash and the girl did not love him, they consented to let him stay to court her in hopes that she would.

"But what none of them knew was that she loved another, a weaker hunter but a more gentle and noble man. When the hunter learned of this other suitor, he saw to it that he spent every waking moment around the girl, keeping the suitor at bay except for when he was away hunting. Even then, the hunter saw to it to kill quickly only game close to camp in order to limit her exposure to his competition.

"Finally, after he could bear it no longer, the hunter proposed to the girl, finally asking for her hand in marriage. She denied him, telling him for once and for all that she did not love him and never could. Well, the hunter, angered by this, picked her up and slung her over his shoulder to bring her back to his own people. He ran and the girl's tribe ran after them, the young suitor running fastest of all. But as she was slight and he was strong, and there was little but open ground between the two camps, the suitor and his tribesmen were unable to catch up to them.

"At last, the hunter reached sight of his old camp, just over there in the hills behind you." Mandu pointed at a rocky outcropping in the distance, at the edge of a dry billabong—a small, rain-created lake. "But he saw no fires, and the shelters had been taken down. It was then that he realized how much time had passed since he had last seen his people—the months he had spent pining for this girl—and he now knew that they had long ago moved on to some other watering hole. He was angry as ever, and threw the girl down on the ground, intent on whipping her with his spear for what she had made him do. He threw her there, right where you're sitting."

Colby looked down at the ground around him. "Here?"

Mandu nodded, walking toward Colby, casting a long shadow over him. "Right there. And the hunter stood here, unslinging his spear."

"What happened next?"

"The other suitor showed up."

Colby's eyes went wide, and he leaned forward, desperate to hear what happened next. "And?"

"He called out to the hunter, demanding he let her go. But the hunter sneered and cast his spear at the young man, killing him instantly. The girl leaped to her feet and climbed atop that rock, crying over her dead love. And as the hunter went to retrieve his spear, she realized she had nothing left keeping her here on this world and jumped—right there from atop that rock—into the sky!"

"What?"

"She leaped so hard and so far that she crossed over from this world into the sky world where she became a constellation. And the hunter, madly in love and ever the angrier, climbed atop that rock and jumped into the sky after her. There, he grabbed stars from the night sky to throw at her, trying to stop her so he could catch her for once and for all, but the stars burned his hands and he missed. And he missed again. And again. And again. And now, on dark nights, once a year, you can look above you in the night sky and see the rocks he throws fall from the heavens, burning through the night, missing the woman he wants and loves so much."

Colby crossed his arms and peered up at Mandu, who still loomed over him from the vantage point of the hunter. "But what does that have to do with magic?" he asked.

"Close your eyes."

Colby closed his eyes.

"Concentrate on the rock. Can you feel it?"

"Yes," said Colby, as if it was the most obvious thing in the world.

"No, can you *feel* it? Like you can the dream in the air?"

Colby focused and his indignation fell away. He could feel the tickle of the rock, a slight pulsing vibration. It tasted like love and agony, loss and anger. "Yeah! It's really just a little bit, but it's there."

"Concentrate harder now. Try to touch that energy with your mind."

Colby reached out again, his mind wandering through the essence of the stone. "I feel it. It's cold. Permanent. Like ice to water."

"Yes. Yes," said Mandu. "That's djang."

"Djang?"

"How do you think the girl jumped so far?"

"I don't think she really jumped that far. That's just a story."

"She jumped that far because she used the same dream you did to make your dragon. But when she did, she left a little of that energy behind, in the land—in the rock—and now, if someone wants, they can tap into that rock to leap across to the sky world."

"Really?" asked Colby.

"Yes, really. That's how we use magic out here. We learn the land, we learn its stories, and we learn to use the spots where magic already exists. The dream, it is all around us, dreaming even as we are awake. Borrow the magic of the land and the land remains magical. Use it up and you end up, well, with the world of the white fella—with a burned-out husk where wonder used to be. You see how powerful your magic is out here?"

Colby nodded. "Yeah. It's really strong."

"Let's keep it that way. From now on, I teach you the magic of the land. The songs. The history. You will learn how to make the land your ally. And then, it won't matter how little magic there is around you. I'll teach you to use djang. You won't need anything else."

CHAPTER 23

ON DJANG

AN EXCERPT BY DR. THADDEUS RAY, PH.D.,
FROM HIS BOOK *DREAMSPEAKING, DREAM-
WALKING, AND DREAMTIME: THE WORLD ON
THE OTHER SIDE OF DOWN UNDER*

Once one has his mind wrapped around the concept of dreamstuff, understanding djang should be no great leap. It is, after all, something akin to the condensed residue of dream-stuff that has been exerted upon an object. If inanimate objects had a soul, it would be djang, which is really the easiest way to think about it, except that it should be stressed that it doesn't lead to sentience.

Throughout history mankind has revered artifacts, places, and the heroes who utilized them in their great feats. Tales have been told of magic swords, holy grails, places of power, even lucky pieces of clothing. These items, the ones used by the heroes in their great deeds, or the places where they performed those deeds, possess djang.

The mechanics of djang aren't quite understood, leading to a number of theories of their creation, two of which seem the most likely. One theory argues that great deeds accomplished through the use of dreamstuff—or that had a profound effect on the dreamstuff of an area—leave an imprint on certain objects, a spiritual fingerprint, if you will.

A dagger is used to sacrifice a virgin before a powerful god, the divinity of that "deity" flowing through the priest. That dagger retains some of the dreamstuff released when the virgin is killed, as it also captures a bit of the essence of the priest delivering a soul. While the portion might be very small, it fundamentally restructures the object and imparts properties that the actor, either consciously or unconsciously, wills it to have. When used by someone who understands how to unlock djang, the dagger above might possess the ability to offer any life snuffed out by it to that god. Or it might stay incredibly sharp, never dulling or rusting. It might also be attracted to the heart of a victim when used in a fight. Or it could serve as a way to communicate with the "deity" to which it was dedicated, no matter where on earth it might be.

The second theory holds that it is not the act that imprints the dreamstuff upon an object, but rather the belief by others in the power of the object or place. People believing a place to be holy, reweave the nature of that place and make it so. The more people who put their faith in the nature of such a place, the stronger that place's connection is to those properties. This theory mirrors the creation of supernatural creatures, which makes it more likely, but as the mechanism of accessing the abilities is different, there is still plenty of reason to believe the former might still be correct. Someone simply believing they can access the powers of a thing or a place does not necessarily allow them to do so, which runs counter to the way supernatural creatures function with belief.

Accessing the djang of a thing takes practice. It usually requires a thorough knowledge of its history, its handlers, and its powers, though some practitioners have mastered the ability to sense and tap into the djang of an object on a purely primal level, able to feel their way through what an object is both capable of and "wants" to do.

The word *djang* comes from the Aboriginal people of Australia, who impart the term purely to places or naturally occurring objects, like trees, rocks, billabongs, or mountains. To the Aborigines, a holy place grants those knowledgeable of the location's history to tap into the energy of the past and use that energy to accomplish similar feats. A rock used as the spot to launch oneself into the sky might become the place Clever Men use to cross over into the land of the dead. A watering hole used to trick another tribe into drowning themselves might become a meditation spot for others to discern how to best outsmart their own enemies. A tree a Clever Man used to travel farther than any Clever Man before him might become a doorway to any other tree in the outback.

All of this can be accomplished by understanding and tapping into the djang.

CHAPTER 24

FISHING

"Mind the trees," said Mandu, pointing to the canopy above them. "Dangerous things in the dark up there."

"Snakes?" asked Colby.

"Worse. Snakes'll just eat you. Yara-ma-yha-who will spit you back out. And you don't want that. They'll drop right out of the trees."

These were the wetlands just south of Arnhem Land; trees were everywhere. There was no avoiding them. Gray trunks like spires, fields of them, growing up and out of the thick morass of brown mud, reaching to the cloud-darkened sky. Mosquitoes as big as a quarter, flies working in mobs, leeches in every puddle.

Colby looked suspiciously toward the treetops. "What are they? What am I looking for?"

"Bright red, can't miss 'em. Just keep your eye out and don't stand too close to low branches."

Colby looked around, horrified. Mandu secretly smiled.

They came upon a large stone plateau, rising like a giant mushroom out of the sea of mangrove trees, its faces sheer, wider at the top than the middle, reds and browns dripping down the sides, jagged rocks climbing the western face like chiseled stone steps. It was like an abandoned Aztec temple, overgrown and swallowed by time, overlooking a wide billabong. Hammer Rock.

As they got closer, Colby spied ten-thousand-year-old rock art, ancient but bright, unmolested by time. Reds, ochers, blues, blacks. Smears and stains, depictions of stick men covering it from top to bottom, colors often inverted with negative space, detailing the magic aura of dreamtime with pigments, leaving the stick men colored by the rock, dotted with little dabs of paint.

The billabong was a dark, murky brown, reeds rising up and out of it, the ripples of fish sweeping bugs off the surface lapping gentle waves along the bank. It was a picturesque place woven wholly of magic, kept out of the hands of anyone who couldn't appreciate it.

"Good a place as any," said Mandu, pulling a hatchet from his dilly bag. "Come here."

Colby rushed to his side. "Yeah?"

"Time you learned how to fish, proper."

"I know how to fish," he said with a sigh.

"With a hatchet?" asked Mandu, holding up a battered, weathered, sharpened hunk of metal, slightly rusted around the edges.

Colby's eyes grew wide. "No!" he said excitedly.

"Today you will." He swung the hatchet, peeling a layer of bark off a nearby emu apple tree. Then he did it again. And again, repeating the process until he'd stripped the tree raw, oozing from a dozen wide gashes. "Follow me."

He walked Colby to the billabong with an armload of sticky bark, then dropped it in a pile by the bank, sitting down, inviting Colby to do the same. Then he began to pound the bark mercilessly with the blunt end of the hatchet. "That's an emu apple tree," he said. "Its sap is found deep inside its bark. You have to pound it free."

"What do we need the sap for?"

"Fishing."

"Is it bait?"

Mandu shook his head. "No, it's not bait."

"What does it do?"

"You'll see."

"Why don't we just make a rod? Or a spear?"

Mandu smiled as if Colby had walked into his trap. "You white fellas always think about the land as if it is something to fight against. To struggle with. You would rather try to lure in a fish and fight with it. But here is a tree by the water that will do all the work for you. The land isn't your enemy, Colby. It is your ally. Learn from it. Use it. We have many friends out here in the bush. Start thinking of it that way, and the land will keep you alive. Even when all else is trying to kill you. Now," he said, filling Colby's hands with a molasses of chewed-up wood. "Sprinkle this in the water. Enjoy the swim. We'll be cooking up fish soon enough."

"Mandu?" asked Colby, hesitantly.

"Yeah?"

"Why are we fishing?"

"Because I'm hungry. And we're having company. It's always polite to feed company."

Colby felt silly, dog-paddling through the water, tossing clumps of gooey bark into the bottom of the billabong. But within moments the fish started floating to the top. The first were merely disoriented, gasping for air at the waterline, puckered mouths desperate, gills flapping furiously. They ducked and dodged as best they could, wriggling out of Colby's grip as he tried to catch them barehanded, but he made easy work of them, tossing them to Mandu like footballs.

The next batch, however, floated up on their sides, some even belly up. Colby scooped them up by the armful, throwing them to shore, each time giving Mandu an inquisitive look, as if to ask, *"Do we have enough yet?"* before Mandu responded with a stiff arm and stern finger pointing him back into the water.

"The sap of the emu apple tree absorbs lots of oxygen when it gets wet. Sucks it all up, eh? Soon after, the fish get light-headed and pass out. Either that or they swim to the surface looking for air. They float to the top, we take the fish. Very easy."

"Mandu," asked Colby, tossing two more fish onshore. "You know a lot about spirits, right?"

"I get by."

"Can I ask you something?"

"Anything."

"Why do spirits always keep their promises, even if it means dying?"

Mandu smiled, nodding knowingly. "Ah, the spirits, they cannot tell you why, can they?"

Colby shook his head, wading back deep into the billabong.

"Because they themselves do not understand. Look around you. What do you see?"

"Trees, mostly. A big rock."

"Do you see any laws?"

"What? No. You can't see laws."

"Nah. Because they don't really exist, eh? We make them

up, convince ourselves they're real. They're only enforced when someone believes they should be. Whole world put together by rules other people believe should exist."

"What does that have to do with spirits though?"

"The spirits only exist because we believe they do. We dream them and they become real."

"No," said Colby. "That's not right. You don't have to believe in a spirit for it to exist."

"Not once it believes in itself. Once it believes in its own existence, it doesn't need anyone else. But that which is made up of belief is bound by it. Act against the nature that holds you together, violate the things that you believe make you exist, and you are unmade as that belief evaporates."

Colby scooped a few more fish off the surface. "So if they believe they have to keep a promise, they have to, or they cease to exist?"

"Yes."

"Oh!"

"The power of man over spirits is that he is a physical thing. Only the self and the society around him exist entirely because he believes it does. But when he stops believing in those things, he can just remake them. He doesn't have to keep his word, doesn't have to find a loophole to cheat. He just can. Thus man can never be trusted. But if he's smart, he can always get more out of the spirits than the spirits get out of him."

"Is that what a Clever Man does?"

"That's exactly what a Clever Man does."

"How many fish do we need, Mandu?" he finally asked, exasperated.

"How many do we have?"

Colby looked down at his feet. Seven trips he'd made, making a pile tall and deep of wriggling, dying fish. Mandu eyed the pile, shrugging. "A lot," said Colby, pointing.

"And how many of those do you reckon you'd have caught with a rod or a spear?"

Colby scuffed his feet, still staring at the ground, embarrassed by the lesson. "Not that many."

"I reckon not. When you're up against great numbers, never fight them head on. Be clever. Know the land. Know the rules. And rather than struggle with them, get them to do exactly what you want." He eyed the pile, doing the math in his head. "That oughta do." Then he reached into his dilly bag and pulled from it his bullroarer, which he whirled about, making a louder, shriller noise than Colby had yet heard from it.

And then the forest came alive with motion.

Mimis poured out of every imaginable place. From under rocks, behind trees, out of bushes, beneath roots, out of the water, seemingly out of the sky, dropping from the canopy. They were long and thin, their bodies a series of lines, like dried branches—painted red with white dots, or blue with yellow, black with red, or green with white—stuck together to make the crude shape of a person. Though half as tall as a grown man, not a one could have weighed more than five pounds, each wispy enough that a stiff wind could have snapped it in half. Before long, a throng of painted stick men stood before them, bobbing, chanting, some fifty strong, the tallest no more than three feet high, looking exactly like they did in the rock paintings.

Mandu let the bullroarer wind down, raising his other hand. "Friends," he said. "This is Colby. He's going to be out here with us for a while."

The mimis let out shrill twitters and hoots, crying out in languages and dialects Colby couldn't even fathom. And though he had no idea what any one of them was saying, he got the general idea.

"Good. Good," said Mandu. "I want you all to meet him. But first, we eat!"

CHAPTER 25

THE RUM THIEF

"Tell me about your dreams," said Wade, his breath strong with coffee, his hands still red, nicked and sore from the cannery. "Where are you going to go tonight?"

"You don't believe my dreams," said Kaycee. She was tucked in bed, tattered covers up around her neck, her father hovering over her, perching on the edge of the bed.

"I believe that you believe them."

"That doesn't mean you believe anything."

"I believe in you. And I believe in your dreams. So where you going tonight? To see your friend?"

Kaycee nodded.

"Are you looking for the bunyip again?"

Again she nodded. "He's out there somewhere."

"Yes he is. And if anyone can find him, you will."

"I wish you could come with me. Then I could show you. I could introduce you to my friend and show you the way the stars look and the way the air dances. There are so many colors, so many more than when we're awake."

"I wish I could go too. But you're with me, you know. In my dreams."

"You dream about me?" she asked, her lips curling into a slight smile, her eyes twinkling a bit.

Wade leaned in, spoke softly, as if sharing a secret. "All the time. I dream about the cannery too. But I try not to think about those. Your dreams sound much better than those."

"Do you dream about Mom?"

Wade looked down at his daughter, his eyes welling with sadness. He gritted his teeth and fought back the tingles of tears. "Every night."

"Tell me about her."

"Kaycee, I—"

"I tell you about *my* dreams. But I never get to see her in those. I only know her from the pictures. Please?"

He paused, weighing the ache of his heart against the thought of disappointing his daughter. Then he nodded, trying to smile. "She was the most beautiful girl in all the world, your mother. Everything you said about the colors and the air and the stars. That's what she was like. Being with her did that to everything. She was my dreamtime. She was—" He broke off, held back the stutter of a sudden sob. "Hold on, Dad needs a drink."

Wade tried to stand up, but Kaycee grabbed him by the cuff of his sleeve, shaking her head. "No. Stay here. Tell me about her."

"I'll be right back. I'm really thirsty."

"Dad, no. Stay here."

He relaxed, put his meaty hand, abraded with scars, on Kaycee's thick black hair, stroking it gently. "She had hair like yours. Exactly like yours. Curly. Never wanted to do what she wanted it to in the morning. On days when it was hot and the rains were coming, it would frizz out—and because she was tall and thin, she looked like a woolly tree fern." Wade boomed out a laugh, trying to mask how hard the words were to get out. "But she was beautiful, even then."

"Did you tell her?"

"Every day. Even on the hot wet ones when she banged on and on about how her hair was a tangle."

"If you had to choose, would you pick—"

Wade's eyes went wide and his face went red. The monstrous Wade Looes now hovered, terrifying, over his daughter. "Don't you dare! Don't you ask me that!" His sudden anger caught her off guard. She'd never seen him this angry, not when he was stone-cold sober.

"But if you could—"

"No! Don't you ever think about that."

"But why did she have to . . . I mean, I never even got to see her."

Wade calmed, trying hard not to scare his little girl. "Because sometimes things are like that. Some people are only allowed to have one truly amazing person in their life at a time. If I had both of you, I would have been too blessed for words. That much joy, it makes a man soft. We're Looeses. Looeses are hard. Tough. Nothing can stop us. So I had many years with her and now I get many years with you. If I didn't have you, well . . . I'm not sure even a Looes is tough enough for that."

"I love you, Dad."

Wade stroked his daughter's cheek, a tear forming defiantly in his eye. "I love you, darlin'. Now get to sleep. Dreamtime's waitin'."

THE PRETTY LITTLE girl in the purple pajamas was racing beneath the stars once again, the moon bright, the land effulgent. She ran past the black stump and knew that she was free. Time bent and the universe bowed and all the world became a dream; there was nothing that was going to stop her from finding bunyip tonight. Not a thing in the world. Not even the murder of crows trailing behind her.

They'd been following her since just outside her house, a mass of chirping, onyx-black beasts slightly larger than the average crow, their eyes glistening a sickly yellow, their beaks shiny, polished, sharp. Their wings beat loudly behind her, their squawks screaming for her to wait up.

Then they changed, their feathers molting, their bodies shifting. Black became pure darkness, and their sleek avian features gave way to oblong shadows. They were at once like squashed men, their heads bent in odd directions, and their arms cocked every which way.

They ran, scurrying, galloping across the land on all fours, barking shrill chirrups into the night. One of them, the fastest among them, trailed very close, so close she could feel its hot breath on her neck.

"Why are you running so fast?" it asked, galloping up alongside her.

"I'm hunting bunyip," said the girl.

"Why would you be looking for a bunyip?"

"Because I was told that I would find one."

"But they're very dangerous. You could be eaten."

"I won't be eaten," she said.

"But how do you know you won't be eaten?"

"Because finding the bunyip is my destiny. And being eaten by a bunyip would be a terrible destiny that no one would bother telling me about."

The shadow thought about this for a moment—his feet wheeling furiously to keep up with her—then nodded. "That's an excellent point. But you won't find a bunyip going this way."

"And how do you know that?"

"Because we see them all the time. And they're never out in this direction."

The pretty little girl stopped in her tracks. The shadows swarmed, forming a circle around her, each ten feet out, not a one of them standing too close. "You know where the bunyip are?" she asked.

The shadow nodded, waving his stubby, handless arms in the air. "Of course we do."

She looked around at all the other shadows, every last one nodding as she glanced their way. Each was about three feet tall, boxy, malformed, their proportions all out of whack, with one hand at the end of one arm and a blurry stump at the end of the other. "Would you show me?"

The shadows silently exchanged curious looks before turning to look at the fastest of them—the handless one. Jeronimus. He nodded. "Of course we can show you where the bunyip are. But only if you do something for us first."

"Why do I have to do something for you?"

"Because those are the rules."

She put her hands on her hips, cocking her head. "And just what would I have to do?"

"You have to appease us."

"How do I do that?"

"Through a test."

"I don't want to take any tests."

The shadow crept ever closer, nodding and waving a stump as if it still possessed a hand and finger to gesture with. "But I thought you said finding a bunyip was your destiny."

"It is."

"But you haven't found one yet, have you?"

She shook her head. "No."

"But you found someone who knows where they are."

She hesitated. "I guess."

"So what makes you think this test isn't your destiny—that it isn't part of the big thing that will happen?"

The girl let that rattle around in her head for a moment. The strange little shadow man had a point. The Clever Man never said just *how* she would go about finding a bunyip, just that finding one would change her life. He could very well have been talking about this encounter.

"Okay," she said with a determined smile. "What's the test?"

The shadow grinned. "Tonight you must go home, crawl up into your father's liquor cabinet, and pull down every bottle of rum you find."

"I can't take Daddy's liquor! He'll be so mad that, well, I can't do it."

"Oh," said the shadow. "I understand. I thought you were serious about finding bunyip."

"I am serious."

"No, you're not."

"I am, I swear. What do I have to do next? With the bottles. Tell me. I'll prove I'm serious."

"Well, next you must fetch a wooden bucket—you'll find it waiting out back by the shed—then pour all of the rum into it, leaving it in your backyard."

"Then what?"

"Then you wait. You go back inside, crawl back into bed, and when you fall asleep, we'll be waiting. And we will show you where the bunyip wallow."

The pretty little girl in the purple pajamas looked around nervously. "Do you want me to go and do that . . . now?"

The shadows nodded excitedly. "Yes! Oh yes, please," they

each muttered, their heads bobbing, torsos bouncing. "Bring us a bucket of rum! A bucket of rum!"

She smiled, turned, and ran, leaving the shadows behind, her heart racing, her feet carrying her faster than they ever had. She was finally going to see the bunyip. Things were finally going to change. All she had to do now was get home.

KAYCEE AWOKE, HER head swimming with visions of shadows still dancing around her. She looked, but they were gone. She'd left them behind, hundreds of miles away. It was dark out and the stars still wheeled slowly above, hours from being chased away by morning's light, but close enough that her father would have already passed out in his chair. It was the perfect time for her crime.

But the TV wasn't on. Most nights her father passed out before shutting it off and slept through the night to the infomercials and, eventually, the static. Other nights, however, he took pity on her and shut it off. In truth, he believed he did this most nights, thinking Kaycee had simply turned the set on to help him wake up. She never did, but never contradicted him about it.

Were the TV on, she could stroll out singing a song and dancing on the creaky old floors without waking him. But the TV wasn't on. The house was silent save for the raucous din of his snoring.

Quietly she swung her legs out over the side of the bed, sliding her backside down the edge of the mattress, slowly easing her weight onto the wooden floorboards beneath until her hands were the last parts of her touching. First with her good foot, then with the club. She took a deep breath and let go, her body now standing up straight without having squeezed out the slightest groan from the boards. Then she stepped each limping step one at a time, her gate wide, pace slow, like a cat burglar in a cartoon show. Kaycee dared not make a sound. Drunk though he was and hard to wake as he might be, if her father caught her skulking through the house after bedtime, especially on a quest for his liquor, he would put a stop to it right away.

And that couldn't happen. Not tonight.

Her toes came down on a loose floorboard and it squeaked, just a little, causing her eyes to clench and her stomach to tighten. *CREeeeeeak.* As her clubfoot came to a rest, she sighed, convinced that this was the sound that would disturb her father, drag him out of his chair swearing, and lead him right to her malfeasance. She held her breath, listened close. Snoring. So she took another exaggerated step, making not a peep. More snoring. This was going well. Very well.

At this pace, it took her nearly five minutes to cross the meager house, three of which she spent on the stairs alone, afraid that every tiny groan would be the end of her. But time and again, these squeaks went unnoticed and she pressed on, trudging through the dark toward the pantry. It was only near the end of her slog that she thought about how quickly she could cross an entire continent in her dreams, but how slowly she had to go in waking life. The thought wasn't comforting.

Kaycee reached the kitchen with its slick linoleum floor and its wide open space. She skated on stockinged feet, crossing the room in seconds, a giddy little smile on her face. Then a turn of the knob and the pantry opened, its dark innards beckoning, the thick smell of mixing foods belching out into the night. Beans. Crackers. Peanut butter. Honey. Smells so sweet, blending; a frothy, hearty stew, tickling her nose.

She looked up at the deep black in the corner of the topmost shelf. Though she couldn't see it, she knew it was there. Booze. Liquor of all sorts. Vodka. Whiskey. And most important, rum. She could picture them. The distinct shape of the bottle, square with a narrowing bottom like the jaw of a thick yobbo; the proud white polar bear peeking out from the yellow label ringed with red and brown racing stripes.

Kaycee knew the bottle well. Not only was it her father's favorite drink, but it also tempted and teased her. Polar bear juice. For years she had pined for it before sneaking a sip that she spat out on the couch. The stain was still there. Daddy had laughed. *Learn to keep it down or don't drink it. You don't waste good booze.*

Tonight she wouldn't waste it.

Tonight she would feed it to the spirits in her backyard, spirits that would lead the way to the bunyip. Her insides tickled, dancing a little at the thought. She was so close now. All she had to do was climb this pantry shelf. In the dark. Silently. *Piece of cake.*

She grabbed the shoulder-level shelf with both hands, gripping it between her chin and neck, raising her one good stockinged foot into the air, carefully feeling her way around. There it was; the shelf beneath her. Her foot came down gracefully, her weight shifting onto it. The shelf cried out a little at the added weight, the brackets holding it up straining to keep steady.

Kaycee held her breath once more. Snoring.

She raised her second foot, all of her weight bearing down on the two shelves. *So far, so good.* Then she pushed up, ascending a level, her hands grasping the next shelf, her weight for a moment on her bad foot. *Almost there.* Her hands trembled, equal parts nervousness and effort. The shelves rattled a bit, the food shifting as the boards began to bow. Once more she brought up a single foot. Then the other. And she pushed up again, rising to halfway up the pantry.

She stretched, her fingers tickling the top shelf, batting a blunted square bottle, spinning it blindly in the dark.

Kaycee had to climb one more shelf.

Her stomach tightened. She was too high up now. If she fell, she was going to get hurt. *No time to think about that. Think of the bunyip. Think about anything but how high up you are. Think about anything but the ground down there. Think of the bunyip. Think of the bunyip.*

Her muscles were aching now, her hands shaking more violently than before, tightly grasped around a wobbly shelf. She raised a foot. Then the other. And she pushed up once more.

Victory.

The shelves groaned again beneath her weight. Bottles clanked as she grabbed them, shuffling them down a level. Her hands were cramping; her legs were giving out. *Just a few. More. Bottles.*

That's when she heard them. Like gremlins. Scampering. Scraping. Clawing. Giggling, chuckling to themselves, hushing one another like teenage girls sneaking out of a house at a slumber party. She couldn't see them, couldn't make them out in the dark, but she knew they were there, climbing over one another just feet beneath her.

She looked down, her grip loosening, arms unsteady as ever.

Then a single clawed hand reached up, grabbing her ankle.

"Stop it!" she whispered loudly. "Let go!"

She acted quickly, shaking off the grip of the hand, leaping up to the next highest shelf. And with that, the shelf snapped beneath her.

She tumbled, her fall so brief that she never even knew what was happening.

Kaycee's head smacked hard onto the floor, the dull concussive shock blunting the sound of the back of her skull shattering.

THE PRETTY LITTLE girl in the purple pajamas stood above her own broken, tiny body, watching as a large puddle of blood pooled beneath her head. Her hair had already soaked up all the blood it could and the rest spilled across the floor, racing to reach the walls. The shadows stood around her, watching the life drain onto the linoleum.

"Does this mean we're not getting any rum?" asked one of the shadows.

"Quiet," said another.

"I wanted rum."

"Me too."

"We all wanted rum," said Jeronimus. "But she doesn't have a body to get it with anymore. She broke it."

"I didn't!" said the girl.

"You did," said Jeronimus. "You broke it."

"Fix it!" shouted a shadow. "Fix it and bring us the rum!"

"I can't!"

"Fix it!"

The pretty little girl in the purple pajamas ran from the pantry, her incorporeal body leaping over the kutji, through the kitchen, and into the living room in the span of a breath. There, in his chair, her father slumbered loudly. She couldn't smell him, couldn't feel him. She shouted, "Dad! Dad, wake up! Dad, please!" But still he slept. "Dad, wake up! I need you!"

Wade muttered quietly, shifting in his sleep as if he could hear her like distant whispers in a dream. Louder and louder she screamed but couldn't rouse him. He was out, thick with the sleep of the drink, and she *wasn't real*. She was in the dream. The colors of the house were brighter, the shadows were all alive, and her father would never see or hear her, no matter how hard she tried.

"Dad, I'm dying," she whispered, her voice choking with tears. She reached out with her dreamlike hand and stroked a face and chin she could not feel. "I love you."

"I love you, darlin'," muttered Wade, unaware that he was saying good-bye to his daughter.

"You're not dying," said Jeronimus as he crept softly behind her. "You're just beginning. The dream is out there *waiting*. The bunyip is out there *waiting*. Your destiny—"

"My destiny is waiting."

"It is."

She leaned in and gave her father a final kiss, trying to stroke his hair as he did hers, even if only for show. "Good-bye, Dad."

CHAPTER 26

NIGHT OF THE BUNYIP

Mandu sat before the fire, the crisp, crystal-clear night sky wheeling above him, his didgeridoo—thin, wavy, painted the colors of a poisonous snake—pressed firmly between his lips. He blew, the long, droning hum, electrifying the air with the mystic buzz of its note, twittering deep like a three-foot-long locust.

Colby watched, entranced. He'd read about didgeridoos in school, but he'd never seen what one actually did to dreamstuff. The night grew colorful, ancient stories becoming songs, song-lines taking shape in hallucinatory plays. The fire crackled and popped, long-dead spirits seemingly coming alive again to tell their side of it.

"What are you doing?" asked Colby, his knuckles white, fists clenched tight, eyes wide and excited.

Mandu finished his note, his breaths long and evenly paced, not having winded himself in the slightest despite the lengthy performance. "I'm calling out the things of the night. Telling them we're coming."

"Telling what we're coming?"

Mandu paused, searching for the right words. "Tonight is an important night. I've had dreams about it for years, seen fragments that have slowly pieced together like a puzzle. Tonight is the night you and I go to the lake, drink of its waters, and see a bunyip."

"A bunyip? What's a bunyip?"

"The most dangerous creature in all of the outback. Capable of drowning those who camp too close to the water while they sleep. Able to grasp a fella in its mouth and chomp him in half. It's large and furry, massive, really, like a horse, but broad and thick like a wombat. It's got teeth like tusks, but dozens of them. It can change shape, looking like whatever will scare you most. And it wants nothing more than to drag your corpse back into the water to feed on your innards for days."

Colby gaped at Mandu, both baffled and terrified. Then nodded, coolly. "Oh," he said. "You're sure?"

"You have no idea how sure I am."

Colby mulled this over for a moment. "How does it work?" he asked.

"How does what work?"

"Your dreams. Seeing the future. How does that work?"

Mandu smiled, nodding, admiring Colby's curiosity. "The dreams come to me in pieces. We all see the future in dreams. We just have so many dreams that it's hard to tell them apart. In mine though, I have a dingo. A big one." Mandu held his arms out wide, stretching them as far as he could. "Huge. Eyes black as black can be. He shows up, slips out of the night, and just looks at me. He's my familiar, my spirit animal. And when he's in a dream, I know that this is something that is going to happen.

"It only comes in fragments though. Never the whole thing at once. Sometimes it's just a few images. Other times it is whole scenes. But over the years, if your mind is sharp, you can stitch all the memories together like a movie and get an idea of what the future is going to be."

"So you know what's going to happen tonight?"

Shrugging, Mandu looked at the stars and juggled the answer. "Some. Not all. We'll see how it all shakes out. The dreams haven't lied before. But you can never trust nothin'." He grabbed his walking stick, braced it in the dirt, and climbed it to his feet. "Even dreams lie. Let's go."

THE PRETTY LITTLE girl in the purple pajamas hid behind a large rock atop an outcrop overlooking the marshy billabong below—surrounding her on all sides was a flock of black crows, wriggling, dancing, ruffling their feathers, unable to contain their excitement. It was *the* night. Everything changed tonight. Everything. For everyone. Tonight a path would be chosen and set; they need only wait to see the moment for sure.

For the pretty little girl in the purple pajamas, tonight was the night she saw her destiny up close. For the crows it meant being one step closer to having one more piece of the puzzle that would set them free.

At first she heard them. The Clever Man was blowing his didgeridoo, buzzing sweet the night. Then the figures appeared, two blue-tinted silhouettes in the moonlight. The water began to ripple and dance, the reflection of the moon and the stars going hazy, then wavy, then vanishing to flash on and off in the waves.

And that's when she saw it rise out of the water.

The bunyip.

It was massive, like a furry rhinoceros, its head elongated, stretched out and squished at the end of a long neck as if it were clay pressed together too hard by giant fingers. It flicked a long anteaterlike tongue at the water, tickling past gleaming teeth as long as a man's arm. Six legs sloshed through the water, all of them with claws nearly as long as its teeth.

This wasn't a monster; it was a nightmare. The amalgam of almost everything she feared, dripping wet, creeping quietly toward land.

"That's what you've been looking for?" asked one of the crows. "It doesn't look like much."

"Quiet," said another crow. "It means something to her." Then it turned to the girl. "Doesn't it?"

She nodded, her eyes bright, glistening slightly with tears. "Uh-huh. It's exactly what I've been waiting for." She looked around at all the crows, who watched her expectantly, smiling. "Thank you. Thank you all. I wouldn't be here without you."

"No, you wouldn't," said the second crow. "Remember that when the time comes. Now, get down there."

MANDU AND COLBY stood at the water's edge, the moon rippling in its sheen. They looked out and saw the hulking shadow moving slowly, silently toward them.

"Don't be afraid," said Mandu. "They only charge faster when they sense fear."

"I'm not afraid," said Colby truthfully, his eyes straining to make out the shape of the monster.

Mandu looked down. "You're not, are you?"

"I've seen bigger. And scarier. If he gets too close, I'll—" He gestured with both hands as if he had a rifle. "*Pkew! Pkew!*"

"I have no doubt about that." Mandu reached into his pouch

and pulled from it his bullroarer, immediately spinning the wooden charm through the air on the end of its cord. It hummed and whistled, seemingly whispering something unintelligible into the night air.

The bunyip stopped where it stood, scratching its ear with a paw, trying to chase away the noise. It whinnied and growled and stomped in the mud. Then it turned and sank back into the water, hiding in the deeps. The water rippled a bit more, then became unnaturally calm, inviting.

"You see, that's what will hold you back, Colby. You fight with strength, not cleverness. Cleverness is good for victory. Strength is good for killing. And killing never ends well."

"I don't fight with strength. I fight with magic. And magic is cleverness."

Mandu shook his head. "No. Strength is for using against others. Cleverness is getting someone to act against themselves. You can do that with magic. But you don't think like that."

"Yeah I do," said Colby, indignant.

"Then how were you going to stop the bunyip if it attacked?"

"I was, well, I . . . that's different. If it was going to attack, I should be able to defend myself."

"I confused it. Sent it away. Clever. You were just going to make it go *poof*! Strength."

Colby looked down shamefully at his feet. "I was going to make it go *poof*!"

"Men study their whole lives to master what comes to you so naturally. Nothing that comes so easily can ever have value. Do not take your skills for granted or a man cleverer than you will rob you of all you have and leave you for the earth to take back." Mandu smiled. "I know why you're here now, what I have to teach you. But there's someone you need to meet first." He waved out into the bush. "Come on, come on. Don't stand out there with your jaw hanging loose. Come out and introduce yourself."

From the darkness emerged the pretty little girl in the purple pajamas. She was a little younger than Colby, but beautiful, athletic, taller, her hair and dark skin almost sparkling in the light.

Colby turned to Mandu. "What is she?"

"I'm a girl," she said.

"She's a girl," said Mandu.

"No," said Colby. "She's not real."

"I'm real!"

"No, I mean, she's . . . she's . . ."

Mandu motioned to her. "She's a dreamwalker, Colby. She can leave her body when she's asleep and walk through dreamtime like you and I. It's her gift."

"So she can see beyond the veil, but only when asleep?"

Mandu nodded. "Uh-huh."

"So she's not really here, but she is?"

"Yes."

"Okay," he said, smiling at her. "I'm Colby."

The pretty little girl in the purple pajamas smiled big and wide, her heart racing. This was a boy. A real boy. He was looking right at her. And he was talking to her. For the first time in her life, to someone other than her father, she was not invisible. "Hi, Colby. I've been waiting a long time to meet you."

"You have?"

"Uh-huh."

"What's your name?"

"It doesn't matter," she said, shrugging.

"What do you mean it doesn't matter?"

"It doesn't matter."

"Of course it matters. What am I supposed to call you?"

"Whatever you like, I guess. But you don't have to call me anything. When you talk to me, I know you're talking to me. And when you talk to the Clever Man—"

"Mandu."

"Whatever. When you talk to him, and you say *she*, he'll know exactly who you're talking about. So why do you need a name at all?"

"You want me to call you *she*?"

"I want you to call me whatever you want."

"But what's your name?"

"I don't have one."

"We all have names."

"I have one back when I'm awake. But now I'm asleep. You don't need names when you're asleep."

"But I'm not asleep."

"Of course not. That's why you told me your name."

"Why don't you just tell me your name?"

"Because names don't mean anything. A name won't tell you who I am. It doesn't tell you what a person is. It tells you what their parents thought was a cute name when they were born. That's it. Does a name tell you that I'm faster than you? Taller than you? Can cross the whole of Australia in a single night if I tried? No. It doesn't. And it never will. Because names are just that. So call me whatever you like. I'll only answer to it if I like you."

Colby turned to Mandu. "She's weird."

Mandu nodded, agreeing. "But a very powerful spirit." He waved to the girl and motioned back toward their fire a mile away. "Go, tend the fire and wait for us. We'll be there shortly."

"Not yet," she said, shaking her head. "I haven't seen the bunyip."

"Weren't you watching from up on that rock?"

"Yeah, but I didn't get to see it up close." She walked over to Mandu and put a gentle hand on his elbow. "Don't worry about me, Clever Man. I'm fast. Faster than anything else out here. I'll be fine."

The pretty little girl hiked up her pajama pants above her knees, rolling tight cuffs to keep them in place, then ran out into the water, slapping it with an open palm.

"She's a lot like you," said Mandu to Colby. "She doesn't yet know how powerful she is. And she doesn't understand her destiny."

"You can see her destiny?"

"I see a lot I can't speak of."

"In your dreams?"

Mandu nodded silently, watching the girl play in the water.

"Have you seen mine?"

"Parts of it."

"Really? What is it?"

Mandu grimaced, looking down at Colby as if he'd just sworn. "It is exactly as you wish, just not as you expect."

"You have to tell me more than that."

"The spirits don't bring dreams to the people who talk too much about them. I'd rather listen to you pester me the whole rest of the walkabout than shut you up and never receive the gifts of the spirits again."

"So that's a no?"

"That's a no." Mandu pointed at the water. "Now watch this. It's one of the best things I ever dreamed about."

The bunyip poked only the top of its head out of the black water, its eyes, each almost as big as a grown man's skull, peering out at the girl splashing loudly about.

"She's quite clever, but so is the bunyip. Look at the edge there." The water began lapping against the shore, creeping up inches at a time but never receding.

"It's rising!" said Colby.

"I wonder who will win," said Mandu, tickled. He looked at Colby with a wry smile.

The pretty little girl in the purple pajamas crept closer to the bunyip, pretending not to see it, slapping the water as if still looking for it.

The bunyip stood still, spying, waiting.

She waded closer.

It waited still.

She turned back to shore, smiling at the pair, rolling her eyes back toward the bunyip playfully as if to say, *Get a load of this guy*.

Then, without warning, the bunyip lunged, its massive paws swinging, its gaping maw wide open, teeth bared, snarling. Water sprayed, the lake exploding as if someone had dropped in a stick of dynamite. It descended upon her, chomping down to make a meal out of her.

But true to her word, she was faster. She leaped up upon the water, running so fast that her feet never sank in. She grabbed hold of its fur, flung a leg up and over, straddled the beast, mounting it. It flailed, cartwheeling in the water, bucking, kicking, but she held on. Try as it might, it couldn't shake her.

Splashing furiously it arched its long neck, gnashed its teeth, tried to bite her off its back like a dog chewing fleas. But she would not let go.

She only laughed, giggling, playing a game, dodging teeth, and mocking with childish faces. Completely unafraid.

Then the bunyip bucked one last time, finally shaking her loose. She flew back across the lake, flopping painfully against a large stone jutting out of the billabong, then dropping back into the water. But she ran again, her feet barely breaking the surface, bolting back out to shore, laughing all the way.

Mandu spun his bullroarer in the air, making the night again uneasy. The bunyip got the message, sank once more back into the dark, muddy water, letting the night at last settle back into peace. The water receded, slowly draining back into the billabong.

The pretty little girl in the purple pajamas smiled, waved, and ran back toward camp, vanishing almost instantly, leaving Colby and Mandu alone again.

"So," said Colby. "Was that supposed to be *fighting with cleverness?*"

Mandu shrugged sheepishly. "Meh. Sometimes bravery trumps cleverness. But you shouldn't make a habit of it."

CHAPTER 27

A BREAK IN THE SIEGE

I'm taking this seat," said a sweet, lilting voice as it pulled a stool noisily away from the bar with an angry din.

Colby, Yashar, and Gossamer each looked up, saw a flash of blond hair, straw cowboy hat.

Austin plopped down on the stool with all the grace of a factory worker after a long day, sighing loudly. Her skin was sweaty, pallid, her eyes bloodshot and wide, as if she was keeping them open by force of will alone. "You know," she said. "These hipster dive bars get harder and harder to find." She waved a finger at the place, pointing almost to every corner. "I mean, I see the appeal. You already know everybody, no douchebags wander in and act like they're at a kegger. But at some point you just gotta draw the line and let a bar be a bar instead of a damn scavenger hunt."

Yashar nodded politely. "Austin," he said, his tone nervous, reserved. "I didn't hear you come in."

Austin looked up at the ceiling, as if lost in thought for a second, then smiled coyly, looking right at him. "No one ever does."

"This isn't a hipster bar," said Colby.

"No?"

"No."

"Because it used to be a fairy bar. Buuuuuut someone kicked out all the fairies. So what is it now?"

Yashar shuffled nervously behind the bar. "Outside . . . are they still—"

"The demons? All over the place." She leaned forward on her stool, grasping her stomach to massage away a sudden discomfort. "Oh, I think I'm gonna hurl."

"Not here you won't," said Yashar.

Austin looked up at him through a strained grimace, her gaze made ever the more intimidating by her seeming illness. "In a bar? I'm not allowed to throw up . . . in a bar? If there was one place I should be allowed to chuck, I'd think—" She took a deep breath, regaining a little of her composure.

"What do you want?" asked Colby, pointedly.

Austin smiled weakly, suddenly pouring on the charm. "You don't want to talk to me?"

"I . . . well. I mean . . ."

"Elevated heart rate, dilated pupils. The way you feel like someone is sitting on your chest when you look at me. Colby Stevens, if I didn't know better, I'd say you have a crush."

Colby stared into his drink, wishing he was invisible. "Oh God. This is happening."

Yashar nodded, half embarrassed himself. "Yep. It's happening."

"It. Is. Happening," said Austin.

"Can I get you something to drink," asked Yashar, "or are you just here to humiliate my buddy?"

"It's a little early to be drinking, don't you think?"

"It's never too early for drinking," he replied. He looked out toward the street even though there was no view from the bar. "Especially on a day like today."

"I think you boys might have a problem. You know you're allowed to feel emotions without liquor being involved, right?"

"Yeah," said Colby. "But the liquor lets us be a bit more honest about them."

"It's just our way," said Yashar.

Austin gaped at the two, her mouth chewing on a pregnant pause before winking slyly, eyes twinkling mischievously. "I'm just fucking with you," she said. "I'm still drunk from last night. *Una cerveza, por favor.*"

"*Una cerveza,*" said Yashar, sliding an ice-cold IPA across the bar.

"How'd you know?" she asked, eyeing the label.

"You mean aside from the fact that I know the secret desires and wishes of a person's heart?"

"Yeah."

"Well, you joke about hipster bars, but I can't imagine there's one in town you don't drink at."

"Guilty." She sipped her beer, her face puckering as if it was sour.

"No good?" asked Yashar. "I've got others."

"It's not the beer."

"Then maybe you're a drink or two past the point of drinking."

"It's not me being drunk either."

"Then what?"

She clenched her fist and thumbed out toward the street. "It's them."

"The Seventy-two?"

She nodded. "I've never felt anything like this before. They're making me sick."

Colby tried to remain invisible, outside the conversation. He sipped his whiskey casually, but couldn't help peeking over to eye her up and down. Even ill appearing as she was, there was still something about her. Something that glowed without light, felt warm without heat. She wore a pair of faded skinny jeans with the knee torn out of one of the legs, a pair of painted Converse, different from the ones she'd worn the night before, and a black T-shirt that read: LIMESTONE KINGDOM. That stung a little and his heart sank, just a little farther, and he found that he needed the whiskey more than ever.

"You're rejecting them," said Yashar, nodding. "You've never had this many in town at once, have you?"

Austin shook her head, sipping her beer. "The city. It's like the sewers have overflowed and all the deep, dark, hidden shit that has been festering beneath it for years has spilled out and stunk up the whole damn place. These things, they're the worst of the worst. Corruption seeps off 'em into the air like cheap cologne. And anyone who gets a whiff gets nervous. Or angry. The whole city is on edge. They can't see 'em, but they sure as shit can feel 'em. People are doing things they ordinarily wouldn't. Getting downright mean. Hurting people they love. I've never had this much taint in the city at once. It feels like I ate a pound of fried shit and now I've just got to sweat it out until it passes."

"When they leave," said Yashar.

"Yeah," she said, eyeing Colby suspiciously. "When they leave."

He frowned, his heart still sinking. "Nice shirt," he said coldly, his anger getting the better of him.

"It's an original."

"Do you listen to yourself when you say shit like that?"

"I do. But are *you* listening? I said it's original. There were only about a dozen made. The only way to have gotten one of these is—"

Colby's jaw dropped and he pointed a limp finger at her. "You were there. That night."

She nodded. "Amazing show. Your boy really had it in him."

"So you were there when—"

"He got jumped? Yeah."

"And you didn't . . ."

"What? Intervene? Why? He handled that himself. He made his own choice."

"But that led to—"

"A dozen different decisions that were all his own. And your own. I'll step in when it protects my city, but I'm not its mother. I don't protect the people from themselves. It's not my way."

"And what is your way?"

She thought hard for a moment, her eyes steeled on his, her gaze fierce, intimidating. Colby couldn't help but hold his breath at the way she looked mulling over his question, the slope of her neck, the cut of her chin, the light sprinkle of freckles across her cheek. "Well," she said. "When someone gets into trouble, if they don't deserve it, I like to see what I can do to help them out. But when they bring trouble upon themselves, when, say, two greater demons of the worst kind show up for them—"

Colby's head fell into his free hand while the other gripped his drink tightly. "Oh God, you're here to bust my balls again. Didn't we just do this last night?"

"Last night I didn't know the trouble you would be in by morning. You really work fast, Colby Stevens."

"I had nothing to do with that."

"Oh, so this has nothing to do with you?"

Colby hesitated, flustered. "Not directly, no."

"Not directly?"

"No."

"So this girl who's coming for you, she's not super pissed at you or dangerous or anything?"

Yashar shook his head. "This isn't about him."

"It's all about him. *Entirely* about him."

"So you're here to scold me again."

Austin sipped her beer, swallowed, shaking her head. "I don't know what I'm here to do. I think I'm here for the beer, mostly."

Colby looked over at her, baffled. "I don't get you."

"Not much to get. I'm just a girl, Colby. I'm a lot like you. Someone extraordinary on the outside, but ordinary on the inside. This is Austin, and I'm just its reflection. I don't owe this city anything. What I give it I give because I love it. I love what this city has made me, and I watch out for it. Aside from that, I'm as normal as the next girl."

"You interfered with me but not Ewan?"

"You're really hung up on that, aren't you? Ewan wasn't threatening my city. You on the other hand want to choke the magic out. You want to make it mundane. Safe. Unremarkable. And then you bring a bunch of baddies like Amy and Oro—"

"Stop saying their names!"

Austin looked quizzically across the bar at Yashar. "Is there something I missed?"

Yashar nodded. "He thinks if he doesn't say their names—"

"That's not what I think," said Colby. "I just don't need to draw any more attention to myself."

"If they're watching you, Colby," said Austin, "then they're watching you. You can't hide. Not here anyway."

"I wasn't, I mean . . ." Colby paused and took a big sip of whiskey. "I'm not trying to choke the magic out. I just wanted to . . ."

"Wanted to what?"

"To . . . protect children."

"I know," she said. "And that's why I like you."

"You like me?"

"Sure," she said playfully, the twinkle returning to her eye. "I get it. You want to feel like you've done something. Like you've left something behind. You're not alone. You're idealistic. Like a politician." She looked at him sternly. "Except that you weren't elected."

"Neither were you."

"Touché." She smiled. That thought hadn't dawned on her. "Well, I mean I was, but I wasn't." She thought some more, trying to find the right words. "I just want what's best for everyone, but I don't know the future. I see what's happening here. I see what you're getting into. And I'm worried about you."

"There's nothing to worry about."

Austin looked at him longingly, her pretenses dropped, face awash in worry. "Please," she said. "Don't get involved in this."

Colby leaned back on his stool, confused. "I don't understand."

"Whatever they're asking you to do, don't do it."

"I don't know what they're asking me to do. All I know is that she's coming."

"The girl?"

"The girl."

"Whatever they need you to go do with her, you can't go. I need you here."

Colby grew cold. "Need me for what?"

"Don't make me say it."

"Need me for what?"

"I just—" She stammered a little, trying to keep cool. "I need you here."

"Need. Me. For—"

Austin stroked the top of Colby's hand with her fingertips, setting his arm ablaze with tingles, then folded her fingers into his. She stroked his hair back over his ear with her free hand, running a single finger down along it to the lobe. "Don't. Do. This," she whispered. Then she batted her eyelashes ever so slightly, almost imperceptibly, her eyes large and pleading. "Please."

Colby squeezed her hand tight, his chest caving in on itself. "I don't even know what they want me to do."

"Austin," said Yashar, paternally. "Please don't mess with Colby like that."

She slipped her hand away from Colby's. "Would you rather I do this the other way?"

"Which way would that be?"

She scowled, spoke with bass in her voice. "The fire and brimstone don't-make-me-kick-your-ass-and-rain-a-world-of-shit-down-on-you way."

Yashar put both hands up. "Okay, the first way was fine."

Colby shook his head. "I didn't do anything. Why are you doing this?"

"Someone died today, Colby. A demon took one of my people."

"You act as if that doesn't happen every day in this city, in one way or another."

"Not for show," she said, bitterly. "Never for show! That demon killed someone just to fuck with you. And I'll be damned if I'm going to let him get what he came for."

"Is that what this is about? Making a point?"

Austin teared up, just a little, the slight glisten making her eyes bluer, glassier, more like the open sea. "His name was Ernesto. He had two kids, Julian and Selena. He met his wife bagging groceries when they were seventeen. She was a cashier. The first day they worked the same line together was like . . . well, you could have powered the whole building with the sparks those two were giving off. He loved his wife and kids as much as anyone I've ever known and he never hurt anyone.

"I had a beer with him once. He sat there the whole time nervous that I was going to hit on him. Nervous. Most guys, especially the married ones, they have a beer with a girl, they *hope* she flirts. Even if they haven't the faintest inclination to cheat. Makes 'em feel good. Like they're *still a man*. Not Ernesto. He was terrified of his wife thinking he might be flirting with another girl. Didn't want her to think for a second that he might find another woman in the world to be as pretty as her. Because he didn't. So we talked about the Spurs and about his kids and then his kids some more." She giggled, her eyes smiling for a second as she thought back, before darkening all at once atop a sneer. "So fuck Asmodeus. And I don't care if he hears me." She looked up at the ceiling. "You hear me, asshole? Asmodeus! Come on down here and look me in the eyes, you little bitch!"

"Whoa, whoa, whoa!" yelled Yashar, waving his hands. "There's no need for that."

"Oh sure," said Colby. "Now you're not cool with invoking them by name."

"He won't come," she said, before yelling at the ceiling again. "He's a FUCKING PUSSY!"

"Jesus," said Colby. "You *are* still drunk from last night."

"I lied about that," she said, taking another sip of her beer. "I started drinking again this morning."

Austin stood up, slammed the rest of her beer, then tossed the bottle to Yashar, pointing at him. Yashar caught it single-handedly, a little pissed at the disrespect, but not wanting to offend his guest.

"Make sure he doesn't get any deeper in this," she said, before turning to Colby. "Let them sort out their mess themselves." Then she walked out of the bar, muttering to herself about god-damned demons.

CHAPTER 28

THE ORPHAN STORY

The Clever Man, the pretty little girl in the purple pajamas, and the boy Colby sat around the fire, Mandu once again blowing his didgeridoo. The night was alive, the fire crackling with hints of stories, the flames momentary spirits that whispered secrets before fluttering away toward the stars. The pretty little girl huddled closer to the fire than the others, her arms crossed, rubbing her hands up and down, trying to warm herself through her pajamas, shivering slightly.

Mandu looked over the fire at the two. "Once, very long ago," he began, "there was an orphan boy whose mother and father had both died in terrible ways. The mother had been careless, wandering too close to the water's edge during the rainy season, while not paying enough attention to the crocs swimming in the river. The father had been loud and boisterous and picked one too many fights with other fellas. Neither died particularly well. So it was very sad for the boy, who now lived with his grandmother.

"The grandmother took good care of him. Fed him, taught him, treated him in all ways like a son. But the other children of the camp were cruel to him. Having no one to teach him how to hunt or properly throw a spear, he fell out of favor with them, and they taunted him for being an orphan. One day he went to his grandmother, saying, 'Grandmother, they won't play with me or share their food.' His grandmother asked, 'Who won't?' To which he replied, 'The other children.'

"Grandmother understood. She handed him a snack of honey and cakes and said, 'Don't you concern yourself with them. They are greedy, terrible children, and one day their bellies will ache with hunger and they will know of their cruelty.' But the boy wasn't comforted. He refused to eat and only cried louder.

"His crying grew so loud that it awoke the Rainbow Serpent from his dreaming. He uncoiled himself from under the earth and followed the crying to the village. He burrowed his way under and into the hut where the orphan was crying and swallowed both him and his grandmother whole. The serpent was so large that as he emerged, the hut lodged on its head like a hat. Hungry from his long slumber, he began eating villagers, swallowing families one by one.

"The people ran, terrified by the Rainbow Serpent trying to end the world. Soon the village was completely empty, but the Rainbow Serpent, he was still hungry. So he moved along the earth, his body weighed down by all the people in his belly, carving a groove in it. Finally, he came upon another village and set about eating it as well.

"By this time, he had swallowed so many warriors, all of whom poked the serpent from the inside with their spears, that he looked like he was covered in a thousand thorns. As he ate, he grew slower and slower, and finally a few warriors were able to climb upon his head and deliver the deathblow, killing the Rainbow Serpent for good and for all. Then they cut open its belly and set free all the people."

"What happened next?" asked Colby.

"Nothing," said Mandu. "That's the end of the story."

"I don't get it."

"Neither do I," said the girl.

"The Rainbow Serpent helped dream the world into existence. He was one of the most powerful creatures in history. But he was woken from his sleep by the tiniest, most insignificant of people. And he was killed by mere men who possessed nothing more than spears and bravery. Normal men. Great and terrible things can come about because of a single person wanting nothing more than attention. And the end of the world can be stopped by men brave enough to try. No one is too big or too small to change the world, for better or for worse. That's the lesson."

"Oh," said Colby. "I get it now."

"I hope so," said Mandu. "That story will mean more to you than most." Mandu put the didgeridoo back to his lips, playing again, letting Colby meditate for a moment on his words.

"Can I ask you something, boy?" said the pretty little girl in the purple pajamas, still trying to warm herself.

"My name is Colby."

"I don't care what your name is."

"I do. And I don't like being called *boy*. What's your deal with names?"

"My *deal*?"

"Yeah, your *deal*. What is it?"

"Names don't mean anything out here. Who we were doesn't

mean anything out here. All that matters out here is who we *are*. Out here I am who I *want* to be, not what anyone tells me I *have* to be."

"Everything out here has a name, you know," said Colby.

The pretty little girl in the purple pajamas gave him a dirty look, her face pinched and puckered as if to say, *I know that*. "I don't have a name out here yet."

"Why not?"

"No one has given me one."

"I'll give you one."

She shook her head. "No. It doesn't work that way. You have to earn it."

"What's your question?"

"What?"

Colby leaned forward. "Your question. The one you wanted to ask me."

"What are you doing out here? I mean, you clearly aren't, you know . . . indigenous."

"Indigiwhat?"

"Aboriginal."

"I don't understand."

"You're not a black."

"Oh! No. I'm not."

"But you can see me."

"Yeah."

"How? And why are you on walkabout?"

"Oh," said Colby, thinking for a second about how best to explain it.

"You ever hear of a djinn?"

"No."

"How 'bout a genie?"

She nodded, smiling queerly. "You mean like from a lamp? Like on TV?"

"Yes. But never, ever, ever say that to one. Because they hate that."

"They? You mean they're real?"

"Why wouldn't they be? Little girls who fly around in their dreams are real. And bunyips are real."

"Yeah, but genies? That just sounds . . . silly."

"They're called djinn. And I made a wish with one. Well, two actually."

"So you haven't gotten your third?"

"It doesn't work that way. You know, you'd think it would, but . . ."

"What did you wish for?"

"To see the things other people couldn't. Fairies, bunyips . . ." He motioned to her. "Dreamwalkers."

"Why?"

"Because I didn't like it at home and I thought that this would be better."

"Is it?" she asked.

"Sometimes. No one ever tries to kill me at home. But there's no one around there I really like either."

"You like people out here?" She motioned to the desert around her.

Colby nodded. "Oh yeah! Mandu is great. Yashar—he's my djinn—he's awesome. I've got this friend Ewan who is a fairy boy. I've met angels and mermen and all sorts of things. You."

"Me? You don't know me."

"Not real well. But I can tell you're cool. I like you already."

She shuffled around awkwardly. "Why? Because you think I'm pretty or something?"

Colby looked away bashfully, his cheeks reddening. "Nooooo. That's not it."

Mandu smiled secretly behind his didgeridoo.

"You don't think I'm pretty? I'm pretty and I'm tall and I'm fast. You don't like that?"

"I like you because you're . . . you know . . . the way you jumped on the bunyip and you weren't afraid of it."

"Why would I be afraid of it?" she asked.

"I was afraid of it."

"Oh, well . . . you think I'm cool?"

"Yeah."

"And it's not because you think I'm pretty or something."

"No."

She smiled, tucking her hair behind her ear and dragging the back of her hand under her chin. "Thank you."

"So will you tell me your name already?"

Her smile evaporated and she frowned, pushing him away playfully. "No," she said in all seriousness. Then she looked up at the stars, the sky so black this far out that there were literally thousands of them swimming together in a deep sea of night. "You know, the Clever Man told me once that in the Skyworld, each star was a campfire of the dead. That they come together with their dreaming or tribe and at night we can peer across the gulf of time and see their fires winking back at us."

Colby seemed incredulous. "Campfires?" He looked at Mandu, who only nodded, still playing his one, droning note.

"Campfires on the other side of the sky," she said, mired in the romance of it, her teeth chattering lightly. "I like the idea. You know that where we go when we die is a place like this. Around a fire. With friends. Telling stories. Where everyone gets to be exactly who they dream they were meant to be."

"I like that," said Colby. "That place sounds nice."

"Why is it so cold out here?" she asked, her body almost convulsing with shivers.

Mandu stopped playing. The night grew quiet except for the

crackling of the fire. "Oh," he said sadly. "Our time is again too short."

The pretty little girl in the purple pajamas looked over at him, terrified, the cord attached to the back of her head growing suddenly taut, yanking her backward. She vanished into the dark.

Colby looked at Mandu, his eyes wide, confused. "Where did she—"

"Home," said Mandu. "She'll be back. She always is."

"Who is she?"

"I told you. She's a dreamwalker."

"No, I mean, what's her name?"

Mandu smiled, shaking his head. "You know, I never thought to ask."

CHAPTER 29

BESIDE HERSELF

Light. Blinding. Almost green. Then it goes out, fading. Tracers trickling across the eyes, fireworks soaring through space. Then light again. A whine, high-pitched ringing in the ears. Everything too bright to make out. Shapes in the light, not a one of them clear, crisp. The whine again, then light. The sound of a truck hitting a wall.

"Clear!" shouts a voice.

Then a circle of light. Bright. Blinding. Tracers across the eyes. Then nothing.

The pretty little girl in the purple pajamas stood in back near the wall of a severe white room, doctors and nurses surrounding a cold steel table on which lay her tiny, blood-soaked body. Beside them, a large box beeped—*beep beep beep*—with a display tracking her heartbeat, a bag of blood in the hands of a nurse fed through a tube into her arm.

"She's back," said one of the nurses while another put away a set of defibrillator paddles.

The girl watched the doctors fiddle with her limp body, flipping it over, trying to sew together the back of her head. She looked so small. Tiny. She'd never seen herself like this. She'd stood outside her body, looking down on it as it slept, but never while other people were around. The adults didn't look like giants, they looked normal. She was the one who looked delicate, slight, a kitten in the mouth of its mother.

It was the first time in her life she realized just how young she was.

She walked over to the table, stood by the doctors, bathed in the glow of the fluorescent light at the end of a robot's arm affixed to the ceiling. The pretty little girl was warmer now. Her shakes were subsiding, and she felt cool instead of cold, warmer every minute.

She couldn't be sure how long she stood there watching, time was different out here, outside of her body, her perceptions warped, bent by the dream. But when she was relatively certain she was okay, and they had put most of the eggshell mess of her skull back together around her silver cord, she knew it was time to go. So she soared to the back of the room, passing through the doors as if they weren't there, out into a long, glaring hallway, the lights dazzling, a white so bright she had never quite seen its shade.

The hallway seemed impossibly long, as if it went on forever. She floated, passing a nurses' station blaring with sounds, flashing lights, then on to the waiting area. That's when she saw him. Over to the side, sobbing into his hands—her father, Wade. Next to him sat a doctor with a serious face.

" . . . coma," the doctor said, the only word she'd arrived in time to make out.

Wade cried openly, almost wailing as he talked, his speech still slurred with drink. "It's my fault," he said. "I should have been there. For her. If I hadn't been, you know, I mean, I could have heard her. Could have gotten her here sooner."

The doctor put an understanding hand on his shoulder. "At times like this, it's best to think about what we *can* do rather than what we didn't."

"She didn't want me to drink. She was gonna pour it out again. Hadn't done it in a while. Though she probably should've. She deserved better. She was trying to make me better. Now—" He cried more.

"We're going to do the best for her we can. But there's no telling how extensive the damage is."

The pretty little girl in the purple pajamas moved closer to put her hand on his, tell him, even if he couldn't hear, that it was all going to be okay. That she was fine. But she didn't get the chance. Because that's when she heard the scratching. Claws across windows, walls, marble floors. Scratches like animals digging under a house, like nails on a chalkboard. The whole hospital shuddered with the sounds.

Then the lights went out and the whole hospital, for an instant, went black. Time slowed, and the black went on seemingly forever. Then the building convulsed, groaning slowly back to life, emergency floodlights winking awake, rooms and hall corners bathed in electric daylight. Were she awake, she might note the dingy dullness to the light, the way it made the dim outskirts seem brown and neglected. But in the dream, those lights blazed a thousand megawatts strong, like rays of the harnessed sun shot into blinding white spots amid the lonely black between them.

She looked down the hall, staggered spotlights like islands

in the night, and then she saw them. The shadows. Kutji. Jet black against stinging white marble and paint. Crawling on all fours, some across the floor, others across the ceiling, others still scampering toward her along the walls. Each avoiding the light when they could; tearing through it, sizzling in agony when they couldn't. Mouths open, teeth bared, eyes wide with a hungry hate. A squirming mass of black overtaking the white inch by inch.

"Get her," slavered Jeronimus.

"Wait!" she shouted. "I thought you said you'd help me."

"We did," said one.

"We took you to the bunyip," said another. "Our business is done."

They poured toward her along every surface, a black wave of shadowy mayhem, nipping at the air in front of them, clawing to get ever closer.

At once the girl realized these things were not her friends; they were trouble. So she ran, ran as hard and as fast as she could, silvery cord trailing behind her. Down another hallway. Around another corner. Smack into another writhing wall of caterwauling kutji, drooling, pounding theirs fists on the walls and floor as they skittered closer toward her.

The halls echoed with the sounds of screaming shadows.

The pretty little girl wound her way through an endless sea of twists and turns and abandoned gurneys, black shapes shuffling past bright white spots, disappearing into the dark after her. She was confused, turned upside down and backward, not used to navigating the world of man when in the dream. At last she came to a four-way intersection, the point at which two corridors crossed, a single floodlight illuminating the center like a theater spot on a dark stage.

There she stood, dead center, watching the shadowy mass of kutji crawl over one another just past the event horizon of the light. She was surrounded, the vicious creatures snapping their teeth together, scratching the marble, taunting her to step out into the dark.

"Come out and play with us!" shouted one.

"Yes! Out into the dark!" shouted another.

"Out into the dark to become one of us! One of us forever!" shouted a third.

One of the kutji hovered at the edge of the light, sticking a cautious stump of an arm out into it. The nub smoked, hissed, searing like it had been thrown into a fire. It howled, yanking the arm back into the dark, blowing on it to soothe the pain.

"You can't stay in the light forever," said Jeronimus. "You have to become one of us sometime."

"No, I don't," said the little girl.

"Yes, you do. It's what we were promised, what we were tasked to do. Two more souls and we can go home. We can find peace. Like we were promised."

"No!"

"You have no choice. We are what you were born to become."

The pretty little girl in the purple pajamas, bathed in the bright light of the emergency floods, screamed, her shriek rippling like waves from a pebble through the hospital, the walls undulating, quivering.

The shadows stopped, silent, for a moment fearful.

Then she shot away, traveling at a thousand feet per second, the shadows left wondering where she'd gone.

Jeronimus howled, calling the pack together. "Take to the skies," he said. "Find her. Tonight she is ours, and let nothing get in our way. Nothing."

And with that they shuffled back into the black, turned into crows, and flew out into the night after her.

CHAPTER 30

CUT THE CORD

Mandu grew suddenly nervous, his head cocking a little to better hear, his eyes wide and alert.

"What is it?" asked Colby.

Mandu shook his head, his didgeridoo gripped tight in his hands. "I don't know," he said. "Something's not right." He looked around with a cockeyed concern weighing on his troubled brow.

It was growing chilly, the warm desert sands cooling in the night. The sky was clear, the moon bright, the air still and quiet as the dead. If something was amiss, it was both silent and well hidden.

She emerged from the dark as she had a short while before, wiping tears from her eyes with her sleeve—the pretty little girl in the purple pajamas. Her eyes were red, bloodshot, and bleary with tears, but she smiled, pretending nothing was wrong.

"Child, you're back so soon," said Mandu.

"I know," she said. "I—I missed you."

Colby pointed at her, but looked instead at Mandu. "Was that what you were—"

"Sshhhht!" he said, hushing him. "No. It wasn't." Mandu looked up toward the pretty little girl in the purple pajamas and motioned to her to get low. "Get down. Something . . . is out there."

The three looked out into the dark, the light stretching only a couple of dozen feet out from the fire before the world became pitch-black. Mandu lowered his didgeridoo, picked up his walking stick. With his free hand he reached into his dilly bag and pulled out his bullroarer.

"If I say run," he said, whispering, "you run like the willy-willy. You don't look back. Do you both understand?"

They both nodded.

"But—" said Colby.

"No buts, eh? You run. I run. We all run."

"Okay."

The night remained silent. No wild things howling or barking. Only fire. Cracking, popping, dwindling.

A burst of beating wings nearby, crows erupting into a flapping flock of caws and wings beating.

Colby sighed loudly. "It's only birds," he said. "Crows."

Mandu looked at him gravely, his skin taking on a strange pallor. "Ain't no crows out here this time of year, Colby. Those are spirits. Kutji."

"Yeah," said the girl. "They're the ones that showed me the bunyip. So I could meet Colby."

"Oh no," said Mandu, his eyes full of fear. "What have you done?" He waved his walking stick over the fire and it fizzled, fading out with a green flicker before flaring up again. "Run."

The night erupted with the sounds of anguished torment, braying, cackling, setting the whole desert on edge. Everyone ran.

Mandu's pace was furious, barefoot over the desert, his feet always knowing just where to fall, as if he'd run it a thousand times. His jaw was open in shock, eyes wide with terror. He had seen a great many things. He had not seen this.

The pretty little girl was close on his heels, trying not to outrun him.

"Away with you," he said. "Run faster! Don't wait for us!"

"I'm not leaving you," she said.

"It will not end well if you follow us. Not for a long while."

"Don't leave me alone."

"Girl, you—"

"This is my fault, isn't it?"

Mandu fell quiet for a second, his steady, controlled breathing and his footfalls the only sound he made. "Yes," he said, finally. "They followed your cord."

Colby was right behind them, pushing himself as hard as he could. Over the past few years he had seen his fair share of trouble and learned the value of being in shape. He walked everywhere, ran when he could, and found mortal terror to be an adequate motivator. He could run like this for hours. "It doesn't matter whose fault it is," he said. "Listen to Mandu. Get out of here!"

The pretty little girl burst into tears. "I don't want to be alone," she said, sobbing.

"You're only putting yourself in danger," said Mandu. "Putting all of us in danger."

"Please don't make me go."

Colby caught up to the two, exchanged glances with Mandu, both nodding to the other.

"You were warned," said Colby.

Mandu looked up into the sky above him, the beating of wings surrounding them on all sides, dark shapes coasting across the star field, outlined by the cloudy arm of the Milky Way. Crows.

Kutji.

Shaking his head he looked at Colby, then nodded ahead of them. Colby knew what he meant. They were about to have company.

Colby took a deep breath, drawing in the universe, feeling out the rippling waves of dreamstuff surrounding them—the energy so thick, so bright this far out in the wilderness that he could feel them coming, like flies in a web. They were descending right ahead of them, driving them into a trap as would a sheepdog, swarming like maddened bees, shifting into shadowy, demihuman shapes as their talons touched the ground.

Clever, he thought to himself. *Think clever. Not strong. Clever.* Nothing came.

So, being eleven years old, he reacted anyway.

Colby's muscles bulged, his hair fell away, and his eyes glowed the color of the sun winking out at dusk. Everything about Colby became wrong for a second, his insides folding out from within. He jumped, wings sprouting behind his arms, scales creeping over his flesh. Within a moment, he had become a dragon, a pillar of flame erupting from his gaping mouth, lighting the night.

Several dozen shadows stood before them, waiting, looking for a fight.

Colby didn't hesitate. He took to the air, letting loose a fire so hot it turned the ground beneath him to glass. Mandu reeled from the heat, hair singeing off his body, still running. The shadows didn't care about the heat. But the light chased them behind their own hands and stumps, stung them like a thousand bees at once, the fire lighting small patches of brush around them like candles.

This was no normal light. This was raw, lambent dreamstuff, brighter even than the sun. The whole landscape lit up with the fire, blazing like noonday, incinerating every bit of brush nearby.

Inspired, Mandu pointed a wild, excited finger. "Colby," he yelled. "The tree!"

Colby soared around the shadows, his wings beating with a mighty *THWUMP*. He looked down, saw the white bark of a towering ghost gum, its crisp green eucalyptus leaves glimmering in the light of the dwindling brush fires. And he let loose another gout, setting it ablaze.

The night grew bright as day, the fire white hot and hateful.

Colby swooped down on the cowering mass of shadows, grabbed two with his massive clawed feet, and cast them shrieking into the fire. The shadows didn't perish, but for a moment they wished they had. The remaining shadows scattered into the night, fleeing for the dark as if they were, themselves, on fire, seeking out the darkest spots nearby.

Mandu waved frantically for Colby to join him on the ground, the girl hiding behind him, cowering from both shadow and flame.

Colby landed, his taloned claw turning back into a foot as it touched the ground, the transformation creeping up his legs, washing across his torso, shifting him back into a boy.

Mandu pointed again at the tree. "That tree is our only way out of here. Quickly, before the trunk is consumed."

"I don't understand," said Colby.

"Trees in the outback do not grow by accident. They are connected. If you know the way, you can find your way from one tree to another. It will buy us some time."

"Why are we running and not fighting? You've seen our destinies. You know we survive."

Mandu looked back over his shoulder into the night. "Too many. It's not our time yet to face them. You're not ready."

"I'm ready."

Mandu shook his head. "I have seen you in dreams. I have seen her in dreams. You know what I haven't seen in dreams?"

"What?"

"Me," he said. "So into the tree."

"But how?"

"Take my hand, close your eyes, and try to feel the road you cannot see. Whatever you do, don't let go."

Colby nodded, taking the hand of the pretty little girl just as she took Mandu's. The tree stood before them, a towering blaze, the leaves already burned away, branches blackening. They held their breath, took two steps toward the fire, eyes closed.

The air crackled with the sound of the fire, masking the all but silent footfalls on the desert sand. Mandu's eyes shot open and he turned in time to see several shadows barreling at them, single-clawed hands outstretched. He flinched, pulling the children behind him, diving into the tree.

Mandu sank into it like a stone into water, enveloped by the bark, dragging the girl's arm with him. But as the pretty little girl in the purple pajamas followed, the kutji caught her by the hair, dangling from the silvery cord on the back of her head.

She screamed as they tugged.

Colby beat at them with a solid fist, too distracted to do anything else. He yelled with as much bass as he could muster. "Get away! Get the hell away!"

They scratched at her, tugged at her hair, screeching, the black shadow of their flesh sizzling away in the light of the fire. But they would not yield. This was too important. She couldn't get away. Not this time. They yanked hard, halting her descent into the tree, bending her neck so far back that her skull touched her spine. Mandu pulled hard on her arm, but she would not budge.

The horde of shadows emerged from the night, bunched together in a serpentine mass, pressing forward like a long, thin school of fish, using one another's bodies to shield themselves, only to suffer a second of the harsh firelight before ducking back behind another.

Within seconds they would be on them, overtaking Colby and the girl completely.

Colby didn't have time to think; he only had time left to act. And so he did.

In his hand appeared a giant, gleaming sword, glowing ghostly white and brilliant. He swung, cleaving in two a shadow perched atop the girl's back, narrowly missing the cord. Then he swung again, one hand still holding hers, bisecting another. The shadows of their bodies fell away into nothing, shattering first into a thousand pieces, fizzling away before they hit the ground.

The mass of shadows leaped up, engulfed the silver cord, shimmying along it ever closer to the two, tugging on it to keep the girl from moving an inch closer to the tree.

Colby swung with all his might, his arc wide, the blade leaving tracers in its wake. Half a dozen shadows scattered at once, a heartbeat away from meeting the end of their brothers. The blade caught nothing. Nothing but the cord.

It snapped, severed in two without the slightest bit of give. Then the long end disintegrated without a sound.

The school of shadows broke, taking off in all directions, some turning back to crows, others scampering away on foot. Mandu tugged again and the children followed him at once into the tree, their bodies vanishing into it.

The tree erupted, exploding, spraying splinters and ash in a circle around the blaze.

For a moment the night was hushed. And then the kutji slowly returned, one by one, to survey the wreckage of the gum tree.

They stood around the smoldering remnants, its fire no longer too bright to hurt them. Jeronimus stepped forward, a sickly, proud smile on his crooked lips. "It is done. Our business with the Clever Man is finished."

"What now?" hissed a kutji from the pack.

"Now we find her, we take her, and we kill anyone who tries to stop us."

"But we can't kill the Clever Man," said another.

"No," said Jeronimus. "But we can kill the boy."

CHAPTER 31

THE OTHER SIDE OF THE TREE

Mandu stared at the tree, waiting to see if anything followed. Colby in turn waited, ready to unleash on anything that stepped through. But nothing came.

"That was a powerful fire, Colby," said Mandu.

"I'm sorry," said Colby. "I tried to be clever."

"Oh, but you were."

"I was?"

"You scared them, scattered them, threw them off their plan. You were aces. They didn't expect that. But they will next time. Trying it again would not be so clever."

Colby smiled weakly. "I'll try something else next time."

"It would be best if there were no next time."

The pretty little girl in the purple pajamas stood to the side, fiddling with the fragment of silvery thread dangling from the back of her head. Mandu looked sadly upon her, his expression one both concerned and sympathetic. It was done. There was no going back now.

"How bad is it, Clever Man?" she asked, trying to look tough, like a TV gangster, squinting and strong jawed. "Give it to me straight."

"It's very bad," he said. "The worst. You've lost the cord back to your body. You have to find it now. Reconnect. Put yourself back together before it is too late."

"That shouldn't be too hard," said Colby. "You remember where you live, right?"

Mandu waved a finger, shaking his head. "It's not that easy. Without her cord she can't move like she used to. She can't run anymore. She has to walk through dreamtime."

"I don't mind that," she said. "I can walk."

"The body that spends too much time away from its spirit begins to wither. It can't eat. It doesn't really sleep. Too long without food and water and the body dies. Body dies, spirit dies with it."

"Wait!" said Colby. "So if she doesn't get back to her body in time—"

"I'll die?"

Mandu nodded. "Too right. But it gets worse."

"How could it get worse?" she asked.

"Your cord's been severed. Once we get you back in your body, you'll never dreamwalk again."

"No," she said. "No, no, no. I can't do that. I won't do that."

"But we have to," said Colby.

"No! I won't go back. I won't go back there. Not to that body. Not without being able to dream. No."

"But you'll die," said Mandu.

"I'll die there. I can't go back there. And you can't make me."

Colby looked at Mandu. "There's got to be a way to teach her to dreamwalk again."

"Teach? There is no teaching. She already knows how. The spirit must be anchored to its body; the cord is what lets it leave, not what holds it back. You get one cord. She sacrificed hers when she chose to stay with us."

Her eyes grew furious, her silky black hair sweeping back as if caught in some deliberate wind. "Are you saying this is my fault?" she yelled. "Are you blaming me?"

Mandu nodded. "There is no blame. There is no fault. There is only choice and consequence. We must all face the consequences for the choices we make. Sometimes we get to know the outcome, other times, like much of what is to come now, the future is invisible to us. But it will be our choices that take us there."

"You're saying it's my fault. Colby cut my cord!"

"I—I didn't!" said Colby, lying even to himself.

"But you did," said Mandu. "You cut her cord. But it was she who chose to stay, she who brought the shadows to our fire. There is no blame. There is only what has happened." He turned to the girl. "You have a destiny before you. One we've talked about many times. One you could not wait to encounter. This is the road to that destiny. These are the choices we talked about. If you don't take responsibility for them, you will never be able to become who you must. The kutji . . . you said they came to you?"

"We made a deal," she said.

"What was the deal?"

"They would show me where the bunyip was. That was all."

Mandu rubbed his hands together. "Did you first make a deal with the spirits demanding that they would not and could not harm you or your people?"

The pretty little girl in the purple pajamas at once felt very stupid and she shook her head, tears forming in her eyes. "No," she said with a whimper.

"And what did these spirits demand of you in return for their favor?"

"All they wanted was rum."

"Rum?"

"They wanted a bucket of rum to drink in the backyard."

"And where did you get all this rum?"

"From the cupboard," she said, looking at her feet.

"Which cupboard? Whose rum was it?"

"My father's."

"And does your father know you stole his rum and gave it to the spirits?"

She began to cry again, sobbing. "I never got the rum."

"Why not?"

"I fell."

"You fell?"

"I hurt myself," she said.

"How bad, child?"

"I'm in the hospital."

"Well, let's get you back there," said Colby.

"No! I'm not going back. Not if I can't dream again!"

"But if you stay out here—"

Her eyes were swollen with tears now, her cheeks glistening. She turned, running off into the night, refusing to hear the next words coming out of Colby's mouth. Somehow, she believed that if she didn't hear them, they couldn't be true.

Colby made a move to follow her, but Mandu interrupted him with a wave. "Colby, no. Look at her. That girl isn't going to go back to her body. No way, no how. She's going to die out here. And that's exactly what the spirits want her to do."

"Why?"

"They have their reasons."

"What are they?" asked Colby.

"The reasons?"

"No. The spirits."

"The kutji? Shadows. Spirits with great magic."

Colby shook his head. "What were they before?"

"What do you mean?"

"I've met a lot of shadows," he said. "Most of them used to be people. If we know who they were before, then we might be able to figure out what they want now."

"They're very old. I've heard that these were once pirates. Murderers. Thieves. They mostly keep to themselves. Haunt the deserts. Not many Clever Men trade favors with them."

"Because they're dangerous?"

"No," said Mandu. "They never seem interested in anything. Not that we have. Now they are. They wanted her to be cut from her cord. What do they want with a little girl?"

"What most shadows want, I reckon. An end to being shadows."

Colby looked out into the dark for the pretty little girl in the purple pajamas, but she was nowhere in sight. "We should find her," he said.

Mandu shook his head. "She'll be back in her own time. She has a very important decision to make. One that will tell us which direction to walk."

"What if she decides to not go home?"

"Then she dies. And we protect her from the spirits as long as we can until she does."

"Wait here," said Colby decisively.

"Colby, I wouldn't—"

"Wait here," he said again, even more firmly. "I got this."

Colby wandered out into the dark, his eyes closed, feeling the ripples in the energy around him. There she was, fifty yards out, sitting on a small boulder, head down, sobbing. He slowly made his way behind her, being sure to keep a short distance between them as he did.

He wanted to touch her, to put a hand on her shoulder or to throw his arms around her, hold her, and tell her everything was going to be okay. But it wasn't okay. And she would most likely push him away anyway. Girls were weird like that.

"My parents sucked too," he said.

The girl looked up indignantly, annoyed, a hair away from being angry. "What?"

"My parents. It's why I'm here. Like you."

"You don't know anything," she said.

"My mom drinks. A lot."

She softened, just a hair, but enough to let Colby know he was on the right track. "Really?"

"Yeah. Not rum though. She liked vodka."

"Dad says vodka is for commies and sluts."

"What's a commie?" he asked.

"I don't know."

"Well, I'm pretty sure my mom isn't a commie."

"Oh," she said.

"Yeah. So I kinda get it."

"No, you don't. I love my dad. I love him more than anything."

"Does he drink a lot?"

"Every night. I've tried to stop him, but, he, he has his reasons."

"There aren't any good reasons to drink like that."

"You really don't know anything, Colby."

"Yeah I do. But what could be a good reason to drink like that?"

"He misses my mom."

Colby looked down, solemnly. "Oh. Is she—"

"Yeah. I killed her."

"You what?" he asked, looking back up at her.

"When I was born. Dad said it was a tough birth. I almost died. It was her or me." She looked at Colby with deadly serious eyes. "I was the thing that killed my mother, and now I'm the cancer eating my father. He drinks because he misses her, which means he drinks because of me. It's not fair."

"No, it's not."

"Maybe if I don't go back. Maybe if I stay here, he can forget. Go on. He's better off without me."

"That's crap."

"It's not."

"That's not how love works. You don't just forget."

"Yes you can," she said. "Anyone can."

"If it stops hurting, it isn't really love."

She sighed. "I wish I could walk in the dream forever and never go home."

"But you can't."

"I don't like that world."

The two exchanged knowing looks. "Yeah, I don't like it either. All I understand is this." He waved at the ground. "I understand how a lot of this works. This makes sense to me. You make sense to me."

"I do?"

Colby sat next to her on the rock, his elbow gently brushing against hers. "Yeah. I don't want to go back either."

"You can't make me."

"I know. But you know what I don't understand?"

"What?"

"How the girl who stared down a bunyip could be afraid of anything. Anything at all."

She turned and looked at Colby, their faces only a few inches apart, her eyes still moist with tears. "How old are you?"

"Eleven," he said.

"You don't sound eleven."

"I get that a lot. How old are you?"

"Eleven."

"No, really."

"I'm eleven," she said.

"You don't look eleven."

"I know. I get to be whoever I want to be out here. Back home it's different. I'm a different person there."

"No," he said. "You're not. You only think you are. You're strong there too."

Her breath shivered, stuttering as she inhaled. She leaned in, putting a hand on his chest, their lips brushing against each other, eyes closed, hearts thundering. And they kissed their first kiss. Gentle. Sweet. The universe falling away.

Then she pulled away.

"You kissed me," he said, startled.

"Yeah," she said. "I told you. I can do whatever I want out here. That's what I wanted to do." She smiled bravely.

"I'm sorry."

"For kissing me?"

"No. For . . . for cutting your cord."

She looked down at the ground, trying to scuff her incorporeal feet in the dirt. "I'm sorry too."

"For what?"

"Bringing them with me. For making a deal with them. I just . . ."

"You just what?"

She looked Colby in the eyes. "Wanted to meet you. My destiny."

Colby nodded. "We'll find a way," he said. "We'll figure this out."

"I believe you." Then she leaned close. "Kaycee," she whispered into his ear.

"What?"

"My name. It's Kaycee."

He smiled and took her hand. "Come on, let's find Mandu."

MANDU SAT CROSS-LEGGED before a fire, rocking gently, singing an incoherent song with words Colby didn't recognize.

"Mandu," said Colby. "MANDU!"

But Mandu didn't respond. He wasn't there. While his body chanted, Mandu's spirit was away, elsewhere in the dream. Colby walked around him, then saw the silvery cord trailing out of the back of his head and off into the night.

His eyes opened, first dazed by reentry, then terrified and desperate. "We have to leave," he said, breathlessly. "Now. They're coming to kill us before morning." He looked at the girl. "We have to get you back to your body. Now."

"No!" she said, stamping a foot in the dirt. "I told you, I'm not going back. I'm staying out here. With you."

"I'm afraid that's what they want you to do."

"I don't care. If they want me, they'll have to come and get me. I'll die before I go home."

"That is exactly what will happen. It is exactly what I've seen."

Colby looked at him, his jaw out, his chest puffed up. He took the girl's hand in his. "If they're coming to kill us, then we should stay right here. I'd rather fight them without having to run several hours to do it."

"Your boldness will get us killed. This isn't where we fight. This, right here, is where we die. For us to fight, to stand a chance, there's somewhere else we have to be."

"Where?" asked Colby.

"Arnhem Land."

"How are we going to outrun them?"

"They can't track her as easy without her cord. We'll sing the land up quicker. These are our songlines, not theirs. It will take them hours before they finally have us. By then, let's hope we're ready."

"Mandu, where did you go?"

"I needed to speak with my spirit. And there were things that needed to be done. Come, it's a long run until morning."

CHAPTER 32

THE NIGHT THE DEMONS CAME

Wade Looes was as drunk as he'd ever been while still able to stand upright, staggering through the streets, muttering in what may as well have been a foreign language. His daughter, his tiny little girl who had once been so small he could carry her cradled in the hollow between his arm and his chest, was lying, skull shattered, in a coma next to a machine that beeped with the sound of her heart.

Coma. There was no mistaking that word for any other word in the English language. She wasn't coming back. The doctors were sure about that. But he couldn't bring himself to pull the plug.

So day in, day out, his daughter lay there. Just beeping. All the rum in the world couldn't chase the beeping away, but he sure tried. *Beep. Beep. Beep.*

He heard the sound everywhere. Echoing off the walls. Trailing down the streets. It haunted him. Even when he closed his eyes and drifted off, exhausted, it crept into his dreams.

Wade was short on sleep now. The only way he could get more than a few minutes' rest was to drink himself out. But he was running out of things to sell for booze.

Wade stumbled to his knees, the world wobbling with him. Nothing would stand still. Not the ground. Not the lampposts. And not the shadows. In fact, the shadows moved most of all.

Beep. Beep. Beep.

He tried to stand up, to push himself off the pavement, but he only managed his way closer to it. The ground began to feel cozy. Perhaps this was as good a place as any to finally . . .

"Hey," whispered a voice.

"Huh?" he mumbled, drifting off to sleep.

The voice whispered again. "Hey! Wake the fuck up!"

Wade swatted, as if chasing flies. "Go away. I'm sleeping."

"Wake up, you miserable piece of shit. Would you want your daughter to see you like this?"

"No, I . . ." Wade sat up, scrambling slowly to all fours, his eyes wide open. There was no one there. "Shit." His head was a blur of jumbled thoughts, none of them coherent, not a one of them bothering to work itself out to its logical conclusion.

"Hey," said the voice again. "Hey, I'm talking to you."

"Who? Who is talking to you? Was I talking to you? Us. Us I mean. What was th—?"

Beep.

"Where the fuck did that . . . ?" Wade looked around, fearful. He was too confused now. Had no idea whether he was even inside or out. It felt like pavement beneath him, but he couldn't be sure. "What's going on?"

"You killed her, you worthless son of a bitch. You killed her."

"No, I didn't mean—"

"Oh, you're happy she's gone, aren't you? No more little mutant with the clubfoot. No more split lip. No more looks of pity. *Oh, that poor man. He can't even fuck a girl right without popping out a broken little beast.*"

"Who the fuck . . . ? WHERE ARE YOU?"

The shadows moved, shuffled, like the walls themselves were collapsing, reshaping to move the light around. Then they started peeling themselves out of the dark, breaking off in tiny chunks. Several strange goblinoid shapes, boxy, like Cubist paintings done solely in black, creeping in, bending with the spinning of the world.

"You liked it, didn't you?" asked one of the shadows. "You liked seeing her broken on the ground."

"No!" Wade shouted.

"Prove it."

Beep.

Wade began crying. "I . . . I don't know how. No one believes me."

"We don't believe you. Prove it."

"HOW?"

A large, rusty butcher's knife clattered to the ground.

"Prove it."

Wade shook his head, his eyes swollen red with tears. "I don't understand."

"Is that the hand?" asked the shadow. "Is that the hand that killed your daughter?"

"No, it—"

"The hand that held the glass all night. The hand that drank you to sleep. The hand that rested limp in the chair while your daughter lay bleeding on the ground?"

No. That's . . . it wasn't like that."

"Clench it."

"What?"

"Clench it. Your fist. Clench it!"

Wade clenched his right hand into a fist.

"Look at it."

Wade stared at his fist, clenching and unclenching it, his fingers scarred stubs from years at the cannery, the dark skin nicked almost entirely white. He could see the way it wanted to naturally curl around a glass, picture it resting in his fingers, the cold condensation chilling his skin.

"That's the hand, isn't it? That killed her?"

"She's not dead."

"That's the hand, isn't it?"

Wade nodded with a sob. "Yes," he whispered. "This is the one."

"You have to remove it," said the shadow. "You have to take it off at the wrist. Before it infects the rest of you with its evil."

"It's too late. I'm already infected."

"It's not too late, Wade. Take it. Take it off at the wrist."

Wade swallowed hard. Picked up the old butcher knife with his left hand. Put his right hand flat on the pavement. The whole world was woozy, spinning. This felt right.

"Just take it, Wade."

He swung.

He screamed.

He'd missed, managing only to sever three fingers at the knuckle.

Blood sprayed across the pavement.

The shadows, however, did not waver. They crept closer. "Again," said the shadow. "Again. Do it right this time or it will infect your whole arm."

Wade nodded, his eyes streaming, his face contorted. "Okay," he said, whimpering.

He looked down, saw the blood pooling around his hand.

The knife came down again, this time at the wrist, his hand coming off cleanly.

Wade howled into the night, the pain too much even for his drunken numb. "OH MY GOD! OHMYGODOHMYGOD!"

"He can't help you now," said the shadow with a hint of delighted irony. "There's only one way to dull that pain."

"What?" screamed Wade, clutching his severed arm with his left hand.

"Over here," said another spirit. "Put this around your neck."

Wade nodded, lumbering to his feet. He took a wide, uneven step, losing his balance, slamming into a wall. He could see a lamppost, shadows circling it, crows sitting atop it—a rope, heavy and thick, swinging slowly back and forth from it, a noose at the end.

"I'm sorry, baby," he muttered, slogging against the drink, reaching toward the rope. "Daddy's gonna make it better. Daddy's gonna make the pain go away. I'm sorry."

"There, there. It's almost done. Just put this on. Just put this on."

Wade slung the rope around his neck and tightened the noose. "I'm sorry," he whimpered again. "I'm sorry."

"Pull," said the shadow. And the shadows pulled.

CHAPTER 33

FOUR MEN SINGING IN A TRUCK

And then the singing stopped, for they didn't own the song to this part of the line. For a moment, they sat in silence.

"It just ain't right," said Jirra, sitting in the passenger seat, nervously picking at a hangnail. "I have a right to know." He was young, handsome, the youthful brown skin of his cheek peppered with a light sprinkling of stubble.

Kami frowned through his thick, curly black beard, shaking his head without taking his eyes off the road. He had a potbelly trying to peek out from under a stained shirt, but the arms of a man who worked for a living, hands that knew the outdoors better than the in gripping the wheel. "You drew the straw, you knew the risks."

"But I should know. I didn't know I wasn't gonna know."

"Well, now you know that you don't get to know. And all is right with the world."

"But it ain't right." Jirra paused for a moment, thinking about how best to say it. "I'm scared."

The night was nothing but darkness, the desert entirely swallowed up in it, the moon hiding behind a bank of thick clouds. It was a palpable dark, the kind you could see the shape of a flashlight's beam in, the kind that was more like a fog than an absence.

The truck was battered, old, culled together with parts from a dozen abandoned wrecks, both fenders mismatched, its body scraped of paint long ago. But its engine sang like a growling mastiff as it ambled down the dirt road at a steady clip, headlights cutting the black, two passengers in the cab, two in its bed. It had, over the years, hauled lumber, rocks, wedding parties, and beer. But tonight's cargo was perhaps the most important of its long, labored life.

"Don't be scared," said Kami. "Whatever happens, it'll be okay."

"Just don't panic, eh? Is that what you're saying?"

"No. You should definitely panic. That's the point, mate. You just don't gotta be scared."

"That doesn't make any sense."

"It doesn't have to."

"Do Daku and Mulga know?" asked Jirra. "Because I could just ask them."

"Nah, bru. I'm the only one who knows."

"How's it fair that you get to know?"

"Cause I'm the fella that's gotta do it, eh?"

The truck veered quickly off the dirt road onto the blacktop highway, neon reflectors stinging in the dark, lit up hundreds of feet out. They could make out the building in the distance, the lights of the parking lot so bright it looked like an airfield or a military base. Isolated, alone in the desert, drenched in halogen.

It wasn't long now.

Jirra shifted in his seat, growing ever the more anxious as they approached, still plucking at his hangnail. "Are you sure this is the only way?" he asked.

"Nah, it's just the best way. Quick, easy, in and out."

"I got rooted on this one, eh?"

"You wanted to come along. Wanted to go on the big job."

"Yeah. I reckon I did."

"We're almost there. It'll all be over soon."

The truck rumbled around another corner, headed dead on toward the light. The signs were visible now, though still too far away to be read. Any minute now they would be deep in it, but for the moment there was nothing but nervous silence and a truck engine.

The truck rolled into the parking lot and rattled to a stop just past the front door. Kami turned off the lights but left the engine running. He looked over at Jirra with a hint of remorse, his hand slipping down between the seat and the door. "Now remember," he said. "Whatever you do, just keep screaming."

The knife he pulled out was long, sharp, glinting in the glare of the parking lot's lamps. He flicked his wrist, cutting a wide gash across Jirra's forearm. Jirra screamed with all the air in his lungs, the sound deafening in the cramped rusty cab. "Fuck, man!"

Kami reached out the open window and slapped the door twice before passing Jirra a greasy white rag to staunch the bleeding. Daku and Mulga hopped soundlessly out of the back of the truck, disappearing around the building. Jirra, on the other hand, still hollered.

"Good, mate. Good," said Kami. "Just like that."

The inside of the building was well lit, all white, but quiet.

Waiting room, empty chairs facing a television. Scattered clip-boards. A nurse sat behind the admissions window, staring at the rerun of some old American show they only bothered to air in the middle of the night. She looked up, scared half to death at the sound of Jirra's bellowing, bolting straight from her chair.

Jirra pressed the rag, now soaked through and dripping, hard against his arm. He wailed as if his hand at any moment might fall off onto the ground, gone for good. He was pissed, glaring whenever he had the chance at Kami, who in turn avoided eye contact altogether. The nurse rushed out, trying both to assess the situation and calm Jirra enough to keep from waking everyone else in the hospital.

"Sir," she said. "Sir! I'm going to need you to keep it down. Stay calm, you're okay now. Sir? SIR?" She looked at Kami, trying to speak over the bawling. "What happened?"

"We were having a few drinks at a pub and this bloke was looking to have a blue. And Willy here, well he didn't reckon he wanted a thing to do with him. And then out came a knife as big as your arm."

"Willy?" she asked Jirra, trying to remove the rag from the wound. "Willy, I'm going to need you to stop screaming."

"It hurts!" yelled Jirra. "It hurts!"

"I know, but you're going to have to calm down. DOCTOR!" she yelled back into the hall. "Doctor, I need you!"

"It's gonna fall off! It's gonna fall off!"

"It's not gonna fall off," said the nurse. "Let me look at it." She gently pulled away the rag, his arm slick with red. He howled. The nurse looked back at Kami. "Is he on anything?"

"Nah," said Kami. "Just grog."

"Because if he's on something and we don't know, it might have an adverse reaction with the painkillers."

"We just had a couple o' coldies at the pub. Nothin' else."

"He thinks his hand is going to fall off."

"He's young. He's stupid like that."

"DOCTOR?"

Kami looked over the nurse's shoulder, holding his breath. Behind her, Daku and Mulga quietly wheeled out a gurney, covered in a light blue bedsheet. He quickly gave Jirra a dire look and Jirra screamed even louder.

The nurse was rattled, her buttoned-up exterior shedding, giving way to full-on confusion. She turned sharply, looking for the doctor, just missing Daku and Mulga as they slipped out the automated sliding glass doors. Ordinarily she would have heard it, looked up reflexively, but she couldn't hear a damned thing over the ruckus. She ran to her station, grabbing a piece of sterile gauze, returning to place it over the gash.

"Stay here," she said. "I'm going to get the doctor." Then she vanished to the back, wondering where the hell the attending physician was at this hour.

Kami and Jirra didn't waste a second. They were out the door and in the truck before the nurse was halfway down the hall. Daku and Mulga were already in back, the body of a little girl wrapped in a pile of blankets between them. With the engine already running, Kami shifted gears and floored it, taking off out of the parking lot, racing back into the thick black.

Jirra held the gauze to his arm, saying nothing but giving Kami the dirtiest look he could muster.

"Does it hurt?" asked Kami, his eyes glued to the small patch of lit road ahead of him.

"Nah," said Jirra. "But it sure as shit looks like it does, eh?"

"He was right about you, you know."

"He was?"

"Yeah. Said you'd pull through just fine. That you'd do it up right. This would all go down right as rain as long as I didn't spoil the surprise."

Jirra nodded. "He knew I'd draw the straw."

"What doesn't that old codger know? You might turn out all right after all."

Mulga slid the cab's rear window open, leaning in. "She was hooked up to an awful lot of machines. You reckon she'll be okay back here?"

Kami nodded. "Mandu says she's just out walkin'. She'll be fine as long as we get her back to town."

"You sure?" asked Mulga. "There really were a lot of 'em."

"If he's sure, I'm sure."

"What then?" asked Jirra.

"Only Mandu knows for sure. And he'll tell you as soon as he sees fit to tell you."

Mulga slid the window closed, settling back in for the long ride back to town. He looked down at the little girl sleeping peacefully next to him, wondering what she might be dreaming about, where she might be walking.

Then the men all sat quiet, waiting to round the coming pass when they could sing their way along the line back home.

Chapter 34

Songlines

An excerpt by Dr. Thaddeus Ray, Ph.D., from his book *Dreamspeaking, Dreamwalking, and Dreamtime: The World on the Other Side of Down Under*

Ownership of a song in a songline is a complicated and alien thing to the uninitiated. When the heir to a songline is born, his birthright is to inherit one. He will learn, through drilling and memorization, the names of his ancestors, the history of his tribe and the surrounding area, and a portion of the song to a songline. Others will come and ask to borrow his song; he, in turn, will generously loan it out. It cannot be bought, traded, or sold, and the heir can never be rid of it. He can only sing it and let it be sung by others.

The origin of a songline finds its roots in survival. The bulk of Australia is a hostile wilderness many liken to a wasteland, with weather patterns that vary wildly from year to year. In order to survive, the Aborigines had to become nomadic. In turn, these nomadic practices inspired a number of philosophies about ownership that simply don't translate easily to the West. To these nomads, property was fluid. The land provided, and since people needed to carry everything they owned from one place to another from time to time, the idea arose that property was something of a burden. Thus one didn't want to hold on to one thing for too long, lest it weigh one down. This began as a necessity, but continued as a philosophy. If one possessed an object for too long, it could weigh down one's very life, and thus one should never be too attached to anything, being willing to trade it away at any moment.

At the same time, a tribe might find itself in a place over-abundant with one type of provision, but short of another. For example one might find oneself in the woods filled with fowl and game, but short on fruit and ocher. The solution was of course to trade. But since all of the tribes were nomadic, knowing where resources were located or abundant was tricky. So trade routes emerged. The Aborigines imagined them as lines, and they learned them and passed information about them along in the form of song.

These songs described the route to a location, as well as contained the history of those locations. Through these songlines tribes would pass information, news, goods, even trinkets in a way to be connected with other peoples around the continent. But what began as a song describing the rock formation one was looking for to find a billabong became a story about a group of men who fought and died there. Later would come a verse about the couple who fell in love there and the hero who would be born of that love. Later still the song would tell the tale of mythic creatures said to haunt it. Over the course of generations a simple method of learning how to get from one place to another became the medium that contained the history of an entire continent.

Soon the songs became so long, so involved, so intricate that no one man could ever learn all of them. Few could memorize every bit of a single line. From this evolved the practice of passing down portions of the song. It is both an honor and a burden, a gift with strings attached. And every so often, a tribe will gather to sing the whole of its line, requiring all of the owners of a piece of the song to perform, in order, their portion.

It is in these recitations that we begin to see the more powerful, religious applications of the songlines. Aborigines believe that if you sing a songline out of order, you can undo the line itself, singing the elements out of existence. While the exact repercussions vary from tribe to tribe, the end result is always cataclysmic, ranging from the restructuring of reality, the redrawing of maps, to the complete annihilation of creation itself. While there appears to be no real basis for this, the belief in these events is dangerous enough. In a land as rich with dreamstuff as Australia, a large gathering of powerful believers singing ancient magicks, all believing something has gone wrong at once, could be the explanation of any number of their history's natural disasters.

This, of course, covers the more mundane aspects of the history. Enter the Clever Men, also known as the Men of High Degree. These medicine men learn the more esoteric meaning to the songs. In short, the magic of them. Through song, these Clever Men can reweave their own surroundings, ward off supernatural creatures, and even travel more quickly via a songline.

It is believed by many that singing a songline while traveling will actually conjure up the location more quickly. And while this is clearly untrue, it is based primarily upon the Clever Men's ability to "hop" from location to location. In truth, Clever Men memorize not only the physical locations and histories, but their hidden, supernatural ones as well. They learn about the spaces between the spaces and memorize their properties within the elements of the song.

There are a number of different theories and explanations as to the nature of the universe, none of which seems to be wholly accurate. I prefer to look at reality as having begun as a balled-up sheet of paper. Over time, it has slowly unfolded, leaving creases and crinkles where portions of it are actually a bit closer than they appear to be when viewed from overhead. People with the ability to perceive beyond the veil can sense these crinkles and creases, and use them to slip from one part of the universe to another without having to cross all of the physical space. This allows someone to travel faster than normal and, when viewed by an outsider, appears as if the person is "hopping."

Clever Men make extensive use of this, traveling between places much faster than the ordinary person, or evading pursuers by simply disappearing and reappearing hundreds of feet away. To the casual observer this appears to happen as if the Clever Man sings it into being. In truth, he is singing to guide himself to the right spot to pass through.

One of the most important secrets to the magical nature of the songs is that the power is not in the words. Like all true magick, the secret is in the belief and execution. Here, in the case of songlines, the magick is from the music. The belief in the tune is the crux of it. While the many tribes of Australia share a common mythology and belief system, they do not share the same language. Even though songlines belong to people of a specific *dreaming* (an extended form of tribe tied into the belief of a people's origin), those people do not necessarily all speak the same language. They do, however, sing the same song. Thus it is not the words that matter, simply the land they describe and the tune by which they do it.

Their belief in the power of their song affects the song itself, weaving in subtle alterations to the way the tune exists and ultimately the way it can fundamentally shape the reality around it. In other words, as long as someone knows the tune, the landmarks and the stories that go along with them, they can sing a song without knowing the specific words and still utilize the knowledge and power of that songline.

CHAPTER 35

THE SWAMPS
JUST SOUTH OF ARNHEM

Where are we headed?" asked the pretty little girl in the purple pajamas.

"Not much farther. Few more hours. A billabong near my home. Great power. Very holy. Delicious fish. You'll like it."

It was afternoon. They had run all night and seen nary a crow. Now that the sun was up, they ran still. There was no time to stop, to rest. But there was time for a lesson as they hoofed it due north.

Colby stopped, looking around at the tree above him, then, confident he was safe, closed his eyes. He put his hand on one of the thin gray trunks, his hand disappearing into it. Though the tree was many times smaller than Colby, he squeezed himself in, emerging from another tree fifty feet ahead.

Mandu nodded, jogging with a proud smile. "Good. Good! You've got it." Colby waved as he stepped completely out. "Now feel out again. See if you can find one with a sister tree farther out."

"Okay!" Colby yelled, turning around and trying again.

"This is stupid," said the girl, just loud enough for Mandu to hear her.

"For you, yes. Which is why I'm not having you do it."

"Then why him?"

"You and he are very similar. Both clever. Both headstrong. Both very good with your heads. But Colby was given too much too soon. He can wipe a being out of existence with a thought or summon terrible nightmares from the dream. So he thinks big. He thinks like a bully. Brute force. We must break him of that or he will do something very, very terrible."

"Like what?" she asked.

"Like something else that cannot be undone."

"Why don't I have to do it, then?"

Mandu smiled. "Because you started with nothing. You think clever, only limited by your age and power. If you get *too* clever, you too will do things that cannot be undone. What you need is to think more like Colby, just as he needs to think more like you."

"Found one!" yelled Colby, vanishing into the much larger trunk of a black walnut tree.

The girl ran quietly for a spell, mulling over what Mandu had said. "Clever Man?"

"Yes?"

"Am I really going to die out here?"

Mandu shrugged. "Child, if you survive this, it will only be because they want you to survive this and only if it serves their plans. Odds are, if you live, it won't be a life worth living."

She deflated, scuffing her foot in frustration. "Oh," she said, thinking about the last time she saw her body. The pain of waking up to fresh scars and a shattered skull scared her less than dying out here, but never being able to dreamwalk again scared her most of all.

"You know," he said, "there is a rock, far out in the desert, well off every road and songline. Big one. Just a boulder in the middle of nowhere. Many Clever Men know where it is. Spirits have been known to sleep there from time to time. One day, you might find everything you're looking for under that rock."

"One day?" she asked, hopeful.

"If you live to see that day, you'll know it when it comes."

Mandu kept his eyes on the horizon, tracking the sun, doing the math silently in his head. They might not make it in time. But he was afraid of telling the children, afraid that they might spend the last few hours of their lives running.

"Mandu!" Colby shouted from a hundred yards away. "This is awesome!"

It was nightfall and they were quickly approaching the border into Arnhem. Both Colby and Mandu were exhausted, their bodies run well past their breaking points. Though both were accustomed to long runs, neither was prepared for this. It was getting harder to be able to keep a straight thought in their heads. All Mandu could think about was crossing the border. *Get into Arnhem. Then they would be safe.* He repeated it over and over.

The pretty little girl in the purple pajamas, however, wasn't even winded. She was a thing of the dream and could run for as long as she wanted, just not as fast anymore. But she kept pace with the others, as fast as her legs could now carry her, scared of what might happen if she found herself too far behind them.

The sound of the first crow cawing in the dark broke Mandu's heart. This was the moment he was dreading. No future was set in stone, he knew that. But even the best outcomes here were unappealing. Both of these children were about to make some of the most important decisions of their lives, but if he dared tell them, dared hint at the true outcome, they would never choose the right path. Either of them.

While the first caw broke his heart, the second was utterly devastating. It came from ahead of them. And it was followed by a terrifying volley of them.

The kutji were waiting, lined across the forest, standing between them and Arnhem.

"Keep running," said Mandu. "Don't stop."

"But they're right ahead of us," said Colby.

Mandu pointed at the horizon. "You see that ridgeline?"

"Yeah."

"That's Arnhem Land."

"So?"

"They can't follow us into Arnhem. They're not allowed."

"Why not?" asked Colby.

"Because that was the deal I made with them."

"You what?"

"Our friend here is not the only one who has trafficked with these spirits. My deal with them keeps them out. If we can get to that ridge—"

"We'll be safe!" Colby ran harder than before, getting his second wind. "But how do we get past them?"

Mandu smiled, reaching into his dilly bag. "I have a surprise." He pulled out his bullroarer, winging it through the air with a *WHUMP-WHUMP-WHUMP*.

The kutji descended from the trees, feathers molting into shadows, wings changing into arms, running at full speed the moment they touched the ground.

And then the forest came alive.

The mimis crawled out from every crevice imaginable, from under rocks and logs, from cracks in the mud, from between the leaves in trees. Their colors varied from black and white to red and purple, yellow and green. Each looked as if it was finger-painted to life, thin as a rail but vicious, fearless.

They rained stones from slings on the incoming shadows; they hurled boomerangs through the air; lobbed spears tipped with flame. The first wave of shadows toppled to the ground, some merely felled by rocks, others screaming, flaming spears sticking out of their chests, boomerangs lodged in their heads. Then the mimis descended on the fallen with clubs, kicking, beating, scratching.

Jeronimus yelled, realizing he'd once again been lured into a trap. He would not spend another night trapped in a pit, plucking the feathers from birds, waiting for death. He yipped twice, waved his stubby arms around in the air, and called back his shadows to rally with him.

The shadows pulled their fallen behind them, dragging them back, mimis chasing them, casting rocks and spears after them as they did. They crawled into the shadows of trees, hiding from the advancing fairy mob, staying still and silent, hoping not to be spotted. Then Jeronimus yelled again. "To the skies!" And the shadows burst into a flock of birds, flapping wildly, chasing the stars.

Colby, Mandu, and the pretty little girl ran even harder than before. This was their only chance.

The crows, still dozens strong and wounded, raced toward the heavens, the stars crystal clear and beaming, the sky black and cloudless. They powered their way up, fighting against the pull of the earth, tiny wings pushing as hard as they could. Then Jeronimus evaporated, his feathers falling away. His form broke down into mist, the blackness of his sheen swelling into the night, obscuring the night sky.

Jeronimus had become a storm cloud, ever expanding and ominous, his companions dutifully following suit.

The horde of crows dissolved into a storm front all their own; dark, bulbous, rolling clouds surging out across the sky, flashes of lightning belching within. The wind kicked up, fierce and steady, gusts whipping between the trees, a torrent of leaves scattering through the swamp like buckshot. Then the rains came.

The winds tore through the forest, microbursts tearing mimis in half, snapping their brittle limbs, tossing them around like tumbleweeds. The mimis scattered, desperately clawing their way between rocks, back into tree hollows, bracing themselves against the gales. The entire forest shook, balding trees waving, shedding leaves by the pile; branches tearing free, crashing into the mud. Storm raging, loud and unrelenting; earth trembling below with the bellows of thunder. It was a sound like the end of the world.

Colby ran. Mandu ran. But the pretty little girl in the purple pajamas huddled behind a dug-in boulder, head between her knees, hands behind her head, fingers laced together. She couldn't outrun the storm anymore; she couldn't ignore its winds or its lightning. With her tether gone, she was slow, clumsy, and exposed. And she was scared to death.

She mumbled quietly to herself, asking for unseen help, praying that the rains soaking her would soon pass, that the winds would soon die down. But the tempest still howled, the storm getting angrier and angrier by the moment. The twisted, broken, red-painted body of a mimi tumbled by, a single splintered hand twitching to grab her as it passed before being thrown into a billabong.

Four clouds broke away from the front, drifting down, letting the gusts tear them apart. They shredded, the wisps becoming feathers, the feathers fluttering together. The four became crows again, dropping through the rain, straight toward the pretty little girl in the purple pajamas.

At once the rest of the clouds burst, the rain stopping, the stars emerging in swaths of sky. Crows formed, flapping back down toward the earth, mist trailing from their feathers. Dozens of birds once again dove down, the thunder having trailed off into the distance, the storm nothing but a memory.

She cowered still behind a boulder, unaware of the hell coming for her.

With the winds gone, the mimis emerged from their holes. This time, however, the kutji were ready, swooping in on the stick men, claws out, tearing them off their trees, snapping them in half against boulders and branches. It had been hundreds of years since the kutji were afforded the chance to be this savage, memories of cobbled-together maces crushing skulls, splattered blood across coral sands flooding back. They felt alive. In a bloodthirsty rage, the spirits relived the heady days of wanton brutality, unleashing centuries of pent-up fury on the mimis they could get their claws on.

What few mimis remained unseen stayed hidden, sure that they would be the next dead against a rock or snapped into pieces by bare hands.

The carnage was over almost as soon as it began, the shadows looking around, eager for other victims, bleeding pieces of mimi in their hands like clubs, crows soaring about them as spotters.

Then the crows formed a murder around the pretty little girl. Some sat on branches, watching, others shifted back into their more human forms. Jeronimus was the last to flap down, dropping to the ground, a stub-fisted shadow, smiling from ear to ear.

"Hello, Kaycee," he said.

"That's not my name," she said. "Not out here."

"It was always your name. It will always be your name. Kaycee Looes. Daughter of Wade Looes. Last and furthest descendant of Wouter Looes. We've waited a long time for you, Kaycee. A lot of years."

"A *lot* of years," hooted one of the other shadows.

"And now we can right the four-hundred-year-old wrong. Can you help us do that?"

The pretty little girl in the purple pajamas shook her head. "No."

Jeronimus leaned in, inches from her face. "Too bad you don't get a say in the matter."

Several kutji landed in the swamp just ahead of Colby and Mandu, running toward them at alarming speeds.

"Colby!" shouted Mandu. "The trees! Take to the trees!"

Colby knew exactly what he meant. He felt out for the trees, sensed their connections. A kutji leaped into the air, claws out, raking at Colby. It came down, inches from him, a heartbeat away from striking. Then Colby vanished, running headlong into a tree and out another twenty feet away.

He was alone now, his legs burning, aching, barely able to carry him. And he ran into another tree. And another. And another.

The kutji couldn't keep up.

The ridge was only a few tree hops away now.

Behind him he heard the screams of the chittering mob, but dared not look back. *Run*, he thought. *Just keep running.*

Another tree. And then another.

And then the ground was different. He looked down, saw the rock beneath his feet.

Colby had made it to the ridge.

He turned, looked back to see Mandu just below him in the swamp, running into a tree of his own. Then he felt the

WHOOSH of air as Mandu blew past him, turning as he did and slowing to a stop. Both doubled over in agony, trying to catch their breath. Colby, hands on his knees for support, looked up for the little girl in the purple pajamas, but she was nowhere nearby.

He looked out farther, then farther still, and finally he saw her, swarmed with maddened kutji, too numerous for her to escape. "KAYCEE!" he screamed. She looked up, as scared as he'd ever seen her, held out a pleading arm, begging him to come back.

Colby ran for the nearest tree, but Mandu put out a stiff arm and stopped him cold.

"You can't," said Mandu, panting.

"They're going to kill her."

"Not tonight they aren't."

"We have to help her!"

"We can't." He pointed to the edge of the ridge. Below them stood a half dozen furious kutji, braying madly, but refusing to take another step. "We're in Arnhem now. You pass that ridge, they will kill you."

"We can't leave her."

"We have to. It is the choice she made. I told you both it would come to this. I told you at the campfire. If she followed, it would not end well. If she didn't go home, she would die before she returned to her body. She *chose* this. This was what she has worked so long and hard for."

"No! That's not fair."

"Not all destinies are fair, Colby. Hers isn't, yours isn't. We get the lives we choose, even when we don't know we're making a choice."

Colby and the little girl stared at each other across the wide gulf of the swamp, both with tears in their eyes. "I don't leave my friends."

"This time you do."

"We're staying."

"Colby, what's about to happen, you don't want to see. I've seen it. And it will haunt me for as long as I live. Don't do this. Come."

"No. I'm not—"

"Come, before you see something you can never unsee." Mandu looked out over the valley ahead of them in Arnhem. "I have something to show you. Something very important."

Colby turned, crying. "But, Mandu—"

"I have seen many versions of tonight in my dreams. There is one in which you didn't make it up here. And another in which you went back. They both end the same. Those were terrible dreams. Please, let them remain dreams. Come on."

Colby turned back to the swamps, sobbing, raising a hand to wave good-bye to his friend.

Below, the pretty little girl in the purple pajamas simply watched him, stunned, unable to speak.

Then Colby turned around one last time and walked sadly into Arnhem with Mandu.

CHAPTER 36

QUEEN OF THE DARK THINGS

The shadows watched as Colby vanished into the forest, out of their reach.

The pretty little girl in the purple pajamas couldn't watch. She stood crestfallen, defeated, eyes cast to the ground. "Are you going to kill me?" she asked.

Jeronimus shook his head. "We don't have to. You already did the heavy lifting on that for us. You'll be dead any day now for sure. We just have to wait for your body to die."

"Where is it?"

"In the hospital where we left it. You're on machines. But they'll pull the plug any day now."

The tears began to flow steadier now and she sobbed openly into her hands. "And what will happen to me then?"

"You'll become one of us. And then we can all move on."

"My dad won't let that happen."

Jeronimus smiled wickedly. "He doesn't have a choice." He gave a shrill whistle, nodding to a pack of kutji standing behind her.

Out from the pack emerged a single shadow, larger than the others, its limbs long and lanky, having died in much different light than the others. She knew exactly who it was, could feel him, feel his pain, knew it was once her father. Wade.

She fell to her knees, weeping. Destroyed. "No! Dad!"

"Your friends are gone," said Jeronimus. "Your family is gone. There is only us now. Shadows! Show her what will happen if she tries to run away!"

They descended upon her with a ravenous fury, kicking, hitting, scratching, clawing. They beat her mercilessly. But she wouldn't budge; she wouldn't flinch. In fact, she didn't move at all. Nor even blink. She just knelt there, thinking about her father. The blows landed but she couldn't feel them. Hits as strong as the kutji could throw glanced off perfect, radiant skin leaving nary a mark.

She growled, shaking her head at the shadows around her. Slowly, but surely, the ferocity waned, each shadow backing away until none was close enough to hit her anymore.

Then the pretty little girl in the purple pajamas stood up, taking one step toward Jeronimus. "I lied to Colby," she said hatefully, taking another step. "I told him what he wanted to hear. I'm not Kaycee. Not here. Here I get to be whoever I want to be. I'm taller here. Faster here. Stronger here. And here . . . no one can hit me. No one can hurt me. Especially not you." She strode up to Jeronimus, her eyes bitter, staring down at him as he looked bravely up at her.

"You have no idea what we can—"

She grabbed his forehead with a single hand, pushing it all the way back on his neck, his mouth open wide and screaming. Then she jammed her fist down his throat, her arm going in all the way to the elbow, grabbed hold of his innards and tugged, turning his soul inside out. Hands gripped tight, she pulled him apart, piece by piece, tearing him to shreds as the kutji shrieked and howled around her like terrified monkeys. Jeronimus was torn into twenty pieces before his pleading stopped and the remains scattered to the ground, melting away into the darkness around them.

And then he was gone.

The kutji went berserk, leaping around frantically, waving their arms, shaking their fists, as confused as they were angry.

"QUIET!" she boomed, her voice echoing through the swamp like an explosion.

The kutji stopped, held in place by sheer terror.

"On your knees. NOW!"

They fell obediently to their knees.

"Who am I?" she asked.

They looked around at one another, murmuring a dozen unintelligible answers.

"Who?" she demanded of them again.

"You're Kaycee Looes," said one of them. Several others nodded in agreement.

"No. Kaycee Looes is in a bed somewhere. I am your Queen. And you serve me now."

The kutji eyed one another, hoping for boldness out of one of their companions. But none came.

"We have business," she said. "I promise never to kill you like I did your master. And you swear, here and now, that you serve me and obey my every command. And no one, not a one of you, ever touches me again."

One of the kutji near her shook his head. "No. We do not swear." She attacked far quicker than before, shredding him before he could stand up again. His tattered remnants evaporated in the night.

"Swear!"

"We swear," they said in unison.

"What do you swear?"

"To serve and obey your every command and never, ever touch you again."

The pretty little girl in the purple pajamas smiled brutally. She walked over to the shadow that was once Wade Looes, took him by the hand, helped him to his feet. "Dad, what did they do to you?"

"Nothing," he said. "I did it myself, darlin'. This is what we are. It is what you and I are supposed to be."

"No. This is not what we are. We're better than this. Better than them. And starting tonight, we prove it."

"What are we going to do?"

She looked out into the outback, took a deep breath. "We're going to make sure no one ever does anything like this to anyone else again."

CHAPTER 37

THE SHE-DEVILS
OF NANMAMNROOTMEE

Large boulders stood erect, upright in the dirt, dozens of them, perhaps a hundred such stones, the soft tinkling notes of a song ringing sweetly between them. A campfire, tall and bright, blazed coolly within their center. And before that fire sat a devil woman, her flesh pale, her hair a flat black. She had no eyes, just smooth skin where the sockets should be, and a handful of crooked, rotten teeth clinging desperately to puss-dripping gums. She sat cross-legged, grinding plums on a large, polished doughnut of a stone. It was clear that the stone had been ground down in just that manner, worn from centuries of grinding plums against it. In a pile below the stone sat an ever growing sludge of delicious-looking purple pulp.

From out of the desert it came, a whirlwind, a dust devil the size of a tree. It twisted furiously across the plum-pit-strewn sands, coming to a rest on the opposite side of the fire from the old witch. As the winds died down, the dust became a man, large, fat, sweaty—still as tall as a tree—his curly hair matted, colored red by the outback he'd picked up along the way. His skin was clay, his eyes like polished onyx.

The eyeless she-devil paid him no mind, instead continuing to grind plums on her stone, tossing away the pits in a different direction each time.

"Oy!" said the desert man. "Marm."

"I know you, willy-willy," she said, her voice like wind whistling through dried leather straps. "There's no need to shout. You don't belong here. That song was not for you."

"It's a beautiful song, though."

"Yeah, it is. But not yours."

The willy-willy looked around nervously, beads of sweat forming on his brow. "Nice night for it, eh?"

"For what?" asked Marm. Though she had no eyes, she seemed to gaze suspiciously at him. "Why are you here?"

Shadows awoke. From behind the rocks they crawled, slow, methodical, their movements rigid, measured, like sloths. A slow-motion dance formed in the firelight, flickering specters, naked, their flesh withered, breasts sagging to their stomachs, nipples raw and bleeding, sharpened teeth bared.

They sang, the notes intoxicating.

She-devils.

The willy-willy looked up and waved a dismissive hand. "There's no need for that, ladies. Just a friendly visit is all."

"You're not here for the plums, are you?" asked Marm.

"No," he said, wiping sweat from his brow with the back of his dusty arm.

Marm spoke more slowly now, more deliberately, more forcefully. The air seemed to chill a bit more at the utterance of each word. "Then why . . . are you . . . here?"

"I'm sorry," he said. "She made me." He turned and looked over his shoulder just as the massive shadow slunk in from out of the dark of the outback. It was taller than a man, though smaller still than the willy-willy, with six legs, a long neck, a fur the color of night. It was a bunyip. And astride it rode a little girl. A little girl in purple pajamas.

She wore a confident smile, her eyes unflinching, like a gunfighter's. The bunyip bowed, lowering its head to the ground, and the girl slid off it.

"You can go, Virra," she said to the willy-willy.

"Thank you, my Queen." Then he turned to the old witch, whispering. "Listen to her, Marm. Trust me." The winds rose up and his skin turned to sand and in an instant he was gone, whipping across the desert as fast as his gusts would carry him.

The Queen of the Dark Things stepped to the fire, sat down cross-legged in the dirt, smiled politely at the old witch, full of the knowledge that she could not see her.

The devil woman held up a hand dripping pulp, offering it to the Queen. "Plum?" she asked.

The Queen of the Dark Things shook her head. "I know better than that. I will not become one of your she-devils."

With that the note of the song came to an abrupt halt, replaced by a chorus of ear-piercing howls.

"I will not call you Queen," said Marm.

"I was hoping we could change that."

"No. *We* can't."

The Queen of the Dark Things put two stiff fingers between her lips and whistled shrilly.

Then from out of the dark came an army of shadows, kutji swooping in from all sides. They went for the she-devils, their single clawed hands rending their naked flesh. The howls turned to shrieks, terror-stricken devils batting futilely at their attackers. The night filled with the sounds of slaughter, of flaying skin and severed limbs.

Marm rose to her feet screaming. "No! Not my girls!"

"Then call me Queen."

"No!"

"The creatures of the night belong to me now. You either join me or you join the campfires on the other side of the sky. Only you can end this."

"No! I won't! I serve no one!"

"You serve me now."

Marm listened as the she-devils she had collected over a thousand years begged for their lives, wincing as they cried out for their mistress to save them. Tears of blood formed in the corner of her hollow sockets, her fists balled up at her sides. "Save us!" they shouted. "Do something!"

And she did.

The devil woman fell to one knee, head bowed, arms out, palms extended to the sky. "My Queen," she said. "Please make this stop."

"Swear to me," said the Queen of the Dark Things.

"I swear to you."

"And only me."

"And only you."

With that, the Queen nodded and her shadows beat a hasty retreat, vanishing immediately back into the night.

The she-devils, what few remained, at once fell to their knees, sobbing, the blood of their sisters covering them from head to toe.

The Queen of the Dark Things rose to her feet, pointing

sternly at Marm. "Your days of grinding plums are done. You will never again seduce another young girl to your fire. You will never again trick one into eating your pulp. And you will never again turn another little girl into one of your monsters. Cherish the devils you have, witch, for you will never make another."

Marm nodded, knowing full well she had no other choice.

"When I call, and I will call, you come."

"I will, my Queen."

The Queen put a gentle hand on her shoulder and offered a soft smile. "I know," she said. "I know."

CHAPTER 38

THE HELL OUTSIDE

Colby slammed back the last bit of whiskey, draining the glass dry. Then he stood up from his stool, cracking his neck from side to side.

"Colby," said Yashar, hesitantly. "What are you doing?"

Colby popped his knuckles. "I'm not going to sit in here circling the damn wagons all day. If they were going to do something, they would have done it. Their little game has run its course."

"They just want to scare you."

"I was done being scared two whiskeys ago. Now it's time to have a talk. I'm going to march out there and tell them that I want no part of this. Whatever mess they're in, they can handle it themselves. I won't be bullied. Not by the likes of them."

"If ever there was anyone *to* bully you, it would be exactly the likes of them. Don't let the fact that they haven't killed you make you think that they won't. Right now they think you're useful, not indispensable. If you go out there and tell them to fuck off—"

"What?" asked Colby. "They might kill me? What good would that do?"

"It'd go a long way toward convincing the next guy to do exactly as they asked."

"There is no next guy. You know that. There's a reason they came to me. I want to know what it is."

"If they wanted you to know, they would have told you. Maybe it's for the best that you don't know."

"So what am I supposed to do? Stay in here?"

"No," said Yashar. "We should go out there. There's just no need to be an asshole about it. We'll talk. We'll find out what they want and then we'll find a very gentle way to tell them no."

"And you think they'll take no for an answer?"

"Hell no. But we might be able to come up with a solution better than *go fuck yourselves and find someone else*."

"All right then, we'll call that one plan B."

"Can we slide it down to D? Maybe E?"

"Afraid not." Colby made his way to the door.

"Hold up!"

Colby shook his head. "I've spent enough time in here. Let's go bust some heads." He tossed back the inside door, waltzing into the cramped entry, then pushed wide the heavy metal door that opened into the alley.

The glare through the doorway was a bright, blinding blue, the world outside a hazy smudge slowly racking into focus. Colby squinted, imagining it made him look like Clint Eastwood. Instead he looked like a kid who had lost his glasses. He turned to face the street, fists clenched, reworking the scant dreamstuff around him into a crackling aura that popped and sizzled against the air.

He strode out toward the street, Yashar following close behind. Gossamer tore out of the door, catching up quickly, leaving no more than six inches between himself and Colby after that.

They reached the street, looked up, Colby with his arms out, taking the fight to *them*. And they saw nothing.

The city was empty of demons, not a sign that they'd ever been there. Traffic was normal, people made their way up and down the street, a couple trying hard not to make eye contact with the strange man with wild eyes and sweat-matted hair making as if he was about to talk to God. Everything was as it should be. The siege, it would seem, was over.

"They made their point," said Yashar. "There was no other reason to stay."

Colby sighed. "Yeah. They did."

"So what now?" asked Gossamer.

"Now we need to find out what we're up against."

"You mean . . . *her*," said Yashar.

"That's exactly what I mean. I need to talk to someone who traffics in just the sort of things we're dealing with."

"And where are you going to find someone like that?"

"The Limestone Kingdom."

Yashar shook his head, dismissing him with a wave. "Colby, you can't go out there. Not now."

"Don't worry," said Colby. "I'll sober up first."

CHAPTER 39

THE GWYLLION OVER THE HILL

Rhiamon the Gwyllion looked at least 140 years old. Her eyes were sunken, black, in a sea of wrinkles, her hair a straw-like white that could snap in a stiff breeze. A single horn curled, knobby and yellow, along the side of her face. She rasped as she breathed, her lungs gurgling, her throat phlegmy, constricted. She tugged at the knots in a goat's beard with a comb, her arms too weak to work it out. It looked as if she could expire at any moment, as if she couldn't possibly make it another night.

And yet, as she saw him, striding up the steep hill to her flock of goats, she aged further still. Colby Stevens was back. And nothing good could come of that.

Her skin went from pale to gray, her hair peeling away in layers. Wrinkles sagged further; breasts flattened against her stomach. The flap of skin on her neck dangling beneath her chin wiggled with the arthritic chattering of her teeth. The blood in her veins went cold, barely pumping through her weak, shriveled heart.

Rhiamon the Gwyllion was dying, the youthful vigor that had once sustained her drained by defeat, drowning in the fear that Colby would one day learn of what she'd done—the full extent of her involvement in Ewan's death—and he would come for her. She was on the council that had chosen Ewan; she had aided his changeling doppelgänger and the redcaps that followed him; and she had all but entirely orchestrated the events that led to each of their deaths. Yet somehow, she'd managed to keep her involvement secret. But she always knew he would come. It seemed inevitable.

And here he was, approaching up the hill, golden retriever by his side, a dangerous, bold look in his eyes, as if he wasn't afraid of anything—especially not her. Terror gripped her. Pain seized her chest. Her eyes widened as she trembled.

This was it, she thought. This was how her several thousand years would come to an end.

"I've come for counsel," said Colby, sitting beside her in the dirt. He pulled a comb from his pocket and began working the knot out of a beard of a nearby billy goat. Gossamer hung back, rigid and poised, watching over them.

"What?" she asked, her trembling hands steadying.

"Your counsel," he said again. "I need your help."

The fluid in her lungs evaporated, the skin around her eyes tightening ever so slightly. The gray of her skin flushed to a soft white. She stared at him, her jaw loose, her eyes as puzzled as they had ever been. "My help? However do you mean?"

"I know you have no reason to help me," he said, struggling

with a knot, the billy goat growing ever more frustrated with each pass of his comb. "But there is no one in the Limestone Kingdom as old, as wise, or as . . ."

"As what?"

"As . . . ruthless . . . as you. To traffic in such creatures as to know the one I seek."

Rhiamon's eyes widened and she shed sixty years in mere seconds. She smiled, teeth swelling out from bloody gums. "The Queen," she said. "The Queen of the Dark Things comes for you after all. She comes for her vengeance."

"I didn't do what she thinks I did."

Rhiamon cackled and lost another decade from her face. Her eyes were bright and beaming now, her hair still white, but full and lustrous. "That doesn't matter, Colby Stevens. Truth is irrelevant when the heart is at play. What we're afraid of, what we believe, those are the only truths when human frailty is involved. Whether you like it or not, you hurt her, Colby. You left her. Alone. With the dark things. And she will have her revenge."

"And that's why I need your help."

"Make a pact with one devil to stave off another? I never imagined you so desperate." She pondered that for a moment. "No. I take that back. That's what you've always done."

"I don't want to hurt her. But I have no idea what I'm up against."

"So you've come to ask."

"I've come to ask."

"You've come to beg."

Colby swallowed hard, the words choking in his throat. "I've come to beg."

Rhiamon was twenty-five, her heart leaping in her chest, her skin radiant, the vibrant spark of life electrifying the air around her.

If Colby didn't know the hag within, it wouldn't take him

long to fall in love with her. But he knew of the dark rot within her heart, the seething hatred that burned like an ulcer in her stomach. She was a living cancer, feeding off everything nearby.

"The Queen, she terrifies even me. I have lived several thousand years and I have never known her like."

"So she's more powerful than me now?"

Rhiamon squinted, eyeing him from top to bottom and back again. "Don't speak to me about power as if you understand it, boy. You don't know what power is. You twiddle your fingers and deconstruct a thing in front of you and you think that's power. That's not power; that's ability. Power is another thing entirely. The Queen, she fears nothing. Her belief in herself is total. She knows nothing of doubt, never for a moment questions herself. She will stare you down and know the best of three different ways she will kill you if you answer her questions wrong. Not can. Will. The things of the night in the dreamtime listen to her without fail; they obey her every command. And they know the penalty for failure. She doesn't give second chances, and she only affords a swift death to those who fail despite their best efforts.

"Yes, Colby Stevens. She's more powerful than you. Because she's willing to do the things you aren't to get what she wants. Cruelty is a power all its own; belief is a power all its own. You question yourself, let your emotions cloud your judgment. You walked up here ready to bargain, and in that time she would have laid you waste. You're nothing to fear, Colby. And even if you were, she wouldn't anyway."

"I'm willing to do what needs to be done."

"Are you? Prove it. Pay my price and I'll tell you everything I know. I'll weave powerful magicks for you that will protect you from her wrath, help you slay her where she stands. Pay it and prove you will do anything to bring an end to this."

"Name it."

She raised a crooked finger at Gossamer. "Your dog."

"No."

"It's all I ask. One soul, and not even a fully formed one at that. I'll need it for my magicks."

"Absolutely not!"

"Don't come to beg the favor of a witch only to balk at the price of her services. You knew who I was when you walked up. You knew my price was steep. If you didn't walk up that hill ready to pay whatever I asked, then this was a fool's errand. I can give you what you seek, the answers to the riddles that vex you, the secrets kept locked up in that little girl's heart. But to do so, I need a soul. One pet. Your dog. And you will live to see this through."

"No. That's ridiculous. I won't."

"Then you will die, Colby Stevens. You will die. Here I've told you that the thing you face will stop at nothing to get what she wants, but you, you have a point at which you will go no farther. Even to protect yourself. You are doomed to meet Ewan's fate. And you will lie there, staring at the stars as your friend did, as the light fades from your eyes, wishing you'd just given me the damn dog."

Colby's eyes narrowed, his temper flaring.

At once Rhiamon realized what she'd done, aging forty years in a heartbeat. Her face was once again awash in wrinkles, her eyes pleading for mercy.

The air around them crackled, Colby's rage tickling the rich stream of dreamstuff surrounding them. He looked at the old woman cowering before him and at once he understood the nature of her power. "This form," he said. "I'm supposed to feel pity for an old woman when I'm not seduced by the allure of the young one?"

She nodded. "Maybe you're smarter than I ever gave you credit for."

"And maybe I vaporize you right here and now."

"Maybe you do. Maybe you continue down that road. Maybe you become more like us every day."

Colby's ire waned, the sudden pangs of his conscience dragging it screaming back into his belly. "I'm not like you, witch."

Rhiamon eased back forward, cautious not to further aggravate him. "That's what I mean. The Queen, she's more like us than you'll ever be. She has given in to her nature and that nature is a decisive one. She doesn't fear the creatures of the night; she conquers them. You still think you can reason with them. You'll try to reason with her . . . when you have to."

"If you won't help me, why even talk to me?"

"Because you fascinate me."

"I do?"

"Yes. You are unburdened by destiny. It holds no sway over you. The others around you, they see what you can become—the potential within you—and they assume that this is your destiny."

"It's not?"

"No. It's not. It is your potential. They're right in believing what you could become. But you stay ever perched upon the precipice of greatness, staring into it as if it were the abyss itself—a gulf of terrible things that you shan't even gaze upon lest it swallow you whole. No, you have no destiny. And you squander what little else you have. You're like a keg of soggy dynamite with a lit fuse. Maybe you'll change the landscape of the very world. And maybe everyone is just tiptoeing around you for nothing. And that fascinates me."

"You don't think I can? Change the landscape?"

"No. I just don't think you will. You don't have the guts. The only time a pure soul ever changes anything is by dying. It's the ones with the stomach to do bad things that change the world. You've done things that showed potential, but you've been regretting them ever since. The Queen of the Dark Things knows no remorse. She will change the world."

"How do you know she's coming for me?"

"The only ones who know aren't talking. We just know she's coming. We can feel it. And we know that we can either run or we can serve."

"Which will you do?"

"I hadn't thought about it," said Rhiamon. "Honestly, I was certain you'd have killed me before she even got here. But now? Now I know I will most likely outlive you."

"Damnit," said Colby.

"What is it?"

"I know now what I have to do." Colby stood up. "Thank you, Rhiamon."

"So that's it? I have done this for you, what now will you give me?"

Colby pointed at Gossamer. Gossamer's eyes went wide with worry. "You see my friend over there?"

"Yes," she said, growing younger by the second.

"He's awakened. I did it myself."

"I know this. It's why he's such a valuable prize."

"I did it with the soul of a redcap." He looked at her with stern, bitter eyes. "And what do you think that redcap told me, screaming, in the last seconds of his life? What information do you think he tried to bargain with?"

Rhiamon was 150 years old, the whole of her body wrinkling in on itself, her eyes sunk an inch deep in their sockets. He knew.

"Today you've earned another day. You'll see another sunrise. Maybe another after that. I won't kill you today, witch. I give you today. That's what you get. Today."

"I'll take it," she said, cowering behind a skeletal hand dripping in liver spots.

Colby stormed off with Gossamer in tow. Gossamer looked

up, tail wagging. "For a second there, boss, I thought you were going to do it."

Colby looked down at his friend, his expression uneasy, breathing labored. "I would never do that, Goss. Instead, I have to do something far, far worse."

CHAPTER 40

THE DUKE AT
THE FOOT OF A ROCK

Duke Dantalion the djinn, seventy-first of the Seventy-two and master of a thousand faces, was in the throes of the most wonderful dream. He stood atop a spire, surrounded on all sides by luscious flesh, begging for his cock, moaning to be fulfilled, as he stared down at the city beneath them, its towers burning, pillars of smoke trailing into the sky, its empire crumbling from his deceptions. He'd done it. He'd brought the world to a glorious, debaucherous end. And now, as his fellow brothers looted the city for souls, he would while away the hours with its most beautiful women. He would make love to them, each and every one, with the face of their own lovers, before revealing himself, just before he came, to revel in the terror of the moment.

He took one of them by the hand, and laid her back so he could watch the city burn as he fucked her. She looked up at him, legs spread wide, eyes insatiable, and said, "Wake up, asshole."

The world trembled, shook, his side burned. He screamed as the universe cracked, shards of it falling away like a broken mirror. Then everything went bright yellow, his eyes burning with the stinging rays of the sun.

"I SAID WAKE up, asshole," said the Queen of the Dark Things, throwing another handful of salt at him.

Dantalion's eyes shot open. The desert. He was in the desert. Leaning against a rock. The dream was over. And he was in trouble.

He jumped to his feet, took in his surroundings. The dirt around the rock had been marred by colorful sand and salt, drawn into the shape of a pentagram. Symbols of warding and binding adorned it. He was trapped.

"Do you know who I am?" asked the Queen.

Dantalion nodded stoically. "You are Kaycee Looes."

The Queen hurled another handful of salt at him, his flesh burning as if sprayed with acid. He cried out, unable to bear the agony.

"Do you know who I am?"

"You are the Queen of the Dark Things," he said through the pain. "And I am in a lot of trouble, aren't I?"

"The worst kind."

"Is this about the bet?"

"What bet?"

He breathed a sigh of relief. She didn't know. "It's nothing. A silly bet some friends made centuries ago. I was just dreaming about it. I'm still a little confused from being awakened so abruptly."

The Queen reached into a kangaroo skin dilly bag on her hip, and pulled from it another handful of salt.

"Okay! Okay!" he shouted. "The bet that made you what you are. That brought about the kutji."

"You know how I came to be like this?"

"I do."

She scattered the salt on the ground then reached once again into her bag. This time she pulled from it a crystal bottle—etched with Persian, inlaid with gold and jewels, stoppered with an ancient cork, its glass a golden yellow. "You know this bottle?" she asked.

"I do. It is Mehrang. It means 'Color of the Sun.' I knew its last occupant. He was a friend."

"I can reunite you."

"No you can't," he sneered. "You know who I am, don't you?"

"I do."

"Then you know my name appears in tens of thousands of books. I have been written into holy texts and books of sorcery. I cannot be so easily forgotten. Nor would my brothers allow me to be."

"But you can be bottled. Stoppered with the seal of Solomon so your brothers will never find you, sealed in concrete and buried deep in the sands of the outback."

Dantalion's boldness failed him, and his fear showed through. "Yes. I can be bottled. Have you come to me for wishes? Because I can't grant those. It is not in my power."

"No. I've come for information."

"That I can grant."

"You know my curse."

"I do."

"I want you to break it. I want to be free."

"No spirit can break your curse, demon or otherwise. Your curse cannot be broken."

"Then I have no need for you." She pulled the stopper loose from the bottle.

"Wait! Waitwaitwait!"

"Why should I?"

"I said no *spirit* can break your curse, that it could not be broken. I didn't say you couldn't be free."

"Go on."

"It is possible for you to free your spirit from the binds of your body, but it requires a lot."

"Like?"

"A willing spirit capable of possessing your mortal body."

"That I have."

"I said *willing* spirit. And capable. Your body is in Arnhem Land and your kutji are forbidden from going there. And what must be done, your spirits will not do."

"I know where my body is. And I know of a thing that can go there. A thing willing to do anything it has to."

"Ahhhhhhh," he said, waving a knowing finger. "You do, don't you?"

"Yes. What then?"

"What then what?" he asked, trying to concentrate against the searing pain.

"Once a thing has taken my body, what then?"

"Then your body and that spirit must be disbelieved. Ripped out of reality. Restructured anew."

"And you can do that?"

Dantalion shook his head, a sick little grin creeping across his lips. He was almost laughing. "No spirit can disbelieve a thing. Only a thing of the flesh can do that. But to dissolve both flesh and spirit as one takes great power. And of the flesh, there is only one being alive with such a power, a man who can will almost anything away with a wave. But he'd never do so willingly. Especially not for you."

"Who is he? Why won't he help me?"

"You know him. His name is Colby Stevens. And he hates the things of the night even more than you. What you're asking for is immortality. To be free to continue your crusade without limits. Colby would never, ever allow such a thing unless he had to."

"Perhaps he will if I ask him," she said.

"Ask? Colby Stevens? He's a prickly little cocksucker. When was the last time you saw him?"

"When he left me here in the desert to die."

"What, then, do you think has changed about him in the years since? He won't help you. Not after what you've become."

"What do you mean by that?"

"What? By what you've become?"

She fumbled for another handful of salt. "Yes."

Dantalion chose his words very carefully, crouching defensively, staying her with a worried hand. "A dreamwalker without the need for a body and a will as strong as yours. Doing that would make you more powerful than he would allow. You have become the Queen of the Dark Things. And the dark things are what Colby Stevens hates most."

"Then we'll have to change his mind."

"He would destroy you first. His temper is quick and his arrogance knows no bounds."

"Then we'll have to find something he bloody cares about and tell him to choose."

Dantalion smiled, the pain fading away. He nodded, beginning to take a liking to the girl. "Yes. Yes. Make him suffer and choose. This could work. You could be free after all."

"I've been told," she said, unstoppering the bottle and sieving in a fistful of salt, "that if you salt the inside of a bottle before putting in a genie, he feels its burn for as long as he's in there. How long do you suppose you'll be in the desert before someone finds you? A hundred years? Five hundred? A thousand?" She swished the salt around the inside of the bottle.

"What? I've answered everything you've asked."

"There's one more thing I need from you."

"Anything. Ask it."

"Swear to me. Swear that you will grant me one last request and I promise that you will never see the inside of this bottle."

"I swear it." He said. "Anything."

"I need for you to get me . . . the ring."

CHAPTER 41

THE FIVE DUKES OF THE *BATAVIA*

This may be the worst idea you've ever had," said Yashar through clenched teeth.

"What choice do I have?" asked Colby, seated once more at the bar, Gossamer panting with concern beside him.

"You have the choice either to do it or not to do it. I vote not."

"Rhiamon said the things that knew what was going on weren't talking. She meant them. The Seventy-two."

"You can't trust that old witch and you know it."

"Do you think she's wrong? That they don't know what's going on?"

"No. I think they know exactly what's going on. I just don't believe that you're really involved in this. I think they want you to be."

"I only want to summon the Horse. He speaks nothing but the truth. He's their oracle, nothing more. He's already appeared to me. He's already watching me. You said as much. How much more trouble can I really get into with him?"

"The answer to that question is entirely what concerns me."

"It's not like I'm going to make a pact with him or anything. We need information. He has it."

"We can get it other ways."

"HOW?"

Yashar looked long and hard at Colby from across the bar. "I . . . I don't know."

"Rhiamon said that what the Queen has over me is the fact that she'll do anything to get what she wants, but I won't. Maybe it's time I took a risk. Did what no one expects me to do."

"Trafficking with demons. That's a *risk*?"

"Yes."

"This is how it starts."

"No. Hopefully this is how it ends."

"Don't say things that might be far too prophetic for your own good. How much of your soul are you willing to leverage for this?"

"To make things right? As much as it takes."

Yashar tapped the bar nervously, mulling over Colby's rash decision. "Just Orobas?"

"Just the Horse."

Yashar sighed. "Do it. Make it quick before—"

"Before what?"

"Before I lose my nerve."

Colby looked down at Gossamer. "You should go home. You don't need to be here for this."

"I'm not going anywhere, boss."

"This isn't something you want to be around for."

"I've been shot at by Sidhe and chased by monsters. What makes you think I'm going to get spooked by a horse?"

"Because he's not really a horse."

Gossamer nuzzled up to Colby, putting his forehead against his leg, tail wagging. "I won't leave you."

Colby scratched Gossamer behind the ear, melting a little. "Stay behind the bar, close to Yashar."

"Okay, boss."

Colby stepped back, letting Gossamer slip between his legs as he trotted behind the bar. Then he took a deep breath, held out his arms, and the world began to ripple, swirl, bend against the flow of time. Everything slowed down, the single bulb dangling on a wire from the ceiling flickered and buzzed. A hole opened in space, the gravity of it bending even the light around it.

"Colby . . . ," muttered Yashar, terrified.

"I haven't said anything yet."

"I noticed."

The hole contorted, shimmered, took the form of a horse. And then it was a horse, its fur an inky black darkness, its eyes darker still.

"I didn't summon you yet," said Colby.

"You didn't have to," said the Horse.

"You were listening."

"For some time now, yes." The Horse, Orobas, took one trotting step forward, its body melting, morphing into the shape of a man—a man with hooves where his feet should be and the head of a stallion. "I can change further, if you'd like. Appear in the form of a man if that will make you more comfortable."

"No," said Colby, harshly. "I don't want to forget for a moment what you really are."

"As you wish. What is it you need of me?"

"I need to know what's going on."

The Horse took a seat at the bar, turning its large equine head toward Colby. "We don't entirely know."

"Tell me what you do know."

"Have a seat."

"I think I'll stand."

"Have a seat, Colby. The tale is a long one, going back quite some time."

Colby sat at the bar next to Orobas, placed his hands together on the battered plywood bar top. "Tell it."

Orobas nodded. "This began many years ago, in the year 1628."

"Oh shit, you weren't kidding."

"Five dukes met in Amsterdam, each there for the same reason. The Dutch East India Trading Company had just built the biggest, boldest ship ever then to sail the seas. Over one hundred and eighty-six feet long. Thirty-four feet wide. One hundred and eighty feet at its highest point. It carried in its belly twenty-four cast-iron cannons and could accommodate up to three hundred and fifty souls on board. It was christened . . . the *Batavia*.

"In their hubris, the Dutch East India Trading Company proclaimed repeatedly that she was not only unsinkable, but that *God himself could not put her beneath the waves*. God himself. As you can imagine, many of my brothers couldn't resist such a dare. And five of them answered the call. Duke Astaroth, the Naked Angel. Duke Berith, the Alchemist. Duke Bune, the Three-headed Dragon. Duke Focalor, the Stormbringer. And Duke Dantalion."

Yashar sighed. "The Thousand-faced Djinn," he said.

"Yes. The five squabbled from sundown to sunup over who would get to sink her but could find no accord. Until, that is, Duke Dantalion proposed a wager. He bet the other four dukes that he could bring to an end more lives aboard the vessel and connected to the ship than any of the other dukes. The rules were simple. They could use any of the powers at their disposal but could not sink the ship in open water nor kill anyone by their own hands. Once the remaining crew and passengers had reached their destination, outside involvement was strictly forbidden, and they would watch the wager play out to its last. The remaining four dukes were intrigued by this, realizing that together, dueling against one another, they could take the grandest ship yet to sail the seas, and destroy her in the most glorious fashion imaginable.

"Duke Astaroth, who was already in Amsterdam, seducing many to heresy and sin through the perversion of a local Rosicrucian order, inspired a series of events and secured a position aboard the ship for one of his most corrupted playthings: one Jeronimus Cornelisz. Cornelisz was already a man of little moral character when Astaroth found him, but by the time he was done with him, he was absolutely diabolical. Astaroth knew that such a man, aboard a vessel carrying a kingdom's worth of riches, would not be able to resist trying to take them for himself. And thus the game began.

"Dantalion made the next play on the day the ship's passengers came aboard. He inspired a number of the crew, chief among them the ship's master merchant and fleet commander Francisco Palsaert, to fall in love with a wealthy young traveler named Lucretia Jans. Such was the power of Palsaert's affection for the woman that he would try night after night to ply her out of her garments with wine and liquor. But Dantalion saw to it only to strengthen Jans's love for her husband, whom she was sailing to reunite with—a man she had no idea was already dead of the fever. Travel by ship takes a long time and there is little privacy, and the passions of the men for her overwhelmed them, consumed them, and brought them to squabble amongst themselves.

"Focalor's play was much more masterful. Dantalion's wager was wise. He knew that Focalor could bring down a ship with a single storm, and often did, but wanted to reserve the right to run the ship aground if he needed to. While he expected Focalor to use his powers over the wind and sea to steer the ship toward some deserted island, he was no master of the sea. He didn't know about the isolated reef and chain of small dead islands off the coast of Australia that Focalor would subtly nudge them toward.

"And now the stage was set. Cornelisz had begun arranging a mutiny, supported by a number of the men as equally in love with Jans as Palsaert, and it would have been bloody and violent were it not for Focalor's impeccable timing. When the ship finally ran aground on the reef, the chaos that ensued was assured. The ship's most essential and highest-ranking crew members manned a lifeboat headed for their original destination, with the aim of sending a rescue party, leaving none other than Cornelisz in charge. Terrified of having his mutinous plans revealed to the survivors, Cornelisz arranged to divide them among the several small islands.

"Focalor kept the rains away, dwindling the supply of water much faster than anticipated. Some died of thirst, others for stealing rations to stay alive. Berith inspired many to murderous rages, while Astaroth drove even moral men to execute thieves and the mortally ill. Dantalion convinced Cornelisz to draft a loyalty pledge, which he made the few remaining sign. But it would be Bune who would make the most daring and brilliant play.

"By this point, Bune had not claimed a single soul for his own. His gift was far less direct than most, and so he had long learned to be patient in applying it. Bune's touch can turn a dying soul he is responsible for condemning into a demon of his choosing. Instead of staying behind for the carnage of the islands, he chose to follow the lifeboat. He knew that Focalor couldn't resist the chance to drive men to thirst, so he followed the officers, keeping them safe from storm and tide. With his help, they arrived safely at port and sent back the rescue party they had promised.

"By the time they arrived, full-scale war had broken out among the survivors, and it was left to the rescue party to quell it. And this is where Bune's genius had become clear to everyone. As he was responsible for the rescue, he was also responsible for the capture and execution of Jeronimus Cornelisz and his fellow mutineers. Their souls were rightfully his. Before they were finally hanged for treason, each had one of his hands cut off at the wrist. Cornelisz in turn lost both. There they were, dangling in the sun, their last breaths escaping their bodies, Bune touching each one, swallowing their last breath for himself, turning them into demons under his thrall."

Colby's eyes went wide. "Kutji. He turned them into kutji."

Orobas nodded. "Indeed. Their souls were his now, and he commanded them to seek out everyone who had signed that traitorous pledge of loyalty or who had escaped prosecution for their mutiny, and—here was the stroke of genius—their descendants. They were to take their victims' hands and then their souls, and turn them into kutji, just like them. In that way, Bune's play was potentially limitless. Dantalion had stipulated *connected* to the ship in his wager. And these unborn souls were now connected. Bune promised the kutji that once they had secured the soul of the last remaining descendant and made themselves whole by finding their basket of hands, they would have peace. And thus, that is exactly what they've done for the last four hundred years."

"Why has it taken so long?" asked Colby.

"Two mutineers, both of whom had committed terrible crimes, threw themselves upon the mercy of the court and were afforded special circumstances. Their death sentence was commuted and they were instead punished to banishment, given a rowboat, and pointed to Australia. Australia was not yet settled by colonists and the Aboriginals thought them simply to be of a dreaming from across the sea. With two of the ship's crew still technically at sea, the wager was unfinished, and Bune spoke with a Clever Man belonging to the nearest tribe. He tasked the Clever Man with finding the strangers, taking them in, and protecting them from any spirits that might come for them. This the Clever Man did in exchange for wisdom and an abundance of food in the coming season.

"When the kutji finally arrived to claim their souls, they found themselves at odds with a Clever Man more clever than they, and the two survivors soon wed and fathered children whose lineage went on now for four hundred years. Once the Clever Man was gone, they were free to claim the souls of the descendants, but by then, they were scattered throughout the land, protected by a dozen other Clever Men. It has taken them four centuries to track down every last descendant of the *Batavia*'s mutineers. Now, only one remains."

"Kaycee," said Colby.

"Kaycee Looes, direct descendant of Wouter Looes."

"Why didn't they just kill her?"

"They can't find their hands. To this day, they have chopped off the hand of every soul they've gathered, sending a kutji after its shadow to find its final resting place. But they've never found it. Once they discovered that Kaycee could dreamwalk, they believed it to be divine providence. She would lead them to their hands. So they made a pact with a wise old Clever Man already in league with another powerful spirit. He agreed to help cut the cord that tethered her to her body in exchange for the assurances he would need to keep her body alive and protect his people from their wrath once they found out."

"Mandu?"

"Yes."

"But he didn't cut the cord. I did."

Orobas looked long and hard at Colby, waiting for all the new information to sink in.

"I cut it. I cut the . . ." Then it hit him. "Mandu tricked me into doing it."

"He did."

"WHY?"

"No one knows but Mandu."

"Well, if this is Bune's curse, why don't you just have him remove it?"

Orobas stamped a hoof on the ground and pointed to Colby. "Good thinking. But he can't."

"Why not?"

"Two reasons. One, a curse is just a bargain struck without benefits. Bune set the rules of the curse, and now he cannot renege on them. He set the rules of the kutjis' existence, and now it has to play out to its last. And two, Bune is missing."

"He's one of the five miss . . ." Colby trailed off. "The five. Your missing five demons. They're—"

"The five dukes of the *Batavia*."

"She's trying to unmake her curse."

"I told you, she can't. The five dukes, no matter how involved they are in her . . . *situation* . . . they cannot unmake what they have made. And she knows that."

"So this is revenge," said Colby.

Orobas nodded, his mane bouncing behind him. "This is revenge."

"She's binding them to pay for their part in having bound her?"

"Yes."

"I'm not seeing my part in this."

"The part where the girl whose cord you cut and left in the desert with a horde of shadows has begun amassing an army of the damned, meting out revenge on those she feels have wronged her?"

"You just said Mandu—"

"Does she know that? Does she even care? She's been out there in that desert for ten years, wandering without a body, unable to go home. Never sleeping, never eating. Consumed only by rage at her own confinement. We'd heard of the terrible things she was doing, the rounding up of the spirits of dreamtime. But we had no idea it would lead to this."

"How did she even summon a demon to begin with? I mean, if you know—"

"Dantalion was the first to go. She didn't summon Dantalion. She found him."

"Found him? How do you *find* a demon?"

"Weema's Rock," said Yashar. Again Orobas nodded.

"I don't understand," said Colby.

"Dantalion is a djinn," said Yashar. "The Thousand-faced Djinn. He can look like anyone. Put thoughts in the heads of men. Can inspire love even between the worst enemies. But he's still a djinn. And powerful though he is, he still has to sleep. Weema's Rock. You've been there."

"The place where we met Mandu? And you . . . ooooh."

"It's in the middle of the desert, far from any songline. No one goes out there. You can sleep for years without ever being disturbed. Only a precious few Clever Men know of its existence— the ones we trust to watch over us while we sleep."

"Oh my God. Mandu told her. I remember now. He pointed out to the desert, described it, and told her that one day she would . . ."

"She would what?" asked Yashar.

"Find her destiny. She was always going on about some destiny. Wouldn't stop talking about it. There was something great in her future that she couldn't wait to get to."

"Destiny is a thing crafted by spirits but chosen by men," said Orobas. "It may have been born in the will of others, but she has chosen the path set before her."

"You're the great oracle. So what's her destiny?"

"I don't know."

"What do you mean you don't know? You have to know. It's the one thing you do."

"We can no longer see her future. Just as we can no longer see yours. That's how we know that you're involved."

"You can't see my destiny?"

"No. Your future has become . . . uncertain."

"Because this involves you?"

"Because it involves the Seventy-two."

"How did she even bind a demon, anyway? She shouldn't have that power."

Yashar shook his head, waving a dismissive hand. "There are dozens of ways to bind spirits, Colby. You know that. Bottles, sacred objects, permanent triangles and pentagrams. Even I know how to trap a demon. I just know better not to try."

"But to summon and bind five?" asked Colby. "There's got to be something more to it. Someone has to be helping her."

"It would appear not," said Orobas. "She is doing this entirely on her own."

"On her own with an army of spirits."

"Yes. But none that could do *this*."

"Okay, but what I still don't understand is why you all don't just get together and form some super-demon assault force of doom and just rain on Australia like it was fucking Judgment Day. Binding one demon is a terrifying enough proposition. But sixty-seven? There's no way. She's not that powerful. She can't be."

"We just . . . can't."

"You just . . . ca—" Colby broke off his mockery, the color in his face draining, leaving him a pale, ghostly white. "Oh my God. She found the ring."

Orobas didn't answer, instead looking away, across the bar, his expression strained.

"Kaycee found the ring, didn't she?"

Orobas looked back at Colby, nodding bitterly. "Yes. She has the ring."

CHAPTER 42

SOLOMON THE WANDERER

AN EXCERPT BY JONATHON WALTERS FROM
HIS BOOK *ABANDONED RELIGION: STORIES
AND EPICS OF THE OLD WORLD*

While there is no empirical evidence of his existence, King Solomon is mostly considered an historical figure rather than a religious one. No artifacts remain from his reign, nor is he mentioned in historical documents of any kind. And yet, he is a pivotal figure in most of the major religions, assumed to be, at least in part, based upon an historical one. That said, the beliefs surrounding him differ from religion to religion. While it is generally accepted that he was gifted with almost supernatural wisdom, many of the stories revolving around him involve his suffering at the hands of his own foolish decisions. Meanwhile, other stories hail him as a demon summoner, only able to overcome their trickery by God's intervention. In the strangest tale, Solomon is gifted with a powerful ring that both gives him great power and sends him on a most unlikely adventure.

Just after the death of David, King Solomon found himself ruler of a wealthy and growing kingdom. While David's rule had been great, his son sought to move quickly out of the shadow of his father. He commissioned the building of the largest temple the world had ever seen, but its construction proved problematic. Surrounding his kingdom were stones of marble that shone bright pink in the sun. But the Torah forbade the use of iron cutting tools, iron being considered the unholy alloy of the Devil. So he tasked, at great expense, every available man in the kingdom to its completion, including his own young concubines.

One, a young boy, soon fell ill while working on it. When Solomon saw the boy so thin and pale he asked of him, "Do I not give you twice the pay and food of any other man? Why are you so thin and sickly?"

And the boy answered, with shame in his eyes, "My king, you would not believe me if I told you."

"You are my most favored and I trust you with all my heart. Tell me what is wrong with you and I will not be angry."

"My king, at night, while asleep, a demon visits me and sucks at my thumb. He steals half my pay, half my food, and each night half my remaining life."

Solomon, love him though he did, was not sure whether to believe the boy. So that night he crept into the boy's chambers and waited in hiding. To his surprise, in the darkest hour of the night, appeared Ornias, a lesser demon, who stole the boy's rations and wages before suckling his thumb.

Unsure of what to do about the demon, Solomon fell to his knees in the temple and prayed that God give him the means to protect the boy. It was then that the Archangel Gabriel appeared before him, throwing a ring before Solomon's feet. Gabriel instructed him to cast the ring at the demon and that the symbol upon it would burn a brand in its flesh. Any demon so branded would have to obey the wearer's every command and could not in any way harm him.

So Solomon waited again and in the darkest hour of the night Ornias again appeared. This time, as he set to suck at the thumb of the boy, Solomon cast the ring as he was commanded, and the ring then burned a glowing brand in the demon's flesh. Solomon put the ring back on, commanding the demon to stop and kneel before him. And thus the demon did.

It was then that Solomon realized the solution to his construction problems. "Tell me," he said to Ornias, "where I might find the rest of your brothers."

Ornias shook his head. "I cannot tell you that," he said. "For I do not know. But I do know where Asmodeus is, and he is the lord of us all. He knows where to find each of us and his word is our law. Find him and find us all."

"Summon him," Solomon commanded, and he did.

Asmodeus appeared, moving immediately to smite the king, but Solomon cast his ring at him and burned the brand into his chest. Asmodeus howled in pain, but fell to his knees when commanded.

"Bring to me the demons under your command," said Solomon, "so that they might build me the greatest temple to God the world has ever seen." And though he did not want to, Asmodeus began to summon them one by one. Soon Solomon had an army of demons thirty-six strong with which to build his temple.

The demons built it quickly, raising a temple higher than any man knew how, burnished with gold and sculptures of the angels. When it was done, Solomon marveled at the mastery of its craftsmanship. And so he turned to Asmodeus and asked him, "How is it that these demons follow you so loyally? This temple exalts all which they oppose. How could they build so well a temple to the Lord?"

"My powers, my king, are weakened by your ring. Perhaps if you took it off I could show you."

Solomon consented and took off the ring.

"Hand it here and I will show you why they obey me."

Solomon handed the ring to Asmodeus, trusting that the demon could not harm him. At once the demon grew in size, one wing touching the earth, the other reaching well into the sky. The demon grabbed Solomon and swallowed him whole. The ring burned in his hand, so he cast it away as far as he could throw it, sinking it deep into the sea. Then he belched out Solomon, hurling him four hundred miles, well out past his kingdom and over several others before dumping him alone in the desert.

King Solomon was shamed, having been fooled by the demon, and set about making his way home, though he knew not which way it was.

Back in Solomon's kingdom, Asmodeus disguised himself as the king, took his place on the throne, and, with his throng of demons, took to slowly corrupting the kingdom. He started small, corrupting officials and tempting the weak willed. Then, as his boldness grew, he convinced the virtuous to throw off their piety, to seek their comforts in prostitutes and profane acts.

Four hundred miles away, Solomon trekked across barren lands and for three years wandered, begging or doing odd jobs to earn his keep until he found himself in the city of Ammon. There, starving and poor, he took the first job he found, as a cook in the king's palace. Solomon quickly showed a talent for cooking and worked his way up to assistant, just beneath the head cook. One night the head cook took ill and Solomon was forced to prepare the meal himself. So pleased was the king with the meal that he immediately promoted Solomon to the position of head cook. And it was then, when he was working directly for the Ammonite king, that he met the king's daughter, Naamah.

Naamah was by far the most beautiful woman in all of Ammon, and said to be more beautiful than anyone in any of the surrounding lands. So beautiful was she that her father kept her from the sight of visiting dignitaries and kings in hopes of saving her for a most beneficial marriage. Only the servants in his palace were allowed to see her, though they were not permitted to speak in her presence. The first moment Solomon laid eyes upon her he was bewitched. Most fortunate for Solomon, the first time she spied him she felt the same.

Every night he served her and every night their hearts pattered faster when the other was near. And after months of suffering in silence, he whispered to her as he set a plate of food before her, "Meet me after sunset." Later, when sunset came, she snuck down to the kitchen where he had begun roasting the next night's meal. Without a word, they embraced and kissed.

They carried on in secret for weeks until Naamah could bear it no longer. She approached her father with Solomon and asked permission to wed. The Ammonite king was furious, convinced that a commoner had stolen her purity. He ordered her disinherited and cast them both out of the kingdom in disgrace. The two wed at once in the first town they came to and spent the last of their money on a meager meal of small fish.

Naamah insisted on cooking their first meal together for her husband and selected the fish herself. When she sliced open the first fish, a silver ring bearing the seal of Solomon tumbled out. Overjoyed with the sudden windfall, she ran to Solomon and presented the ring to him. "We're rich!" she proclaimed. "We need not worry about starving any longer!"

Solomon smiled at this good fortune, saying unto her, "It is true. We will never have to worry about money." With that, he put on the ring and they were transported at once back to Israel.

Solomon found his kingdom in disarray. The poor were uncared for. Houses of ill repute advertised their wares in the streets. Temples of worship were empty or defiled. Angered, Solomon stormed into his throne room and saw the demon Asmodeus sitting upon his throne, disguised as him.

Solomon raised the ring and commanded Asmodeus to reveal himself in his true form. "I think you would not like it," said the demon. But Solomon insisted. It was then that the demon revealed himself for what he was, not as Solomon had seen him before, but in the form he spared only for Hell. Trembling at the horror, Solomon remained firm and ordered the demon out.

With that, Solomon took back his throne and announced his queen to all his kingdom.

That night, and for every night after, Solomon suffered terrible dreams, visited by visions of Asmodeus's true self. Plagued night after night by nightmares, Solomon devised a plan to rid himself of them. He had his artisans construct a brass vessel, and summoned demon after demon, commanding them, one by one, into it. Once full, it was sealed with the sign of Solomon and branded with the ring. Then he commanded his men to dump it deep into the sea where even he knew not where to find it.

Though this did not cure his affliction and he thus dreamed of Asmodeus every night, the kingdom prospered, no other demon daring to set foot into Israel for the rest of his days.

CHAPTER 43

THE FAVOR OF OROBAS

You're not afraid for your brothers," said Colby to Orobas. "You're afraid she may come for you."

"Yes," said the Horse. "And she will."

"Once she's had her revenge, why would she?"

"Because they always do, the bearers of the ring. Hide it though we do, someone always manages to find it. And once they have it, and get a taste of what we can do for them, they have to have us all. Whether out of greed or fear that we might come for them, they trap us all. And we either trick our way out of servitude, or have to wait until their death."

"And once dead?"

"We make them suffer torments beyond that which they could ever have imagined."

"You're afraid this might be about more than revenge."

"Her avengement is not just about punishing those responsible for her predicament. It's about punishing all the creatures of the night. All of the *dark things*. She will not rest until we are all under her thumb."

"What then?"

"Maybe she binds us into another box and throws us into the sea. Maybe she becomes drunk with power and uses us to remake the world as she sees fit. Kaycee Wooes was once a bright-eyed little girl who simply wanted to live in her dreams. After ten years of nightmares, she's become this. What might she be once she has the power of the Seventy-two at her disposal?"

"Maybe she makes the night safe for everyone," said Colby.

"And maybe she brings her nightmares to the rest of the world," said Yashar. "Orobas is right. No one who traffics with the Seventy-two can stop themselves. I know the stories of the half dozen who have tried just since I've been alive."

"But not the others," said Orobas, "who we've wiped from the very face of history."

"I imagine not."

Colby took a seat at a nearby table, staring off into the distance. He was crestfallen, defeated. There was no talking his way out of this one, no brokering a deal to remove himself. Orobas was right. Regardless of his intentions or what the Queen of the Dark Things was really up to, it involved him, even if in some small way, and the Seventy-two were never going to let it go. They'd involve themselves in his life, torment him, stalk him every minute of the day until he was dead or the Queen herself showed up for her revenge.

"Maybe I could go see her. Talk sense into her. Tell her this doesn't end well."

"You think she'll give up the ring?" asked Orobas.

"She won't, Colby," said Yashar. "The minute she does, she's a goner. Those demons will tear her apart for what she's done. And that'll just be the beginning of it. That ring is the only thing protecting her now."

"He's right," said Orobas. "We will make her suffer in ways most unimaginable."

"I thought I'd already killed her once. Now you're telling me I have to do it a second time."

"Yes."

"Let me ask you something, Orobas. Solomon—I've always wondered. He's always referred to as one of the wisest men who ever lived, and yet most of the stories have him acting foolishly, doing things only an idiot would do."

"Like giving Asmodeus the ring?"

"And being tricked into making a sacrifice to another god. And every other stupid thing he did for a piece of tail. Especially considering just how many wives he had. It's all bullshit, isn't it, the parts about him being a fool?"

"There are those who say that history is written by the winners. Those men did not know King Solomon. The truth is that history is simply written by those who live the longest, the last ones standing."

"You rewrote history. With propaganda."

"I didn't. I couldn't. But the others did. We needed to be protected. We would have cleansed the story of the ring entirely, but it was widespread long before we were dredged out of the sea. So we changed it. Told a more interesting version. That's the one that was penned in the books and made sense alongside the rumors after his passing."

"You knew him. What was he like?"

"He was the cleverest man I have ever met, the only man ever to live to outwit the Seventy-two."

"But you made him suffer, as you did the others?"

"No. He was too pure for us. The ring never corrupted him. But then, it was he who forged it to begin with. He never wanted the power we offered. He only wanted to put us down, buried for a thousand years."

"He only got five hundred," said Colby.

"His one fault. He wasn't forward thinking enough to imagine the technological advances that would follow his death or acknowledge things as simple as a tide against an ever changing landscape. Solomon believed he lived in a world that would never change, that the temple he built would stand until the end of time. Now all that remains of him is that ring and the stories."

"And you, bound together as you are."

"And us."

Colby took a deep breath. "So you guys can't go anywhere near her, or see anything involving the ring?"

"That is correct."

"And you need me to free your five friends and kill the Queen of the Dark Things?"

"Yes."

"Then we'll bargain for it."

"Colby!" shouted Yashar. "Don't!"

Orobas shook his head. "Bargain, I'm afraid you don't understand—"

"I understand just fine. The Seventy-two have gotten themselves into a world of shit. They have lost five demons and one of the most powerful relics in the world to a little girl and you need me to get them back. And this you expect I'll do for free, or rather, just so my life doesn't turn to shit? At your hands?"

Yashar shook his head, waving his hands from behind the bar. "Don't. This is how they work. This is what they wanted all along."

"Yashar, I know what I'm doing."

"No. You don't."

"Orobas, bargain with me now. I will give you back the souls of your five friends in exchange for five favors, each granted by the demon of my choosing. When I call, they will appear, and they will give me one boon each."

"I cannot bargain for them."

"Yes you can. Because you're going to go back to them and tell them of the bargain you've made. And I'm certain that they will find my terms far more agreeable than the Queen's."

"They won't come. Not here, not now."

"They'll come," said Colby.

"No. She could be anywhere. She could be here now, or arrive at any moment. I'm risking myself just by being here."

"Then I'll go to them."

Yashar pounded his fist on the bar. "Colby!"

Colby waved him off. "You'll send the Angel on Horseback."

"Seere will want to have nothing to do with this," said Orobas.

"He'll have little choice."

"So you will kill the Queen and retrieve the ring—"

"I cannot see the future and I don't know how I'll have to do it when the time comes. The bargain is this: five favors for five souls. I will release your friends or I will die trying."

"My brothers will want more assurances."

"But they will get only this. Any demon I summon who refuses to do my bidding, granting exactly the boon I ask for, fulfilled in its entirety, will forfeit *your soul* and service over to me. Do we have a deal?"

"My soul?" asked Orobas angrily.

"My deal is with you. But I need it to be with them. I need assurances that they will grant me the boons I need to defeat the Queen. And you are all bound by your oath to protect one another from enslavement. Is that correct?"

"That is in our vow."

Colby spoke coldly, deliberately, each word dripping with arrogance. "Do. We. Have. A. Deal?"

"You know the price of failure?"

"I do."

Orobas nodded. "Then we have a deal. Five favors for five souls."

"Go speak with your brothers. I have preparations to make."

Orobas vanished, the world once again warping around him.

Yashar leaped over the bar, angry, tears in his eyes. "Damnit, Colby! That's exactly what they wanted. For you to make a deal with them. It wasn't enough for you to summon the Wild Hunt. Now you're making deals with devils."

"You said it yourself, Yashar. I was already damned. What's a little more damnation on the pile?"

"It's everything, Colby. It's everything."

CHAPTER 44

THE ANGEL ON HORSEBACK

Seere. He is a Mighty Prince, and Powerful, under Amaymon, King of the East. He appears in the form of a Beautiful Man, riding upon a Winged Horse. His office is to go and come; and to bring abundance of things to pass on a sudden, and to carry or re-carry anything whither thou wouldst have it to go, or whence thou wouldst have it from. He can pass over the whole Earth in the twinkling of an Eye. He gives a True relation of all sorts of Theft, and of Treasure hid, and of many other things. He is of an indifferent Good Nature, and is willing to do anything which the exorcist desires. He governs 26 Legions of Spirits.

—*Ars Goetia*

You can't do that here, Colby," said Yashar, his arms folded, a tattered rag hanging from his belt, a reminder of his new position. "Not here. I won't let you."

Colby shuffled around the back of the bar, haphazardly placing dozens of candles on tables and in corners, eyes squinting as if working out algebra in his head. Everything had to be perfect. "Well, I'm not going to summon demons at my house."

"But this *is* my house."

"This is a bar."

"But it's my bar. It's not pretty and it's not busy, but it's mine. And I'm not going to let you conjure up some of the very worst things in the world into it. Orobas was one thing, but this?"

"Scraps had one rule about this place. What was it?"

"Colby, Scraps is dead."

"What was the rule?"

"Only the cursed and the damned could drink here."

"You're goddamned right. What else is a bar for, if not for entertaining the very worst sorts?"

"Are you going to try to get him drunk?"

"It might be worth a shot."

"This isn't funny."

"No, it's not." Colby placed the last candle and turned to face the djinn, his arms out, trying to reason with him. "Yashar, how many of the Seventy-two have you met over the years?"

Yashar thought for a moment, sifting through his memories. "All of them at one time or another. But some of them not for a thousand years."

"But you know them."

"I do."

"I know. You're the one who told me their stories. Who cautioned me against ever trafficking with them. Your knowledge—your abilities—they're invaluable right now."

"So what do you want me to do?"

"Stand with me. Keep me sane. Grounded."

"And be ready to throw down if I have to?"

Colby nodded, shrugging shamefully. "Yeah."

"So I'm your muscle?"

"No. You're my friend."

Yashar put his hand on the bar, leaned forward, sighing. "Damnit, Colby. That's cold-blooded."

Colby took a deep breath. "You're going to make me say it, aren't you?"

"Say what?"

"I'm scared."

"You don't look it."

"I'm terrified. The things visiting me—"

"I know. They're bad hombres."

"The worst."

"All right." He raised one of his thick, muscular arms, pointing a strong finger at a row of candles along the back wall. "But your candle placement sucks. Those things are going to go nuts, and you're going to burn this place to the ground."

Colby grinned sheepishly, his ears meeting his shoulders. "I . . . I've never done this before."

"It certainly looks it. Who's up first?"

Colby walked over to the wall, shifting the candles farther away. "I have to summon Seere first, but he'll be taking me to . . . the Leopard."

"Jesus, you're not exactly starting off easy."

"I know."

"He's charming. Charming as hell. But—"

"Evil," said Colby, matter-of-factly.

"Rotten to the core. He'll try to get into your head."

"I imagine they all will."

"Without a doubt." Yashar drew a rune in the air with his finger. "You know about the triangle, right?"

"Yeah."

"He's not going to like it. He'll want out. He'll beg and threaten if he has to."

"We have no other choice."

Yashar reached into his pocket, pulling out a large piece of pink chalk. "Use this." He tossed it underhanded across the room. Colby caught it like a wild pitch to the outside.

"Seriously? You keep this on you?"

"Not usually. But I thought it might come in handy. Be sure to salt it after you draw it. It will burn like a mother if he tries to mess with it."

"How do you know that?"

"I've done my time in plenty of circles over the years." He reached up, unconsciously fondling the scars left on him by Knocks and the redcaps. "He won't budge. Not if you do it right. But make it big enough for him to move around a little, or else he'll be pissed from the start."

Colby pulled a salt shaker from his pocket.

"Table salt?" asked Yashar.

"Sea. Dead Sea, actually."

"You keep it in a salt shaker?"

"Yeah. Where do you keep yours?"

"As far away as possible." Yashar casually reached under the bar, fished out a bottle of his best. Uncorking it, he smiled weakly. "I never wanted to see you go down this road."

Colby softened. "Yashar—"

"It's been my worst fear. Since the beginning. There are wizards and there are sorcerers. I never wanted you to be either, but if you had to be one of them—"

"I know. I never wanted this either. But there isn't any other way."

"People who traffic don't come back. Not the same, at least. They're never the same. Once they've seen these things, felt their touch, tasted the power . . ." He poured two glasses of whiskey. "Colby, this is the last drink I get to have with my friend. After this—" He waved around the room. "After *all this*, you won't be the Colby I knew."

"I can try."

"They all try. Everyone tries. But it's a dark road, and lonely. And when the fallen are their only comfort, it's hard not to end up like them."

"I'm not dead yet. Don't eulogize me."

"I always knew that one day I would have to. But not like this. So." He picked up both glasses and offered one to Colby. "One for the road."

"I need to stay clear."

"It's not to get drunk on. It's for courage. For the road."

Colby took the glass, swirled it, took a whiff. It smelled rich, deep, like the fresh-baked apple pie of whiskeys, memories swelling to the surface filled with laughter and rain and angels. It was Old Scraps's private reserve. "Wait, this is—"

"I finally found out where he was getting it." Yashar raised his glass to Colby. "To getting better of the road than it gets of you."

Colby raised his glass in return, hesitating. "It seems wrong to slam it down."

"There really is a lot more where that came from." Yashar tossed back the whiskey and so too did Colby. It tasted like old times. "Now," he said, his voice horse, recovering from the drink. "About that angel."

Colby put down his glass, took a deep breath. He closed his eyes, waved his arms, and all the candles lit at once. Yashar turned down the lights and the room flickered, alive with the zeal of a hundred wax candles. Then Colby stood up, holding his palms out, and said the words. It was a garbled tongue, filled with furious vowels and consonants that ran together like a bad cough. The very world quivered at their utterance, walls bending away to get as far as possible from them. Then, at their climax, Colby yelled, "Seere, I summon thee! Appear and speak!"

Then from outside came a tremendous clatter, the din of the world breaking in half and spitting something out.

Colby looked warily around. "Shouldn't he be—"

"He's going to arrive outside," said Yashar.

"Not inside?"

"He always brings that fucking horse."

"You would think—"

"You would, but he brings it anyway. Come on."

Yashar and Colby ran out into the midnight alley, the air gamy with rotting fish, standing paces away from both the Dumpster in which they were laid to rest and the door to the Cursed and the Damned. The city blazed halogen orange, spilling faintly into the narrow access.

THE OTHER END of the alley swelled with smoke, a swirling haze hanging in place that obscured the city lights but glowed with its own unearthly golden hue. A shadow appeared in the mist, a figure on horseback, large feathered wings splayed out from both steed and rider. The horse trotted forward with an elegant prance, a dancing pony angling for a blue ribbon.

"You've got to be kidding me," whispered Colby to Yashar.

"I told you. Get ready for the show."

Seere was beautiful, his skin a pristine milky white ivory, fragile like a china doll's; his hair black, flowing, waving as if caught in a slow river current. He still wore his armor, head to toe polished silvery plate, gold inlay gleaming even in the dim light, depicting the great battle for Heaven. And his wings were massive, each feather no smaller than the size of a man's forearm, each perfect, unmolested by time.

His horse was equally majestic. A fine-bred stallion, his coat unblemished, muscles rippling with each step. Its wings were so large that it had to flex them back to keep its feathers from dragging along the walls on both sides of the alley. But its eyes were solid black orbs, cold, dead, like a possum's. Steam erupted from its nostrils as it breathed, but it made no sounds other than the *clack clack clack* of its hooves on the concrete.

The pair trotted up before Colby, stopping just a few feet away.

"I appear," said the angel, his voice like a virgin's, sweet and unassuming. "And I speak." He slid off the side of the horse, folding his wings behind his back as he did, striding forward from his dismount without breaking stride. He walked past Colby, toward the door of the bar without so much as eye contact. "Look after my horse, will you, Yashar?" he said, not expecting any argument. "He's the last of his kind."

The door opened without him touching it and he entered quickly.

"Wait," said Colby quietly to Yashar, pointing at the horse. "This isn't—"

"One and the same."

"*The*—"

"There were skies full of them once. But they're just a story now. One no one believes anymore. Get in there. I'd rather not have to deal with Seere anyway."

INSIDE, THE ANGEL strolled through the bar, hands clasped tightly behind his back, admiring every nook and cranny as if he were in a gallery, committing every detail to memory, trying to understand the meaning of the placement of each individual thing. He seemed at once both keenly interested and completely detached. *Pretentious.* Everything about him read *pretentious*.

Seere stopped at the painting *Dogs Playing Poker*—still the only art hanging in the whole of the bar—pointing at it with an appreciative finger, eyes brightening for a moment. "I always liked this one," he said. "The whimsy of it. The idea that if dogs were more like people, they too would cheat at something as meaningless as a game."

He turned and looked at Colby, then took a seat at the nearest table.

"Can I get you something to drink?" asked Colby.

"No. I don't need a reason to stay longer than I have to. It would be impolite to not finish a drink, and I'd rather not be here that long. So go ahead, ask me. Everyone does."

"Ask you what?"

"About God. All of us were angels, every last one. But for some reason, because I still look the part, everyone only asks me. Did God dream man or did man dream God?"

"I wasn't going to—"

"There's no shame in it, Colby. We all wonder that. Truth is, we don't know. None of us remembers a time before there was man. The earliest we can recall is a time when there was God, there was man, and there was us. And God loved you more. So here we are. A great war and several thousand years later and I am pressed into your service for the sins of my accursed brothers. I'd sooner have them rot in servitude to that girl, but I swore an oath, and I am bound to it." He looked around at the candles, burning brighter in his presence. "They're angry, you know."

"The others?"

"Yes. Quite. All of them. You have them very, very concerned."

"You don't seem to care."

"You and I have a lot more in common with each other than I have with them. Damned though we are, we make the best of it and try to remain pure. While I certainly think your arrogance is capable of convincing you that you can outthink us, I doubt you'll do anything worth terrifying us over."

"You don't like them very much, do you?"

"I hate them. As much as I can. It's probably what binds me here, but I can't let it go."

"What did they do?"

Seere ran his fingers through his black hair, holding a tress of his ever flowing locks—still waving, even inside—up before his eyes, lost in a memory of the time it was still blond. "They changed. They didn't have to. But they were so bitter, so angry. They made their home in the hollows of Hell and began to make it in the image of their own suffering. Soon they began to believe that this suffering was all they were. That's the curse of the fallen. We so felt loss at his loving of you more, that our punishment was to become like you. The others embraced the very worst of you. Colby, do you know why the world hasn't been overrun with evil?"

"It hasn't?"

"No. Not like one would imagine it. Angels, they fall all the time, and they turn. Get seduced by all this down here. So why haven't they risen up and bent men under their will?"

"I have no idea."

"Because we hate one another. All of us. We can't stop fighting. Each wishes to be a lord on his own. So we spend all of our time squabbling, arguing, sometimes even brawling. We can't agree on anything, not the way the world should be, or who should run it. We undermine one another's schemes, cheat one another out of spoils. There is no legion of Hell setting out to corrupt the world. Just a disorganized mess of creatures who have only ever come together on one point, at one time, and are together bound by that one moment. I hate them. I really hate them. But I am bound to them."

"Why?"

"A moment of weakness. Down in that box, beneath the sea, we thought we might never again see the light of day. And when we did, we had to make sure that nothing like that ever happened again. The ring, it can't be destroyed, Colby. It's God's cruel joke. We were given free will only to know that there was something out there that could rob us of it. It's desperation that damns us, Colby. But you know that better than most." He paused, looking around the room, taking it all in. "So which of my brothers are we visiting first?"

"The Leopard," said Colby, trying his damnedest to sound stoic as he said it.

Seere smiled weakly. "If he's your first visit, I'm terrified to know who you're saving for your last."

CHAPTER 45

THE LEOPARD

Flauros, a strong duke, is seen in the form of a terrible, strong leopard; in human shape, he shows a terrible countenance, and fiery eyes; he answers truly and fully of things present, past, and to come; unless he be in a triangle, he lies in all things and deceives in other things, and beguiles in other business, he gladly talks of the divinity, and of the creation of the world, and of the fall; he is constrained by divine virtue, and so are all devils or spirits, to burn and destroy all the conjurer's adversaries. And if he be commanded, he suffers the conjurer not to be tempted, and he hath twenty legions under him.

—Pseudomonarchia Daemonum

Colby arrived atop the back of the winged horse, his arms held tightly around Seere. The mountainside they'd landed on was misty, thick, milky fog wisping past in a stern wind. Jungle enveloped them, ancient trees with dark gnarled roots growing up toward a canopy that blackened even the brightest of burning stars. It was a cold but muggy night in a waxing spring.

"Where are we?" asked Colby, peering out into the dark.

"South America. I think it's safe to tell you that. You'd deduce that yourself, eventually. But I won't say any more."

"Is this the place?"

Seere pointed farther up the slope. "No. But it's as far as I'm allowed. Past that tree and up the trail you'll find a city hidden amidst the trees where no man has trod for a thousand years. Even the dead have left. It is now just a relic waiting to be rediscovered. Until then, Flauros calls it home."

"You don't enter each other's lairs?"

"It's better that way. Even demons deserve some privacy. But I'll be here when you return."

Colby slid off the back of the horse to trek up the mountain, swallowed immediately by the jungle. Fifty paces in he turned but couldn't see Seere back through the mist and foliage. The air seemed to further cool with each step and it was only after a few paces more that he realized this was no fog around him but clouds. Dreamstuff ran rich here, a virginal flood of energy surging past, pooling in pockets, swirling in eddies. Seere wasn't exaggerating. This place was truly unspoiled, save for the corruption that no doubt rotted at its center.

It wasn't but a few steps more before he saw the first stones of the forgotten city. They were well worn and battered by time, smooth, pockmarked with the sanded-down nicks of tools that had rusted into nothing centuries ago. Soon scattered stones began to hint at patterns, then walls, and finally structures swollen and broken apart by jungle growth. And as the mist of the clouds parted, he found himself standing in the middle of a crumbling fortress that once housed a people only time was able to conquer.

Somewhere, deep in the murk, the glowing eyes of an animal peered out at him, and a chill took to his bones.

He swallowed hard, steadied himself, and pulled the chalk from his pocket.

Colby began to draw arcane symbols on the cold, dark, antediluvian stone of a sundered domicile—each by memory, esoteric though they were. Then he outlined the entire thing with a large, perfect equilateral triangle, five feet on each side. Finally, he reached into his pocket and pulled out his salt shaker. He unscrewed the cap, sprinkling it liberally over the chalk. The chalk and the salt sizzled, the triangle lighting up for a second like magnesium set ablaze.

At once the ancient city came alive, bright as day, severe shadows cast out into the glowing jungle. And there they were, a hundred devilish animals staring at him from the boughs of trees and beneath the cover of bushes. None moved; they only stared.

He was watching.

As the image burned into his eyes, Colby saw blackened mounds sprinkled across the city. Twisted, curled, charred, it was at once apparent that these were no mere mounds, but bodies, burned beyond recognition, carbonized by Hell's flames. All victims of Flauros's wrath, trophies left out with no wall to hang on, their message crystal clear.

Colby stepped forward, his arms spread wide, palms to the heavens, and once again he belted out a flurry of unrepeatable demonic jargon. The triangle grew bright, a thousand megawatt spotlight pointed straight down into it, not a single ray spilling past the chalk. Then he yelled, "Flauros, I summon thee. Appear and speak."

And then the form appeared—a shadow at first, melting into place. A man, hunched over, long Herculean arms, sharpened claws dancing at the end of wispy fingers. Fur, black and sleek, gray leopard spots flaring out from its chest along its back. A cat's face, pointed ears, whiskers, a snout laced with razor fangs. Flauros, the Leopard, scowled, his eyes lighting on fire, the lambent flames burning cold, trickling toward the sky.

"You chose me," he said, his voice heavy, proud, the notes lingering on the air.

"I did," said Colby.

Flauros looked down at the triangle, then cast a sneering grin back at Colby. "I don't suppose that we could do away with the formalities?"

"The triangle?"

"Yes."

"Not on your life."

The demon nodded, the flames of his eyes dimming to a febrile smolder. He leered at the jungle around him and with a nod sent the beasts scampering silently back into the dark.

Flauros cracked his neck, adjusted his posture. He no longer hunched, but stood, dignified, like a visiting professor at a symposium, a poised hand tickling the fur of his chest. "I've waited a long time for this conversation," he said. "You were due."

Colby shook his head. "Let's get on with this. I have a long night ahead of me."

"The longest. But that's not how this works. *You* summoned *me*. You have entered a bargain for my boon. My boons, my rules. You should know this."

"I was hoping we could skip all that."

Flauros turned, wagging a disapproving academic finger. Though his visage was terrible and alien, his expression was statesmanlike, majestic, profoundly arrogant. "We could skip all that, I guess, if you were to erase a corner of this triangle and let me walk out, so we could talk as men. I mean, if we're skipping things."

"You know I can't do that."

"No, I know you *won't* do that. So we're going to talk until I'm satisfied."

"Then talk."

The demon's leopard snout curled back into a wicked smile, daggerlike fangs piercing through the snarl. "Once, not so long ago, you sat atop a tower with Bertrand, the angel."

"You know Bertrand?"

"I know all of the fallen. It is my task to keep track of them. To bring those worthy into the fold of Hell."

"That's not Bertrand."

"No. He has too much pride, even for Hell."

"What about him?" asked Colby.

"What, indeed. He spoke to you, at length, about sacrifice. Selflessness."

"Yeah."

"And I'm here now to undo the damage of that night."

"And just how do you plan on doing that?"

Flauros looked down at the chalk triangle keeping him in check. "By telling you the truth about him. He told you he jumped, didn't he?"

"He implied it."

"He only thinks he jumped. It's why he can't go back. Bertrand questioned his plan. He questioned the way things worked. And he thought, if he jumped, he could do more good down here, on the ground, in the thick of it, than he could elsewhere. But it was pride. From the beginning, it was pride. He stepped to the edge to jump only instead to fall. All because he thought he knew better. And once he was here, he couldn't find his way back, because he never realized it was his pride chaining him here. At any moment he could free himself, fall onto his knees, and cry out to the heavens, begging for forgiveness, forgiving himself. But his pride looms so large, that its shadow keeps him from ever seeing it.

"Now he's spent too much time down here. Clouded his mind with too much drink. This world, the physical world, it takes its toll on you if you let it. You begin to become part of its chaos, its mundanities. You forget the things of the spirit and worry only about those you can see, touch. And that's what he did. He began to see the world from this point of view and lost sight of what real morality is."

"And that is?"

"Perspective."

"That's not exactly news."

"Oh, but it is. You see, Bertrand explains goodness as if it is a single point on a line. Black on one end, white on the other. In the middle are the things you paint gray."

"You're not wowing me here, demon. Come to your point or—"

"There is no gray, Colby. That's the point. It's a flawed model. The idea that ethics and morality can be summed up two dimensionally, as a binary system riddled with aberrations, is primitive. The aberrations are the proof that the model doesn't work. Morality isn't a line; it is a series of spheres, beginning first at a point in the center. That point is the singular person against whom any action is made. You have to ask yourself *what is best for that person*. That decision is binary."

Colby shook his head, pursing his lips. "No. There's not always a right and a wrong."

"There is!" Flauros spoke excitedly now, eyes a searing blue flame, the passion of his point bubbling into froth. His lecture was in full swing and Colby was playing right along, ever the eager student. "The gray areas you're thinking of only happen when you flatten the spheres to a line. We leave the point now for the first sphere—the actors. Those performing the action. We have to ask now *what is best for them*? If the action against the person in the center is not in the center's best interest, it is wrong . . . from the point of view of the center. But from the sphere outside it, that decision may be what's best for them. In this case, it could be right."

"Yeah, yeah. What's right for one—"

"There's more than one sphere, Colby. There are several. The next sphere is the community. Then the state. Then the world. And just beyond that is civilization. History itself. Is an action right or wrong for the state of history? For the human race? And finally, the universe?"

"You want me to ask myself whether something is right or wrong for the universe?"

"No. The question is never whether or not something is right or wrong. It can be both right and wrong, alternating between the spheres. Something that could be inarguably just in all of the lower spheres—like caring for the sick—can be morally wrong in the wider spheres as history becomes replete with the descendants of the weak and sickly, dooming mankind to extinction for its inability to cope with its own poor selection. The question must never be about right and wrong but whose perspective we are choosing to value most. This is how so many people argue with one another with absolute certainty. It is not always because one is ignorant; it is most often because they both are. They refuse to argue and form a consensus on the perspective while they babble about the minutiae of their own.

"Bertrand was wrong because he believes that doing a thing wrong in one sphere because it is right in another can damn a man. Because Bertrand has already chosen his point in the spheres and judges them all from there. And that point is in the center. He's caught up in the idea of the individual and his pride makes that point of view unshakable. That pride has rubbed off on you. You think yourself in some sort of gray area, that your choices are somehow nebulous and murky. You weren't damned because you let in the Wild Hunt. You were damned because the point you chose to defend, which seems so right, is so wrong in all the others." Flauros paused for a moment, as if choosing his next words very carefully. "Colby, why did you save Ewan? The first time, when you were children."

"Because he was my friend."

"So you did it for yourself?"

"I did it for him."

"Did you?"

"Yes."

"Because killing an innocent child was wrong."

"Yes."

"Despite all the death and violence that surround that rescue and the subsequent massacre it led to?"

"Those things had it coming."

"They were a menace? They were going to cause more harm?"

"Exactly."

"To the community. The children of Austin. The third sphere." Flauros leaned forward as far as he could without coming into contact with the barrier of the triangle. His eyes narrowed, flames glinting, a self-satisfied smile on his face, baring his fangs once more. "Colby, you're not lost because you find yourself in the gray area; you're lost because you can't reconcile your priorities. You're scared to ask yourself who is more important because you might not like the answer. Your ethics are arbitrary. You want to be good and just. You just don't know for whom."

"And what do you know about *the good*? What, exactly, would happen if I scuffed away that triangle and let you out? Could I expect you to be good then?"

"I wouldn't kill you, Colby. I can't. We need you. However, since I have to be honest, I probably would hurt you a bit. Scare you. Get inside that head of yours and dig out some true terror just so you know who you're dealing with."

"And that's good?"

"No. But is it really bad? I have outlived empires, Colby. I watched man crawl out of the caves and erect temples to gods who were dead and forgotten before the days of Babylon. I judge my actions based on the good of the farthest spheres. I play a long game. That means, in the short run, little that I do for my own amusement has any real impact. Who cares if I consume the soul of someone who was never going to amount to anything?" He leaned back and stroked his dark fur with his long, clawed fingers, delighting in memories. "Only others who don't matter. I can't kill you because, in the long run, that might actually be bad. At least until you've served your purpose. So I stay my more loathsome desires for the Seventy-two, because we, ultimately, serve a purpose of our own. One far greater than yours. And what's good for me, and good for my fellow fallen angels, is that you see this night through. No matter how much I would enjoy tearing you apart and feasting on your innards."

"Do you feel better? Getting that off your chest?"

"Hardly. You're not listening. You're just waiting for me to spin myself out so you can ask me what we both know you're going to ask me, without caring that I might be preparing you for the weight of your decision."

"Is that right?"

"Yes."

"Then what am I going to ask you?"

"The same thing every sorcerer of your ilk asks for. The one reason to summon me over all the other demons you could have asked for. You want my one great boon. You want my rain of fire."

"I don't."

"Oh, but you do. I can do it. Just say the words and fire will rain from the heavens upon those who have wronged you, those who stand against you now. I may not be able to bring my holocaust upon the girl making her way here, but the shadows she brings with her? The beasts in her legion? All gone in a single gout of flame. But why stop there? The Limestone Kingdom is full of those who deserve to roast alive."

"No. That's not why you're here."

"You can smell it, can't you? The scent of their immolation. You can hear the sound of their wings popping as they curl into ash. The sound of their terrified, confused screams. That's my favorite part. Make no mistake. What you ask me to do, I do willingly. Have me collect their souls, Colby. Say the words."

"No," said Colby, shaking his head defiantly.

"Say the words. Tell me what to do."

"Okay. Great Duke Flauros, master of thirty-six legions, bearer of the rain of fire. I ask of you a boon, your offering in exchange for one of the souls of the five dukes."

"I agree to this bargain. What is it you would have me do?"

"Bestow upon me the gift of an iron will, that I may see through the lies and temptations of spirits and be not by them corrupted."

Flauros's smile disappeared, the flames in his eyes smoldering with contempt. "That's not the bargain."

"But it is. We have a deal. And you, as I understand it, have more than one boon to bestow. Do you not?"

"I do," he growled.

"Then please, spirit, grant me the boon."

Flauros took a step back, unballing his fists, the slow, deliberate smile of understanding creeping back into place. "Ahhhh. You are indeed craftier than anyone has given you credit for, boy. I see what you're doing. You face five spirits, and you hope a protection from their lies and temptations will see you through to their more powerful gifts. Clever."

"Sometimes it's wiser to pick up a shield before bothering with the sword."

"Yes. Yes it is! Then I grant you this boon. It will do little to help you against some of my brothers. I might be among the most frightening of them, but some of them don't need lies or temptations to twist you apart."

Flauros held his right hand open, brought it to his lips, kissing his fingers lightly. Then he held out his hand and spoke with bone-rattling tones in a language far older than civilization, sharp consonants like the wet hiss of a knife going into a stomach. Colby's skin prickled, a blistering cold washing over him, his heart pounding, his blood thickening to ice. His head grew cloudy, vision fuzzy, every muscle in his body trembling. He doubled over, shivering on the ground, grunting against a sudden flu, his whole body rejecting the magic at once.

Colby threw up, chest heaving, blood vessels in his eyes bursting. He screamed and the ground shook.

And then it passed.

Everything became clearer, the intentions of the demon before him crystallizing in his thoughts. This was the boon Flauros was most frightened he would ask for. Had he chosen the fire, that meant Colby was as weak and easily manipulated as most. But if he chose an immunity from deceit, it meant he was much more of a wild card.

But the demon hadn't lied. He couldn't. Not in the triangle. He honestly believed Colby to be weak-willed, filled with anger, and absolutely out of control. With that one decision, everything changed. Colby, it would appear, was something else entirely. And now Flauros would tell his brothers what was coming for them.

Colby rose to his feet, his blood pumping again, heart no longer struggling in his chest. The air had returned to normal, the boon's only lingering remnants a cold layer of sweat pooling on Colby's brow.

"Thank you, demon. Our deal is struck. I will release your friend."

Flauros nodded, the flames in his eyes fading. "You know what happens if you don't?"

"I do."

"Then, for your sake, I hope you keep your end of the bargain." Then he winked away with a puff of smoke and the bitter stench of brimstone, leaving Colby alone in the dark, terrible jungle.

CHAPTER 46

MEATPUPPET

Wade Looes was no more, but the kutji that was the shadow of Wade Looes very much still was. And while it didn't remember all the details of Wade's sad and unfulfilled life, it remembered very well how much he loved his daughter, which was very much indeed. It also remembered that he had done something very, very bad to her. Wade couldn't remember what, exactly, but it felt an overwhelming sense of guilt about it. Self-loathing. Despair. Anger. And it knew that, above all, it had to set things right.

So when Wade's daughter came and asked it to make the long journey alone, across Arnhem Land, to bring something back to her, it did not question; it simply did as she asked. For some reason it didn't quite understand, all of the other kutji had promised never to go there. But Wade hadn't. So it fell upon it and it alone to trek across the untamed wilderness to bring back the barely breathing corpse of Kaycee Looes.

The forest was still, dead quiet despite the life teeming throughout. No insects chirped, no cane toads croaked, everything dug well into their holes and hollows or instead wallowed in the mud. It was as if the swamps had been cleared of every living thing, the eerie calm unsettling, dreamlike. Mist rose up off the billabongs like a ghostly militia setting the charge, the forest beginning to take on the night's chill. The kutji Wade Looes had no idea that it was him they were afraid of.

Having flown most of the way, it now crept through the muck and mud, staying in the shadows cast by trees in the moonlight, darting out only long enough to find another. As he drew closer to the outskirts of the small village, he crept slower and slower. There was a Clever Man here, possibly even a powerful one, and if Clever Man saw it, it was cooked. It had to get the body. It could not let its daughter down. Not again. Not ever again.

At the outskirts of the tree line, it saw what it was looking for. The house, just as she had described it, silhouetted by the moon, towering three stories above the fresh mud. The windows were dark and the porch light off. Easy pickings. In. Out. Quick and easy.

Be like the shadow, it thought. *Be like the shadow.* Flattening itself, wafer thin, it slipped in through the crack between the door and the floor. Inside it was pitch-black and silent as the grave, the only sound the soft, distant beeping of a heart monitor. It followed the sound, slinking soundlessly through the hallway, eyes peeled for any signs of life.

The door to the room was shut, but unlocked, and the handle squeaked ever so slightly as it turned, the creaking hinges whining only that much more. The loudest sound was the heart monitor that, while set to its lowest volume, still pulsed like a sonar ping against the dead of night. *Beep. Beep. Beep.* That sound rung in its head like a hangover, fragmented memories bubbling to the surface at each one. Pounding. Aching. Scratching to get out.

The shadow crept forward, and for the first time in ten years, laid eyes upon its daughter.

Kaycee didn't look anything like it remembered. She was taller now, gaunt, frail, so much skin draped over too small a skeleton. Her eyes were open and lifeless, a feeding tube running in through her mouth, an IV dripping water into her drop by drop. A thin blue bedsheet covered her from breast to toe, and as the kutji tugged it away, it saw that it was Wade's daughter for sure.

The shadow stroked the nubs along her clubfoot, then moved up and ran its wispy claws along the trace of her cleft palate. Though older and sickly, she was still every bit as beautiful as he remembered. Memories a decade old loosed themselves from piles of misery and angst, set free to run barefoot across the tracks of its mind. Flashes of a little girl tugging his arm awake. Of holding her in his arms, eyes warm with tears, as his wife lay lifeless beside them. Of a tiny hand grasping his thumb as they walked because she was not yet big enough to slip her fingers between his.

The shadow that was Wade Looes had no heart, but its insides broke as if it had. It had to set things right. This little girl had to go home. Once and for all. It wouldn't let her down. Not again. Not ever again.

Reaching down, it pulled the feeding tube out from her mouth, pulling her jaw back as wide as it would go, then squeezed itself inside. It pulled itself as tight and as thin as it could, forcing itself, headfirst, down her throat and into her belly.

Eyes blinked. Limbs twitched. She was possessed.

The shadow of Wade Looes stared at the ceiling, skin prickling with discomfort, trying to move against years of disused muscles. The legs didn't work, the arms didn't work, the neck couldn't so much as swivel the head connected to it. Everything had atrophied. It was going to have to carry her out.

Focus. Harder. HARDER.

It spread itself thinner, worked its way into every cell of her body, lifted with all the force it could muster.

A toe twitched. Then a hand. A fist clenched. An arm jumped.

Wade dug deeper. He saw his daughter on the floor, in a puddle of her own blood, already drying in her hair and clothes. It was like electricity, a live wire of anguish.

Kaycee Looes shot upright in bed like a marionette whose strings had been suddenly jerked. Her eyes were wide but still lifeless. Her jaw dangled limply, open. She spun in the bed, legs hanging over the side, slumping out onto wobbly legs. The shadow worked each limb, pulling and tugging with the power of its own soul. *Keep thinking about her,* it thought. *Think about her.* It plumbed the depths of its own memories, birthdays and bedtimes, smiles and tears. Whatever was left. Anything it could remember it threw into the furnace of its own soul, chugging forward like a lumbering steam engine.

It worked the body across the room, missing the door entirely, slamming headfirst into the wall. Kaycee backed up. Turned. Moved forward again. The shadow was pushing the body forward as if it was working levers from the inside—every move disconnected from what it actually had to do to make it happen. Each step was a chore, painful, agonizing.

But worth it.

Into the hallway. Step. Step. Step.

It thumped into another wall.

"Oy! What the bloody—" called a voice from farther down the hall.

A tall, limber man in his early thirties appeared, a tangled mop of black hair in a T-shirt and boxers. It was Jirra, who had years before taken a blade to the arm to secure the very body now standing in the hallway before him. He was older now, rugged, wise wrinkles setting in where his youthful vigor and good looks had once been.

He looked at Kaycee, confused for a moment. Then he smiled. "Oh, you're awake."

The shadow panicked. *Shit!* "Yeah," it forced out, working the jaw and tongue as best as it could manage while managing to remain upright.

"Well, where are you off to?"

"Out."

"Well, careful out there. It's a long walk, wherever you're goin'."

The shadow gave a clumsy, instinctive wave, stomping as quickly as it could toward the door.

The man rushed past, quickly unlocked the door, held it open, a beaming smile on his lips.

This had to be a trap. *Run*, it thought. It barreled out the door, uneasy feet barely able to keep it standing. *I'm coming, darlin'. Dad's coming. I'm gonna make this right. I'm gonna make this right.* He couldn't let her down. Not again. Not ever again.

CHAPTER 47

THE SECOND
PRESSED INTO SERVICE

Yashar was right, you know," said Seere, still sitting atop his horse. "You won't make it through this. Not as you were."

"I'm doing fine so far," said Colby. The dark of the mountain still closed in around them, but he felt safer now, with the angel so close.

Seere laughed as much as he could, a stifled chuckle that came out more like a cough. "Already Flauros's words are devouring you from the inside. I can feel it, his arguments sitting on the tip of your thoughts. You're wondering if he's right. If you've just been looking at it all wrong."

"Is he?"

"The difference between angels and demons is more than just whether or not we've fallen and given ourselves over to something . . . else. Angels see morality as a simple set of laws; there is right and there is wrong. There is no room for deviation, only law. Demons, on the other hand, believe that right and wrong are based solely upon the outcome, not the act. Measuring that outcome in years or decades or even millennia creates a decidedly different set of morals. Flauros is a master of rhetoric, but he's also the bearer of Hell's fire. His philosophy is blunted by the hundreds of thousands he's charred to ash at the behest of others. A thing like that forces you to distance yourself as far as possible. He's not wrong, but his view is . . . corrupted . . . by his need for perspective. It's the humanity in him."

"I didn't see much humanity."

"That's because you, like most of your kind, only use that word to describe your best qualities. To be fair to Flauros, you really weren't looking for what little of those he still has. When this is all over, the same might even be said about you."

Colby stared, unwavering, at the angel. "You know the gift I asked for."

"We *all* do. Even now, as we speak, my brethren are no doubt convening to decide what should best be done about you, to parse out what you might be up to. Make no mistake, when I'm done here, I too will return to their conclave and I'll have to tell them what you asked *me* for. What we discuss here is in no way said in confidence. Every word, every gesture, plays a role in your future."

"You're saying it's only going to get harder."

"No matter whom among us you choose."

"And this boon Flauros gave me—"

"Only serves to let you know you are being tempted and to resist the supernatural attempts to overcome your free will. You can see through the lies of spirits, but you still have to make your own decisions. So, with that in mind . . . who's next?"

"You."

"Me? You already have my service."

"To take me to see whichever of the Seventy-two I choose. What I need, I can only ask you for."

"And what, exactly, is that?"

"I need you to take me somewhere," said Colby. "Somewhere your brothers don't tread."

"Of course. But there were several of us that could have done that."

"Yeah. And you're the only one of the Seventy-two whom I can trust to keep me safe while I do what needs doing."

"Colby, where, exactly, are we going?"

"There is a house, in Arnhem Land, that belongs to a Clever Man where I lived for a while as a child. And I need to go there."

"But Arnhem Land is in—"

"I know where it is."

"She has the ring! If she finds us, she could bind me as she did the others."

"Even if she were still in Australia, which she isn't, she won't come near us. She won't set foot in Arnhem Land."

"How can you be so sure?"

"Because that's where her body is kept."

"It's too dangerous. I can't risk servitude again. Not for this."

"Then it's a good thing for me that you don't have a choice."

Seere looked bitterly at Colby, silently grinding his teeth.

"Are you going to make me say the words?"

Seere shook his head. "No. The less you treat me like them the better."

"Then take me there."

CHAPTER 48

THE STALE ROOM AND THE GRAVE AT THE EDGE OF THE WORLD

Buwulla, Australia, was a ramshackle little town, nestled in the marshy wastes of the Northern Territory, Aboriginal land, where only natives and those with the proper permits were allowed to travel. It was also one of the most beautiful places on earth, speckled with rocks covered in paintings older than Western civilization.

Colby slid once more off the back of the horse, having only in the blink of an eye before been in South America. He breathed deeply through his nose. Nothing quite smelled like the outback, especially Arnhem Land, the smells ancient, swampy, lived in. He looked around, singing to himself stories of the surrounding village, recognizing so much of it, far-flung memories finding their way back to the horizon of his thoughts. A broken-down truck, at least fifty years old, rusted completely through, stood exactly where he remembered it, swallowed up by spear grass, a paperbark tree growing up from the ground into the cab and out the passenger-side window that had long since shattered out. Behind it stood a farmhouse, its white paint chipped and peeling, graying weathered wood peeking out from beneath it.

The sky was a deep cerulean, a row of black clouds gathering in the distance, ready to douse the village with an afternoon thunderstorm. It was Gunumeleng, the first of the six seasons in Arnhem Land—a hot, mostly dry season broken up by regular afternoon storms. Soon, however, monsoon season would set in, flooding the region and filling the billabongs that had at this point mostly dried up for the year. Arnhem Land didn't have a "winter," but this was as close as it got to the beginning of spring.

Colby looked back over his shoulder at Seere, still astride his horse. "This is dangerous, Colby," he said. "We shouldn't spend too long here. Even if she is halfway across the world, she still commands the things of this place."

"I know. But I have to be here. It's important."

"I want my freedom returned to me. Let's get this over with."

The curtains on the kitchen window of the farmhouse peeled back, a face emerging from the black behind it. Colby's arrival had not gone unnoticed. It took only a moment before a young man emerged from the house, his skin a dark, rich coffee brown, his hair black and curly. He was only ten years Colby's senior, but walked as if he were five years younger, buoyant and carefree.

"'ey, fella," he said. "I think you've got the wrong place."

"No," said Colby. "I'm exactly where I need to be. I'm looking for the owner of that house."

The stranger threw a stiff thumb over his shoulder and smiled. "This house? The one behind me?"

"That's the one."

"Well, that's my house, eh?"

"That would make you the new Clever Man."

The stranger's smile weakened, his eyes squinting. "Yeah. I reckon it would."

"I'm looking for Mandu Merijedi. Where can I find him?"

"'Fraid you're a bit too late, fella," said the man, soberly. He smiled bigger now, as if Colby wasn't in on some joke.

"I'm sorry?"

"You're too late. Mandu's dead. Been dead for ages."

Colby stared the man straight in the eye, unshaken. He cleared his throat. "I didn't ask whether or not he was still alive. I asked you where I can find him. Do you know, or will I have to ask someone else?"

The man looked at Colby with disbelief. It was only then that he noticed Colby's red tangle of hair, the awkward shape of the nose. His eyes widened, his slackened jaw dropping slowly down into a stunned gape. "You ain't no fella. You ain't no fella at all. You're Colby Stevens."

Colby nodded silently.

"I think you better come inside, bru. I have beer. It's cold."

Colby smiled. "Now you're talking."

"But the other fella will have to stay out here."

"Other fella?"

"No spirits in the house."

Colby looked back over his shoulder once more, and Seere nodded.

"One beer," said Seere.

"You really don't know why we're here, do you?"

"I haven't the faintest."

Colby nodded. "Make yourself comfortable. We're going to be here a spell."

The inside of the farmhouse was sparsely decorated, looking very much like Colby remembered. The walls were water stained, old, tattered wallpaper curling away in spots. He walked into the house, past the door to the kitchen, and down toward a long hallway.

"Kitchen's back this way," said the man.

"I know where it is," said Colby, still walking.

Down the hallway he saw it, the old room whose memories still haunted him. The door was open, the smell of ten years of stale sweat wafting out past a well-worn door frame, paint chipped around the edges, stained at just the place Mandu would rest his hand and lean against it to look in. Inside was a bed, empty, still unmade, sheets crisp and clean on the edges, but thin and ragged where an unmoving body had slumbered for a decade. There was a chair beside the bed, cushion ragged beyond repair, and thirty-year-old medical equipment scattered about the room—a heart monitor, feeding tube, stainless steel IV tree with an empty plastic water bottle still dangling from it.

"Shit," said Colby, under his breath.

The man came up behind him, but Colby couldn't shake his gaze. "I still remember," he said, "you just sitting in that chair for hours, watching her sleep."

"I was waiting for her to wake up."

"Or die?"

"Either. I just never wanted to think about the latter."

"That's how I remember you best. Just a little fella, looking after his friend."

"How long?"

"I'm sorry?"

"How long ago did she wake up?"

"'Bout a week."

"Her muscles had to be atrophied. How did she—"

"Too right. It was the damnedest thing. Bloody body just stood up and wobbled away. Must've bumped every wall on the way out. Made a hell of a racket. Middle of the night, it was. Just wheelin' and thumpin'. Made it outside and just shuffled off like some kinda bloody zombie."

"How is that even possible?"

"Weren't her. Spirits be powerful things. Whatever took her away had an awful lot of fight in it."

"Why did you let it leave?"

The man shrugged. "Mandu said to. Said if it ever got up on its own and wanted to walk away to let it. Come on. Let's get you that beer."

Colby sat at a wobbly metal kitchen table, easily sixty years old, its lacquered top whittled down and chipped in places. The chairs were mismatched, some almost as old as the table, others decades newer but in no better condition. The man opened a rounded, avocado-green icebox, older than anything else in the kitchen, and pulled from it two, frosty, ice-cold beers.

"You don't remember me, do you?" asked the man, popping the bottle caps off on a refrigerator-mounted bottle opener.

Colby nodded, immediately trying to place him. "You're the one who set his tucker bag on fire."

The man laughed. "That'd be me. I thought I could warm up dinner without burning it. Jirra."

"I remember. You took Mandu's place?"

"Yeah," he said, mindlessly thumbing an old, thick white scar across his forearm.

"He trained you?"

"Since I was a kid, yeah. I was already mostly done when you came along, though. I'd already done my first walkabout. That's why we never got to know each other well."

"How did it happen?"

"Mandu? He said it was his time. He'd done his part, trained two great dreamspeakers."

Colby stifled a proud, sad smile. "That's very kind of him."

"More than kind. I was always just thankful he said two and not one. Including me with you was the nicest thing he ever said."

"Oh, that's not—"

"You've got your own songline, Colby. There's no need for modesty. Not here in my kitchen. I know what you did. I teach the children about you. They sing the songs. You can feign your modesty with everyone else. But in here, in this house, we both know who and what you are." Jirra raised his bottle and Colby did the same, glass clinking together. "You're gonna talk to him, ain't ya?"

Colby nodded. "I have to. There are some things I need to know."

"You're looking for something?"

"Yes."

"The little girl? The dreamwalker?"

"Information," said Colby. "About her. What do you know?"

"Only that if it were anyone else wanting to go out there after her, I'd say that fella was mad as a cut snake. But you? You might be the one thing to set her straight."

"Set her straight?"

Jirra grew a bit cold, his words hushed, his tone fearful, reverent. "She's not right. She's not been the same since you left her out there. She's one of them now. Different."

"Different how?"

"Different as in I've never stuck around long enough to find out when she come around. She'd never set foot in Arnhem. 'Fraid we might trap her soul in that body. But I saw her a few times farther south, out in the dreaming. Walking the songlines. But not singin' 'em."

"What was she doing?"

"Trappin' mostly. She'd find herself a spirit out in the wild, then set her swarm of kutji on 'em. Then she'd do business with 'em. Make 'em trade serving her in exchange for their life. Bloody ugly stuff. She's raised an army. Dreamtime's hers now. No one crosses her. Not here."

"Do you know why?"

"No. For that, you'll best be askin' Mandu."

"Take me to him."

MANDU MERIJEDI'S HEADSTONE was the ornately carved trunk of a long dead banyan tree atop the tallest hill in the area, his story carved bit by bit into the thick, fig-tree bark. Colby ran his fingers over it, noting the sheer number of tales recounted about him. There were stories here Colby hadn't thought about in a decade; others he'd never even heard.

"He carved some of that himself," said Jirra, pointing to the center-most relief: a tall man with wild hair holding the hand of a young boy.

"He knew he would be buried here?" asked Colby.

Jirra nodded. "Of course. He told me once, when I was little, that even after he died, he had one more thing to do and he needed to be here to do it. I think he just liked the view. He came up here every day for a year carving parts of that. Worked on it without anyone knowing what he was up to."

Colby smiled. "He was always a step ahead of us all."

"Still is."

"I don't doubt it." Colby looked down. There was a squared ring of painted stones marking the grave. This wasn't common at all.

Jirra pointed at them. "I didn't understand why he wanted those here until just now." He thought for a moment. "Is there anything I can get you?"

"No. I just need some time to myself." Colby raised the back of his hand to the horizon and counted the fingers between it and the sun. "We've got a little over an hour and a half until sunset. I'll just camp up here for the night."

"Of course." Jirra turned, walking back down the hill, stopping a few steps down. "Oh, one more thing," he called over his shoulder.

"Yeah?"

"Would you tell him we miss him?"

"I will."

Colby made camp, first gathering kindling and some branches for a fire, then laying a small bedroll over the grave, between the stones. He sat at the edge of the hill with Seere, neither speaking, watching the sun sink beneath the trees as the sky slowly rolled into shades of orange, rose, and violet. The world darkened and the first stars poked through. Then shadows overtook the land, blackening it completely as campfires dotted it like freckles.

There was no place like the outback at night. Not anymore. Colby hadn't realized how badly he'd missed it.

Finally, Seere spoke up. "What is it you need me to do?"

"Just keep watch. Make sure nothing disturbs my sleep."

"I don't think anything is going to come up here while I'm here."

"That was the idea."

When the world was black save for the stars and the fires, Colby crawled into his bedroll, the dirt beneath it soft, comfortable, molding to the contours of his body. He quickly, quietly, fell into a deep sleep. Mandu had thought of everything.

CHAPTER 49

THE FOOL'S GAMBIT

Tonight was lonelier than most. The Cursed and the Damned was all but empty. Bill was out hunting. Colby was in God-knows-where Australia doing God-knows-what. Even the few regulars Yashar served on the side without telling Colby were off in their homes and hollows, waiting out whatever hell was about to blow into Austin. It was just Yashar and Gossamer, each seated at a table, Yashar in one of the few functioning chairs, Gossamer perched nobly on a small wooden box, play-ing chess.

Chess was one of the few games Gossamer could play, not for lack of understanding, but because most games required thumbs.

Cards to hold, dominoes to maneuver. But with chess, Gossamer could simply call out his move, and Yashar would move the pieces for him. Colby hated chess, called it a two-dimensional game that required only memorization and punished creativity. But Yashar and Gossamer both knew the truth. Colby stunk at it.

"Pawn to e4," said Gossamer, making his opening move.

Yashar reached across the board and moved the piece, then followed by immediately placing his own pawn directly in front of Gossamer's.

"Knight to f3."

Again, Yashar moved the dog's piece. He sat for a moment mulling over his next move.

"I miss the boss."

"He's only been gone a few hours."

"I know that. I mean I miss the old boss."

Yashar passed the dog a bereaved look over his nose, his face still facing the board. "You can call him Colby."

"I like boss."

"I don't think he's coming back. Not the Colby we knew, anyway. Knight to c6."

Gossamer let out a long sigh, his head drooping below his shoulders. "Bishop to c4. Why not? Just because he's making deals?"

"No one *just* makes deals with demons, Goss. They get in your head, futz around with your insides, show you futures where you can get everything you want. You can even get it sometimes. But it comes at a cost. Everything comes at a cost with them. And it's never the price that's advertised. Pawn to d6."

"The boss is strong, though. He *might* be able to get through it all right?"

Yashar shook his head.

"Knight to c3."

"I've been on this earth too long to believe that. Colby's

cursed. It's my fault. And this is the fallout of that curse. There's no point in worrying about it. He'll be who he'll be on the other side of it."

The two stared morosely at the board, examining their next moves.

"Bishop to g4."

"Yashar, what's a familiar?"

Yashar again looked over his nose at the dog. "It's . . . it's a special relationship between a pet and his master."

"I like boss. Knight to e5."

"Between a pet and his boss."

"Boss said it was a best friend."

"It is, kind of."

"What is it really?"

"It's a magical bond. It means he can see what you can see. You can read each other's thoughts. He can weave magic through you. Bishop to d1. Bishop takes queen."

"You took my queen? Already?" Gossamer's eyes grew sad, his muzzle lowering to the board's edge.

"Yes."

"But that's my favorite piece."

"Learn to protect it better, then."

"Bishop to e7. Check."

Yashar eyed the board, looking for a way out of check.

"Why won't boss make me his familiar? That all sounds awesome."

"Because it's not all awesome."

"What's the catch?"

"Catch is that your life forces become linked. You can't ever get too far from each other. You would have had to go to Australia or else you'd both be doubled over, sick, puking your guts out. I've seen it."

"That doesn't sound too bad."

"King to e7. I told you, Goss, your life forces are linked. So if he dies . . ."

Gossamer looked up, suddenly understanding. "Oh," he said solemnly. "I would die too."

"And if something ever happened to you, he would be weakened to near death. It's a position that comes with great benefits, but terrible consequences. Colby doesn't lead a very safe life. And he loves you, Goss. Very much. He doesn't want anything to happen to you."

"Is that how you feel about Colby?"

"Every goddamned day."

"If you could take it back, would you?"

"The wish?"

"Yeah."

Yashar sat silently for a beat. "What do you mean? Do I wish he had made a different wish?"

"No. If you had to choose between Colby's wish and the wish of another child, which would you choose?"

"I don't know. I've thought about that every day for nearly fifteen years now and I still don't know. Every time I sleep, I dream about it. I had a dream once, seven years ago, in which I granted a wish to a different child. It was a wonderful dream. Everything was just how it used to be. The kid's wish was simple, didn't end so badly, and we went about life happy, not involved with . . ." He waved around the bar. "Any of this. But then, what I assume was about a year or so into the dream, I remembered Colby. And he showed up in the dream. I saw him living his life. Normal. Bored. Working behind the counter of some retail chain. I have no idea what he was selling. But I missed him. I missed him so badly. So I talked to him. And he didn't know me. I tried to tell him that we knew each other, but he didn't believe a word of it. And for the rest of the dream, I was miserable. I went about the various unbelievable adventures I have in those dreams and couldn't enjoy a one of them because Colby wasn't there.

"So what would I do, given the choice? Would I spare my friend a lifetime of fear and suffering and damnation? Or would I put him through all that just so I wouldn't be so lonely? I'd like to think that I would be unselfish. I'd like to think that, but all evidence is to the contrary. Does that answer your question?"

"Yeah," said Gossamer. "Knight to d5. Checkmate."

Yashar cast his eyes down incredulously, thinking for a moment that the dog had no idea what he was doing. And he saw it. Checkmate. "Wait! That's the fool's gambit. With a queen sacrifice! Where did you learn that?"

Gossamer's tail wagged furiously, his mouth dropping open with a panting smile. "Learn to protect your queen better, you said. You said that. You mocked me."

"You just sharked me."

"I did."

"You son of a bitch."

"Don't . . ."

"Dog joke."

"That only works on Colby."

"What's good for the goose . . ."

Yashar could feel the doors opening, the metal outer door closing with a slam, the inner door popping open with a WHOOSH. He wasn't expecting anyone, but he wasn't expecting trouble either.

Half a dozen kutji flooded in through the door, their stubby malformed bodies skittering across the floor, scampering up the walls, scooting across the bar. Yashar pushed his seat back slowly, its legs grinding against the concrete.

"Goss," he said beneath his breath. "If I say run, you fucking run."

"I'm not leaving you."

"This is no time for loyalty."

"Screw you. This is exactly the time for loyalty."

"Yashar," hissed the kutji standing tallest atop the bar. "It's my understanding that this place is under new management."

"It is. So get the fuck out of my bar."

"No," it said, hopping down, striding confidently toward the djinn. "I mean it's under new management now." The kutji held out both of his hands, waving to the bar. "This place is ours."

"Like hell it is," said Gossamer, fur bristling, growling deep, as if he was ready to snap at the closest hand.

"Goss," said Yashar. "Ease back."

"This place is ours."

"Not anymore it isn't," said Yashar. "Live to fight another day, my friend."

"Is that all it takes to own a bar? You just walk in and take it?"

The kutji smiled wickedly, teeth pointing every which way out from his black gums. "Sometimes," it said. "Sometimes."

Yashar stood up slowly, waving for Gossamer to follow him. "It's all yours." The two then backed away toward the door, Yashar spinning slowly as they did, trying to keep an eye on all the kutji at once. A single kutji stood between them and the door, for a moment refusing to yield. But as Yashar cautiously closed the distance, he moved, holding the door open for the two.

Yashar gave one last, longing look at the bar, drinking in the sweet nostalgia, took a deep breath, and then stepped outside.

Crows lined the alley, a single kutji in demihuman form standing ten feet from the door. Yashar and Gossamer stopped dead in their tracks. They looked around, saw they were surrounded. Gossamer squatted low, tail back, teeth bared, growling.

"You the guys here to kill me?" asked Yashar, inching ever closer to his companion.

The kutji nodded.

"You doing this because you want to? Or because you have to?"

"What's the difference?" asked the kutji, balling up both of his fists.

"Difference is in how many of you I kill before we call it a night."

The crows all squawked at once, angry, beating their wings against their sides, shaking their feathers while strutting on their perches.

"Oh, you like that, huh?" yelled Yashar over the sound. "I'll ask you again! You doing this because you want to or because you have to?"

"Kill him," said the kutji.

At once the birds took to the air, their speed faster than Yashar imagined, diving toward him and Gossamer.

"Shit!" Yashar picked up Gossamer by his belly, hoisting him awkwardly in the air, then spun, pulling himself tight, vanishing into thin air. The birds swarmed in, finding nothing, some slamming into the wall, others the door—none striking home.

"Where is he?" screamed one of the kutji, shifting back from crow to man.

"He's gone," said another.

"Well, spread out. Find them."

"It's too late," said yet another, sniffing the air. "They're gone."

"What now?"

The lead kutji from inside leaned out of the door, dangling on the knob. "We make sure he doesn't come back. We make sure he gets the message. Everybody inside."

The last of the crows shifted immediately, pouring inside the building. They leaped up on the tables and up on top of the bar. One swung back and forth on the single dangling bulb as if it were a jungle vine. The largest of them began tossing bottles against the wall, pouring liquor over the bartop. "Help me," it said to the others.

In a flash, every bottle in the bar was shattering against any and every surface there was. Every bottle but one. The last bottle of Old Scraps's special reserve. The largest kutji held that bottle in one hand, stuffing a rag in it with the other. Then he picked up a lighter from behind the bar, lit the rag, and screamed, "Everybody out!"

Then he threw the bottle against the bar and the whole place went up in flames.

CHAPTER 50

DREAMSPEAKER

He awoke, a fire crackling beside him, a shadow standing silently at the edge of its light.

Colby sat up, smiling. "Hello, Mandu."

The shadow walked slowly around the fire, a large walking stick preceding it step by step.

Mandu Merijedi looked only vaguely as Colby remembered him, the creases in his face deep from years in the sun, his hair no longer salt and pepper, but fully bleached white with age. His eyes were milky with cataracts, tired, iris and pupil fading into the whites as if he were blind. His teeth gleamed in the firelight, his smile warmer than the blaze.

"Hello, child," he said, his voice darkened, affected by the grave. There was an echo to it, a hollowness, as if he was calling through a cave, recorded, then played back through an old speaker, static and all.

"It's been a long time."

"No, it hasn't. Long for you because you're young. The young always think such a short time is forever. You don't understand forever. Not yet."

Colby nodded. "You're right. I don't understand it."

Mandu laughed, each *ha* trailing off into the night like distant fireworks. "Of course I'm right. That's why you came all this way to speak to a dead man."

"Thank you for waiting for me."

"I had no choice. You were always going to come here and call on me. I just knew in advance."

"I'm sorry."

"No need to apologize. Ain't upset. No need being upset with the inevitable. I might sooner be angry that things fall down instead of up or that rain also darkens the sky. It is how things were meant to be." He paused and beheld the stars as if he hadn't seen them in years. "You're here about the girl," he said, still staring at them.

"Yes. The dreamwalker. Kaycee."

"That's not her name anymore. But don't worry. She'll find you."

"That's what I'm afraid of."

"How did you get here?" Mandu's gaze wandered down from the sky, looking Colby straight in the eye.

"A powerful spirit brought me. On his horse."

Mandu shook his head. "No. Ask yourself. How did you get *here*? To this spot? Now. How did you get to now? Only when you understand what brought you to where you are can you really go farther. If you want to find your friend, you need to retrace your steps. Walk the path you walked as a child. Sing the song of your deeds, walk the songline to the last place you saw her. But do not sing it wrong or you will unsing creation. You will unsing your own story. Remember, Colby, the past is the past. If we try and change it, we only change ourselves."

"You want me to walk my songline?"

"I want to rest. You, you want to remember. Because you want to find your friend. She needs you. To fulfill her destiny and free herself from what ails her, what binds her, she needs you. This was the destiny she has so long pined for and it is so close. You cannot let her down now."

"Is that it? Is that all I have to do?"

Mandu laughed again, this time more heartily than before, though it still chilled Colby to the bone. "No. That's not it. That's just the beginning."

"Tell me. Tell me everything."

"I don't know everything. The spirits only show so much."

"That's damned inconvenient."

"Destinies are fulfilled best by people trying to avoid them. They are not carved into the earth like mountains, but are like water in a billabong. Knowing a destiny is like knowing where the water will go when it rains. You know the water will be there. But you cannot tell the sky to put the water there. You cannot tell it when. You just have to let it. You can carve the earth out yourself, make rivers and reservoirs, guide the water away. And destiny becomes different. But why would you? You want the water in the billabong. Because it will bring the animals that will feed the people. You must think back on your song, you must be the rain. It will fill the billabong. It will bring the animals. It will feed the people.

"I have been given the opportunity to stand back and see history as one might see the land from this hill. It is all laid out. And it was my job to protect it. To sing of it. To be its custodian. I did that. And now that is Jirra's job. And I can rest."

Colby eyed the spirit knowingly. "You're already at rest, aren't you? This is just an echo."

Mandu nodded, waved his arm around the dark of the dream. "Dreams are the one place the spirits cannot hear us."

"You knew that I would need to hear this and that I wouldn't be alone."

"I was wrong to not want to teach you, especially when you learn so well."

"You never wanted to teach me?"

"White fellas don't learn the dream so good. But when a great spirit of the desert comes with the wind and brings you a child, saying, 'Teach him the old ways,' you do not question him. This is proof. The spirits were right to bring you to me. We come from the clay; we return to the clay. It is how it is supposed to be. Over time, the world changes. We can do little about that. But getting to take part, no matter how small, in a great story of such changes? Getting to leave something behind, whether given credit or not, is the greatest gift. I have that now. So thank you."

"I haven't changed anything. Certainly not the world."

"Your wish changed everything, Colby. Changed the order of things. I don't know how it works, or what the dream behind it is doing, but whatever it did, very powerful spirits took an interest in you. They set about changin' the path of your life to get you where they wanted you to be. My spirit had me do the things I did to get you here, to this moment, because he said the choice you make here, at this point in your life, is the one that decides not only who you become, but what becomes of the world. The fate of all the dream rests in your hands. Do you remember the story of the orphan who cried awake the Rainbow Serpent?"

"Yeah. Are you saying I'm the orphan?"

"You were, once, before you made that bloody wish. But then you became the serpent."

"Wait, what?"

"The serpent was just hungry. Been asleep a long time. To him, the people were nothin' but tucker. He never knew how big he was, that his body carved rivers in the earth. Never knew that his very dreams would dream the world awake. That's you. That's you now. In your story, the orphan becomes the serpent. Dreams the world anew."

"I don't even know how that's possible. I'm not that powerful."

"That's the other part of the story. The moral for everyone else. Small people change the world. Bring down great monsters."

"How do I bring this one down?"

"The dreamwalker?"

"Yeah."

"You cut her cord. Severed the link between her spirit and her body."

Colby glared at Mandu. "You tricked me into doing that."

"Too right!"

"Why? Why did you let me think I did that?"

"Because of how you felt after you did it. I didn't understand it at first either. My spirit told me this must be done and I trusted my spirit. But then I saw how you watched over her as she slept; how your guilt made you more conscious of how you used your power. When I met you, you were a boy unafraid to throw magic around, to rob the world of its dream to solve your problems. Now you are a man who hesitates before acting, thinks about the consequences of his actions, protects the dream where he can. Even when you kill a thing, you give its dream back to the world. That's why you had to believe."

"It was another damn lesson?"

"They're all lessons, fella. Everything is a lesson in this life. Even the small things."

"I cut her cord to learn a lesson?"

"Her cord was cut because it had to be. She could not become who she is now if it hadn't been. And this is who she was always meant to be. The reason you did it was to learn a lesson."

"So why did it have to be cut?"

"Because, if her body dies—"

"She dies. I know. That's not an answer."

"That body was not her destiny. She was meant for the world of dreams, not the one of her body. But what if someone were to *disbelieve* her body? Will it away?"

"She would be disbelieved with it. Right?"

"Yes. Unless . . ." Mandu looked across the fire, waiting for Colby to get it.

"Unless . . . ?" Colby's eyes shot wide. "Unless some other spirit had made her body its home."

"Too right again!"

"Then I wouldn't be disbelieving her, I would be disbelieving something else. Is that right?"

"A dreamwalker whose body is taken by another spirit is condemned to walk forever as a spirit."

"She'd be immortal. A spirit. Forever."

"Just as she always dreamed. To walk in the dream forever."

"That's why she's coming for me."

"Partly."

"Is the other part revenge?"

Mandu shook his head. "Those spirits, her kutji. She's as much their slave as they are hers. When she dies, she too will be kutji. She won't remember all of who she is. Only the strongest parts. And the parts strongest in her right now are her anger and her fear. The kutji want her dead. They'll betray her given the chance, if it doesn't break with their business."

"She doesn't just *want* me to give her her immortality. She needs me to."

"Desperation is dangerous, especially with a spirit so strong as hers."

"Why didn't she just ask?"

"Maybe she doesn't think she can. Would you trust the boy who left you in the desert with your nightmares?"

"But I didn't!"

Mandu looked sadly across the fire. "No. I did. And if you don't do this right, I'll have sacrificed a friend for nothing. Her ending doesn't have to be tragic. And no thing worth havin' isn't worth a little suffering for. Give her what she wants, Colby."

"I don't know that I can."

"I hope for all our sakes that you can figure out how. But it won't be easy. Not with what's happening even now."

"What's happening now?"

"You'll see. It'll change everything."

"Shit."

"Yes."

"What do I do?"

"Remember the fish. Do not stab or bait one at a time when you can fish the whole pond at once with a little preparation. You'll know what that means when the time comes." Mandu looked up at the stars once more. "It's time."

"Oh, Jirra asked me to—"

"Tell him I miss him too."

"I'll miss you, Mandu."

Mandu smiled. "Most Clever Men only ever get to teach one other Clever Man. I got to teach three. All very clever. Very clever."

"Three?"

"Yes, three. You, Jirra, and Kaycee." Mandu stepped back toward the shadows then stopped. "Oh, I almost forgot. One more thing."

"What?"

"Wake up."

CHAPTER 51

AS SHADOWS FADE

Meanwhile, as Colby slept beneath the stars of an Australian sky, the skies above Austin had grown unexpectedly stormy. Clouds moved quickly, thunder rumbling without a flash of lightning to betray its origins. A sharp, cold wind blasted the streets, stripping the leaves off trees, dropping the temperature a good thirty degrees in the span of an hour. Winter was setting in and this front was its announcement. Below, a single figure strode flamboyantly, his pace quickening against the storm.

Aaron Brandon strolled down the street as if he was on top of the world. He felt virile, pumped, his parts still tingling. It had taken all night and fifty dollars' worth of drinks to ply that girl out of her panties, and she could barely stand up by the time he had. After he'd finished, she could barely slur out her own name, let alone remember his. Last he saw her, she was still slumped in the alley, all but passed out in his juices, muttering something like, "Wait, where are you going?" before mumbling herself to sleep.

Aaron Brandon was a douchebag. A proud douchebag. All muscles, tribal tattoos, and twenty-four-karat gold. And he was of the decided opinion that if she remembered tonight at all, it would be a blessing to that girl—a memory she would cherish of the time she'd made it with a real man. After all, she was only a six, and sixes were lucky to get it at all from anything but neck-beard IT rats and balding men ten years their senior. She was lucky if she ever got anything close to him again. And now he was off to one of his favorite off-Sixth-Street dives to see if he could catch himself a closing-time loner for round two and a ride home.

Bill the Shadow stood in the darkest corner of the alley between two downtown buildings, just out of reach of the streetlamp up the block. He hated Aaron already. He'd seen him before, trolling the downtown bars for easy tail, and had earmarked him for a last-minute substitution on a light night. Usually Bill preferred darker souls than this—violent souls—but pickings were slim, he was hungry, and Aaron had it coming. The man was human trash, a worthless sperm machine pumping out mediocre sex in three-minute bursts to women who could barely tell what was going on around them.

It was an odd treat, drinking one of those. As big and badass as they might seem, they didn't really understand their own darkness. They didn't regard their own sins as anything of the sort. There was no remorse lurking in their gut. Only entitlement. But Bill loved destroying entitlement.

He crept behind him, keeping a safe distance, occasionally

scuffing the pavement with his boot heel before darting into nearby shadow. Aaron was just drunk enough to be slow, but not so much that he didn't pick up on the sounds.

Aaron repeatedly turned around, hearing the scuff, seeing a flash of dark out of the corner of his eye, a smudgy blur that vanished a second later, wondering if he was jumping at the sound of his own footfalls. By the third time, he began to grow anxious.

"Who the fuck?" he shouted the fourth time he heard it, chest puffed out, fists clenched, arms flexing like the hero on the cover of some old video game. "I will beat the fuck out of you. Who's out there?"

A cigarette lit up in a deep shadow, the cherry peering out like a single tiny light in the brooding dark.

Aaron stormed over, brow furrowed and furious. "You homeless fuck. I will kick you until you piss bl—"

There was nothing in the shadow. Not even a cigarette. He looked around. Nothing. The streets were empty. There was a slight wind coming in off the river, the only sound a paper dancing across the street in the breeze.

"What the—"

Then he saw something. A shadow moving. A man, standing against a wall. Wide hat. Long coat. Aaron was shitting bricks now. That man wasn't there before. And the more he looked at him, the less it looked like a man at all. *Was it the shadow of a pole? An overhang?*

He took a step closer, looking both ways despite there not being a single car.

"Hey! You!"

The shadow didn't move. He raised his arm, fist above his head as if he had a hammer of some sort in it, ready to bring it down.

"I said *you*!"

Still nothing.

"Shit."

Then he doubled over, vomiting into the street, spewing forth a thick spray of green and brown. Then just brown. Then brown and red. Then red and only red. He fell to his knees throwing up blood, his orange tan going pale white, the blood vessels in his eyes bursting purple from the heaves. Veins spider-webbed around his sockets, his eyes thick with tears.

The vomiting stopped and Aaron began to choke. He clutched his throat. Pounded himself in the stomach. Tried to swallow. But his mouth wouldn't shut. His jaw gaped wide, wider than it should, then it broke, snapping out of place. Aaron tried to scream, his head tilted all the way back on his neck, but nothing came out. Just muffled awfulness. Whimpers. Choked pleading.

Two small black hands, neither quite the same size, clawed at the corners of his mouth, breeching a shadowy head out of the unhinged jaw. Then eyes followed. Then a large, square mouth. Within seconds a full-size kutji was squeezing its way up through his throat and out into the street.

Aaron died right there, collapsing, head smacking limply on the pavement, the kutji scraping his blood and vomit from itself in thick handfuls.

Bill emerged from his spot against the wall, bitter, ready for a fight. "Seems you're a long way from home, hombre."

The kutji nodded. "A long way. But in the right place."

"I'm not so sure about that."

Then came the beating of wings, the sound of scurrying in nearby alleys. Bill took a step back, eyeing the street as over a dozen shadows emerged from the dark spaces of the city or out from the night sky. They surrounded him silently in a semicircle.

"Aw, hell. This is gonna be one of those nights, isn't it?"

"Actually," said the lead kutji, still shaking the last remaining bits of Aaron from his body, "it's going to be *that* night."

"Oh, I wouldn't go that far, chief. It's going to take more than a dozen of you to scare me."

"We're not here to scare you. We're here to kill you."

"So it is going to be one of those nights." Bill sighed deeply. "All right. Let's get this over with. I'm starving and there's not a whole lot of night left." Bill adjusted his hat, sliding it back on his head as he took one last drag off his cigarette. He popped his back, cracked his neck, pitched the butt, then growled.

He spat out a sudden cloud of fog as the kutji swarmed toward him. Bill ducked and weaved, the diminutive shadows grasping at him and catching nothing but empty air. One grabbed for his leg but he lifted it in time for the kutji to slip right beneath him as Bill brushed his jacket back like a matador. Then he snuck away, loitering on the outskirts of the cloud, listening as the miscreant mob swore, flailing about to find him.

Bill skulked quietly in the dense mist, his mouth yawning wide, more fog pouring into the streets by the second. Then came the flutter of wings, like an entire flock taking flight at once, their wing beats trailing off into the sky. There were no more scuffs or scuttles, no twitters or chitters. It sounded as if the streets were empty, fog drifting alone, transformers overhead buzzing loudly on their poles from the moisture. It was clear to Bill, however, that this was far from the end of his ordeal.

That's when the thunder rumbled directly overhead.

The wind kicked up and thick drops of rain began to pound the pavement. A stiff gust blew, wiping the fog away from the street like a drawn curtain. And there, standing dead center, stood a tall, time-ravaged man, on fire from top to bottom, flames licking the air around him. The Holocaust Man.

"Hello, Bill," said the demon, his voice deeper and more menacing than Bill imagined.

"I'm getting the distinct impression that this isn't about me," said Bill.

Amy shook his head, smiling a lipless grin, teeth charred black. Spatters of rain slopped steadily around them.

"I don't have a dog in this fight, and if I don't have a dog in this fight, why are we here?"

"Because you do have a dog in this fight," said Amy. "And that dog thinks he can get the better of us. He doesn't want to kill the girl. He has to; he just doesn't know it yet."

"So he's supposed to think that she did this."

"He will think she did this."

"That's a pretty shitty reason to die."

"They're all shit reasons to die, Bill, in the end."

"I couldn't agree more."

The rain stopped, the clouds bursting away, falling to earth in the shape of crows. They soared down, landing on buildings, lampposts, and awnings, watching like a circle of schoolkids, cheering with squawks and caws. Bill looked around at the mess he found himself in. Amy tapped his foot impatiently, the tinny, hollow sound echoing through the empty streets.

"I thought you lot had lost all these," said Bill.

"Most. Not all. The rumors of the Queen's utter domination of her lands are just that."

"Well, I reckon you know that I won't go down easy."

"It wouldn't look real if you did."

Bill nodded, turning into a blob of shadow, flinging himself at Amy faster than Amy could react, bowling him over, knocking him to the ground. Re-forming, Bill towered above him, punching him in the face over and over, a foot on his chest to keep him down, his fists sizzling against the flames.

Amy reached out, grasping wildly for Bill.

Bill grabbed both sides of Amy's face, grabbing him by the ears, staring deep into his eyes, Bill's foot still standing right on top of him, mouth wide to swallow his soul. But nothing came.

He breathed deeper, trying to suck something out of the man beneath him, but there was nothing there. Just a hollow shell brimming with hate. The Holocaust Man stared back at Bill, deep into the dark recesses of the boggart.

"What the hell?" mumbled Bill.

Amy flared up, blazing as if he'd been doused suddenly with gasoline, burning away the shadows surrounding Bill. The boggart was entirely illuminated. There was no flesh that Bill concealed in his darkness; he was entirely hollow, his features floating in what was ordinarily murk. Now he was naked, small bits of face and hands suspended in the air by forces unseen.

Amy laughed. "I see you for what you are, Bill. And there's nothing to you after all." Then the Holocaust Man exploded.

Bill was blasted backward, far across the street, slamming against a building some two stories up. He fell immediately to the ground, face-first, weakened, trying to re-form his shadows.

Bill coughed, spitting a bit of his soul out like phlegm, then rolled over on his back.

Amy's fires died down and he looked once again like he had. He hopped to his feet, almost skipping on his way over to Bill. "It's a shame it had to be like this," he said. "But it did have to be like this. Sometimes the friends we keep are the source of our own undoing."

He plunged a fiery fist into Bill's chest, incinerating his insides.

Bill looked up at the clear sky, the clouds having cleared away with the kutji, the stars starting to grow fuzzy. He reached into his pocket, pulled out a cigarette, and put it in his mouth before fumbling with the lighter. His fingers were fading and the Zippo clanged behind his ear as it slipped out of them.

Amy leaned down, touching the end of the cigarette with a single smoldering finger.

Bill inhaled deeply, lighting it, then exhaled without pulling the butt from his lips, and died, the cigarette going limp over his chin.

Crows descended, the murder flooding the corpse, picking at the shadows with their shiny black beaks. They tore him away in chunks, swallowing Bill bit by bit as the shadows around him began to fade, light creeping in from streetlamps. Within seconds he was gone. Only his coat, hat, and lighter remained.

CHAPTER 52

WINTER OF DISCONTENT

Winter in Austin is brown and yellow, white being something most Texans only dream of. In the odd years, when the rains run long and heavy, late into the season, the grass and trees will stay green well into December. But even then the cold snaps come to chase the green away. The trees turn yellow first, then brown up slowly over the course of weeks. The grass goes yellow almost right away.

Winter is heralded by the day the first strong winds come and wipe the trees of all their leaves over the course of a single night. Then, from that point on, it becomes the long, lingering, earth-tone trod toward springtime, the nights chilly and crisp, but

rarely cold enough to matter. The days are just slightly warmer.
Winter. In all its sudden, spectacular glory.

It was winter again, and Colby Stevens felt the way the city
looked. Haggard, raw, tired, stripped bare. All the mistakes, the
worn cracked surface, exposed, covered in prickly stubble. Just
a few nights before, it was a nice, brisk autumn. Now the city
was in its winter slumber, ugly as it got.

He stood before the smoldering remains of the Cursed and
the Damned and he felt his heart breaking. Yellow tape marked
the area off that, along with swollen puddles, stood as the only
proof the fire department had been there. Moments before, he
thought he'd had it all figured out, that he was thinking steps
ahead of everyone, that he was somehow playing their game
better than they could. And now his arrogance was out in the
open and he wondered just how deep in trouble he had really
gotten himself this time.

Seere stood behind him, his expression almost as solemn as
Colby's. "There's no one in there."

"I know," said Colby, unable to feel the spirits of his friends,
dead or otherwise. "Do you know where they are?"

"Your friends?"

"Yes."

"I do."

"Are they all right?"

"They appear to be."

"Take me there."

COLBY HOPPED OFF the back of the horse and onto the street
in front of his house.

"Call for me," said Seere, "and I'll take you to the next of
your appointments."

Colby looked up to thank him, but he was already gone,

horse and all. He took a deep breath and made his way quickly into the house.

Yashar sat on the couch. He looked up at Colby, unmoving, crestfallen.

"What the hell did you do, Colby?" he asked.

"Where's Gossamer?"

"He's under the bed. He won't come out."

Colby whistled.

Gossamer shot out from the bedroom, rounded the corner, and charged Colby, tail wagging, nuzzling between both of his legs. "Boss!" he said, ecstatic. "You're home."

"What happened?"

Gossamer and Yashar exchanged looks, neither wanting to be the one to say it.

"It was kutji," said Yashar. "A swarm of them."

"I tried to be a good dog. Tried to protect Yashar. But there were too many of them."

"It's okay, Goss. You did good. What's important is that you're both okay."

"They got the bar," said Yashar.

"I saw."

"That's not the worst of it."

"How could it get any worse?"

"Bill," said Yashar. "They killed Bill the Shadow."

Colby's heart dropped into his stomach, his jaw following soon after. His blood ran cold and it became progressively harder to breathe. He wanted to throw up. "How?"

"They tore him apart. There wasn't much left."

"Are you sure he's—"

Yashar reached beside him on the couch, pulling from it Bill's coat and hat. "Yes."

Colby walked over, took the coat and hat into his hands,

eyes misting as he examined them. He knew every fold, every contour. There was no dreamstuff left here, only djang—the etched-in power of who he was. "These are burned," he said, chalky black residue wiping off onto his hands.

"So was the bar," said Yashar.

"They're sending a message," said Gossamer.

"I shouldn't have left."

"No," said Yashar. "You shouldn't have. Did you at least find what you were looking for?"

Colby nodded. "I did."

"And?"

"I know what she's doing. Why she's coming for me."

"What are we going to do?"

"We're going to find her and we're going to kill her for this."

"Are you sure?" asked Yashar.

"Very."

"You know you'll have to do it without me, right?"

Colby glared at him. "I thought we were in this together."

"No," said Yashar condescendingly. "We're not. Not this time."

"What is that even supposed to mean? Are you pissed at *me*?"

"No. It's the ring, Colby. It doesn't only affect the Seventy-two. It affects us all. Every last demon and djinn. If I go near her, I'm as good as hers, and if she turns that ring on me—"

"You'd be her slave," said Colby, voice drowning in under-standing.

"That's not what scares me," said Yashar. "We're all some-body's slave, whether we want to think about it like that or not. I've been through worse than serving someone like her. What scares me is that she might force me to kill you. Or you me."

"Oh, Jesus."

"Yeah. Are you ready to have that fight? Because I'm not."

"You can't come," said Colby. "For both our sakes."

"No, I can't. You're on your own for this one."

"No he's not," said Gossamer.

Colby smiled weakly, scratching his friend behind the ears. "Thanks, Goss."

"I'm serious."

"Not this time, I'm afraid. You need to stay here with Yashar."

"No," said Gossamer. "Don't stay me."

"Goss, this is really—"

"No. Not this time, boss. I'm coming with you."

"We don't have time for this."

"Then just do it."

"Do what?" asked Colby.

"Make me your familiar. Once and for all."

Yashar and Colby exchanged troubled glances. "You don't know what you're asking. What that involves."

"Yes I do, and I don't care. I'm not just your dog anymore. And I'm tired of being just half a thing. Make me the whole thing. Take me the rest of the way. I want to be your familiar."

Colby petted Gossamer, scratching his graying cheek, looking down at him sadly. "If we do this, our souls will be inextricably linked. We'll never be able to—"

"I've heard the sales pitch already. From Yashar. I'm in. Let's do this thing."

"I don't know," said Yashar. "These things, they don't always end so well."

"If anything were to happen to me . . . ," said Colby.

Gossamer rubbed the top of his head against Colby's thigh and looked up at him with solemn, deadly serious eyes. "Colby, the only way anyone is ever going to kill you is if I'm already dead. Just do the thing and say the goddamned words already."

Colby hesitated for a second, mulling it over. "I love you, Gossamer."

"I love you too, boss."

Colby lowered a hand onto Gossamer's mane, rubbing his fingers through his golden red coat. He began mumbling, cursing in arcane languages, focusing every last bit of dreamstuff he could from as far as three city blocks away. The two began to glow, a dark sickly green pulsing underneath their skin. Then the sound of thunder and the nauseating wobble of the universe contracting and expanding around them.

Gossamer felt suddenly ill, every inch of his body tingling, his insides jumbling as if he was strapped into a disintegrating Tilt-A-Whirl held together by duct tape and loose nuts.

"Just breathe," said Colby. "You've got to breathe through it."

"It feels awful."

"It'll pass. Focus."

The pulsing grew to a crescendo, a kaleidoscopic torrent of color wheeling about them. They both winced in pain, a surge like a hundred thousand volts streaming through their souls. And then it stopped and the colors faded away.

Gossamer looked around, freaking out, suddenly very anxious. "What the—? What the hell is going on?" His mind was filled with thoughts, images, complex structures he didn't understand. The air buzzed lightly around him, like it was swarming with gnats. There were colors to the world he never knew existed. His soul felt like it was on fire.

"Relax," said Colby. "You need a few moments to adjust."

"Adjust to what? What the hell is going on inside my head?"

"Your new perceptions. My perceptions. My thoughts. This is what I was talking about. It's going to take a little getting used to."

"No shit. This is . . . this is fucking weird."

"Yes. We're linked for good now. We can think to each other over distances, see and hear and feel what the other can feel, hear, and see. And I can work dreamstuff through you. It'll take awhile for us to work the kinks out, but we'll make it work. But first, I need you to focus. Find a single thought, one thing you can see in your head, and just focus on that."

"Okay." Gossamer saw a campfire. And a man. Not a man. A spirit. He looked up at Colby. Then his mouth dropped open and he began panting with excitement.

Colby and Gossamer looked long and hard at each other, each sifting through the other's thoughts. Gossamer nodded; Colby reeled back a bit, then shook his head. Just as Colby had shared his thoughts and memories with Gossamer, so too had Gossamer shared his with him.

And it was at once clear that all was not as it appeared to be.

Don't say a word, thought Colby. *This stays between us. You hear me?*

"Yeah," said the dog. "Loud and clear." Then he barked once, just to see if he still could. "Okay. Let's do this. Time's wasting." He trotted toward the door, stopping to give a single look over his shoulder to see if Colby and Yashar were following. "*Come on!*"

"Welcome to the club," said Yashar to Colby.

"What do you mean?"

"Now you know what it feels like to be responsible for someone who has no idea what they've asked for."

"Oh," said Colby, slipping into distant thoughts. "Shit."

"Yeah. Shit."

The door burst open and Austin stormed through, hat cocked sideways on her head, rage overflowing with bluster. "What the hell did you bring to my city?" she screamed.

"Whoa, whoa, whoa, whoa! You're not allowed in my house! What the hell do you—"

"This is my city, asshole. I can go wherever the hell I want."

"No you can't, Captain Police State."

"*What the hell did you bring to my city?*"

"I didn't bring—"

"Yes you did. They're here because of you. Everything is here because of you. Demons, shadows, and a little girl who calls herself Queen. They're not here for the fucking music."

"Now you don't know that, they could be—"

"Don't be a smart-ass. Not now. You have fucked up one time too many, Colby Stevens. Bill was one of the good ones. The Cursed and the Damned was a little piece of magic this town can never get back. It was one thing when they came on their own, but when you chose to traffic with them, this became something else entirely. I won't have sorcerers in my town, Colby. I won't have power-hungry jackasses bringing the worst kinds of things here."

"That's not what's happening," said Colby, his voice pinched, defensive.

"It is what's happening. You've done nothing good for this town. Ever. First you clear it out of all the fairies because you had a beef. Then you kill a spirit without consulting me, which, albeit, I had more than a little something to do with. And now, well, now the Seventy-two are showing up one by one while an army of shadowy creeps comes to tear the place apart. I won't have it. You're gone."

"What?"

"Your Austin privileges are revoked. Grab your shit and get the hell out of my town. You're done here."

Colby stepped forward, standing almost nose to nose with her. While she was a slight bit smaller than he was, her posture was more assured, meant business. He tried to remain bold, staring straight in her eyes, but she was far too intimidating. He swallowed hard, trying to raise enough courage to tell her off. "I'm not leaving."

"The hell you aren't. What do I have to do? Level the house? Harry your every move? Make things so bad for you that you can't bear to stand here another moment? I'll do that. I can do all of that. Or you can leave right now. Get out and never look back."

"Not until this is done. I have to finish what I've started."

"No," said Austin. "This is my city they've come to. I'll finish this."

"Then let's do this tog—"

"No! I can't trust you. Someone came to threaten your life and you bargained away your own soul to save it. You're not who I thought you were."

"And who did you think I was?"

"The guy who only thought about damning himself when it meant saving his friends. Get out. Get out of my town. I want you out of here by sunset."

"That's just a couple of hours away."

"Yeah. It is." Austin looked up at the ceiling, her eyes slipping from anger to worry. She looked back at Colby. "She's here."

"I thought she was already here."

"Her shadows, maybe. But not her. She's at the city limits. I'll take care of this. You pack your shit and go."

"No. You can't go talk to her. She's—"

"She's what?"

"Dangerous."

"I can take care of myself. Now get the fuck out of my town." She pointed straight at Yashar. "That goes for you too."

"I figured as much. It was a nice town, while it lasted."

"It was. And then you two had to fuck the whole thing up."

Austin fell away like a shattering piece of glass, shards toppling silently, abating into nothing before they hit the floor. She was gone.

Colby, Yashar, and Gossamer traded glances, wondering what to do next.

"We can't do what you're thinking, Colby," said Yashar.

"And how do you know what I'm thinking?"

"Because I know that look in your eye. Don't let the fact that she's sweet on you distract you from what she really is. She'll tear you apart."

"She's not sweet on me."

"Colby, stop being an idiot. This isn't the time."

"I'm just saying—"

"When a loci tells you to leave, you leave. You don't ask questions."

"It's her or the Seventy-two. Whose wrath do I really want to suffer? She gave us until sundown. That gives us time."

"Time for what?"

"Three more boons."

"Colby!"

"I made a deal."

"A deal you shouldn't have made."

"Five souls for five boons. If I don't deliver, they will hunt me down and *they* will tear me apart, which they were going to do if I didn't make a deal. I never had a choice, Yashar."

"You did then. You do now. Stop trying to pawn this off on them. This is how they work. It is how they've always worked. You're supposed to feel like you had no choice, like every alternative was worse. They weren't. There's nothing worse than selling a little bit of yourself just to save the rest of it. Because once you've done that, there's nothing to stop you the next time and the next time until there's nothing left. When are you going to take responsibility for your own damnation?"

"Right now. Right here. Get the candles. The black ones."

CHAPTER 53

THE PAGEANTRY OF QUEENS

Dawn was rapidly approaching, but darkness still swallowed the city. The Queen of the Dark Things rode gallantly through the trees on the outskirts, poised atop her ambling bunyip like a knight strolling before an adoring crowd. Beside her, hobbling as fast as it could, was her body, still driven by the kutji that had stolen it. Behind her, dozens of kutji scampered across the landscape, none daring to go any faster than their mistress. The five dukes of Hell, each with the mark of Solomon burned into its chest, followed gravely, their faces pained, as if they were marching to their own funerals.

At once, the Queen came to a halt, holding up her hand to stay the procession.

Before her stood Austin, her jaw tight, eyes hidden beneath the brim of her straw hat. "Turn around," she said. "You've come to the wrong city."

"I don't think I have," said the Queen. "I'm pretty sure Colby is in here somewhere."

"Not for long. But while he still is, he's under my protection. This is my town."

"Would you like to keep it?"

The wind whipped up around Austin and the very earth came alive at her feet. Her hair, however, stayed perfectly in place, as if she were unaffected by the gales ramping up at her command.

"Focalor?" trilled the Queen of the Dark Things, as if summoning a child for breakfast.

The beast stepped forward, nearly seven feet tall, with the tan wings of a griffin stretching out from his back. His hands had callouses upon callouses, his arms sculpted from centuries of pulling ropes aboard ships, his eyes the color of sea spray. The stench of the drowned followed him, sharp with salt, heavy with bloated rot. Everything he wore was tattered and drenched. He raised a steady arm and stayed the winds, howling mightily with the sound of an angry sea as he did; he was its master, everyone else merely dabbled.

Austin struggled against the dying winds, trying to muster them back to full strength, but she lacked the power. The earth below her still rumbled, the tremors growing wrathful. But she was losing.

The Queen shook her head. "You're a powerful spirit. I don't want to be on your bad side. Just let us pass and leave us be."

"Not gonna happen."

The Queen looked around at her subjects, smiling. "Take her."

Austin nodded, pulling the brim of her hat farther down over her eyes. She clenched her fists, energy crackling, enkindled.

The shadows charged, sharpened claws on their remaining hands out, grasping, their mouths wide with razor teeth. They sounded calls for her blood, jeering and screaming as they stampeded over one another to be the first to rend her flesh.

Austin began to glow, her skin luminescent, brightening with the glare of the sun. The shadows recoiled, shrieking as the light sizzled away the black of their bodies. They ran, hid behind trees, crawled into the spaces in between the rock and the ground. With a single finger, Austin slid her hat back, grinning. "What's this Queen without her dark things?"

"They aren't the only things of the night." The Queen waved and the five dukes all stepped toward her.

"This isn't between us," said Austin to the five. "Your brothers and I have no qualms."

"Not our choice," said Focalor. "We serve only the ring now." Beside him was Astaroth, the Naked Angel, astride a beastly black dragon, a poisonous serpent writhing in his grasp, golden crown atop his head. The dragon hunched low, creeping rather than walking, its scales grinding with the sound of sawing bones, mouth agape, flaming spit trickling out of the sides of its mouth.

Following behind them was Berith, alabaster skin pulled tight beneath a crimson military uniform, desert style, like a U.S. soldier's that had been dyed haphazardly in a river of blood. His eyes shone blue, his hair short, curly, blond, peeking out beneath a black iron crown. He rode a horse every bit as red as his uniform, even its eyes swirling, sanguine pools, only its onyx hooves and ebony teeth standing apart from its scarlet flesh.

And from the other side came Bune, himself a dragon, large scales the color of twilight, with three heads swaying on long, spindly, serpentine necks. The outside pair were massive, draconic, with teeth like sabers and eyes like puddles of festering piss. The middle-most head, however, was that of a man, portly, hideous, three chins and broken teeth, sweat beading atop its brow.

And lastly came Dantalion, just a little farther back than the rest.

The five made their way slowly, deliberately, toward Austin, more threatening than actively pursuing. After all, they knew her next move better than she.

Austin clenched both her fists, held them out like a tiring pugilist, then threw her arms back, shredding the ground on which she stood. The earth buckled, lines and shapes appearing in it, forming a pentagram twenty feet across with her standing at its center. The five dukes continued advancing, surrounding her at each of the star's five points, unable however to take one step farther.

Focalor cocked his head arrogantly, grimacing. "Keep it up, bitch. Better not falter. The minute you step out of there I'm going to drag you through the fields, drown you in your own lake, and then fuck the corpse." He licked his dry, sea-wind-cracked lips.

Austin held firm, trying not to let him get to her. She could hold this for a while, but do little else. She was powerful, but no more so than any one of the demons. Five to one, she was done for. She'd gotten herself in way too deep.

"This doesn't need to be adversarial," said the Queen, slowly steering her bunyip closer, step by step. "I need to speak with Colby. That's all."

"You mean to kill him."

"Only if he doesn't mend what he's broken. This is all his doing, you know that."

"You have a beef with him? You settle it outside my town."

"Why are you protecting him? He wouldn't do the same for you."

"You don't know that."

"Oh!" said the Queen, clapping excitedly. "You have feelings for Colby."

Austin gritted her teeth. "No. I just do right by my people, that's all."

"No, no, no. I can see it in the way you hold yourself. The way your nostrils flare when I say his name. Does he know?"

"Turn around. Don't come back."

"Does he care about you?"

"Colby only cares about Colby."

"Noooooo. We both know that's not true. We've heard the stories. Dantalion! Tell her the story about the fairies. The one about the tithe!"

Dantalion nodded, a bottle swinging from his waist in mockery. "When Colby Stevens was but a boy—"

"I know the story," said Austin.

"He'll leave you, you know. It's what he does."

"You don't know him. Not really."

"No, *you* don't know him. You're only seeing what you want to see. You don't know what's going on here. You don't know how this is going to play out. This could all end peacefully. He could set me free and my friends and I could be on our way."

"It's too late for that." She pointed at the five demons. "Their friends have seen to it."

The Queen leaned forward on her bunyip steed, eyes concerned, fearful fingers tickling a silver ring on her finger. "The Seventy-two? Colby's given himself over to them?"

"It's not like that."

"Oh. What's it like then?"

"He had to."

"He always has to," said the Queen, bitterly. "That's what he told me, you know. *I'm sorry, but I have to.* But he's really done it? He's bargained with them?"

"He has."

"Then he really means to kill me, doesn't he?"

Austin nodded grimly. "After what you did, why wouldn't he?"

The Queen eyed Austin suspiciously. "Something's happened."

"Of course *something's happened*."

"Someone died? A friend of Colby's?"

"Don't play dumb. Neither of us has time for that."

The Queen grew troubled, her face falling. She slid slowly off the back of her bunyip, slumping sadly onto the ground. The bunyip, in turn, dropped, making itself comfortable, curling up against her back. Tears swelled in her eyes. She looked up at Austin. "This isn't about me, is it?" she asked, no longer the Queen, but a little girl whose heart was irreparably broken.

"I don't—"

"My destiny. It wasn't about me becoming Queen, making the night safe for other children. This was never about me. Colby cut my cord. Colby left me in the desert. Colby sold his soul for the power to kill me. Colby isn't a part of my destiny; I'm just a small part of his. This whole thing was about him. About seducing him. Everyone knows that he's cursed, but I never . . . I never thought—"

"Oh my God," said Austin. "He's—" The earth quit rumbling and all was once again silent.

"He's theirs now. He has to kill me. If he doesn't—"

"They don't want you. They just want the ring. They want their brothers free."

The Queen looked up at Dantalion. "Is that true?"

"I don't know, my Queen," he said. "I cannot see his future any clearer than I can see yours. The ring, it clouds it. But if Colby is as crafty as they say, I would imagine that was the deal he struck."

"Tell me the truth; if I freed you now and gave back the ring—"

"We would kill you where you stand—"

"And then bicker over who got to torment your soul," finished Astaroth.

All five nodded, for they could not lie, not to the wearer of the ring.

"And what of Colby's bargain?" she asked.

"He would have received powers he had not paid for," said Dantalion. "And his soul might then belong to others to squabble over."

"So for one of us to walk away?"

"The other must die."

"And if I ran?"

"He would be bound by his bargain to find you."

The Queen looked back up at Austin. "Mandu lied. All he ever did was lie. He told me I had a great destiny, that things would be different. Maybe I just misunderstood him. Things are different. Now I have a choice between killing the one person who can free me from my curse or dying by his hand so he can be further damned. What kind of destiny is that?"

"I don't know," said Austin. "There has to be another way."

Dantalion shook his head. "There is no other way. We've seen to that."

The Queen stood up, reached into her dilly bag, and pulled out a handful of salt. Dantalion cowered behind both hands.

"Lower your hands," she said.

He did and she approached him.

"Now, swallow this."

His eyes grew large with fear. He trembled, but he did not move, save to lean his head back and open his mouth. The Queen poured the salt down his gullet and he screamed, gurgling on his own boiling insides. Dantalion fell to the ground, writhing, convulsing.

The Queen smeared the tears from her cheek with her purple

sleeve. She hardened, her gaze becoming icy, determined. "Go do what you need to do," she said to Austin. "I don't want to kill you. But I will if I have to. We can fight this out here if you like, but if you lose, I win. I will march on your city to meet Colby. And if you win . . ."

Austin nodded knowingly. "Colby owes five souls he can't pay back."

The Queen whistled loudly and called out into the night. "Dark things! Go find shelter for the day! Find the darkest hollow you can find and dig in! At sunset we meet again to bring an end to all this!" Then she turned back to Austin. "If it's my destiny to die tonight, I will. And I won't cry about it. Not anymore. Tonight we find out whose destiny this is really all about. Tonight I will kill Colby Stevens or he will kill me."

Austin nodded, then vanished.

CHAPTER 54

THE BEARDED HUNTER

Barbatos. A great count or earl, and also a duke, he
appeareth in Signo sagittarii sylvestris, with four
kings, which bring companies and great troops. He
understandeth the singing of birds, the barking of
dogs, the lowings of bullocks, and the voice of all
living creatures. He detecteth treasures hidden by
magicians and enchanters, and is of the order of
virtues, which in part bear rule: he knoweth all
things past, and to come, and reconciles friends
and powers; and governeth thirty legions of devils
by his authority.

—*Pseudomonarchia Daemonum*

Not the fucking woods again," said Colby, trudging through the fresh mud of a cold autumn rain, Gossamer trotting closely at his side. They were deep in the backwoods, somewhere in the Virginias as best Colby could tell. The air was so thick it clung to his skin, and even though it was early in the day, the heavy rain clouds and nigh impenetrable canopy gave off the distinct feeling of twilight.

These were a witches' woods once, lingering trails of incantations, pockets of dreamstuff swirling around three-hundred-year-old trees. It was the sort of place fairies should be running about, claiming as their own.

But even fairies knew better than to run afoul of one of the Seventy-two. Especially Barbatos. The Hunter. It seemed as if even the wild things—the birds, the squirrels, all the things of the forest—knew what lived here and stayed far, far away.

Colby knew what he was looking for but didn't look with his eyes. He sniffed, felt out for the warping of space, the corruption in the roots of trees. And he found it. A shack. Lingering silently off a trail, placed just so as to not be seen from any angle one might happen upon.

It was a hunter's shack, small, like a shed, made of rotten wood and century-old timber. It leaned slightly to one side, the door seemingly giving it more support than its posts. From its porch hung wind chimes made of the skulls of woodland animals, a light breeze clattering them together with the dull, hollow clink of bone on bone. A wind rose up, whispering through the gaps in the boards of the place, threatening at any moment to knock it over into a pile of scrap. But it held, for it was no force of physics that had kept it standing all these years.

Colby took a deep breath and stepped forward onto the porch, the boards squeaking beneath his feet. Then he turned the knob of the door and stepped in. Gossamer lingered behind, only for an instant, hesitating at the first whiff of the brutal, terrible smells wafting out. He looked over his shoulder, gazing out, back into the woods, thinking that they were really no better than whatever was waiting for them inside.

He was wrong.

It was dark and it was large and it was by no means the same building within that it was without. Outside measured maybe ten feet on each side, but inside was a cluster of rooms, each bigger than the shack appeared, and each connected by a doorway with no door. It smelled damp and foul, like festering piss and neglected corpses. The walls were lined with ramshackle wooden shelves, stacked precariously from floor to ceiling with jars of every shape and size—brown, viscous fluid suspending hearts and livers, fairy wings and unicorn horns, eyeballs and snouts. In the spots between the jars—where there were spots— experiments of taxidermy stared out, frightened, molded less to look like vicious or dangerous trophies and more like terrified creatures glimpsed at the moment of their demise.

And from the ceiling hung skulls. Hundreds of skulls. Perhaps thousands. Bird. Wildcat. Dog. Human. It seemed as if Barbatos kept a little piece of everything he'd ever killed. Colby wondered if there was a room here where he also displayed their souls; Gossamer didn't care to know the answer to that question.

In the center of the second room they found the butcher block, a solid piece carved from the heart of a single ancient tree, its wood stained a dark, clotted red from a thousand dismemberments. And stuck in the wood were two dozen knives, their steel hardened with magicks Colby struggled even to identify.

He held out his arms, palms up, fingers splayed precisely, and once more spoke in a demonic tongue. "Barbatos, I summon thee! Appear and speak!"

Barbatos appeared, screaming. His beard was white at the roots, then yellowed and browned the farther it got from his face, festooned with twigs, brush, and bugs, his hair unruly, wild, colored the same as his beard. But his eyes were black, empty, and never caught the light; they were hunter's eyes, remorseless. And they were furious.

"No!" he hollered the moment he arrived, as if he'd been stuck with a knife. He flailed about, naked, covered in mud, his body rigid and muscular, as if he spent every waking moment running, climbing. "Why would you do this to me?"

"Calm down," said Colby.

"No! She's here! She's here with that fucking ring! Get me out of here! Release me. I do not wish to be here."

Colby spoke coolly, calmly, not letting the choler of the demon thrashing in his living room get to him. "This place is yours. We're safe."

"No! She has things! Hundreds of things! At her beck and call every moment! They're following you, looking for you, looking for us. And they won't have me! Release me!"

"We had a deal."

He cowered, almost perching, ready to strike, casting his eyes wildly at the corners of the room. "You took too long. She's here, I know it, and I will not be her slave."

"If she wanted you as her slave, Barbatos, you would be her slave. I want this done as quickly as you do."

Barbatos calmed, his rage seething beneath the surface. "Then speak it, tell me what you want, and I'll grant it. But do it quickly."

"There's something I need you to find. Something hidden. Something very dangerous."

"It's yours. If it is out there to be found, I will find it. Whisper it into my ear, and I'll find it."

Colby looked nervously at the demon, before trading glances with Gossamer, terrified of getting too close to a creature as choleric and unpredictable as Barbatos. "Can't I just ask you from here?"

"Do you want the Queen to know about it?"

"No."

"Then it must remain a secret between us. What is said into my ear is mine alone. Say it. Say it quickly and let me go find what it is you seek."

Colby inched forward, his bravery waning for a moment. Then he stepped quickly up to the wild-haired hunter, parting the tangles around its ear, whispering almost silently into it. Barbatos recoiled, expression steadying for a moment. He looked deeply into Colby's eyes, puzzling over him.

"You are a clever boy, aren't you?" he said. "They've underestimated you. We all have. It's yours. It will take me some time to uncover it, but you'll have it before sunset. I swear it."

"Thank you."

Barbatos scratched his head through the scraggly mess. "You could have asked for something else, you know. There are far more powerful things in this world. I know where or how to find them all."

"But none of them is as powerful as this. Not now. Not tonight."

"I know. Maybe it's not the Queen I should be scared of, after all."

And with a cautious wink, Barbatos spirited away into the ether, leaving behind nothing but the heavy musk of reeking sweat and soil.

CHAPTER 55

THE MASTER OF THE PARADE

Paimon is more obedient in Lucifer than other kings are. Lucifer is here to be understood he that was drowned in the depth of his knowledge: he would needs be like God, and for his arrogance was thrown out into destruction, of whom it is said; every precious stone is thy covering. Paimon is constrained by divine virtue to stand before the exorcist; where he putteth on the likeness of a man: he sitteth on a beast called a dromedarie, which is a swift runner, and weareth a glorious crown, and hath an effeminate countenance. There goeth before him a host of men with trumpets and well-sounding cymbals, and all musical instruments. At the first he appeareth with a great cry and roaring, as in Circulo Salomonis, and in the art is declared. And if this Paimon speak sometime that the conjurer understand him not, let him not therefore be dismayed. But when he hath delivered him the first obligation to observe his desire, he must bid him also answer him distinctly and plainly to the questions he shall ask you, of all philosophy, wisdom, and science, and of all other secret things. And if you will know the disposition of the world, and what the earth is, or what holdeth it up in the water, or any other thing, or what is Abyssus, or where the wind is, or from whence it commeth, he will teach you aboundantly. Consecrations also as well of sacrifices as otherwise may be reckoned. He giveth dignities and confirmations; he bindeth them that resist him in his own chains, and subjecteth them to the conjurer; he prepareth good familiars, and hath the understanding of all arts. Note, that at the calling up of him, the exorcist must look toward the northwest, because there is his house. When he is called up, let the exorcist receive him constantly without fear, let him ask what questions or demands he list, and no doubt he shall obtain the same of him. And the exorcist must beware he forget not the creator, for those things, which have been rehearsed before of Paimon, some say he is of the order of dominations; others say, of the order of cherubim. There follow him two hundred legions, partly of the order of angels, and partly of potestates. Note that if Paimon be cited alone by an offering or sacrifice, two kings follow him; to wit, Beball & Abalam, & other potentates: in his host are twenty-five legions, because the spirits subject to them are not always with them, except they be compelled to appear by divine virtue.

—*Pseudomonarchia Daemonum*

You're going to hate him," said Yashar.

"They're demons," said Colby. "I can't say I like any of them."

"Yeah, but Paimon's different. Of the Seventy-two, some are terrifying, others outlandish, some, like Seere, are downright tolerable. But Paimon. He's—"

"He's what?"

"He's an asshole."

"How bad?"

"Through and through. I've never seen a face in all my life as punchable as his. You'll hate him before he even opens his mouth. Just face northwest, say the words, and let's get this over with. Even thinking about him turns my stomach."

"You don't have to go."

"You asked. And you never ask."

"The stories about it—"

"They're all true."

Colby nodded. "Let's rip off the Band-Aid."

The two stood in the backyard, just outside the sliding glass door into Colby's kitchen, looking out over the scrub of the disused space. The sun was high, creeping toward its zenith, casting shadows from the rickety, well-worn wooden fence that separated Colby's property from five other adjacent lots. There was no lawn furniture, only a trail of dirt around the base of the fence that Gossamer had run down over the last six months.

"Seere," he said softly. And Seere appeared.

Colby jumped astride the back of the horse and Gossamer jumped immediately into his arms. He looked down, wishing for a moment that Seere had a bigger horse.

Yashar looked confused, then smiled sheepishly.

"I don't know how this is going to work," said Colby.

The djinn took a few steps toward the horse and put a hand

gently on its side. Seere turned and looked down at Yashar, nodding.

"I think you need to be on the horse," said Colby.

Yashar shook his head. "No, it doesn't work that way."

"But I've been—"

Seere looked at Colby, then down to Yashar. "I didn't have
the heart to tell him."

IT WAS NIGHT and the desert was cold, Seere having flung them
to the far side of the world. They stood in a vast expanse, a great
valley covered in dunes, the bright moon and stars lighting the
sand a soft blue. Unlike the lairs of the others, there was nothing
creepy or unimaginable waiting. Just sand. Miles upon miles of
sand.

Colby looked up and found his bearing by the stars and
faced northwest. He held his hands before him and said the
words, once more speaking syllables most inhuman. "Paimon, I
summon thee. Appear and speak."

From literally out of nowhere marched a parade, a procession
of clowns, acrobats, musicians-performers of all sorts—each appearing without so much as a flash or a bang. They simply were,
and continued to multiply. Each wore colorful clothes with bells
and baubles, floppy hats and curly-toed boots, playing music, elegant and celebratory. Cymbals clashed, trumpets blared. And all
the while the paraders danced, skipping, frolicking like they were
having the best time in the world. But their faces dripped with
fear, their eyes wide and terror stricken from the horrors they'd
seen. And those that were smiling looked the worse for it, as if
they had hooks on the insides of their cheeks to keep them so.

These were the souls of Paimon's favorite conquests, some
only centuries old, others millennia, and each step they took
pained them, for they never stopped dancing, never stopped
blowing their trumpets, never were allowed a moment of peace

in all their deaths. And behind them, a dromedary, its camel hair carefully manicured, its back saddled with fine silks and ancient leather, carried the most august, handsome creature Colby had ever seen. Paimon.

Paimon was dressed from head to toe in fineries, his eyes ringed perfectly in mascara, his olive skin without blemish, his long, lustrous black hair looped through silver and platinum barrettes, rings, and headbands. He reminded Colby instantly of Rudolph Valentino in a way that made it seem as if Valentino had been nothing but a pale imitation, trying its best to evoke the demon to the best of its earthly constraints. The demon gazed down from its swaying beast, held up a single swishing hand, and stopped his procession at once. He looked at the three companions—his entertainers still dancing in place—grimacing haughtily. Then he locked eyes with Colby, shrieking with an unearthly clamor that vibrated down the bones and back up through the soul.

Colby winced, unprepared for such a caustic pronouncement. He waved his arms, trying to stop him, but the demon spoke in an abyssal argot so foul that Colby found it hard to form his own words. "Stop! Stop!" he finally belted out. "Paimon, speak to me as would a man."

Paimon stopped, pursed his lips, and looked straight down his nose at Colby. "I have appeared. Let us speak then, as men do."

"I'll make this brief. I know you don't want to be anywhere near—"

"Oh, don't concern yourself with that on my account. I'm not going to let a small thing like that little girl and her ring keep me from enjoying my time with the *great Colby Stevens*." Paimon tightened his face as he said the last part, fingers pinched together as if holding a teacup.

Paimon spoke with a gentle, lilting voice, ending each of his sentences with a vocal upturn that made them sound mocking and sarcastic. He couldn't keep his hands still, not while speaking, waving for emphasis in the midst of each word, hands like the blade of a windmill at the end of limp wrists. His poise was the height of pretension; even the way he held his head was conceited. There was a way about him so regal that it could make even the aristocratic feel downright vulgar by comparison. When he cast his eyes around a place, he did so as if he was disappointed by the filth and squalor surrounding him, which Colby imagined he did even in the most lavish of accommodations.

Yashar was right. Colby wanted to punch him square in the jaw long before he spoke, but even more so now that he had. He fidgeted, trying not to make a fist, aggravation pulling taut the muscles in his hand.

Paimon smiled, delighted that he had so easily gotten under the boy's skin. He lifted his leg gracefully, sliding off the side of his dromedary and onto the ground without so much as disturbing a grain of sand. "Let's go inside," he said.

He clapped and a lavish tent appeared, a dozen lanterns lighting it. It seemed to blaze like a star in the sea of moonlight. Paimon turned and made his way toward it.

"I told you," whispered Yashar beneath his breath.

"Shut it," Colby whispered back.

Paimon stepped inside and made another disappointed face. "No, I'll need a rug for the dog." He turned to Colby, who followed distantly behind him. "No dogs on the pillows. You know my rules?"

Colby nodded. "I do."

"Good," he said, taking a seat on an ornately stitched and gilded pillow. "So, have you fucked her yet?"

"What?"

"I said have you fucked her yet? The girl. The loci. The blonde with the ass in the tight jeans you're always pining for. Have you fucked her? Crawled deep inside that tiny little twat and given it to her good? Slipped a finger in and tickled her insides? Rolled her over and taken every hole you can? Have you done that, Colby? Have you given her the good fucking you've been craving? Drenched her in every fluid you have until you can't come anymore? Well, have you, Colby? Colby Stevens?"

Colby's expression dropped, his gut roiling. "No," he said, now terrified of where this conversation was headed.

"Sit, sit. But you want to, don't you?"

"I think I'll stand."

Paimon tsked. "My home, my rules. You'll sit."

Colby slumped onto a pillow of his own, crossing his legs, trying to remain stoic.

"He's just trying to humiliate you, Colby," said Yashar.

"Of course I'm trying to humiliate him. He's a wee little child who wants to play with the men. But you can't play with the men, can you, Colby? Because a man would have fucked the shit out of that tight little piece of ass by now. And you're no man. You can't even talk to her, let alone fuck her. You want to fuck her, don't you?"

"Yes," said Colby, his insides hollowing out, shrinking away into the deepest, darkest, most hidden parts of him. His face was flushed with shame. But he couldn't lie. Not without giving Paimon license to add him to his procession.

"You've thought about it, haven't you?"

"Yes."

"Have you thought about getting her on those pretty little knees while you drench her face in your spunk?"

"No."

Paimon peered severely at Colby, sniffing. "Oh. You haven't, have you? Oh my lord, you imagine that you *respect her*." He laughed, something that sounded like a churlish giggle piped through a calliope. "You poor, pathetic, tiny-cocked little shit. You are worthless. You think that not thinking about that amazing little body on its knees sucking your cock dry and begging for you to fill her holes shows her some kind of dignity. She reads minds, Colby. She knows that's what guys think about. What you *think* about. Every guy who sees her wants to plug those holes. What kind of a sissy must she think you are that you try to think about anything but. She deserves better than you tossing off to her beautiful little pink areolae on those free-floating creamy fair-skinned tits of hers. Oh God, maybe I should fuck her. You think she'd like that?"

"No."

"Would you like to watch that?"

"No."

"You wouldn't, would you? You're ashamed of your little pecker. You think it's not good enough for her, do you? Can't bear the thought of seeing her get it from real manhood?"

"Are you done yet?" asked Yashar.

"I haven't even begun!" shouted Paimon. "Answer the question, Colby! Do you think your cock is big enough to fuck her hairless twat and come on her stomach?"

"I don't know."

"Oh," said the demon, waving him off. "You really don't. You really are that fucking pathetic. What about the little girl?" He stood quickly and did a mocking little dance, lowering his voice as he curtsied. "The Queeeeeeeeeeen."

"What about her?"

"Have? You? Thought? About? Fucking? Her?"

"No!" said Colby.

"What is it with you and fucking?" asked Yashar.

"You don't get to ask questions, Yashar. I ask the questions I feel like until I decide that I'm done. And right now, I feel like asking your chaste little boyfriend about his deviant little sexual fantasies. He's been around the world, but he's never *been around the world*. And he certainly shouldn't feel like an expert in anything if he can't even describe what most thirteen-year-olds can detail from memory. Does that embarrass you, Colby? That most middle school boys know what a pussy feels like and you don't?"

"Yes."

"Of course it does, you despicable little maggot. You can never please a woman. The only girls inexperienced enough to not know how inept you are at fucking are so young you'd be humiliated to fuck them. But you'd like to fuck them, wouldn't you. Little girls?"

"No."

"Oh my God, you are so fucking boring! It's not even fun to make fun of you! Do you think you can save her?"

"What?"

"The girl. The Queeeeeen. Do you think you can save her, Colby?"

"I don't know."

"She's coming to kill you, you know."

"I know."

"But you'd like to, wouldn't you? Save her?"

Colby sighed, resigned. "Yes."

"But you can't save her. Not without damning yourself further. Not without earning our wrath. Are you willing to damn yourself to save her?"

"Is there any better reason to be damned than for a friend?"

"But she's not your friend. She hasn't been your friend for a long time. Amy was right about you, we can't trust you, can we?"

"That depends. What do you have to trust me to do?"

"Keep up your end of the bargain. Kill the girl."

"You can trust me to keep up my end of the bargain. I'll be dead before I renege on our deal. I promise you that."

Paimon eyed Colby closely, once again sniffing deeply, sensing not even the slightest bit of a lie. "I don't like the way you phrased that. What do you have up your sleeve, Colby?"

"A way to kill the Queen that I dare not speak of lest its revelation ruins the surprise for her."

"I must know."

"If I tell you, what is spoken between us will be known by Dantalion, will it not?"

Paimon squinted distastefully. The boy was not wrong. "Dantalion," he said, as if spitting out bad fruit. "I rescind the question."

"You didn't actually ask it. The girl is coming. We don't have much time. Are you quite done?"

"No. I have nothing but time. You're the one with the ticking clock. Were she to walk in the tent now, she'd kill you before thinking of enslaving me. I'll be fine. So tell me, do you think by saving her you can absolve yourself of Ewan Thatcher?"

Colby gritted his teeth, his heart pounding as it sank in his chest.

"You do, don't you? You think that if you can help one friend you've wronged, it will somehow balance the ledger. Don't you?"

"Something like that."

"Or exactly like that. Is it exactly like that, *Colby Stevens*?"

Colby swallowed, his mouth growing increasingly dry. "Yes."

"You really are a miserable, sad, obvious little boy." He rolled his eyes and waved Colby off in disgust. "You're no fun anymore. I'm done with you. Ask your boon and be done with it."

Colby nodded. The worst of it was over. Or so he hoped. "Great Paimon, I am told you possess knowledge such that you can create nearly any mystical item from memory."

Paimon stroked his chin. "Of course."

"And what do you remember of Babylon?"

"I remember everything. Every moment. The name of every corrupted soul in that beautiful bastion of sin."

"Then I want you to teach me to make Babylonian Demon Traps."

Paimon's eyes at once fumed, his skin flushed with anger. He waved Colby off with a dismissive flutter. "What? No! I refuse! What do you need those for?"

Colby stood up and took a bold step forward. "I've answered your fucking questions, you foul-mouthed, pompous little pervert. I've done your dance and my soul is safe. Will you not grant me the boon?"

"No! I . . . those were not meant for you, Colby Stevens."

"No. Their knowledge has been wiped from the world, passed down only orally as a legend for centuries. Who, I wonder, would, or even could, have done such a thing?"

Paimon glared at Colby. All of his grace was gone, replaced with blustery indignation.

"Did you do it, Paimon?"

"Yes. Yes I did. I've kept that secret safe for centuries, I will not pass it on to you."

"Excellent. So how does this work? My deal was with Orobas, and your deal with him—so does your eternal servitude come straight to me, or does it go to Orobas and I get Orobas but can trade him his freedom for you?"

"That's not how it works."

"The deal was quite clear. Five boons of my choosing for five souls."

"You haven't paid the souls."

"Demons pay first. Them's the rules. Don't pretend that you don't know them, because I sure as shit do. Do you honestly think I'm that stupid?"

"I was hoping you might be. You're strong, shrewd, but you buckle when someone questions something you might not know and you often take their word for it. It was a gamble."

"Why don't you want to teach me to make . . . Babylonian Demon Traps?"

"Because there are few people in this world more suited to

abuse them than you." Paimon relaxed, steadying himself, at once regaining his calm composure. "But you need these for tonight, don't you?"

"You don't get to ask questions anymore."

"It was rhetorical. There's no other reason you would need them. And I guess I *could* impart the knowledge of their creation to you. Of course, the materials to make them and the time it would take to fashion them would take far too long for you to acquire and craft . . . and you have, what, but one boon left? Which boon might you ask for? The ingredients? Or the demonic skill and powers to make them in the time prescribed? Decisions, decisions."

"What are you proposing, Paimon? That you make them for me?"

"I could. But it's a tough choice. Either ask me *how* to make them or ask me to make them *for you*. Hmm. Nail-biter."

"Make them," said Colby, coolly.

"What?"

"That's my boon. Make me two sets."

Paimon opened his mouth to speak, but hesitated, for a moment slightly embarrassed. "Um, I . . . I can't."

"You what?"

"What I mean to say is that I can *make* them. I can assemble the materials and construct them. But I can't finish them. I can summon the materials, shape them, inscribe them, bake them in the fires of Hell, but I cannot breathe life into them, not the way you need. That requires a tremendous amount of energy, essence."

"Dreamstuff."

"Yes. But once it's there, I can't touch them. Can't manipulate them in any way. That you'll have to do yourself."

"How much will it need?"

"Quite a bit. More than you'll be able to summon natively

here." He hesitated for a moment, thumbing his chin mischievously. "But no more than you might scrape from a powerful artifact."

"And where am I supposed to find a powerful artifact that I can just will away?"

Paimon cast a crooked finger over to the tent's wall, grinning all the while. Upon it appeared the vision of two pegs, a pike resting upon them. Ewan's pike. Ethereal, illusory, but crystal clear in its point. "That will more than suffice."

"I'm . . . I'm not parting with that."

"Do you have any other choice? Or would you prefer I make something else for you?"

"You'll make these."

"It'll take me some time. Not long, but long enough for you to decide how important they are to you. I'll make them. You can finish them. Use whatever you like."

Colby stewed, as angry as he ever was. For a while he'd thought he'd regained the upper hand with Paimon, only to see that lead evaporate in the last moments. He stared at the vision of the pike, brooding over its potential loss. "Make them," he said. "I'll get you what you need."

Paimon smiled crassly, savoring the win. "Don't be sore, Colby. You never should have expected to get the best of us. But as a consolation, I'll deliver the bowls." He cocked an arrogant eyebrow at Colby, pursing his lips. "As I said, I'm not afraid of a little girl and her ring." He clapped once gracefully, and with that, he and his procession were gone, the tent along with them. Once again, the three were plunged into the dark of an empty desert lit only by the moon.

"Colby," said Gossamer. "What are you going to do?"

Colby didn't lift his gaze from the spot where the vision of the pike had been. "I don't know."

CHAPTER 56

THE WEIGHT OF THINGS

Colby sat cross-legged in the center of his living room, the John Brown pike across his lap like a prized new toy. Its blade was still razor sharp, gleaming in the orange-yellow light of the dozens of candles burning about the room. While all the blood that had been shed by it had long since been wiped clean, Colby could hear the screams of the departed, feel the grunts and grip of the death blows. Every molecule of the pike resonated with djang, the stories of its bearers, no matter how short, burned indelibly into its core. This was no mere thing. It was an echo of history, banging off the rocks of forever.

And now Colby had to let it go. Say good-bye. Will it into nothing.

He didn't want to do that. Not at all.

"It's not him, you know," said Yashar, sitting idle but impatient beside Gossamer on the couch.

"What?" asked Colby.

"The pike. It's not him."

"Do you know about djang, Yashar?"

"Colby," he said in a withering tone.

"We all put energy out into the universe. Just a little bit of ourselves that vibrates the things around us, leaves a shadow of our thoughts and emotions on our surroundings."

"I know what djang is, Colby."

"Ewan's shadow is here, on this pike. There's a little bit of him left making it what it is."

"That pike is not Ewan. Not the Ewan you want to remember. He was gone by then."

"I know," said Colby. "But it's the only thing I have left." He picked up the pike, closed his eyes, felt the tremors and fury and brutality of its past. For a split second he could feel him, his grip tight, ferocity overwhelming. He was there, his shadow passing over Colby—more a tingle than a man—but there nonetheless. Ewan.

Colby's eyes stung, wet with tears.

Yashar stood up, putting a firm hand on his friend's shoulder. "He's already gone."

"I know. And he's not coming back." He looked up at Yashar. "Why do I always have to kill my friends?"

"Colby—"

"No. It's all I've ever done. Too many friends over too short a time. Sometimes I think the only reason I've lived so long is that my curse isn't that I end badly, like so many of your other kids, but rather that I'm cursed to end up alone with the knowledge that I'm the one who got everyone killed. If I survive tonight, it will only be because I killed another of my friends. And I'm running low."

"That's not your curse, Colby."

"How do you know?"

"Because that's my curse." Yashar reached down and began fiddling with the countless baubles, trinkets, and other jewelry adorning his outfit. "I've never told you about these, mostly because you never asked."

"Oh," said Colby, never having given them much thought, but now, in an instant, understanding. "Those aren't—"

"They are. Each and every one from a different child. One from each."

Colby looked closer. They hung from chains and loops and short leather cords. Christmas ornaments. Rings. Bracelets. Toys. Each coated in bronze, silver, or gold. It had always struck Colby as being a bit garish, but he'd never really processed it. It was just one of those things, something he assumed was a product of someone from another age.

"Where's mine?" asked Colby.

Yashar reached into his pocket. "I don't wear it until they're gone," he said. "But I keep them with me, nonetheless." He pulled out an ugly, plastic, digital watch with the face of a long-forgotten cartoon character, so far gone that Colby himself couldn't name who it was. But he recognized it. It was the watch he'd worn as a child when Yashar first met him, that he'd used to count the minutes until Yashar would show up again to grant him his wish. The one his mother was always so keen to make sure he was wearing. "It's never easy to have to wear these for the first time. These last six months I've known that it would be any day now. Now I know—the kid who wore this was gone a long time ago."

"Yashar—"

"Don't. I won't wear it. Not yet. But after tonight, no matter how it plays out, you won't be you, not the you I knew. And you know that."

Colby nodded, rolling the pike gently back and forth in his hands. "We can't stay us forever."

"No. We most certainly can't. Ewan's gone and so is the boy he loved. And that little girl you knew. She's gone too. She's something else entirely now. There's no going back. You can't. Everyone tries at some point. But no one ever does."

"You don't think we can be saved?"

"Who? You or the girl?"

"Either of us."

"You've both not only walked with demons, but you also scare them. Frankly, if we're being totally honest here, I'm not certain there's anything of those kids left *to* save." Yashar braced himself, expecting Colby to blow at any moment. Instead, Colby looked down sadly, nodding once more.

"You're probably right. But we can try."

"You won't save her," said Austin, emerging from the shadows beyond the candles. "All you can do now is save yourself."

Colby glared at her. "You gave me till sunset."

"I was wrong," she said.

"I'm not leaving."

"I mean I was wrong about you leaving. She means to kill you, Colby. There's no talking her down from it. But it's not you who brought her here."

"How's that?"

"This is her mess. They're just using you to clean it up."

"That's what I tried to—"

"I told you. I was wrong. But now we're all in it. And I don't know how we're going to get out of it."

Yashar waved her off. "This isn't your mess to get involved in. You can leave at any time."

"Too late for that now. I met her. And the hell she's bringing with her."

"And?" asked Colby. "What did she—"

"She's got no other choice. She knows she'll never be free now. She's made her bed. And they've played you both. Rigged the game. It's you or her. And she knows that for good and for all. For her to have a chance at tomorrow, you have to die tonight. And for you to have a chance—"

"Yeah. We were just discussing that."

"So she means to kill you. Whether I like it or not, my streets are gonna run with blood."

"Again."

"Yeah. Again."

Colby gripped the pike tightly, again the djang of it tickling his senses. So much fear, so much hate, so much death, all packed neatly into a few pounds of wood and metal. "You know, I've been to the land of the dead. Trod where spirits have trod. And I've killed more than my fair share. Honestly, I can't tell you which scares me more. Or if they even scare me at all. I'm becoming numb to the idea of death. The only thing I want now is to avoid being a tool in someone else's shed. If I die, that's fine, as long as it's on my terms. And if I have to kill, I don't want it to be for any reasons other than my own. So tonight, no matter what happens, I'm doing it the way I want to do it for the reasons I need to do it."

Yashar shook his head. "They've thought of everything. Somehow, tonight, no matter what you do, you'll be someone's pawn."

"Yeah. But I'm not going to let them decide whose pawn I end up. I owe myself that much." Colby stood up, looking toward the back of the house, met by the sound of blaring trumpets, crashing cymbals. "We have guests."

He walked over to the sliding glass door, stood the pike on

its end, slid the door open for the demon. Paimon floated into the room, eight clay bowls in his arms. He quickly set them on the table without a word, promptly turning and slinking back outside.

"You'll understand," said Paimon through the open door, "if I leave you to it."

"You don't want to wait around to see if they work?" asked Colby.

Paimon scowled at Colby. "They'll work. And you won't trap me with them. Use them carefully and well. I would not want to be you were my brothers to find one of their own trapped by these."

"I wouldn't want to be you either, seeing that you're the one that made them. I have one boon left. Aren't you curious about who I'm going to call up?"

"No. I'll know soon enough. And if I'm right about you, I'll pity him. For a time."

"For a time?"

"He'll get out eventually. And then you're his. Good-bye, Colby. Don't call on me again."

Paimon faded away, his troupe vanishing along with him.

The bowls were wide as a plate and shallow, cast out of red clay, and inscribed on both sides, covering every square inch, in cuneiform. At their center was an image of a demon carved into the clay, each bowl of the set with a different great king of Hell, the inscriptions surrounding them telling the story of their fall from Heaven. Colby had seen a number of decorative forgeries in museums, but never the real thing. Once he handled them, he understood. The difference was the red clay. That was the secret.

He sounded out the cuneiform, soon piecing together the stories, further understanding why Paimon had been so hesitant to share their secrets. Not only were these dangerous weapons, but to know how to inscribe them was to sing the song of the king it represented. That meant invoking them, possibly trapping them, ultimately commanding them. It was knowledge Colby was immediately thankful he didn't possess.

Colby sat Indian style on the floor, surrounding himself with the bowls, the pike lying in his lap. He ran his fingers along the shaft, grasped it one more time, and felt the shadow of his friend.

"Good-bye, Ewan," he said, closing his eyes. Then he focused and unmade the pike in a single breath.

His whole body prickled, swelling with dreamstuff. He hadn't felt this much run through him since he was a child. He'd forgotten how powerful this thing really had been, how mighty it had grown in such a short time. Colby became woozy, overpowered by the sensation. Gossamer jumped off the couch, running in circles, as if chasing his own tail.

"What the hell?" he asked.

"Relax, Goss," said Yashar. "Just focus with Colby. He needs you."

Colby nodded, unable to speak, trying to tame the energy bubbling over inside him. Gossamer stopped, then slowly trotted over, across from Colby on the other side of the bowls. "What do you want me to do?" he asked.

Colby locked eyes with Goss and the energy calmed. The two passed the energy back and forth in a loop, keeping it flowing, neither having too much energy for too long. Then, taking a deep breath, Colby focused again and unleashed it all into the eight bowls around him.

For a moment, the inscriptions on the bowls glowed as brightly as the sun, the figures in the center burning brightest of all. They pulsated, hummed, the energy baking the clay further, changing the very nature of it. The red became crimson, and as the light began to fade, the inscriptions cooled to a dark, charred black.

"Now," said Colby, sighing. "One last boon before nightfall."

CHAPTER 57

THE SNAKEHANDLER

Purson, alias Curson, a great king, he commeth forth like a man with a lion's face, carrying a most cruel viper, and riding on a bear; and before him go always trumpets; he knoweth things hidden, and can tell all things present, past, and to come: he discloses hidden things, he bequeaths treasure, he can take a body either human or aerie; he answereth truly of all things earthly and secret, of the divinity and creation of the world, and bringeth forth the best familiars; and there obey him two and twenty legions of devils, partly of the order of virtues & partly of the order of thrones.

—*Pseudomonarchia Daemonum*

While no one had lived here for decades, the place seemed remarkably well kept. Buildings still stood—rusted and weather worn though they were—their paint still vibrant in places. Many of the streets remained intact and the grass looked simply unkempt rather than wild. There were trees growing atop some of the buildings and windows broken out all along the way, but there was nothing postapocalyptic about it—it was not at all like Colby thought it would be. This was Pripyat, Ukraine, better known for the facility that used to power it.

Chernobyl.

It was safe now, he was told, or safe enough to walk around for a few hours without protection. But he wouldn't be here long enough to care. It was approaching sundown in Austin, which meant it was still a few hours from sunup here, and it was no town in which to be wandering around. Not at night. Especially not at night.

When the people fled and the town was left to the wilds, it became the perfect place for the things beyond the veil. Anything that wanted privacy or needed a hollow to hole up in could find it here. There was a city's worth of dark places. And only one of those was off-limits, for it had been claimed by another, one more powerful than anything else that took to its Soviet-era concrete and crumbling statues.

His name was Purson, and he held court on a depressing slab of parking lot known as the Pripyat Amusement Park.

Scheduled to open a few days after the meltdown, the park itself was nothing more than a few carnival staples—bumper cars, a paratrooper swing, a meager boat swing, and its now infamous Ferris wheel—and only ever saw a few hours of use. Now to some it was a symbol of the life that was left behind, and to others a marker of the area to avoid.

Colby and Gossamer moved quickly through black streets, the near freezing Ukrainian autumn air harsher than anything they'd encountered through the day. There were angels on the buildings above, staring down at them as they passed, and fairies of all sort and kind following through the fields, using trees as cover. They recognized him, but as he seemed to move with purpose, none wanted to risk getting in his way. So they watched. And waited. And wondered why the most powerful boy in the world was heading straight into the darkest heart of their city.

"They're watching us," said Gossamer.

"Let them. Just stay off the grass."

"Why the grass?"

"Something to do with the fallout. Living things absorbing radiation. I don't understand it myself. But everyone says *stay off the grass*, so I stay off the grass."

"But going to see a demon—"

"Shut it."

As they approached the park, their silent entourage eroded, none willing to get too close, none wanting to see Purson, or worse, have him see them. The lot was cracked, buckling in places, and the rides, up close, were a total disaster. The boat swing was a rusty series of pipes that looked as if it might collapse in a strong wind, its boat smashed to pieces on the ground below it. The disintegrating bumper cars were scattered, covered from top to bottom in graffiti, grass sprouting out of most, a tree growing in the seat of another, all beneath the brittle skeleton of a dying pavilion. The paratrooper swing was nothing more than a rickety platform with a series of park benches welded to a merry-go-round. But the Ferris wheel had kept its bright yellow color, and still, despite its rust, looked as if a little elbow grease could get it running again.

Colby and Gossamer stood on the lot between the four attractions, in the spot that felt the coldest and most devoid of energy. Then Colby raised his palms once more, and spoke, for what he hoped was the last time, in a language he was regretting ever having learned.

"Purson, I summon thee. Appear and speak."

There was a loud crack, the earth wobbling beneath them, the whole of the world feeling numb and out of sorts. And then he appeared.

Purson was a monstrously large man, rigid muscles like hewn granite, hands massive enough to palm a man's skull and lift him one-handed. His face was that of a lion's, all fangs and fur and snout, but his black hair was trimmed conservatively short, like a man's. In his left hand he held a diamondback snake just beneath its head, its tail sounding the soft, threatening rattle of an impending strike. And beneath him, serving as a saddled mount, was a fully grown grizzly, one or two sizes larger than its material cousins, its fur brown and bristling.

"Goddamnit, Colby," said the demon, looking around the park, eyeing the ground at his feet. "Where are they?"

"Where are what?"

"Don't play with me, boy. The bowls. Where are they?"

"Back home. Yashar is watching them."

Purson laughed, a deep, almost reassuring kind of guffaw, like a drunken uncle telling a bad joke. "You scared the shit out of me. To hear Paimon tell it—"

"Let Paimon believe what he wants to believe," said Colby. "I made a deal and your lot has thus far kept up their end of it."

The grizzly roared and the snake rattled and Purson smiled, large and friendly. "She comes ever closer, Colby. You have little time left to squander with me. What boon do you ask?"

"You have no tests? No requests?"

"We don't have time for that. My brothers were fools to waste any of yours. Your time is our time now. So speak. Ask me and I'll grant what I must."

"I have a question."

"One question?"

"Yes."

"And that's your boon?"

"Yes."

"Ask it, then, and be done with me."

"Each of you has a task, a role you play, whether it be to oversee the fallen, or to keep track of the hidden things, or to bear with you some knowledge so it might be kept alive."

"We do."

Colby steadied himself, his question quivering in his throat. "Who," he asked, "is the master of the Hunt?"

"The Wild Hunt?"

"Yes."

Purson cocked his head, now far more curious about Colby than he'd been. Suddenly this boy was of keen interest. He squinted, sizing him up in a way he hadn't thought to. "You want to know who damned you," he said, putting it all together. "Who seduced you into calling the hunt across. Who sought you out to corrupt you, to turn your angelic allies against you."

"I do."

"Why would you want to know that? No good can come of it."

"I have my reasons."

Purson leaned forward atop his bear, his knowing grin growing wider with each word. "You mean to have your revenge."

"That remains to be seen."

Purson laughed, bellowing louder than before, the sound echoing through the empty streets, his grizzly padding the ground nervously beneath him. He turned to the snake. "Did you hear that? He wants to know who damned him."

The snake hissed, tail writhing, rattling furiously.

"It is the boon I ask."

"No man is ever damned by the act of another, Colby Stevens, least of all a demon. He can only damn himself. We seduce, charm, offer alternatives to the indoctrination of the taming societal shepherds keeping you in line. But the choice is yours. Were it so easy to damn someone, Hell would be overflowing with more souls than it is stuffed with now. Your revenge, were it even possible, would be fruitless, and only serve to damn you further. I wish you had asked me this beforehand, before making this your boon. I'd have gladly told you with joy in my heart. The look on your face will be worth more to me than if I were able to deliver your soul to Hell myself. But a deal is a deal, and it is your boon.

"It's true that each of us bears responsibility for some fragment of the duties to keep this place running. We tend fallen angels, keep men at war, sink vessels, bring heat waves that cause fathers to beat their children and mothers to shoot their lovers. But no mere demon oversees the Wild Hunt, and certainly not one of the Seventy-two. The one you seek, Colby, the only one who can loose spirits from Hell to roam free and call them back at a moment's notice, is the high lord and king of Hell itself."

Colby's bravery dropped into his stomach, his skin becoming suddenly flushed and sweaty. His jaw fell loose from its moorings, swinging open, wide, dumbstruck.

"Lucifer, Colby. Lucifer commands the Wild Hunt. They are his personal tools here on earth, their purpose to hunt down those spirits he wants for himself. Or to act as his heralds, warning of his coming. Or to lure the just to their doom. The Devil, Colby. The Devil is the thing against whom you want your revenge. Good luck with that. Your soul is his. And whatever his plans for it, they go beyond our feeble understanding."

The weight of his words wore upon Colby, his heart pounding, head growing dizzy. He looked over at Gossamer, whose eyes held a sudden sadness deeper than Colby had ever seen.

Together they shared a silence in which they said more than they could have with words.

"This isn't why you did all this, is it?" asked the demon jovially.

Colby stammered for half a beat, shaking his head.

"It is, isn't it? You gave yourself over to this thinking you might get a shot at the demon who set you up. Oh, Colby. We all thought you were smarter than that."

"I guess I'm not."

"No, you really aren't. For your sake, I hope the things you asked of us help you more with the five dukes than they do your vengeance."

"Me too."

Purson nodded his feline head, then reared back on his ursine steed, waving his snake with a mocking good-bye. "Keep your promise, Colby Stevens. Five souls. Don't make us squabble over who gets the honor of tearing you apart if you don't."

"If I don't, I'll already be dead."

"And you think that'll stop us? Your death will just be the beginning." He laughed once more, vanishing with the sound of a roar, the whole city shaking with it, the silence on the other side creeping and profound.

COLBY WALKED INTO his house, sullen, bearing the weight of unbearable disappointment on his brow. Yashar and Austin looked up from the couch, eyes hopeful. For a moment, no one said a thing. Then Yashar spoke up.

"Did you get the last thing you needed?" he asked.

"More or less." No one dared ask what he meant. They could tell by the look on his face that he hadn't found what he was looking for. "Come on. There are things we have to do before the sun sets."

"What do you need me to do?" asked Austin.

"You shouldn't be here. The things that are coming, they're a real threat to you."

She stood up from the couch, emboldened, unyielding. "I can handle myself."

"I know. But I only want you here if you want to be here."

"I've nowhere else I'd rather be."

Colby pulled a folded sheet of paper from his pocket, handing it to her. "Memorize these. They have to be perfect, down to the last detail."

Austin unfolded it, eyeing it suspiciously. She frowned a little. "Are these what I think they are?"

"Yes."

"How were you planning to—"

"I wasn't."

"You knew," she said, cocking an eyebrow.

"I guessed."

"You *guessed*."

"When we were kids I watched Kaycee wade into a billabong as a bunyip crawled out. It came after her, tried to kill her. She jumped on its back, laughing, riding it around like she was breaking a bronco. When I think of her, that's what I remember most."

"What does that even have to do with—"

"She's marching around in the dark with an army of kutji. She's gotten herself the ring of Solomon and enslaved five of the most powerful assholes ever to walk the earth. What, do you imagine, she fears? Anything?"

"No."

"You're powerful, Austin. But she isn't afraid of you. And you're smart. It wasn't going to take you long to realize that she wasn't going to stop. I figured you might come around."

Austin glared at Colby as the pieces fell together. "You sent me out there."

"No, I told you *not* to go out there."

"Because you knew I would."

Colby smirked, nodding a little.

"You son of a—"

Colby moved in; he didn't have much time. He ran his hand through her blond tresses, his fingers tickling the top of her ear, then back around to her neck. Pulling her close he kissed her hard. His whole body went wobbly, his stomach flipping, toes curling. Every molecule in his body tingled like he was about to pass out. Austin pushed him back.

"What the hell are you doing?" she asked, her eyes hard, nose wrinkled.

"I didn't want to die not having done that."

"No," she said. "I suppose not."

Then she grabbed him by the collar of his shirt with both hands, pulled his chest to hers, and kissed him back. For a moment there was nothing else in the world. Just two pairs of lips, eyes closed tight, noses brushing. She tasted like the city smelled in the spring, hints of jasmine, mountain laurel. He wrapped his arms around her, pulled her tighter, her own grip on his shirt refusing to yield. They kissed as if nothing else mattered, and for a moment, it didn't.

They relaxed, eased away from each other, eyes locked, hearts thundering beneath the thin fabric of their T-shirts. Their breath short, shallow. "What the hell, Colby?" she whispered.

"It's about damn time," said Yashar. "I was tired of watching you two fumble around like fucking schoolkids."

Colby turned bright red, ran his fingers through his hair nervously, looking away. Austin grabbed his chin with a single hand, pulled his face toward hers. "We will do that again."

Colby swallowed hard. "Even if I live through tonight, you may not want to."

"You will make it through tonight."

"If I do, you buy the beer."

"Deal."

"So now that we've got that out of the way," said Yashar, "what do you need me to do?"

Colby looked over at him, still trying to catch his breath, slow his racing heart. "I need you to get me a gun."

Chapter 58

High Moon

The Barton Creek Greenbelt is a stretch of land over seven miles long running through the southern tip of Austin proper. By day it is a series of hiking and biking trails chiseled out of limestone cliffs and crags, covered with dense trees and scrub, filled with folks of all sorts, trying, for an afternoon, to imagine they don't live in one of the country's largest cities. But at night it shuts down, clears out, and becomes a playground for fairies. At least it used to, before Colby came along.

Now it had emptied for good, leaving the night to loneliness. There were rumors that some fairies had taken to sneaking back in, to dance through the trails and chase the moon across the sky. But those came to an end when Colby happened upon a redcap who had crossed over into the city limits. That's when everyone knew he was serious and that Austin, for a time, was no longer theirs.

It was night and Colby stood wearing a ragged hoodie and an old pair of jeans, shovel in hand, in the middle of a large swath of open ground, a path through which the rainwaters ran when the thunderstorms found their way into the city. After a hard rain, the spot where he stood could be as deep as six feet underwater. Now it was a patch of rock and sand, carved out between two limestone shores. It had been threatening to rain for weeks, but nothing had come of it, Austin slowly browning without it, the land growing dusty, dry.

The sun had set slowly behind him twenty minutes ago and the pinks had turned to violets and soon would turn to black. The shadows crept long over the greenbelt, patches of wood already fully in their grip, dark and ominous. Soon the only light would be that spilled by the rising moon. He needed to finish his hole. It was shallow, six inches deep already. Beside him a mound, hidden beneath an old sheet, rested, waiting for the right moment, a single bowl sitting atop it.

Apart from that, he was alone.

He heard the flapping first, the flutter of wings deep in the woods flanking both sides of him. Then he saw the dark shapes against the fading sky. Soon he'd hear the caws. He knew it. They wouldn't be able to help themselves. She was coming, just over the ridge in front of him, no doubt with her royal court of dukes in tow.

Then she appeared, first as a massive shadow on the ridge, the details filling in with the remaining light as she approached. She was smaller than he remembered, still clad in her purple pajamas with the bright yellow stars, mammoth bunyip beneath her, carrying her toward him with a careful trot. At once Colby recognized the same little girl he'd known without a single detail out of place. The only difference was the look on her face. It was colder now, hateful, unrelenting. Her eyes, when he could finally make them out, held nothing but contempt and confidence.

Behind her strode the five dukes in a V formation, each looking ready for a fight. Just behind them hobbled her emaciated body, so tired and weak that it looked as if it would topple over at any moment. The trees on both sides of the floodplain had lined with crows, the last of them perching as the Queen of the Dark Things came to a stop some twenty feet from him. The bunyip growled, its fur bristling, its head rearing back. She tugged on its fur, shushing it quietly.

Colby spiked the shovel into the dirt, the crisp, shrill sound of metal against dry earth barking into the night. He leaned into the handle, pulling up a healthy clump of earth, dumping it just to the side of the hole.

"You bring that to dig your own grave?" asked the Queen of the Dark Things.

"Nope," said Colby, unconcerned with the threat. "I'm digging yours."

"I doubt that. If you wanted to kill me—the way you do it—there'd be nothing left to bury."

"Oh, I can't do it that way. You're too strong for that and you know it. There's not a creature alive—or dead for that matter—that can best you will against will. No, if I want to kill you, I'm going to have to do it with this hole right here. And a gun. But we'll get to that later."

"You're going to kill me with a hole?"

Colby pointed to the sheet-covered mound beside him. "And this. And a gun." He knelt beside the hole, picking up a handful of earth, smelling it deeply. "This'll do. You should come over and take a whiff."

"Like hell."

"Oh, so it's true. The Queen of the Dark Things is scared of me after all. Me and my hole."

The Queen's bunyip took a contemptuous step toward Colby. Colby wagged a disapproving finger, tsking, then stood back up. The bunyip took a single, anxious step backward.

The Queen gripped the bunyip's fur, spurring it on with her heels.

"I wouldn't," said Colby.

The Queen whistled and her body shuffled forward, struggling over the uneven ground. "This ends tonight."

Colby shook his head. "It's already over. It ended the moment you came over that ridge."

"So you are digging your own grave."

"No, I'm just waiting for the rain to fill the billabong."

"What does that even mean?"

"It's something Mandu said."

"Fuck that old man," she spat.

"I wouldn't be too hasty to condemn him. He liked you."

"He had a funny way of showing it."

"He did. I didn't understand it myself until just a little while ago. But then I saw it."

"Saw what?" she asked, growing impatient.

"The empty billabong waiting for the rain."

"He taught you how to speak in riddles. Cute."

"Destiny. The empty billabong is our destiny. It was dug out by the spirits a long time ago. They were just waiting for someone to bring the rain. And the moment you came over the ridge, here, to find me, you did just that."

"I brought the rain."

"You did," he said.

She looked around, exaggerating her own surprise. "I don't see any rain."

Colby pointed at the kutji and then the demons and then the bunyip beneath her. "And I see nothing but rain."

The kutji grew restless in the trees, pacing to and fro on their branches, cawing angrily into the coming night.

"I'm tired of this," she said. "I'm tired of your riddles. You know what I want, don't you?"

"I do."

"So do it."

"You know I can't. So why don't you just release those demons and give back the ring?"

"Same reason as you, I reckon. They'll tear me apart otherwise."

"They've really got us up against it, don't they?"

She nodded. "One of us has to die."

"And the other has to be damned."

"No way around it," said the Queen.

"None," said Colby.

"I'm sorry it has to end this way."

Colby cocked his head. "You know, I'm really not. It bothered me for a while, really tore me up. But we've had this coming for a long time, you and I. Tonight we pay up. I'm good with that."

"I like the poetry of that," she said. "Especially since you're going to die the way you left me to." She pointed around at the kutji. "At their hands." The kutji went wild, the greenbelt swelling with the cacophony of birdcalls.

Colby smiled. "But you didn't die."

"Only because I wouldn't let them kill me."

"I figure I'll do the same."

"We'll see. Dark things! Kill him!"

The crows took to the air, the thrash of their wings like a thousand drums beating out of sync.

Colby reacted, grabbing the bowl off the top of the mound,

casting it aside, yanking the sheet off with a single tug, revealing what was beneath. It was a basket. A simple, wicker, woven basket, nearly four hundred years old. Inside were the shriveled, shadowy remains of several dozen hands.

He picked up the basket and flung its contents out over the ground, scattering the hands in a wide arc well past the hole.

The kutji shifted forms in midair, their stumpy, malformed bodies flailing as they fell, screaming in unison, "OUR HANDS!" They hit the ground running, tearing across the broken earth, no longer interested in Colby. They lunged, each scrambling for the hand landing nearest him, pouncing to the ground like cats on rodents, clumsily shoving the severed end onto their dull nubs. Few of them actually found their own hands, but that fact didn't stop a one of them from putting them on. Some ended up oversize, almost too big for their bodies, while others ended up too small, their hand looking withered, shrunken, a bit of extra wrist poking out on each side. A few even ended up sideways or upside down, grasping upward, resting out away from the body.

And as the pack hooted, celebrating, making themselves mostly whole, Colby calmly picked up the discarded bowl, dropped it upside down in the hole, and covered it up by sliding the small mound of dirt back in place with his foot. He gave the dirt a few quick stamps to tamp it down, then stepped back with a proud, smarmy smirk.

"Shit," muttered Dantalion, at once recognizing what was happening. He looked around fretfully, terrified of the very ground around him. He motioned to the other demons who were equally disquieted.

"You were saying?" asked Colby.

The kutji looked up from admiring their hands, spying Colby, unafraid of them, no more than twenty feet away.

"Kill him!" yelled the Queen.

They nodded and lunged once more, running on all fours

before slamming headlong into an invisible wall. They stopped in place, stunned, confused. Then they clawed at the wall in front of them, screeching in mortal terror.

"You ever hear of an incantation bowl?" asked Colby of the Queen.

"What?"

"Incantation bowls. Otherwise known by their lesser known name—Babylonian Demon Traps."

"What the hell did you do?"

Colby took a few casual steps backward, putting his hands behind him as if lecturing to a symposium. He looked down, taking one more step, nodding, and stopped. "The Babylonians didn't care much for demons. This was back before the veil fell, of course, so they knew very well that demons were real. They could see them."

"Skip the history lesson."

"I don't think I will. You see, the Babylonians figured out the power of belief. At some point, some genius invented these bowls. They'd mold them, carve symbols into them—often with the names of angels or their god—then bury them in the ground, upside down. Usually at the four corners of the foundation of their house. Spirits can't touch the things. And once there are at least four of them," he said, pointing to the filled-in hole and three more like it around it, "no spirit can cross the unbroken line between them."

The Queen of the Dark Things lunged forward, furious, but stopped again. She looked over at the five dukes and pointed at Colby. They shook their heads, apprehensive. "Kill him."

The demons marched forward, the djinn Dantalion clenching his fists as he walked, his body smoking, his skin turning a golden olive, his muscles swelling as he manifested his spirit form; Focalor pulling a heavy boat chain from seemingly out of nowhere, swinging it with a force that could powder bone;

Astaroth astride his dragon; Berith astride his horse; the draconic Bune, prowling forward on his taloned feet, flames conflating in his growling maw.

Colby whistled and the earth shook. The ground rumbled, splitting apart, lines forming shapes, shapes becoming pictograms and circles. Each demon stopped in place, at once trapped in a circle drawn especially for him, every symbol in its proper place, cut into the dirt and limestone. They scuffed wildly at the symbols, but for each grain of sand they moved, another took its place.

Austin appeared. She stood before Focalor, a wry little grin tugging at her lips. Then she shrugged coyly, playfully shrinking from him. "Does the big mean corpse-raping demon have a problem?"

Focalor growled. "I won't once I'm out of here." He stepped forward menacingly, eyes spiteful, ready to kill her. The ground beneath him shuddered, and the symbols moved, the circle shrinking, an invisible force pushing him ever back.

"Let's see if we can make that a little cozier for you, then. You might be here awhile."

The bunyip reared bitterly, flailing back on its hind legs, batting at the air. The Queen spurred it again, tugging at its fur. "Hold," she said. "Steady!" It settled and she kicked it again, driving it toward Colby.

Colby whistled again and Gossamer tore out from the dark of the woods. As he ran, Colby focused, siphoning the nearby dreamstuff, stronger here in the greenbelt than in the city, funneling it into his familiar. With each step Gossamer grew in size, his golden fur becoming longer, shaggier, a lion's mane growing from the nape of his neck. Before he was halfway across the open field, he was eight feet tall at the shoulder, drool dripping in gobs from teeth the size of a man's thumb.

Gossamer pounced, letting out a fiendish snarl, its eyes

on fire, breath steaming, and bit into the neck of the wincing bunyip.

The bunyip let out a shrill whimper, recoiling, throwing the Queen from her mount.

The two beasts scrambled for ground, nipping, clawing, rending each other's flesh.

The Queen leaped to her feet and tried to hop back atop the bunyip, but the brawl was too chaotic, the creature's craning neck striking at Gossamer like a cobra only to be batted away by the dog's savage paws.

There was only one thing left for her to do. She bolted at Colby with inhuman speed, covering the short distance in less than a breath.

Then she slammed into an invisible wall inches in front of Colby's face. She staggered, dazed, mind shaken loose by the hit.

"I made eight," said Colby, looking at the ground beneath him. There, dug into the dirt, ten feet apart, were four filled-in holes.

She too looked at the ground, realizing what was going on.

"Now," he said. "Let's talk."

"We don't have anything to talk about."

Behind her, the beasts came to a stalemate, each gashed, bleeding, growling with feral ferocity, eyes locked, waiting for the other to make the first move. Meanwhile, Kaycee's possessed body lumbered toward its spirit, the shadow of her father growing very worried for its daughter.

"But we do," said Colby. "Lots to catch up on."

"We better catch up quick. You're going to die tonight."

Colby looked around at the throng of caged kutji, the five demons locked in summoning circles, and the bunyip cowering from Colby's familiar. "That might be true, but not by your hand. You didn't come here to kill me. That's why I'm not freaking out right now. Later? I'll probably piss myself. But here?

Now? We're just two old friends, one of whom is trying to play the other one for an idiot."

The Queen ground her teeth. "Because you are an idiot."

"You don't believe that. Not standing outside my demon trap, you don't. Though I imagine right now you're wondering just how smart I really might be. If I've figured it all out and if this is all going to start to get worse for you."

"Is it? Going to get worse, Colby?" she asked, her voice dripping with sarcasm.

"Pretty bad, yeah."

"I'll find a way out of this, you know. And I'll kill you."

"No you won't. But I can kill you." Colby pointed at Kaycee's shell, still stumbling awkwardly toward her.

The Queen looked back over her shoulder at her body. "Kill it. Turn it to ash or whatever it is you do. See if I care."

Colby pulled a revolver out of his hoodie, cocking back the hammer. He fired, the bullet tearing a hole in Kaycee's emaciated, club-footed leg. The body toppled to the ground, screaming, clutching its massive wound.

"Colby!" she screamed.

Colby's eyes widened and he simpered a little in surprise. "Holy shit. I didn't think I'd hit with the first shot."

"What the hell are you doing?"

"Shooting better than expected, apparently."

"No, what are you—"

"I told you. I worked this out a long time ago." He slid the revolver back into his pocket. "How long do you reckon before your body bleeds out?"

She ran over, knelt beside her body, cradling the wound. Then she screamed at the demons. "Help me! Heal him!"

The demons shook their heads. They were powerless outside the circles.

"Colby, you can't do this."

"Tell me something, Kaycee. Why didn't you call me? You could have just shown up and asked me. Instead . . ." He waved an open palm around, gesturing at all this. "What, are you as much the kutjis' prisoner as their master?"

"Something like that," she said, her eyes cold and narrow.

"And when you die, when that body bleeds out, you'll become one of them."

"Yes."

"And the curse of the *Batavia* will be ended."

She nodded.

"I told you, Kaycee. I was going to kill you."

She began to cry, holding close the body, instead more worried for the spirit inside.

"The Colby I remember didn't kill someone in cold blood like this."

"Yeah, well, that kid died six months ago. He just didn't know it yet. Besides, I don't think you were going to give me much of a choice, were you?"

"No. I wasn't."

"I was going to have to kill that thing, one way or another."

"Yes."

"Who's in there?"

"My father."

"A kutji."

"Yes."

"That's not your father."

"It is."

"No. That's just a shadow of him. He's no more your father than my friend is out in a field waving for me to come back. Your father's dead."

"I know," she said. "But it's all I have left."

"How long do you think before he bleeds out?"

"Bastard!"

"Time's running out. Do you want to deal or not?"

She looked up at him, tears streaming down her face, a little girl terrified, her father dying in her arms. "What?"

"Do you want to deal?"

She jumped up, ran over to Colby. "Yes. Yes! Anything. Name it."

Colby softened, nodding a little, struggling with the truth. "I've lost enough old friends. I don't want to lose another if I can avoid it." He looked at the body, blood pooling on the ground beneath it, then slid the revolver back into his pocket.

The two shared a moment of understanding silence, her gaze confused, heartbroken. "You mean that?" she asked, her voice trembling.

"I didn't leave you behind because I wanted to. I had to. And I didn't understand why until very recently. I had to leave you in the desert to become who you are, so I could become who I am, and so we, together, could do this here. Tonight, you and I get to be the people we always dreamed we could be. Even if just for a few moments. Tonight, you and I get to stand against the darkness and say *fuck you*. Tomorrow we might be damned, or dead, but tonight we own our destinies."

"What do you want?"

"The ring."

The Queen of the Dark Things shook her head. "I can't, they'll—"

"Kill you for what you did?"

"Yes."

"That's for tomorrow. I'll see to that. But they want their friends free and they need to know this won't happen again. So I need the ring."

"I-I—"

"You don't have a choice. Die here with the ring, or fight tomorrow without it."

She nodded, tears streaming faster now. "This was always my fate, wasn't it? The destiny Mandu talked about. This is it?"

"Yes."

"It sucks."

"Not all destinies end the way we imagine. If it makes you feel any better, I'm pretty sure you're not alone."

The Queen twiddled the ring on her finger, too frightened to remove it. She took a deep breath, closed her eyes. Then she tugged, pulling it off.

"You aren't the boy I met in the desert. Not anymore."

"And you aren't the girl. So are we agreed?"

She nodded.

"Don't look so grim. You're about to get everything you came for."

"Not the way I wanted it."

Colby stuck his hand out, palm up, past the barrier of the bowls, and the Queen dropped the ring into it.

Colby motioned to Gossamer, and Gossamer took the hint. He relaxed, his fur lying down, his teeth settling in back behind his gums. He stepped backward a few paces, then trotted around the barrier to stand as near Colby as he could.

The moon was up and the sky was black, littered with the night's first stars. Colby looked around, taking in the young night, slipping the ring into his jeans front pocket. "It's a good night for it, you know."

"A good night for what?" asked the Queen.

"For all of it. When the sun comes up tomorrow, everything will be different. But tonight, tonight is a fine night." He smiled at the stars, as if for the last time. Then he stepped forward, outside the safety of the demon traps, kneeling next to Kaycee's body.

He could feel the kutji writhing inside her, fighting the pain, desperately trying to retain its hold. Her brown skin was a sickly pale, blood still seeping from the leg wound. She had minutes left, at best.

Colby cradled her head in both hands, staring into her lifeless eyes, looking for the spark of the thing inside. It was thunderstruck, barely holding on, about to slip free of its moorings. He concentrated, trying to tear apart the dreamstuff of the thing, restructure it anew.

But it relented. The kutji was just too strong.

Colby focused harder, digging deeper, but the hate inside it for its own existence, the passion to save its own daughter, kept it together, tethered it not only to the body, but to the world.

"Shit," muttered Colby. "He won't break."

"What?" asked the Queen. "I thought you could do this."

"I can."

"They said you could. *Swore* that you could!"

"I can!" He closed his eyes, dug even deeper than before. Only once before had he fought something so unwilling to give up. And that he had thrown to Hell to destroy. "I can do this. I can do this."

"Colby, I'm dying," she said, watching her mortality leak away, drop by drop. "Hurry!" The Queen of the Dark Things closed her eyes, and for the first time in a long time, she felt fear. She took a deep breath, waiting, terrified that she was wrong.

The kutji in the demon trap crawled over one another to see, scampering up the wall, excited, hooting, making catcalls at the Queen. "She's dying! She's really dying!" they told one another. They howled like monkeys, did backflips off one another, pulled one another down in an ever shifting pyramid of celebrating shadows. They were close; they were so close. They had their hands and soon they would have the last of their spirits. The circle would be closed, the curse ended, and they could all slip off to their great reward.

"I can do this."

"Colby, please."

"Talk to him," he said.

"What?"

"Be his daughter. Distract him."

The Queen caressed her own face, her voice no longer domineering, bold, but young, loving, scared. "Dad," she said. "Dad, are you in there?"

Her body nodded, gurgling a little, wheezing.

"You want a drink, Dad? A rum?"

The body shook its head, grimacing. "No more," it said, gasping desperately for breath. "No more." It coughed with the soft hiss of a death rattle.

"Then what can I get you?"

"Eggs," it said.

The Queen of the Dark Things smiled softly, remembering one of the few bright spots of her old life. "How many eggs?" she asked.

"Three?"

"We can spare three today. I think there'll be enough for tomorrow."

Colby carried on, still trying to find the weak point in the kutji's psyche. It still would not crack. He worried he couldn't keep his end of the bargain, that all this had been for naught. And he hoped that as the body teetered toward death, that it might just be weak enough for long enough for him to pull it out. But that was looking less and less likely.

He looked at the Queen and she looked at him, their eyes sadly conferring.

She nodded, resigned. "You're right," she said, looking up at the stars. "It's a fine night for it." Then she leaned in and kissed her body on the forehead. "Dad, I'm dying. Again. This time for real. I love you."

Kaycee's body smiled, rasping. "I love you too, darlin'."

And then the body vanished with a soft puff and the sweet smell of rum and lilacs.

"There you have it," said Colby, having broken the stalemate. "Your immortality."

The Queen stared at Colby in stunned silence, a few lilac petals resting in her otherwise empty hand.

"It wasn't going to work for you, you know," said Colby. "After, I mean."

"What are you talking about?"

"The ring. That's the trick of it. It only works for mortals. They would have torn you apart the second you were free."

"Wait . . . so all of this—"

Colby nodded.

"Was for me?"

"There was no other way out for you. You weren't going to give it up willingly. Not without a fight. I had to take it. So I gave you no other choice but to give it to me."

"So what now?"

"Now you get on your bunyip and ride until you can't ride anymore. Go home. Do what you do. And if anything ever comes for you, you fight it on your terms, on your turf. Go be what you were always destined to be. Go dream forever and never wake up."

She pointed to the kutji, who stood mute, unsure, staring at them from within the trap. "What about them?"

Colby pointed east to the horizon. "The sun will be up soon enough and there isn't so much as a rock for them to hide under in there. It'll be painful, but quicker than they deserve."

The Queen threw her arms around Colby, hugging him as hard as she could. "I don't deserve a friend like you."

"Then go make sure you do. This cost me more than you'll ever know. Don't waste it."

"I won't." She turned, then immediately turned back. "Can I ask you something first? As a friend?"

"Anything," said Colby, happier at the sound of that than he thought he'd be.

"The girl. Do you feel about her the way she feels about you?"

Colby nodded. "Yeah. I reckon I do."

"What is it about her?"

Colby thought hard for a second, scratching his scalp through layers of matted red hair. "I like girls who are smarter than me."

The Queen laughed. "I won't tell her you said that."

"She already knows."

The Queen of the Dark Things whistled, loud, snapping the fingers of a single hand in the air and her bunyip trotted next to her. She turned, put her forehead directly against his, scratching behind its ears with both hands. "You were very brave," she whispered. "Thank you." Then it bowed before her and she launched herself astride its back. She smiled, warm, unencumbered, like an eleven-year-old girl out for her first time in the dream. "Good-bye, Colby."

"Good-bye, Kaycee."

And then she ambled off into the dark of the woods until she vanished completely.

Colby sauntered up to the summoning circles, smiling at Austin. "Thank you," he whispered.

"You're welcome," she mouthed silently back.

"Let us out," said Dantalion.

"Yes," said Astaroth. "That was your deal, was it not?"

"It was," said Colby. "But we never agreed on *when*."

At that, the demons growled and howled in unison, their rage shaking the earth beneath their feet.

"You can't stop us from killing her," said Focalor. "Not after what she did."

"Oh, but I aim to," said Colby. "Austin, how long do you think you could keep this up?"

"Oh," she said, as if thinking deeply. "A couple of days before I get bored, I guess."

The demons thrashed like antagonized baboons in their circles.

"Hmmm, a couple of days. That's an awfully long time."

"What do you want?" gnarred Dantalion.

"One day," said Colby. "I want you to vow right now that you will seek no retribution against me or my friends here."

"We can do that."

"And that you will not pursue Kaycee until sunset tomorrow."

"Just one day?" asked Focalor.

"Yes," said Colby. "I'm hoping after that you'll choose to leave her be of your own accord."

"I doubt that," said Astaroth.

"Doubt is the right word. I like doubt. It leaves a lot open to change. I'll take that. Sunset tomorrow. And no retribution against us. Ever. Agreed?"

"And you will set us free?" asked Dantalion.

"Right this minute."

The demons exchanged glances, nodding one and all. "We swear," said Dantalion.

"We swear," said the rest in unison.

Colby nodded and with a gesture Austin wiped the runes and circles away from the earth. "Go free," he said. "And tell your brothers our deal is done."

"Not yet," said Dantalion. "I believe you have something of ours."

Colby shook his head. "Yeah, but it's not for you. You're the one who lost it. You have to go back and face the music on that. The ring is meant for another of your brothers, the one who's earned it."

"That's not how this works."

"It is today."

"You made a vow."

"Not for the ring. Never for the ring. That I'll give back on my own." Colby slid his hand into his pocket. "We're not going to have a problem, are we?"

Focalor eyed Austin up and down. "Another time," he said.

She smiled, nodding, unfazed. "Another time."

The air sizzled and the ground warped and the wind howled like it was being murdered and the trees swayed their branches away in mortal terror; the entire universe bent in upon itself, threatening to snap, almost giving way. One by one the demons vanished, each unique in their exit. Focalor became a puddle that boiled away in an instant; Astaroth collapsed into a singularity, burning bright, like the sun before winking out; Dantalion simply smoked away into mist; Berith exploded in a gusher of gore; and Bune immolated, burning to ash that fluttered away on the wind. Then the universe bent back; the trees relaxed and the wind died and the ground flattened and the air calmed to a standstill. And they were gone.

Colby looked at Austin, nodding sadly. "Now for the hard part."

"I still don't understand what's going on," said Austin.

Gossamer nuzzled Colby, looking up at the two. "You will," he said. "It'll all make sense by morning."

"Let's go, Goss," said Colby.

"Sure thing, boss."

Colby gave a somber wave, then he and the dog walked off into the woods together, stepped into a tree, and vanished, leaving Austin and the kutji behind.

CHAPTER 59

WITH THIS RING

The night was darker out here, the stars brighter, the light pollution of the city too far to ruin the sky. Half the horizon was covered in clouds, flashes of lightning rippling through their bellies. At last, it seemed, rain was on its way. Maybe this time it wouldn't just be a tease; maybe this time the drought would end.

Colby and Gossamer were nowhere near home, too far out for Austin to hear them. They were deep in the Limestone Kingdom, but nowhere near anyone's haunt. The two were entirely alone.

"This is as good a place as any," said Colby.

"They'll find out eventually."

"Yeah, but not tonight. We get tonight."

"Last chance," said Gossamer.

"The last chance has come and gone. You know that."

"I do. I just thought I'd make it *feel* like we had a choice in the matter."

"I appreciate that."

Colby held out his arms and started screaming in an infernal tongue, chanting once again the means of summoning. Then he shouted, "President Amy, I summon thee. Appear and speak."

The earth clattered awake and the demon appeared in a burst of hellfire. Amy. The Holocaust Man.

"It was my understanding," he said, flames trickling off his tongue, "that our business was concluded."

"Between myself and the Seventy-two it has. But not between me and you."

"There is no business between *me and you*."

"Oh, but there is," said Colby. "You see, I've brought the ring."

Amy eyed the ring nervously. "You should have given it to Dantalion. He's the one who lost it. He should be the one to put it back where it belongs."

"But he didn't fight for it. Not like you did."

"I'm not sure I know what you mean." He was lying. Colby could sense it.

"Thank you," said Colby, smiling politely.

"For what?"

"For lying so directly. You could have played with some version of the truth, kept us going round and round until I had to get direct with you. Now I know for sure what I only suspected."

"Which is?"

"You killed Bill the Shadow. And you torched our bar."

The Holocaust Man stared blankly at him, eyes dimming, curious. "I'm listening."

"From the get-go everything seemed wrong," said Colby. "Orobas consented to my deal too quickly, didn't niggle over the details. He could have demanded the ring, but he didn't. Then, each of the five did exactly as I asked, no exceptions."

"That was the deal."

"That was. But no one tried to pervert it. No one cheated, tried to screw me out of what I asked for through loopholes. I gave each of them ample opportunity for shenanigans, but they didn't take the bait. They were each punctual, exact, and saw to it that they honored our deal in toto. They even played upon my own weakness for knowledge, almost all of them more than happy to engage me in discussion, hand me secrets men have died trying and failing to learn. All because they wanted me to trust them."

"And you did," hissed the demon.

"No. Because there was something else nagging at me."

"What was that?"

"Orobas. He told me that he didn't know why he couldn't see my future anymore. That none of you did."

"We didn't."

"Oh, I know. But for that to be true it meant that merely being involved with the ring wouldn't cloud your sight of my destiny. It meant that I would, at some point, come into possession of the ring. And what Orobas meant when he said he didn't know, was that he didn't know whether I would take the ring and hand it back or if I would keep it for myself."

The Holocaust Man nodded, flames jumping, licking the air, as he did.

"I can only assume there was some debate over which it might be and how best you could convince me to give it back. The prevailing thought must have been to earn my trust. But someone dissented. Thought it best to scare me, make me think the ring was far more trouble than it was worth. Convince me that everyone and everything that I loved would be at risk if I kept it. And that was you."

"How did you know?"

Colby threw a stiff thumb at Gossamer. "My dog."

"Your familiar?"

"He was there when your kutji torched the place."

"And how did you know that wasn't the Queen?"

"Because your kutji had both of their hands." Colby held both of his hands open in the air.

The demon smiled, his charred teeth large, cinders smoldering between them. "You're a clever boy after all, Colby Stevens."

"You couldn't help yourself."

"No, I couldn't."

"No, I mean you couldn't help yourself. You were destined to do it. This had to happen. You were the reason you couldn't see my future. Before you intervened, I wanted nothing to do with the ring. It scared the shit out of me. I didn't want that kind of responsibility, or to earn that much enmity. But the minute you made your play, I saw just how untrustworthy a lot you were. I almost bought into the idea that you were all just fallen angels, doing your own thing. But you're not. You're demons. You're Hell. And I will never be free of you."

Colby reached into his pocket and pulled out the ring. He held it up, pinched between thumb and forefinger, eyeing it as it flickered in the firelight.

"You can't keep it, Colby," said the demon. "We'll never let you keep it."

"But that's just it. I don't have a choice. You robbed me of that choice the moment you interfered. That's why you couldn't see my future. You were always meant to let me know that I was never safe from you, with or without the ring. So my choice was to fear you without it, or fear you with it. Which is no choice at all."

"Colby—"

Colby slipped the ring on his finger. "You killed my friend, you son of a bitch." He punched the demon square in the chest, the brand of Solomon burning immediately into him. Amy reeled back, but not in time. His eyes smoldered black, flames erupting all over his body. He screamed in agony.

"Kneel," growled Colby.

The demon fell to his knees.

"Who do you serve?"

"You."

"You're going to go back to your brothers. You're going to tell them what you've done. You're going to tell them that you're the reason I've kept the ring. Then you're going to give them a message."

"What's the message?" asked the kowtowing demon.

"That I'm going to leave your punishment to them."

The Holocaust Man looked up fearfully. "What?"

"If I'm satisfied with your punishment, I won't use this ring in any other way. But if I'm not, or if a single one of you interferes in my life again, or shows its face without me asking, or goes after one of my friends, I will summon you one by one over the course of a single afternoon and I will bury you so far and deep within the earth that your five hundred years in the sea will feel like a fucking holiday weekend. And that goes for Kaycee too. She's off-limits now. And they have you to blame."

"No. Please. You have no idea what they'll do—"

"You're right. I don't. I lack their capacity for cruelty. I can't even begin to imagine the suffering you're about to endure. You see, that's the illusion of choice. Your brothers can go to war with me for the ring. Or they can just shit on you and wait me out. Do you imagine there will be much of a discussion?"

"No. I don't."

"Neither do I. Bill was good to me. He deserved better than that. I hope it was worth it."

The demon smiled again, laughing. "It was. Now you're truly damned, Colby Stevens. Truly damned."

"Go. Tell your brothers. Accept your punishment."

"Good-bye, Colby," said the demon, still smiling.

"Good-bye, Amy."

Then the Holocaust Man fell away into ashes, a small flaming circle left burning in the ground where he'd knelt.

Colby looked down at Gossamer. "I told you. What you've gotten yourself into with me, it can't be undone."

"All due respect," said Gossamer, "but go fuck yourself. There's nowhere else I'd rather be, boss."

Colby scratched Goss behind the ears. "Let's go home."

"Good idea. I need a beer."

CHAPTER 60

THE BURDEN OF SOLOMON

Colby and Gossamer were only five minutes ahead of the storm, the smell of the rain wafting in from the west, thunder rumbling through the streets. The stars were gone now; only clouds remained. They were only a few blocks from home when they heard a third pair of footsteps. At once, from the barefoot scuff, Colby knew without looking who it was.

"Hello, Coyote," he said without breaking stride, too tired to make a big deal out of it.

"When was the last time you slept?" asked the manitou.

"Australia."

"That was awhile ago."

"And not the best sleep. How can I help you?"

"I'm good. Just a friendly visit."

"There are no friendly visits from Coyote."

"They're all friendly visits, Colby. I don't believe in getting angry."

"Probably because you're very good at helping everyone else with that."

"It's good to have a skill."

Colby stopped, Gossamer stopping with him. "What do you want?"

"To congratulate you."

"For what?"

"What do you think?"

"I really don't know."

Coyote grinned, beaming like a proud father. "Four hundred years ago, five demons decided to sink a ship just because they could. Tonight they paid for their arrogance and lost the one thing they hold most dear."

"The ring?" asked Colby.

"No. Their immunity from repercussions."

"They didn't suffer long for what they did."

"They've only just begun to suffer. You saw to that."

"I have no intention of tangling with them again."

Coyote smiled wider, increasingly pleased. "But they don't know that. You're a being of the flesh, Colby. You aren't bound to your word like they are. From this day forward, they will always want to know where you are because they're always going to be afraid that you might at any moment renege on your end of the deal."

"So they'll come for me instead. Is that what you're saying?"

"What, and ensure that you'll bind them? Mark them with that little ring and make them kneel like you did Amy? They only have the illusion of choice, like they gave you. Either they trust you or they ensure they'll become your slaves."

"That's not a very good choice," said Colby.

"That's why I like it so much," said Coyote through a churlish giggle. "Of all the options presented to you, the wealth of possibilities, and this was your path. You could have asked for power. Immolated your adversaries. Become a god. You could have had any woman in the world, ended all your loneliness. One boon can grant more power than most men ever dream of. You had five. Instead you asked only for what you needed. Knowledge and tools."

"That was the only way to do it."

"It was the only way to do it and retain your soul."

"Like I said. That was the only way to do it."

Coyote nodded, walking again toward Colby's house, waving a lecturing finger. "At night you drink yourself to sleep, wondering why your life has to be so hard. Wondering what it would be like if you hadn't made that wish. And yet every morning you wake up stronger. Smarter. Wiser. And now you have that ring."

Colby walked briskly to catch up, Gossamer in tow. "I don't want it."

"Good. The people who want it shouldn't have it. They say Solomon didn't want it."

"Yeah, but I'm not Solomon."

"Solomon was just a man, Colby. A man who cared about his people. Greatness isn't given to anyone. It's taken after years of hard learning."

"I'm not great."

"No. You're not. But you've become a problem. Almost everyone hates you. No one can trust you. You have grown far more powerful than you have any right to be. And worse yet, you are driven by ideals that run counter to the very world you are a part of. You look around you and see great corruption— dangerous creatures that need to be taught a lesson. And you figure you're just the one to teach them."

"Maybe I am."

"Maybe you are."

"Maybe you could use a lesson or two."

Coyote smiled, shaking his head. "It's not yet time for the student to become the teacher."

"I'm not your student."

"Aren't you?"

"No."

"What was your first boon?"

"What does that have to—"

"You stood before that demon and he gave unto you a mind that could never be deceived by a spirit again. So tell me, oh seer-through-of-bullshit: am I lying?"

He wasn't. Colby stopped in his tracks. "Mandu."

Coyote turned, the biggest, smarmiest smile Colby had ever seen pulled back over pearl white teeth.

"But he said his spirit—"

"Was a dingo. A large dingo."

"Yeah."

"Living in Arnhem as he did, do you imagine he'd ever even seen a coyote?" Coyote returned to walking, his stride now more of a stroll. "Angels have their preachers, Colby. Demons have their sorcerers. And I, I have my Clever Men." The manitou kept walking, fading away as he did, until he was nothing but a shadow dimming in the night. And then he was gone, one with the black.

Colby muttered beneath his breath, but Gossamer knew what he was saying all the same. Then the two continued home, ever more unsure about everything that had just happened.

As they rounded the corner, they saw her, sitting on the front porch, a six-pack of icy Mexican beer at her side. Austin. She gave a slight nod and motioned to the beer. Colby nodded back, then looked down at Gossamer.

"I think I'm going to take a lap or two around the block, boss."

"You don't have to. You'll get caught in the rain."

"Nah, it's about time."

"That it rained?"

"That too. Save me a beer."

"It's a sixer. I'll save you two."

Gossamer rubbed his head against Colby's leg, looked up at him with the kind of love only a golden retriever knows, then loped off down the street, dreaming about beer.

Colby plodded slowly up the front walk, hands in his pockets, eyes on the cracked cement. Austin smiled, pulled a pair of beers from the sixer, and popped off the tops without an opener.

"Mayor," he said, looking at her, hands still in his pockets.

"Sheriff."

He sat down, taking a beer from her hand, and looked out into the night. Austin sipped at hers, staring out with him.

"I'm not the mayor," she said.

"I'm not the sheriff."

"That's not what you said before."

"That's because I was an idiot. I'm no sheriff. This town doesn't need one."

"It doesn't?"

"No. This town needs something else."

"What's that?"

"A Clever Man."

They sat there, together, in silence, drinking, neither saying a word. Neither needing to. Gentle slaps of rain rolling down the street, the storm only seconds away.

EPILOGUE

Once upon a time there was a very clever little girl who possessed the power to walk through dreams. Each night, as she slept, she would traipse out past the black stump, deep into the outback, and dance beneath the moon. She would frolic from billabong to billabong, leaping on top of rocks, scaling cliff faces, climbing trees, visiting all her friends of the dream as she did. And this made her very, very happy.

But one night, as she danced deeper than she ever had before, she came across a barren desert that stank only of the dead. It was soundless, with no bushes or trees for the wind to rustle. But when she heard the wind rise up she grew frightened, for it was unlike any wind she had ever heard before.

There is a vast difference between the large, boisterous sound of the wind tearing across an open plain and that of its twitters through a tight space. In the desert you notice these things. One means bad weather, the other means something is nearby. This was the latter. The whistles were like a stiff wind through a wooden fence, long, labored, the trill changing pitch with the rise and fall of each gust.

The little girl stopped in her tracks, noting the sound was moving with her, surrounding her on nearly all sides. As she came to an abrupt halt, she heard a flapping, scurrying, but the whistles still wailed. She looked around. Nothing. Darkness everywhere the eye could see. Even the stars were afraid of this place.

The little girl pulled a small box of matches from her pocket, plucked one from the tiny cardboard tray, and struck it against the side. The match brightened, growing in intensity until it became a white-hot blaze, like a phosphorous flare against the black of the outback. The darkness withered and twenty skeletal creatures, dressed from head to toe in rags, cowered from the light.

Nomorodo. Desert vampires. Dried skin wrapped tightly around brittle bones; their insides, meat and all, sucked out by their predecessors; their hair long, straggly; finger bones filed down, sharpened to fine, deadly points. They stood there, feral, snarling, cowering behind their hands from the light, stunned for the moment by the surprise of it.

The little girl gasped. Not only had she not expected vampires, but she also hadn't imagined that if there were, there would be so many. She was completely surrounded, some on the ground, some hovering in the air, wind blowing through them making such terrible sounds. And at any moment they would pile on and drain out every last bit of her.

Then, from out in the desert, came the most terrifying sound, like a pig being both strangled and stabbed at the same time. The earth rumbled, tremors like a freight train headed right for her. And then the wind took away her light.

Screeches of a scuffle surrounded her, howls, bloodthirsty and raw, shrill against the night. Bones shattered to dust. Leathery skin shredded. The ever-present whistling began to quiet and the remaining nomorodo began chittering nervously.

Then came a burst of light so bright it lit the desert purple for miles before blinding the little girl, the image of a half dozen nomorodo being mauled by a gigantic beast burned into her eyes. Whatever it was, it was too massive, too malformed to comprehend in so brief an instant.

The nomorodo begged for their lives in dry, sand-mouthed rasps, but whatever this thing was, it showed them no mercy at all. The remaining nomorodo scattered, the whistling fading quickly as they ran for their lives.

A tangle of rags blew in the wind, wrapping loosely around the little girl's ankle, the only reminder left of its former owner. Another gust came along and took it away, dragging it off, lonely, into the desert.

Her eyes adjusted and when she looked again, the stars and moon had come back out. Standing before her was a monstrous beast, six clawed legs, fangs larger and longer than she, bristling fur from stem to stern. Atop it sat another little girl, roughly her own age, wearing purple pajamas with bright yellow stars.

The little girl atop the monster offered her a hand, helped her up onto the beast along with her.

"Thank you," said the little girl.

"You're welcome," said the girl atop the monster.

"Are you . . . are you the Queen of the Dark Things?"

"No," she said, shaking her head. "The Queen of the Dark Things is dead. She died in a land far, far away. My name's Kaycee. Just Kaycee."

And they rode off together to a safer part of the dream.